HAUNTED

A GOTHIC REVERSE HAREM BULLY ROMANCE

STEFFANIE HOLMES

HAUNTED

Ivan, Titus, Dorien.
The bad boys of Baroque, the kings of this school.
They messed with the wrong girl.
I'll topple them from their thrones.

They made me trust them.
They made me *want* them.
Now, I'm going to haunt their asses.
Even if it costs me… everything.

They'll carry their secrets to their graves.
If they don't put me six-feet-under first.

Manderley Academy won't claim another victim.
They can't shove these skeletons back in the closet.
I'll do whatever it takes to get justice.

It's time for Manderley's ghosts to come out and play.

A dark mystery unfolds around musician Faye de Winter in book two of this gripping gothic college reverse harem bully romance by *USA Today* best-selling author Steffanie Holmes. Warning: Proceed with caution – this tale of three spoiled rich boys with unsettling secrets and the girl who refuses to put up with their shit contains dark themes, a creepy house, a smoldering second-chance romance, college angst, cruel bullies and swoon-worthy sex.

Grab a free copy *Cabinet of Curiosities* – a Steffanie Holmes compendium of short stories and bonus scenes – when you sign up for updates with the Steffanie Holmes newsletter.

*To Niccolò, Johann, Wolfgang, and Franz –
the original Bad Boys of Baroque.*

"I know not how it was—but, with the first glimpse
of the building, a sense of insufferable gloom
pervaded my spirit."

– Edgar Allan Poe, *The Fall of the House of Usher*

IVAN

PRAGUE – TWO YEARS AGO

"*W*here is he?" Elena's blue eyes scanned the crowd. "He said he would be here."

We huddled together for warmth. Elena tucked her gloved hands inside my sleeves. Outside, a storm battered the ancient city with bitter fury. Wind whipped rain and hail into the glass of the station building. A shiver twisted through Elena's body, but I didn't know if it was from the cold or because of what we were about to do.

My chest tightened. *He should be here by now. He said he had everything planned. If we can't—*

"There he is." Elena's face lit up as Dorien pushed through the crowds of tourists and commuters huddled around the ticket booths and bracing themselves for the dash to the exposed platforms. His black wool coat flapped around his long legs, and the end of his silk scarf trailed behind him like a ribbon of crimson blood. He darted a glance over his shoulder before pulling an envelope from the pocket of his coat and pressing it into my frozen fingers.

"I had to empty my account to get these, and promise him backstage tickets to future Broken Muse shows, but it was worth

1

it," Dorien's grey eyes twinkled. "Who knew the finest document forger in the world is an angry Czech mobster ex-cellist Broken Muse fan?"

That twinkle unnerved me. I knew even given the seriousness of the situation, part of Dorien loved this – sneaking around the ancient city, making shady deals on the black market for fake passports. It was pure theatre, and Dorien's whole life was a performance.

But he was also my friend, and he'd taken a huge risk for us, for Elena. I took the proffered envelope and slid it into my coat pocket. "What about you?"

"For once, this isn't about me." Dorien reached into his coat pocket and withdrew a mobile phone, a couple of tickets, and a stack of Euros. "This will get you to St. Petersburg. You'll need to exchange the money somewhere. You've got visas in the passports, so you shouldn't be asked any questions. I don't care where you head after that – just make it somewhere far, far away from her. Stay on the move until I can sort things on this end. The phone is a burner and I'm the only one who has the number. Call me when you get there, let me know you're safe, then ditch the phone, too."

"Why Russia?" Elena's lip trembled. "I want to go home to Romania."

"You know that's the first place she'll look." Dorien folded my fingers over the tickets. "First, we get you away. Then Titus and I will expose her for the monster she is. Once we've got your money and she can no longer hurt you, you can go wherever you want."

I met his eyes. A hundred unspoken things passed between us. I'd been all over the world with this guy. I'd seen him at his absolute worst, and until today I'd never felt as if I knew him at all. He certainly hadn't known me. These tickets were more than just scraps of paper – they spoke of the depth of Dorien's friendship, of the way he took the pain of others and bore it on his own shoulders, weaving it into his music as if he hoped he could heal the world.

I swallowed. "I cannot thank you—"

"Don't." He cut me off. "Don't you dare fucking thank me."

I thought of everything Dorien was giving up by putting me on this train. We were only a week into our most successful tour yet – if we didn't perform in Bratislava tomorrow night, we'd be on the hook with our promoter for a ton of money. Not to mention our pissed-off fans. And Madame Usher... I shuddered to think about what punishment she'd dream up for him after she discovered he helped us flee.

Elena squared my hand, pulling me back to myself. As much as I loved Dorien in this moment, it paled in comparison to what I felt for her. Elena was my sunshine, my reason for breathing. The gifts of the Zână flowed from her, and it was my job to protect her. Now I knew Madame Usher's plans for her, I felt in my bones that we had to do this.

We'd been prisoners of Manderley since we were eight years old. The things we'd endured at the hands of that woman still made my skin crawl... and we'd survived it all in the name of a better life. But a respite from her torment would never come. I could live in the shadows – I'd been there all my life – but Elena was made of warmth and sunlight. Locking her away would see her wither and rot. It would break Elena, and watching her break would kill me.

We had no choice. We had to go.

Dorien must've sensed what I was thinking, because he smiled his sad, stormy smile. "I'm sorry, my friend. I thought things could be different for us."

I thought so, too. When Dorien blew into my life like a storm breaking against the shore, I dared to dream of something more for Elena. Now, he may be the only way to save her. I looked into that impish half-smile of his, and for the first time in my life, I felt what it meant to *trust* someone.

A whistle blew. The crowd of passengers surged toward the platform. Dorien gave me a nudge. I squeezed Elena's hand. With a last nod to Dorien, I dragged her into the fray.

Elena and I fought our way through the crowd to the waiting train. We stepped on board, ducking and weaving through people until we found our seats. I slid my violin case into the luggage rack, and Elena clutched a backpack with all our money and a few clothes hastily thrown inside. My heart hammered against my chest so loud I was sure the conductor would hear it and kick us off.

In front of us, a group of tourists from New Zealand in black t-shirts laughed and teased each other. They talked loudly about the bands they were going to see and the mead they'd drink at a heavy metal festival in Germany next week. I longed to be one of them – carefree, thinking only of fun things and friendship.

We were supposed to be playing at that festival. Titus could barely sit still, he was so excited about it. I was pleased I wasn't there to see Titus' face when he found out it wouldn't happen.

Elena huddled against me. As we pulled out of the station, her head drooped on my shoulder, her long eyelashes fluttering shut. I stared out the window, unable to sleep. I wouldn't sleep until we were far from Madame Usher's evil. Maybe not even then.

Prague sped by in a blur of narrow alleys, burgher houses, Soviet blocks, and towering spires. The city lights glittered off the Vltava River, and I wished we could be sitting on one of those open-topped tourist boats, enjoying a beer as though we didn't have the specter of Manderley bearing down on us. My mind cast back to the euphoria of last night – standing on stage with Titus and Dorien at our sold-out show in one of the most beautiful cities in the world. The audience in rapture, clapping and stomping for more, more, more of us. Our music heard and loved and *felt*. It should have been the high point of my career, and yet, here we were, sneaking away as ghosts in the night.

The train chugged on into the gloom. The city lights gave way to darkened fields and ugly villages of concrete brutalism. A cart offering reheated meals – stewed meat with potato dumplings – wheeled by, but the smell of the food made me feel ill. It reminded me of another home across the Carpathian mountains, a tiny walled city I'd once been so desperate to escape.

The roar of the crowd still coursed through my veins, mingled with the ever-present thunder of my racing heart.

The conductor turned out the lights, and the passengers reclined their chairs and pulled on sleeping masks. One by one even the metalheads fell asleep, hugging their enormous backpacks emblazoned with flags and ferns. I stared into the bleak night, knowing I should sleep but finding the idea of closing my eyes impossible. How could I sleep and leave Elena unguarded?

Even on the other side of the world, Manderley squeezed in on us, the walls of that house becoming our prison. Every year another fresh-faced group of music students entered its walls, but Manderley changed them. Hardened them. Extracted their secrets and left them bound to it forever. Now that Victor was gone, Madame Usher had no one to temper her evil, and Master Radcliffe—

My body jerked as the train screeched to a halt. Elena's head whipped up. "Are we in Poland?" she asked sleepily.

"We are not." I peered out the window. Outside was pitch black – no lights from a platform, no glittering city sprawling across the horizon. We were stopped in the middle of nowhere, with rain driving into the train.

A commotion started at the front of the car. Doors swung open and two men barked at the conductor in loud voices. They spoke Czech, so I couldn't understand what they were saying. I didn't need to.

"Get up," I growled. I dragged my violin case from the compartment. Elena opened her mouth to argue, but she must've seen the fear in my eyes because she snapped it shut again. She picked up the backpack containing our worldly possessions and followed me toward the rear of the car.

I tugged Elena past the bathroom and through the next car, moving as quickly as we dared. The lights flickered on and passengers stared bleary-eyed into the gloom, trying to figure out why we stopped. I yanked open the compartment door, and we entered the gangway. A foul smell rose from the bathroom, and Elena pinched her nose in disgust.

I slammed my fist into the button. With a hiss, the external door released. A rush of frigid air tinged with diesel slammed into us. Elena coughed. I grabbed her hand and yanked her down the steps.

"Ivan, where are we going?" She hurried after me as I picked my way along the tracks, away from the lights of the train, away from the whistleblowing and men shouting. Wind battered against us. I slid into a ditch, dragging Elena behind me. My violin case banged against my knee, but I ignored the pain.

We have to run. We can't go back.

I tossed the violin case onto the other side of the ditch, wincing as it bounced against a rock. That violin was precious, and I hoped it wasn't damaged. I scrambled up the slippery slope and reached back to pull Elena up after me. My palms stung where they grazed the rocks, and the driving rain flayed at my skin. Behind me, Elena whimpered as her sneakers sank into the mud. But we didn't stop.

I plunged into the trees. Branches scraped my arms and attacked my violin case. Elena dropped my hand to hold the backpack over her head, trying to shelter her face from the onslaught.

My feet slammed into something hard. I pitched forward. My violin case flew from my hands. *Fuck.* I felt around in the gloom for what had stopped me. A fallen log. *A hiding place.* I tugged Elena down beside me, pressing our back against the log and using it to shelter us from view. She whimpered again as we sank into the mud, but I held my finger to my lips.

The wind howled around us, wild and angry. I pressed Elena into my body, wrapping my arms around her. She trembled – whether from cold or fear, I could not tell.

We needed a little of her *Zâne* magic now.

In the distance, the train blew its whistle. The tracks shuddered as the wheels turned and it took off. I squeezed Elena's hands, pressing them to my heart as we waited. Our breath puffed in clouds of steam. The tips of my fingers had gone worryingly numb.

I lost track of how long we waited, huddled together in the brutal cold. We could no longer hear the train or the people. I couldn't hear anything except the wild wind and the pounding of my heart. I helped Elena to her feet and bent to pick up my violin case.

"We'll follow the train tracks until we find a village. Hopefully, there will be a bus or—"

A hand fell upon my shoulder, snapping my body backward. My grip on Elena broke, and she screamed as another black-clad figure leaped from behind a tree and grabbed her hands, twisting them behind her back.

"You're coming with us," my captor hissed in my ear. "Madame Usher does not like it when her little birds fly the coop."

FAYE

...

FAYE

...

DORIEN

This is completely fucked.

4

FAYE

...

5

IVAN

"Have you seen Faye?" I shoved open the door to the Yellow Room. Titus stood beneath the window, a silhouette against the golden glow of the setting sun. Blades of orange fire pierced the thick canopy of trees to torch the carpet around him. Titus preferred to stand when he played, his feet planted wide and his head bent over the strings of the cello, his braids swinging wild around his face as he practiced his performance piece for this evening. In a normal concert setting he was forced to sit, holding the posture of a 'proper' musician. But when we played Muse shows he stood like this, holding a place of power. Sometimes he'd swing his cello around the stage, stalking and slinking about with the instrument in his enormous hands as girls in the audience grabbed at his legs.

Seeing him standing like that – his statuesque features tight with concentration, his lower lip protruding as he fought with Sibelius for control – sent a rush of memories slamming into my head. Of the first time I met Titus in New Orleans during a choral competition, when he'd snuck me and Elena out from beneath Madame Usher's watchful gaze and took us to see an underground metal show. Of him surging into the mosh pit, dark hair flying, kind eyes glowing with abandon as he unleashed a beast that lurked inside him.

Of Broken Muse shows, of the look of utter rapture on Titus' face when he cast aside the mask he wore every day and lost himself in the music.

Of the tightness in his voice whenever he spoke to his parents – that desperate sense that he was trying to cram himself into a tiny box, but the seams were ready to burst and there was nothing he could do to stop it.

As I strode toward him, he set the bow down and jerked his head up, and I saw he had that desperation about him now. He wasn't comfortable. He didn't fit here, and he knew it. The only things at Manderley that truly made sense to him were Broken Muse, Faye, and that guitar under his bed. Like all of us, Titus was hiding from a truth that gnawed away at him, and tonight, with his parents in the audience, he'd have to be on guard, lest the seams finally broke and his darkness was unleashed.

"She went to her room to get ready." He kept his voice even, begging me to pretend I hadn't just seen what I'd seen. If I'd been Dorien, I might have tried to call him out on it, tried to convince him to come clean to his parents about what he really wanted. But I wasn't Dorien, and right now, we had more important things to worry about.

"She's not there." I cast my eyes around the room, feeling that familiar prickle of someone watching me, of the house itself betraying my secrets. "She's not in the kitchen or out fetching more wood. She's not polishing the silver or dusting the Fazioli. And I can't find Heather or Dorien anywhere, either."

Titus nearly dropped his cello. "Heather's missing?" His chest sank as he pushed out his breath. "We need to find them."

He replaced his cello into its stand, and the two of us barreled upstairs to the attic. Titus had to stoop beneath the low ceiling as he pushed open Faye's door. *Why didn't she lock her room?*

Titus swept through the small space, taking in the absence of her the same way I'd done a few minutes ago – the clothes thrown casually across the bed, the empty garment bag that had held her concert dress crumpled on the floor, the makeup case missing from the bathroom counter. The cold prickle on my skin told me something had happened to her.

Titus unlatched the window and pushed it open, inspecting the latches and windowsill. "This is locked, and I don't see any signs of a shoe scuffing or a struggle..."

His back froze rigid as he peered down at the edge of the sloping roof and the overgrown garden below. I knew he was thinking about Micah. His shoulders sagged in relief, and I knew he hadn't seen Faye's body crumpled and mangled beneath us. Titus pointed at a movement on the edge of the woods. "There's Dorien."

I crossed the room in three strides to stand beside him, peering out over the garden. Heather emerged from the path leading down to the gazebo, a chilling smirk playing across her lips. Dorien trailed behind her, his red shirt and trouser hems covered in dirt and dead leaves. Even more concerning, his shoulders were tight and his cruel mouth was set in a hard line. He stopped and turned to look over his shoulder. He turned back, and even from here I could see the bleak horror flicker in his eyes.

What has he done?

Titus met my eyes, and the unspoken message passed between us. We bolted for the door and crashed down the narrow stairs, meeting Dorien just as he slunk up the main staircase. Titus grabbed him by the scruff of his shirt and dragged him into his bedroom, slamming the door behind us.

"Ow, fuck." Dorien's face twisted as Titus slammed him into the wall. A Broken Muse poster behind his head tore away, the colorful paper hanging in a jagged ribbon.

"Faye's missing." I'd never seen gentle Titus look so dangerous. He shook Dorien, tearing the ribbon of poster away so it floated to the ground. "You wouldn't know anything about that, would you?"

Dorien's gaze flicked toward the window. That one look told us everything. Titus dropped him. As soon as Dorien's feet hit the floor, he seemed to make a decision. The horror in his eyes glazed over and he cast his face into a mask of his usual arrogance. He reached into his closet and pulled out his suit, as if everything was normal. As if Faye wasn't in danger.

"Dorien, *fuck*." Titus' hands curled into fists.

"You must tell us." I picked up the ribbon of poster. It was the Broken Muse band logo, torn through the middle. I balled the paper in my hands and lobbed it at Dorien's head, wishing it was something harder, wishing I could knock some sense into my friend.

"Faye is fine." He removed his shirt. The words IN CAUDA VENENUM stretched and contracted across his pecs as he pulled a fresh white shirt from his closet and buttoned it over his chest.

"She's not here, and the concert starts in *two hours*. The guests will be here soon. Not to mention the fact it's dark outside, and the temperature will drop, and—"

"After everything we've been through, do you honestly believe I'd let anything happen to her?" Dorien slipped his muscled legs into his trousers and looped the belt at his narrow waist. "I'm taking care of Faye. Everything is under control."

I wanted to believe him. I wanted to find reassurance in the deft way he knotted his silk tie, in the casual ease with which he smoothed down his suit. But in his eyes I saw the same boy who'd handed me fake passports at a train station in Prague – the boy who wanted to save the world but was instead being immolated by it.

Dorien Valencourt was not the one in control here, and he was *terrified*.

And Faye – *our* Faye – was in trouble, and he refused to let us help her.

6

FAYE

I awoke in darkness. My head pounded like someone had stuck it inside a church organ and mashed down all the keys.

Once, I'd been invited to a prep-school party at some girl's fancy East Village penthouse. I met a group of stoners out on the fire-escape (what's the collective noun for a group of stoners? I'm going with a *bakery*), downed half a bottle of Southern Comfort, and woke up under a bush in Central Park wearing my panties on my head. The hangover had felt something like this.

Ow. Owie. Owwwwww...

I tried to grab my head to shove my brains back inside. The ground twisted out from beneath me, and my body lurched. I reached out a hand to steady myself, only instead of a wall or the brass head of my bed, my fingers slammed into some kind of slippery fabric.

Huh? Wha—

I lurched again, and though the fog in my brain I registered that I wasn't stationary. My ass jabbed against something hard, and my body jerked and jostled as I was shuffled by invisible hands. I threw out my arms, shoving against the fabric that held me, and my mind searched for a memory of what happened.

I'm not hungover. I've hit my head. And now I'm being moved—

"Fuck. She's woken up." A muffled voice reached my ears from the other side of the fabric barrier. "Dorien, you idiot. You didn't use enough of that stuff."

Heather.

Dorien.

With the hiss of those words, the memories came back to me. Climbing the stairs to my room and encountering that horrid vision – Clare's face staring at me from the gloom, her mouth open in a silent scream as shadows twisted from her body, reaching for me. Staggering back into the arms of an assailant. Fighting with two shadowy figures. The hand over my mouth. The sweet smell in my nostrils as whatever drug they gave me dragged me into oblivion.

And now...

I was trapped inside some sort of enormous bag – the kind of bag a romance reader would bring along to a book signing. And the bag was moving, being carried along by Heather and Dorien.

"It's tough to hold something over her mouth when she's just kicked you in the testicles." Dorien's voice cut through me like a knife. "If you had nuts, Heather, you'd understand."

"I've got more balls than you ever have." Heather laughed. "I'm willing to do whatever is necessary to succeed."

She wasn't lying. Nothing about Heather shocked me now, but...

Dorien.

Dorien the dickweasel.

Hot anger rose inside me. Dorien had convinced me he was on my side. I *trusted* him. He made me agree that he could continue to torment me for Madame Usher's benefit, but in private, he was supposed to be *mine*. He let me believe that we would play my composition together for the world to hear, for his *parents* to hear… but it was all a lie. Instead, he and Heather drugged me and kidnapped me, and were taking me fuck-knows where.

I gave him my heart, and he'd ripped it to pieces in front of me.

Sound the fucktrumpets, I'm so stupid.

My ass bounced on something hard, cracking my tailbone. I howled as pain rocketed up my spine.

"Shut her up!" Heather yelled.

"Don't be so dramatic. No one will hear her out here," Dorien said. "We've come far enough. Let's leave her and get back to the party."

The bag dropped on a hard surface, jolting my throbbing tailbone. Someone kicked the side of the bag, driving the wind from my lungs. I doubled over, gasping for air as fresh pain bloomed across my temples. Outside, Heather giggled. "Now that's what I call taking out the trash."

"You can't leave me here." I punched the side of the bag.

"We just did," Heather called back, her voice already distant. I imagined her flipping her perfect honey-blonde hair over her shoulder as she linked arms with Dorien. I imagined him staring down at me with a satisfied smirk playing across his too-perfect mouth. My hand curled into a fist, but it would only have the empty satisfaction of punching the bag.

"You can't do this," I yelled. "Dorien, let me out!"

I scratched my nails against the bag, but it was no good. The fabric was thick and made of some kind of extra-tough material – maybe leather? I felt for the zipper, trying to push it open, but they must've locked or tied it shut on the outside, because no matter how hard I pulled, it wouldn't budge.

Tears pooled in the corners of my ears. I swiped them away angrily. *Don't lose it now.* I thought of my mother, all alone in that hospital room two hours from Manderley Academy. She should have been here tonight to see me play. But someone poisoned her. Someone attacked her.

I should never have come to Manderley. I should be with her.

But I am here. And I'm not letting Dorien fucking Valencourt win this round.

My jaw set with new determination, I felt around in my pockets and on the bottom of the bag, looking for something I might be able to use. Judging by the feel of the ground, I'd been set down on rock. I could hear an owl hooting and wind rustling through the trees. I was in the woods. But that didn't exactly narrow things down – Manderley was built on the edge of the mountain range, with a vast tract of managed forest and wild woodlands stretching down into the valley. I could be *anywhere*.

I swallowed down a lump of panic and forced myself to consider my circumstances rationally. I couldn't be too far from Manderley. My kidnappers would have left themselves time to get back for the party. *If I can just get out of this bag—*

I felt around for something I might be able to use, or a loose thread I could pull. My fingers brushed a long, thin object in my back pocket. I pulled it out, inspecting it with my hands. *It feels like a tiny flashlight.*

I flicked it on and inspected the inner walls of the bag. I wondered why I had the flashlight. I hadn't been walking around the house with a flashlight in my pocket. Why would Heather and Dorien drug me and drag me out here, then give me a flashlight? It didn't make any sense.

I aimed the light upward to examine the zipper in detail, and gasped. Along the seam of the bag were scrawled the words:

"I'M COMING BACK FOR YOU."

Fuck. Fuck. Fuck.

I sucked in stale air as I struggled to keep my panic in check. My mind flashed back to the message on the pantry wall in Clare's loopy handwriting, or the single word scrawled across my mother's forehead.

I'M COMING BACK FOR YOU. What did it mean? Was it a threat? They were coming back to finish me off? It was obviously from Heather and Dorien – they wanted me to wait in this bag in the cold and imagine all the horrible things they might do to me.

Or was it… something else? Clare's face flashed in my mind again, joining with all the other strange and unexplained things that had happened at Manderley Academy. Was the message from some entity or spirit from beyond the grave?

Don't be such a bitchbadger. Ghosts don't exist. All the weird things were just Dorien fucking with you, which he's gone and proved tonight. And even if there was a ghost, acknowledging that now is not going to get you back to Manderley. Find a way out of this bag and deal with the spectral maid later.

I swallowed once, twice, three times, forcing back my panic. I swung the beam of the flashlight all around me. All I could see were the rough inner surface of the bag, the slash of the zipper I couldn't budge, and my knees poking through holes in my torn jeans. And those words – those evil, malevolent words that swam in my vision and made bile rise in my throat.

"Help! Help me!" I yelled. Hikers used the trails on the mountain that snaked close to Manderley. If there was a chance someone was out there right now, I had to get their attention. I kept yelling as I scrambled around on my hands and knees, shuffling the bag across the ground. If I could rub the fabric over a sharp rock or thorned tree, then—

The zipper tore open. A shaft of moonlight punctured my gloom.

"If you hurry, you'll make it back in time," someone whispered in a voice so quiet I couldn't tell if it was male or female. I was positive I didn't recognize the voice, but something about it seemed familiar.

What the fuck?

"Dorien?"

Footsteps rushed away as I grabbed for the open zipper.

"Hello?" I popped my head outside. "Hey, where did you go?"

It took a moment for my eyes to adjust to the bright moonlight. Trees rustled behind me. I spun in the direction of the sound, but I lost my balance and tripped over the bag. I yelped as my knee cracked against the rocks.

My breath roared in my ears. I rolled out of the bag and scrambled for the flashlight. I clicked it on and trained it on the trees, searching for whoever freed me.

They'd disappeared into the mist.

7

FAYE

*E*ven with the flashlight, the hike back to the academy would take some time. First, I had to climb to the top of the ridge to get my bearings. Luckily, Madame Usher had Manderley lit up like Fourth of July fireworks for the party tonight. Solar torches along the drive acted like a landing strip pointing toward the house, which glowed on the horizon – a beacon.

Not a beacon of hope, because hope had no place at Manderley.

I glanced around again, hoping for some shortcut to present itself, wishing for a knight in shining armor to appear from the trees, throw me over the back of his horse, and ride on to Manderley. I'd settle for a ride on Titus' shoulders or even to hold Ivan's hand for a single moment to steady my fractured nerves.

But Titus and Ivan weren't here. I didn't even know if they were involved in what Dorien did tonight. I remembered Titus throwing himself at Heather when she tried to burn my hand, how Ivan's cold eyes bore into Aroha as he twisted her arms behind her. How they swore to protect me. How they drew me into their world, into their hearts, knowing that they were footnotes against the history that weighed between Dorien and I. I couldn't believe they were involved, but then, I'd been foolish enough to trust Dorien, so what the fuck did I know?

Apart from an owl hooting, I was alone.

I had no choice. I started walking.

Branches tore at my skin as I pushed through the trees. My thighs ached, and every step jolted my stinging tailbone until tears itched the corners of my eyes. Hiking wasn't exactly an extracurricular activity offered at either of my previous schools. And even if it was, I'd never have opted for it. Nature wasn't my jam.

I stepped into a wide clearing. At first, I thought I must be near the poison garden because of the way the forest retreated from the center, as if afraid to accidentally brush against the fatal earth. But no. What stood in the clearing wasn't a Victorian greenhouse but a hexagonal building made of stone and covered so thoroughly with vines and weeds that it appeared to protrude from the mantle of the earth itself, as if thrust up from some deep subterranean city of cyclopean remnants. Curious, I stepped toward it.

As I rounded the building, a loud *CREAK* punctured the stillness. My heart stuttered before I noticed a gate swinging out from the structure, caught by the wind. No, not a gate as such. I stepped closer. It was a door made from a lattice of wrought-iron, elaborately cast to form a crest in the center. I pushed away some of the weeds to look at the crest. The word USHER was written in gothic script in a ribbon across the top, and beneath it, the words IN CAUDA VENENUM.

The same words written above the poison garden.

The same words tattooed across Dorien's chest.

I didn't understand the significance of the phrase. Latin hadn't been on the school curriculum, either. But I thought I knew what the stone structure contained.

This must be the Usher family mausoleum.

I stepped up to the grate, running my hands over the metal, tugging away the vines that held it until I uncovered a narrow doorway accessed by three stone steps. The doorway was flanked by two columns – their style echoing the columns holding up Manderley's crumbling front porch. A later, Victorian construction, then.

Inside, all was in gloom. I trained the beam of my flashlight into the depths. The hairs on my arms stood on end, and I felt a kind of twang in the air – a violin-string pulled too tight, ready to snap at any moment. Like the heroine in a horror film, I knew this was a bad idea, but I couldn't tear myself away. I had to see.

I stepped inside.

The temperature dropped as I descended three stone steps into a hexagonal room. I rubbed my hands on my prickling arms as I gazed around the space. Like so much of Manderley, the mausoleum was in great need of TLC, and I didn't mean the 90s hip hop group. The building was topped with an impressive cupola adorned with sculptures depicting the Stations of the Cross, but the stone had cracked in several places and many of the sculptures existed only as pieces of rubble littering the ground. Vines twisted through the cracks, hanging down into the space like a living chandelier. Spiderwebs glittered from the grated windows on either side of the hexagon, and my feet crunched as I moved through piles of dead leaves that had blown inside and piled up over the steps and the stone dais in the center.

There were three blocks of niches in the walls, some empty, others covered with capstones carved with names and dates. Between them were statues of weeping angels beneath the windows. The angels' eyes seemed to follow me as I moved toward the center of the room, where an above-ground stone tomb dominated the space. My eyes scanned the names and dates on the niches in the walls. Most of the graves were from the

1800s, except for two closest to the door – Victor and Mary – who I presumed were Victor Usher's parents.

I stepped up onto the edge of the stone dais, my shoes crushing piles of dead leaves and fuckadoodle-knows what else. I scraped a hand through the detritus shrouding the stone – vines and weeds, and dried bunches of stalks tied with crimson ribbon, the remnants of floral bouquets and wreaths – pushing it away to reveal the stone sculpted into the figure of a sleeping man, holding a sword and a tablet upon which a name was carved – Victor Usher. Madame Usher's husband.

He died only last year, six months before Madame Usher invited me to Manderley. But this place looked like it hadn't been touched in centuries. Madame Usher didn't believe in keeping her husband's final resting place tidy. I remembered what she told me when we first met – that she planned to leave Victor Usher for my father before he disappeared. And even though that was over ten years ago, I wondered how much it had tainted their relationship since, as Madame Usher had tainted everything at Manderley.

I moved down the tomb, pushing away more leaves and vines. My fingers pressed into a crack running across the stone – the whole thing looked so heavy, but I wondered if this section would come away if I lifted it—

"Faye. Fayeee..."

What the fuck?

My name echoed across the stones. My heart thundered, and a fresh wave of agony pounded against my skull. I spun toward the sound, flicking the flashlight across the walls. *Sound the fuck-trumpets, what now?*

"Hello? Who's there?"

"Fayeeeee..."

The hairs on my neck prickled.

It's just the wind whistling through the grated window. It's just—

A shadow thrust itself from one of the unoccupied niches,

barreling toward me with malicious intent. I staggered back. The flashlight beam trembled as the shadows resolved themselves into the shape of a girl. A girl with frizzy brown hair pulled back into a bun, with the most adorable tiny nose, with green eyes that shone with pain, through which I could see the capstones on the wall behind her.

Clare.

"Fayeeeee…" The voice swirled around me, everywhere and nowhere.

My mouth moved, but I couldn't speak, couldn't scream. Wind lashed against me, and the fear tore away my voice. I stood, frozen, the flashlight shaking in my hands, as Clare moved across the tomb, gliding toward me without moving her legs.

Clare raised her hands. Shadows crawled from her skin and spilled from her mouth, swirling around her. She reached Victor's tomb, but instead of going around it, the figure went right through it like it wasn't there at all.

Like *she* wasn't there at all.

I forced my legs to move, staggering backward until my ankles clipped the edge of the step.

No. No no no no no. This can't be real—

"*Fayeeee,*" Clare's voice rasped against my skull, almost as if it came from inside my own head. "*Only you can save Manderley from the voice in the walls.*"

8

FAYE

"*Fayeeeeee...*"

BANG.

The mausoleum gate slammed shut.

Clare's voice hissed at me, dry as the grave from which it had come. I swallowed back my fear and forced my legs to move again. I scrambled back up the stone steps, my chest heaving and heart racing. My head swam with a pulsing agony punctuated by the loathsome scratch of Clare's voice as I spun in a daze, pushing against the grate until it flew open.

I tripped on the step and sprawled into the dirt outside, driving the air from my lungs. I looked back as the grate swung in the wind, slamming shut with an ominous *CLANG.*

An owl hooted.

Dead leaves skittered across the damp ground.

My ears rang with a noise made of silence and fear.

I pressed my hand to my chest, against my galloping heart. I listened. I waited. Clare didn't appear, but I fancied I caught the whisper of her voice on the wind.

Fayeee...

I dragged myself to my feet and sprinted into the trees,

gasping for air as I fought to keep moving through the cold. Some oppressive force bore down on me, driving me away from the mausoleum. I skidded over the damp ground, my fingers clawing at tree branches that attacked my face. I crashed forward into the gloom, letting the lights of Manderley guide me.

My chest heaving, I crested the steep slope where the stream trickled into the valley, and Manderley's glory came into view. I broke into a run. I'd never been so happy to see that oppressive building. Lights blazed from the downstairs rooms, and I could see from the figures moving in the windows the party was already in full swing.

The horror of what I'd seen in the mausoleum faded as I surged toward the very real reason I'd been stuck out in the forest to begin with. Dorien and Heather wanted me to fail. But I wasn't broken yet.

What time is it? Am I too late?

I raced through the dead forest surrounding the poison garden, my feet splashing in puddles left on the path by the retreating rain. I bolted across the overgrown kitchen garden and slammed into the back door. I twisted the handle – locked. I pounded my fists against the wood. "Help, help! Let me in."

Someone yanked the door back. Harrison's face appeared, haloed by the warm lights of the kitchen. "Miss de Winter? I was so worried about you. I wanted to call the police—"

"Harrison, was it you?" I gripped his collar. "Please, tell me if it was you who let me out of the bag."

"I don't know what you're talking about, love." He stared down at my filthy clothes. "But you'd best get yourself cleaned up before you join the party. All the guests have gathered in the ball-room for the performances."

Shit. Shit. Shit. I burst into the kitchen just as the first snatches of Elena's performance piece jarred in the air. My knee twinged with pain, and my head spun. I knew I was covered in dirt, my clothes soaked through, my hair a rat's nest.

How the hell am I going to get up to my room to change without anyone seeing me? I took a step toward the door—

—and stopped dead.

There, sitting on the corner of the kitchen table, was a stack of clothes. *My* clothes. The crimson gown I'd laid out to wear tonight sat neatly folded with some toiletries and a jewelry box on top of my violin case.

A note stuck to the box read, 'break a leg, Faye.'

9

FAYE

Cold dread settled in my chest as I stared at the pile of my belongings, here in the kitchen instead of behind the locked door to my bedroom. This was one too many creepy-ass things to happen today. "Harrison, where did these come from?"

He shook his head. "I've no idea, I'm sorry. When we couldn't find you, I came in to help with the food, and there they were. And a godsend, too, by the looks of it. Hurry, love, there's still time for you to make it."

He was right – I didn't have time to question who had broken into my locked room and placed this stuff for me to find. I grabbed the stack of clothes. Whoever had left them for me had even thought to add my makeup bag. Harrison left to carry out trays of food, giving me a wink as he shut the kitchen door behind him. I tossed my soiled clothes into a corner, scrubbed the dirt from my skin and hair over the kitchen sink, and pulled on my dress. I did the best job I could on my face with the tiny compact mirror and the horrendous lighting. All the while, the jewelry box stared at me from the top of the range, its presence unnerving.

I could have just left it there, unopened, unacknowledged. But

39

I was far too curious. I flipped open the lid to reveal a beautiful set of jewels. A necklace glittering with droplets of red rubies, and earrings to match. They complimented my dress perfectly. I threaded the earrings through my ears, clasped the necklace to my throat, picked up my beautiful new violin, and raced through to the ballroom as the final bewitching notes of Elena's performance swirled around me.

I lingered at the doorway as Elena rose from the piano stool, her silver hair streaming down her back and a serene smile playing across her lips. She looked every bit a fae queen from some otherworldly realm, indulging her earthly subjects with a song that wove magic in the air.

Behind her, a semicircle of guests stood in rapt attention. Some clapped, others bowed their heads in silent acknowledgment of Elena's genius. Master Radcliffe rushed forward to present her with a bouquet of roses. In the low light, I could just make out Dorien and Heather standing behind him. Heather leaned over to whisper something to Dorien, but he didn't appear to have heard her. His face was hard, his mouth set, but his stormy grey eyes were drenched in misery. I glanced away, unable to face him. I couldn't let myself be drawn into his beguiling darkness again.

"Brava, brava, Elena." Madame Usher basked in the glow of Elena's glory. Tonight, she eschewed her usual funereal black gowns for a silk and taffeta number in a deep, royal purple. With her hair twisted back and a necklace of ruby droplets at her throat, I caught a flicker of what Victor Usher and my father might've seen in her. She had nothing on my mother, but there *was* a statuesque, powerful beauty about her – like a crash of a violent wave before it tossed a helpless boat against the rocks.

Madame Usher thrust her hands in the air as Master Radcliffe led Elena back into the crowd and Dorien shuffled forward to take his seat at the piano for our piece. "Thank you, Elena. That was perfection. Unfortunately, our next student, Faye de Winter, wasn't feeling well and couldn't join us tonight, so Dorien Valencourt will perform her piece accompanied by Heather Danvers—"

"Good news." I swept into the room. "I feel much better now, so I thought I'd join the party."

If looks could kill, I'd be dead and buried. Madame Usher's face froze in disbelief, her fingers dangling in midair. Heather swore. Titus started toward me, but Ivan held him back. I could tell from their faces they'd had no idea what happened to me, and the relief of that surged through my veins, driving my defiant spirit onward as I stepped into the light.

Dorien kept his head turned away from me. His shoulders stiffened. His back fused ramrod straight.

A collective gasp swept through the room as I glided across the floor in my crimson dress, my violin clutched in my hands. I kept my chin high, my eyes locked with Madame Usher, daring her to deny me.

Behind Madame Usher, Heather's cheeks burned with fire.

Titus broke free of Ivan's grasp. He crossed the room in three strides and took my hand in his, escorting me to my place in front of the piano. "Where have you been?" he whispered. "We were so worried about you."

I shook my head. I couldn't think about it now. I needed every ounce of strength within me to make it through this piece with Dorien.

Madame Usher composed herself. She clearly hadn't expected me to be here tonight, but whether that meant she had anything to do with my kidnapping I couldn't determine. "We're so pleased to hear it, Faye. If you'd like to join Dorien for your piece..." She turned to the people behind her. "Faye has made a study of Paganini this year, and she's inspired by his showy style. Her little finger can be quite weak, but she's managing."

I'll show you managing.

I rested my instrument against my chin. Dorien lifted his eyes to mine, and I reveled in the pain and regret swimming in those orbs. *Fuck you, Dorien.* With a smugness born of hiking through a fucking forest and twice seeing a ghostly visage I couldn't yet explain, I struck the first note.

The music soared through the ballroom, wild and vibrant and filled with my distinctive fire. Master Radcliffe's breath hitched as note after perfect note fell from my bow. At the piano, Dorien's fingers trailed along the keys – perfect as always, but this time fading away, becoming part of the background so I could shine.

I closed my eyes and poured all my pain and rage and hurt into the piece. I played better than I'd ever played before. Dorien and I soared together as the notes flew from my fingers, as the melody took the entire room on a journey with me, into the fires of hell and back. Even the near-impossible arpeggios felt like butterflies fluttering against my skin. Sometimes playing music was about remembering the notes, and sometimes it was this – this magical, ethereal presence that takes over your body and makes you soar.

Smells circled around me – the scented memories I conjured whenever I played. This time, the air sang with polished wood flooring and Victor Usher's distinctive cigars – the smell of the old New York music school where Dorien and I first met, where we'd first started down the destructive path that led to this moment.

When I finished and took my bow, a deathly silence clung to the room. Master Radcliffe stood and applauded. "Brava." He kissed my cheeks. "I see our fears about your unconventional training were unjustified. You are a rare talent, Ms. de Winter. I see so much of your father in you."

BAM. Just like that, my good mood evaporated. No matter what I did, my father was always in the room with me, his legacy hanging over my head like my own personal sword of Damocles.

Dorien strode toward me, his eyes dark. He looked like he was going to be sick. "Sprite, I—"

Titus and Ivan were at my side in moments, pulling me back through the crowd. Dorien's eyes burned into my back, but I refused to turn and acknowledge him. Titus and Ivan pulled me right to the back of the room, into the small alcove formed at the base of one of the turrets. A table had been set up here, laden with the food I prepared and bottles of Champagne in silver buckets. The first tinkling notes of Heather's piece sounded in the vast room, muffled by the thick curtains – just as well, because she sounded as vapid and lifeless as ever.

"You were remarkable." Ivan pressed a Champagne flute into my fingers.

I lifted the glass to my lips and realized my hands were trembling. Titus' warm hands fell on my shoulders, and he moved me away from the table and into the alcove of the windows. I gripped the sill, my gaze flickering outside to where the trees bent toward the house, branches reaching like fingers beckoning, threatening to drag me back out into the cold forest. I remembered that creepy mausoleum and Clare's horrific visage gliding toward me, and the words written inside the bag. A shiver cascaded down my spine.

"Where were you?" Titus demanded again. "And what did Dorien have to do with it? He's been acting fucking weird all evening, and then we couldn't find you anywhere."

Now that my piece was over, the full horror of what they did to me and what I'd seen tonight washed over me. I gripped Titus' arm as my knees buckled. "It was horrible. You swear you didn't know anything about what... what they did..."

"Hell no. We've been looking for you all afternoon." Titus wrapped his arms around me, holding me upright, steadying me against his bulk. "We were going to call the police, but someone stole our phones from our room and Madame Usher refused to let us use the house phone."

"We couldn't find Heather, either," Ivan said. "We thought that at least if Dorien went after you, you'd be safe."

"I'm never safe with Dorien Valencourt," I hissed. As Titus held me steady, I relayed everything that happened since I saw them last – going up to my room, being attacked and drugged, waking up in the bag, being let out by an unknown source, running back to Manderley, the mausoleum, then finding my clothes in the kitchen, waiting for me. As I spoke, the full horror of it weighed on me, and the headache bloomed across my temples once more. I couldn't believe it had all transpired in a few short hours. It felt like a lifetime had passed.

When I woke up this morning, Dorien Valencourt had my heart, along with his fellow Muses. Now, all he had was my hatred, and I'd make damn sure he suffered for what he did.

The only bits I left out were the words I found scrawled in the pantry and inside the bag, and seeing Clare's face. Now that I was back at Manderley and faced with the very real horror of what Dorien and Heather tried to do, I couldn't believe it was anything other than a trick of the drugs Dorien used on me. And in the mausoleum, it was the shadows and the wind playing a trick on me.

It *had* to be.

Because Clare's message makes no sense. There are no ghosts at Manderley – only evil, spiteful dickwizards who are going down.

I thought Dorien cared about me, and then he drugged me. All so he could play my song – *our* song – with Heather? As far as I was concerned, they deserved each other.

Titus and Ivan exchanged glances as I finished my tale in a breathless rush. "I'll kill him right now." Ivan's fists tightened at his sides. In his Romanian accent, the harsh words took on a sinister tone. In that moment, I truly believed my ice prince capable of murdering his so-called friend.

"We'll kill him together." Titus cracked his knuckles. His fingers were so large the sound was like approaching thunder.

"But not tonight. His parents are here. That's torture enough for him for now."

Dorien's parents are here? I pulled the edge of the curtain back and peered into the room, searching the unfamiliar faces. Despite myself, I couldn't help being interested to see them. His mother was always a Grade A bitchbadger at Dorien's rehearsals and recitals. He said they were involved in that weird cult and hadn't been outside their compound for nearly a decade, so I hadn't expected them to show up, but I kind of wanted to see what cult membership did to a woman like her.

Also, I wanted to see Dorien *squirm.*

"You are just afraid to do anything in front of your own parents," Ivan shot back at Titus.

"Damn right." Titus made a face. "I don't like any of this. Dorien and Heather working together... something feels off. He wanted you so much he was willing to share you with us, Faye. He was genuine about his feelings. I don't understand what could have made him do this."

"I can." Ivan's gaze swiveled to the curtains. I leaped away just as a pale hand drew them back from the other side, revealing Madame Usher, her cheeks flushed with pride from the performances.

"Don't hide back here." She flapped her hands toward the ballroom. The cloying scent of her floral perfume wafted around her – she reminded me of the decaying blooms placed on her husband's tomb. She might have once been beautiful, but not even she could hide from the rot that devoured her from within. "Tonight, you are my stars. Your public awaits."

I opened my mouth, but her steel gaze stole my accusations from my lips before they could be spoken aloud. Ivan's nails dug into my arm. Madame Usher turned on her heel and glided back into the room, expecting us to follow her.

Titus sighed. "We should get out there."

"Don't leave our side." Ivan held me close.

"I wouldn't dream of it." I placed my hand on top of his. Titus filled wine glasses for all three of us. I knew I'd need the drink to get through the rest of this event with Dorien's eyes boring into me from across the room.

We stepped out from behind the curtain. Immediately, the tension in the room shifted. Conversations dimmed. Eyes roved over my body, and I heard the words 'Donovan de Winter' slip from several lips. I moved through the crowd, flanked by Ivan and Titus, and it was as if an invisible shield slammed down around me. The stares and whispers that might once have infected me rolled off my skin, leaving me unscathed. The unique intensity of Dorien's gaze touched my skin, but it was dimmed by the light of my two Muses.

I was Faye de Winter, and tonight, I was *untouchable*.

Ivan made a beeline for Elena, who stood with Master Radcliffe, making conversation with three of his friends from the New York Opera. All three men laughed at something Elena said, and Master Radcliffe stared at her with a look of utter enchantment.

Ivan's jaw set in a hard line, and he tugged my arm. But the crowd closed in on us before we could make it to them. "Faye, you were *sublime*." A woman drenched in sickly vanilla perfume and dripping with strings of pearls clasped my hands. "I must have you in my company. Get Gizella to call me. We'll talk about a summer tour—"

"Have you ever thought about joining the theatre, Faye?" A wiry man with horn-rimmed glasses thrust a card under my nose. "We're always in need of musicians, and with your stage presence, you'll be a star—"

"I cannot believe Gizella's had you locked up in this house for months and she didn't even tell us." A portly woman leaned in and pinched my cheek so hard it made tears pool in my eyes. "Wait until I tell my donors about this – the daughter of Donovan de Winter on stage at last. You are poised to be even greater than your father—"

Their voices swirled around me, and I drank in the praise that had never before been directed at me behind the walls of Manderley. I tried to ignore the comments and comparisons to my father, but his name made a burning rage coil down my spine.

Beside me, Titus beamed. He talked in his booming, sexy voice about my talents, while Ivan's fingers dug into my skin as he watched his sister over my shoulder. *What's his deal? Elena is perfectly safe in this room filled with people. She's the real star here, not me. And that's exactly as it should be.*

If I didn't know better, I'd say Ivan was jealous of the attention Elena got from Master Radcliffe and his guests. But I knew him better than that. Ivan lived for his sister – her life was more to him than his own. So what caused his spine to go rigid and his jaw to lock so? If it wasn't jealousy, what did he have to fear from this party?

As we moved across the room, I saw Madame Usher deep in conversation with a white-haired, square-jawed man standing military-straight. "Who's that?" I asked. Somehow, I couldn't picture that man as Madame Usher's type.

"That's the New York City police commissioner," Titus said. "His wife is a huge classical music buff. Madame gives him tickets to all the events, and they come for dinner several times a year."

I watched the two bend their heads together. They certainly appeared to be friendly. Which was odd, because I was certain Madame Usher didn't know how to have a normal human relationship.

Aroha stood at the edge of the room with a couple who bore a striking resemblance to her angular features and shimmering dark hair. They could only be her parents – her mother wore a deep blue evening gown, and over it, a short cape/cloak stitched with feathers. Her father's face was tattooed with similar swirls and lines to the ink Aroha had on her own skin. Aroha wore a similar cloak to her mother, although shorter. All three of them looked thoroughly uncomfortable, and I noticed no one else in the room was talking to them.

"Aroha, hi." I needed to know if she was involved. "I'm sorry I missed your performance. How did it go?"

Aroha touched her nose and winked at me. "Perfectly."

She was on drugs again. I guessed her parents couldn't tell.

"Kia ora, Faye." His father took my hand and leaned in. I thought he would kiss my cheeks – a greeting I was well used to after years of being around pretentious classical music types – but instead, he touched my nose with his. "Aroha has told us so much about you."

"She has?" I didn't believe Aroha wasted a single breath thinking or talking about me. She'd always made it clear she was here for the prize money and nothing else.

"Dad is *trying* not to be weird," Aroha rolled her eyes. "But he's failing miserably."

Her dad hugged Aroha to him, letting out a deep, kind laugh. "My daughter, she is the strong, silent type. Kiri and I, we beg her for news, for stories. We want her to tell us all about her exciting life in America. She says that you're the life of this school, you and your many boyfriends and your bold songs and your kindness. She says you're the one to beat for the Manderley Prize, and that she would not feel dishonored to lose to you. We worry about our daughter, coming all the way around the world to study on her own. It makes us so happy to see her with such accomplished friends."

Friends? I guess he doesn't know about the time Aroha tried to hold my hand over a stove element. I glanced at Ivan for support, but he was too busy glaring at Master Radcliffe as he handed Elena another glass of Champagne.

Aroha stared at me with wild eyes. "Dad, why don't you get us some kai? I want to talk to Faye for a sec."

"Excellent idea." Aroha's parents held hands as they made their way across the room toward the food table.

"Yeah, so… you can ignore all that stuff he said." Aroha stared at a spot on the wall behind me, her vision swimming. "Sometimes I have to tell them shit so they don't put me on the next plane back to New Zealand."

"It's okay," I said, without thinking. It wasn't really okay. I was still angry and afraid of this girl. I didn't trust her one bit. But I had enough shit to worry about tonight – I didn't have it in me to remain pissed off at Aroha, especially not when I'd just got a glimpse of what was going on with her. I already knew about the crippling stage fright she masked with drugs. I think she told her parents we were friends because she didn't have a friend here. She was lonely and out of place, in the same way I was lonely and out of place. So I decided to ignore it. For now.

"I know it's weird," she shrugged. "But you're all right, trash."

"What was the nose thing?" I asked.

"It's called *hongi*. It's the traditional greeting where the breath of life is exchanged. I figure if I have to spend all evening being wet-kissed on my cheeks from gross old white dudes, they can deal with a little nose-bumping from my fam."

"Agreed." I dared a smile, which she returned with a grin that was almost manic.

Two faces appeared at the back of the crowd behind Aroha, buried in shadows so I could not distinguish their features. Something about them made my heart hammer against my chest. I felt their eyes raking across my skin, lifting up the corners to peek underneath.

Aroha wandered off to find her parents. The crowd parted, splitting off into smaller groups, and I got a view of the unsettling faces. I gasped as I recognized them.

Dorien's parents bent their heads together, whispering harsh words and darting glances at me. Now that I was no longer the center of attention, I could take the opportunity to study them. And what I saw was… confusing.

While everyone else in the room strutted around in designer cocktail dresses and elegant suits, Mr. and Mrs. Valencourt wore floor-length robes made of rough grey cloth, belted at the waist with white cords. Their features were as aristocratic and imperious as I remembered, which made their attire stand out even further. It was as if the Valencourts *knew* beyond a shadow of a doubt that they were better than every other person in this room. Not despite their strangeness, but *because* of it.

I'd barely been able to believe it when Dorien said his parents were in a cult – I couldn't imagine his stern mother taking orders from anyone. And yet seeing them here, bold in their devotion, I understood exactly how they'd come under the spell of this 'Father Aaron.' Dorien's parents craved power – they always had. That was why they pushed Dorien so much, because in his talent they saw a world opening up to them, a world they so obviously *deserved*. Why limit their power to the earthly realm? The cult, whatever it was, would open up the heavens to them.

Another couple moved toward them – Heather's parents, I guessed, as they both bore the same honey-blonde hair and California good-looks – and they leaned in for the typical cheek kisses. I watched Dorien's mother's face as the honey-blonde woman turned toward her, the way her features pinched with surprise. I wished I could get closer to hear what was being said—

No. I don't care. Dorien Valencourt is dead to me.

"Are those Heather's parents?" I whispered to Ivan, jabbing my elbow at the new couple. Ivan was still watching Elena, who held Master Radcliffe's arm as he escorted her from group to group. I had to jab him again to get him to turn back to me, and when he did, his lips were drawn in a tight line. I'd yanked him out of some obsession.

What does he think will happen to Elena in this room, in front of all these people?

Or is it simply that after over a decade in this house, he knows tonight's display of convivial finery is only a mask to hide the real Manderley – the Manderley of ghosts and shadows...

Wow, I sound like Edgar Allan Poe after an absinthe bender. Must've been all the creepy things I've seen.

I forced down the images of Clare's face and that creepy writing inside the bag, and shook Ivan's arm again. He cursed under his breath, his icicle eyes swirling to meet mine. All I saw were glaciers – old and immovable. I repeated my question, and Ivan nodded. "Yes. Those are Heather's parents."

"There's something about them..." As I watched, Heather's mother turned to accept a glass of Champagne from her husband. The candlelight caught something glittering at her throat – a brooch she wore pinned to the nape of her neck. It was a strange cluster of fiery jewels set in a circle with a crescent moon on top and a cross beneath – it looked a little like an occult symbol or something, but completely blinged out.

Odd, I swear I've seen that before...

The memory rushed at me, transporting me back ten years to another city, another Faye, another room filled with musicians and fancy people we were supposed to impress. I *had* seen that piece of jewelry before. Back at Madame Usher's music school, at an end-of-year recital. Dorien gave an almost flawless perfor- mance. In the last bar, his finger slid on a note – it was a mistake, but barely perceptible. I could tell he was aware of it, for his shoulders tensed as he stood to give his bow, and he stormed off- stage without acknowledging me waiting for him in the wings.

Backstage, I wrapped my arms around him, whispering that he'd been incredible, that no one apart from his tutor Master Usher would have noticed the bum note. That he was special and everyone in the room could see and hear it. The corner of

Dorien's lip had tugged upward, and I thought I'd almost managed to make him smile when we were interrupted.

"Dorien!" He stiffened at the sound of her voice – a shrill whistle that bounced off the floorboards. I resisted the urge to clamp my hands over my ears. I glared up at Dorien's mother as she loomed over us, her elegant arms crossed over a severe brown dress, her only adornment a black mesh veil and that *same glittering brooch* at her throat.

"Mom, I—"

She grabbed Dorien's ear, dragging him backward across the hardwood floor. Dorien's face twisted in pain as he scratched at her wrist. She let go, shoving him roughly and sending him sprawling. He cupped his ear, and blood trickled through his fingers.

"You *disgusting* boy. You are a failure and a disgrace. We indulge your every wanton desire, give in to your every whim. And this is how you repay us? You have spat in the face of our God. You cannot be saved."

You cannot be saved. At the time I thought it such a strange thing to say. But I never gave it a second thought. My heart was too busy breaking for Dorien.

The words hit Dorien as if they were a physical blow. He reeled, curling his body in on himself and wrapping his hands over his head, trying to protect himself from further attacks. His mother watched him, a satisfied smirk tugging at the corner of her mouth – the same expression I'd seen mirrored on Dorien's lips when he pulled some ridiculous prank. Only what Dorien craved was love and affection, and what she desired above all else was to cause pain. She took pleasure from the hurt she'd done to him.

My back pressed into the wall. I stood frozen, torn between the desire to run to comfort him and the vicious urge to step forward and kick her ankles out from under her, or to tug the brooch from her neck and stab her with the pin.

"Leave him alone." The words fell from my mouth before I could stop them. I was my mother's daughter, after all.

The woman turned to me. "You were supposed to make him great for us," she said. "It was all planned. But I see now he is beyond redemption."

With that weirdness said, she turned on her heel and left the room. I rushed to Dorien, but he shoved me away.

"Dorien?"

His eyes flashed with pain. He spun on his heel and fled out into the concert hall, where the parents gathered with the Ushers' prominent guests. I chased after him, but before I could reach him, warm arms reached around me and scooped me into the air.

"There's my Maestra." Dad's scent washed over me – that smoky aroma of cigarettes and expensive cologne, of his achievements and his vices colliding against my nostrils. He so rarely stepped back from his shining career to notice I existed, and this was the first time in years he'd actually been in the city to see me perform, that for a moment I forgot about Dorien and reveled in his attention, burying my head into his shoulder and kissing his neck.

"Darling, you were amazing." My mom swept me up into a hug. She wore her pride in her easy smile, and my heart stuttered as I wished more than anything that Dorien could have what I had, that his parents could see who he truly was. I held my mom tightly. Behind her, my father watched Dorien's retreating figure, a strange expression on his face, almost as if he—

"Faye?" Titus snapped his fingers in front of my face. "You disappeared somewhere inside that beautiful brain of yours."

"Do you have a concussion?" Ivan's eyes narrowed. "I will *kill* Dorien. I do not care who watches."

"I'm fine. Save the killing until after dessert. I made tres leches cakes and they are incredible. I don't want them covered in blood." I watched Heather's parents as they moved away from Dorien's family and surrounded their daughter. "I was just remembering something. It's probably nothing, but that brooch Heather's mother is wearing used to belong to Dorien's mother."

Titus rolled his eyes. "They probably brought it from the same designer store."

I nodded, but I wasn't convinced. "It looks more like a one-off piece or family heirloom."

"The Danvers and the Valencourts are prominent old-money families, and they definitely have business dealings," Titus said. "Dorien told me that his parents even have this written agreement that he and Heather will marry. Like an arranged marriage. From the way she carries on around him, she wants it to happen."

"I think they'd be perfect together." I was too busy watching the strange people of this party to say it with any real venom. No matter how much closer I got to understanding the secrets of Manderley, the old house revealed another layer. Why was Heather's mother wearing Dorien's mother's brooch? And did that have anything to do with Dorien's sudden desire to hurt me?

10

DORIEN

*E*very moment of the party was agony. I couldn't keep my eyes off Faye as she circled the room with Ivan and Titus at her side. She greeted every guest with grace and mirth – no trace of what Heather and I had done penetrated her loveliness.

Meanwhile, I was a wreck. I couldn't eat, couldn't drink. During my second performance, I slipped on the keys. Heather glared at me over her violin as my clunky playing ruined her mediocre melody. Behind her head, I saw my parents exchange that familiar look of disdain and disappointment that had shadowed me my entire life. I was not living up to the standards they'd set – and it just wouldn't do.

Little did they know, I was just as bad as them. Father Aaron pulled their strings, and they danced for him. I let Madame Usher and Heather control me, and I lost one great love to save another.

I hated Heather for finding a way to manipulate me into hurting Faye. She'd been taking lessons from Madame Usher. But that hatred paled to what I felt for myself. I *loathed* my weakness.

I'd been conditioned to see myself as disgusting, useless, a pointless stain on existence. And I'd proven them right. Now it was like a tide pushing against the breakwater, and I could no longer bear the weight of holding it all back.

Having my parents here made everything worse. My heart was already raw and bruised, but they threw salt into the wound. Mother insisted Madame Usher send Harrison into the village to collect them. I knew they'd come in on the train but didn't want anyone to know. Father Aaron destroyed their car. He said fossil fuels were of the Devil. I was surprised he let them out to see me at all, but then, they were only here to remind me of my duty.

People stared at them in their strange outfits, and they stared at me as if I had a third head. Whispers followed me as I circled the room, staying as far from them as possible. I spoke with conductors and producers and classical musicians of renown. I swung my infamous Dorien charm like it was a weapon. I even had an awkward conversation with the commissioner – he asked if I was staying out of trouble, and the guests tittered as if it was a brilliant joke, but he and I both locked eyes because it was no joke. Madame Usher had brought him tonight for a reason – to remind me to toe the line, or she would send the whole house of cards falling down around me.

I tried not to stare at Faye, but it was impossible. Her light burned bright in the dull room, blotting over every nightmare that lurked in the dark places.

As the party wound down, my parents cornered me. They got my back against a wall (literally. I dug my nails into a gap between the paneling and felt a rush of air and wished like fuck it was a secret passage that would swing open and swallow me). Father beckoned me into the shadows of the Red Room.

"Dorien, you've been ignoring our letters." My mother leaned against the door so I couldn't escape.

"You could use the phone like normal people," I bit back. I sounded like a petulant child, but I couldn't bring myself to care.

"You know that mobile phones are not secure." My father stood by the window, his hands resting on the back of the chaise lounge. I noticed the callouses and cuts covering his fingers. My father once managed a vast real estate empire. For my entire life, his hands bore the smooth, soft touch of someone who barked orders and made deals on the golf course. He still bore that air of callous authority, but his hands betrayed what was happening behind the compound walls. What did Father Aaron have my father doing that had changed him so drastically?

"After all we've done for you, you repay us with this insolence?" Mother's voice dripped with poison. "You have forgotten all we taught you living in this house of privilege and frivolity. You've never done anything worthwhile."

Why, why, why, even when they're fucking looney-tunes, do they still have this power over me? I knew the answer to that question – because I knew what they were capable of. I lived through their hell and thought I finally escaped, but as long as they had Jacob, I was trapped and they knew it.

"If you've come all this way to hurl insults at me, you should have written a list and posted it to 69 Go Fuck Yourself Avenue." I moved to the port decanter on the sideboard and poured myself a glass, hoping like fuck they didn't notice my hand tremble as I sloshed the liquid. "You're not paying for my education. You cut me off because I wouldn't agree to be part of your barbaric religion. I'm legally an adult, so you don't have a say over my life any longer."

My life is controlled by someone else now. I have another puppet master pulling the strings.

"Son," my father warned. His face remained still and impassive as stone, but one hand balled into a fist beneath the bell sleeve of his robe. I noticed how thin his wrist appeared, the veins protruding through thin skin. Must've been that vegan diet.

"We came because we want to see our firstborn do what he

was born to do – to move hearts and transform minds with music." My mother swung at my hand, flinging the glass at the wall. It smashed to pieces, leaving a stain of blood-red alcohol dripping down the molding. "Instead, we find a shallow brat who's pissed away his talent on sex, drugs, and rock'n'roll. It's not too late to return to your family. Give up this world of heathen debauchery and instead use your gift as God intended – to bring new disciples to his True Path."

"Not interested." I gestured to the door. "If that's all, I've got some heathen debauchery to get back to—"

"You didn't tell us you were seeing Faye de Winter," my father said.

I must be imagining that hopeful strain in his voice.

"I'm not *seeing* her. We just performed together. Why do you care?" I leaned back in the piano stool and fiddled with the lid, pretending I didn't give a shit that Faye's name was on his lips. "She has as much right to be here as any other student. Just because you don't want anything to do with such a 'volatile' family, doesn't mean I can't—"

"Madame Usher told us the two of you have become close, but that you were attempting poorly to hide it." My mother's lip curled. "She also told us this Faye was involved with those two other boys who play in your little band."

That fucking bitch. I let the corner of my mouth twist into a smirk. "I thought you cult types were all into free love?"

"Dorien, you can't allow those two to get in your way." My mother folded her arms. "Faye is your destiny. You must fight—"

SLAM.

I dropped the lid of the piano, narrowly missing jamming my fingers inside. "You can't be serious."

My parents exchanged a glance, and in their eyes, I read something that made horror tingle down my spine. I knew they weren't here to 'invite me back into the family.' I thought they'd come to make sure I was getting cozy with my future wife,

Heather. But this, this was worse – now they had some plan involving Faye?

My mind flashed back to earlier today when Heather had come to my room to force me to do her bidding. She mentioned the Temple of Earthly Truths and my assault charges. I assumed Madame Usher had given her that information so Heather had leverage over me, and that was probably true. But there could also be something else going on here.

I knew one thing, I'd give my life to keep the Temple of Earthly Truths away from Faye.

I leaned back again, folding my hands in my lap and glaring up at them both. I hoped they couldn't hear my heart pounding in my chest. "Nothing's going on between Faye and I. I thought this would please you. I thought you wanted me to marry Heather. That's certainly what she wants—"

"You cannot marry Heather Danvers," my mother hissed.

"Son, this is important." Father came around the chaise lounge to stand over me. "You need to listen to us. We know what's best for you. And seeing your performance tonight has cinched it – Heather is not a good match for you. But Faye has her father's gift. She is an unorthodox choice, sure, but the Lord has placed her back in your path for a reason. He wants you and Faye to be together, to spread his message through your music. Did you hear how many conductors and producers in that room want you to tour with them?"

My hands balled into fists. I knew why they were here. They needed money. They always needed money. They were checking that their investment in me would be paying off.

"Why did you have to come?" I growled. "You should have just stayed at the compound."

"And miss seeing our baby play?" Mother cooed, her voice dripping with false sentiment. "Dorien, we need you at the Temple. With your talent and Faye at your side, you could spread our message across the world."

"What about Jacob?" I demanded. "What's his role in all this?"

"Your brother's star doesn't shine like yours. He is not made to be a Conduit of Truth, as you are. He is a disciple of the True Path, and he will serve the new world in his own way." Dad glanced out the window. "Father Aaron says the time of ascension is approaching, and we must be prepared."

"What does that even *mean?*"

"We can only reveal the truth to those who take the oath. Dorien, we want you to visit us at the compound. We're having an open day where we talk to our families and loved ones about the True Path."

"A recruitment drive, you mean."

Mother flashed me a self-satisfied smile. "Your brother misses you. He asks after you every day."

"That's your fault," I growled. "You won't allow him to speak to me, or see me when I visit."

"He's not ready to face the temptations of the outside world. Please, son, come home. The open day is next Saturday."

"I have a recital."

"Even better." She patted my shoulder. The contact made my skin crawl. "Come before your recital and pray with us, and the light of the Lord will shine on your performance."

The day of ascension. I didn't like the sound of that. My mind played over that famous recording from Jonestown – of prayers and words of faith, of women crying and children screaming, of gasps and thuds as hundreds of bodies dropped around them after they drank Flavor Aid poisoned with cyanide. The deathly silence that followed.

I suppressed a shudder. I knew what I had to do. I'd been putting it off because I thought I could save Jacob without making his life even harder than it had to be. Or maybe I'd just been trying to keep the ugly side of myself hidden from the world. Maybe my sacrifice was buried in selfishness and bullshit.

No more.

I'll come home, all right. I'll come and take my brother far, far away from your evil.

I forced a smile. "Sure, Mom. I wouldn't miss it."

"And you'll bring Faye?"

Faye will never speak to me again. She's sensible like that. "Sure. I'll try."

11

FAYE

I spent the rest of the evening sneaking looks at Dorien's parents and trying to steer myself close enough to overhear what they whispered to each other. But lucky for me, I was suddenly Miss Popularity. Everyone wanted to gush over my performance and hand me their business cards and talk about my father's mysterious disappearance, so I couldn't get any sleuthing in.

While a British musician with dreamy shale-grey eyes talked my ear off about his band, and his theory that my father had run away to join the circus, my mind wandered back to the cult that had Dorien's parents in its thrall. He hadn't told me much about it. I thought back to what I'd seen when Harrison dropped him off at his parents' estate – the barbed wire, the high stone wall, the pile of trash, and NO TRESPASSING signs. And that creepy guy Dorien called Father Aaron who'd watched us play that one time I visited Dorien as a kid – I guessed he was the cult leader.

"Gabriel, so good to see you." Titus came up behind me, slipping his hand through mine and clapping the other guy on the shoulder. "I can't wait to get back out on tour with Octavia's Ruin. Faye, can I tear you away? My parents want to meet you."

Titus' parents. Nerves twisted in my gut. I'd never had a boyfriend before, so I'd never had to meet anyone's parents. In fact, I still wasn't sure I was allowed to call Titus or Ivan my boyfriend, and Dorien… fuck Dorien. And Titus' parents weren't just anyone – Amos and Delphine Thibodeaux were famous in our world. I wanted them to think well of me. But also, I knew they were the reason Titus hid his electric guitar and played in a damp woodshed out the back of the school.

Before I could protest or beg for a moment to prepare myself, Titus swept me across the room, where his parents held court around the piano. Amos sat on the stool, his fingers tinkling the keys as Delphine leaned over the lid, her long fingers caressing the stem of a Champagne flute as she sang in a low, sultry voice. They may have been a classical duet, but they were born and raised in New Orleans – jazz was in their blood.

Titus' warm hand settled in mine as he drew me forward. Amos caught his eye and waved him over with a sweeping hand, keeping his other on the keys, playing through the scales. "Son, come join us for a song."

"Maybe later." Titus' jaw tightened, and I sensed a tension flicker between him and his father that hid behind their easy smiles and booming, kind voices. "I wanted you to meet my girl-friend, Faye de Winter."

My girlfriend. I started at the very words I wasn't sure I was allowed to utter falling so easily from Titus' sexy mouth. Behind me, Ivan stiffened. I wondered if this was Titus' attempt to stake a claim on me.

No, not him. Titus didn't believe in stirring trouble for the sake of it. That wasn't his style. He always wanted everyone around him to be happy and at ease. If he said the words, it was because he believed them.

My girlfriend.

A jolt of heat surged through me. I squeezed Titus' hand, my heart skipping as he turned to smile at me. *I like it.*

"The famous Faye de Winter." Amos rose from the piano stool and clasped his hands together. The sound was like thunder clapping before a ferocious storm. With his barrel chest and booming voice, Amos Thibodeaux had an imposing stage presence, but in person the sheer force of his personality filled the whole room. He took my hand in his and led me to sit beside him on the stool, where he tapped out a cheerful ditty on the keys. "It's a pleasure to meet you. We enjoyed your performance this evening. You are a vision."

"In the hands of a lesser musician, that piece might have sounded somber, but you inject a liveliness and vivacity into your playing that elevates you," Delphine said. "I understand you composed that piece yourself? Rarely are talented composers also exquisite performers, but it seems you are the exception."

"Thank you." I beamed at them both, wallowing in the joy of their praise. I could see why Titus wanted so badly to please his parents, even at the expense of losing himself. It felt amazing to have Amos' smile on me, his attention rapt, his fingers lacing in mine like I was some precious object he couldn't let go of in case I floated away. They did not mention my father, and I immediately liked them all the more for that.

"Son, your girlfriend's glass is empty." Delphine glittered from head-to-toe in a stunning designer dress as she leaned over to top up my glass with Champagne. "Never mind, it is easily remedied. Amos and I are trying to inject some life into this stuffy affair. Honestly, once you spend any time in New Orleans, you will find every other function dull and dreary."

"I do hope to visit one day," I said.

"We should arrange that. Amos and I will be on tour during Christmas, but perhaps in the new year? We would show you the sights, all the jazz bars and music venues, perhaps arrange a recital for some of our friends?" She stroked my arm. "I'd love to see you and my son play together."

I beamed up at Titus, thinking of the new composition I'd

started working on – a bombastic piece of violin and cello. "I'd love that, too."

"Son," Amos' enormous hand landed on Titus' shoulder. "We must discuss your fingering. You got lazy toward the end, and I don't want to see it—"

He led Titus away, his voice rising into a boom as he went over every second of Titus' performance, critiquing and offering suggestions. To an outsider, it might have sounded like a friendly and helpful critique, but I knew better. As his father talked, Titus shrunk into himself, nodding and staring at his shoes. The Thibodeauxes were not like Dorien's parents, deliberately setting out to tear him down for their own twisted joy, so I knew there was a deeper issue that Titus couldn't – or wouldn't – face.

I didn't like to see him with his back up like that, cornered by his father's critique, when I knew he needed love and kindness. But I couldn't go after him. Delphine still held my arm, studying me intently with the heavy-lidded dark eyes of hers. She had her short, curly hair cut in a stylish afro that accentuated her sharp cheekbones, and diamond earrings glittered from her ears.

"It's an honor to meet you," I said. "I'm a huge fan of your music."

"Amos and I have fought hard for our careers." Her eyes penetrated mine. "You have Latina heritage, I see. Perhaps you know of what I speak. There are many in our world – in this room, even – who believe the music halls belong to those with a certain *pedigree*, and that perhaps we should stick to our own world."

"Music isn't owned," I said. "It's universal, bigger than any of us."

"I could not agree more," her eyes twinkled. "Titus' brother had a Plato quote written on the inside of his cello case. 'Music gives a soul to the universe, wings to the mind, flight to the imagination, and life to everything.'"

"That's beautiful."

"It is. And not attributable to Plato. Micah found it on a Facebook post and never thought to check if the famous philosopher ever spoke the words. Micah was no historian, but he loved anything beautiful."

"I didn't know Titus had a brother?"

A shadow of pain passed over her eyes. It was gone in an instant, but I knew I said the wrong thing. "Micah is with the Lord."

Shit. Titus' brother is dead? I felt awful, like that was something I should have known. "I'm so sorry for your loss."

"Yes. As we all are." She smiled then, an attempt to put me at ease. Her smile was so warm and kind, but that sadness flickered in her eyes again, and I knew she was well practiced at masking her pain. "Titus is a good boy, so talented, so full of spark. I always knew with the right partner by his side he would soar to the heavens. It's time for him to give up on his silly pop music and allow his real career begin, and I know you'll help him soar."

I couldn't believe she called Broken Muse 'silly pop music.' I thought of Titus hiding in that shed outside, his long, beautiful fingers shredding the strings of an electric guitar. How at peace he looked in that moment, how free.

But no one was ever free at Manderley.

As Delphine spoke, I could see the wheels turning in her head. She had visions of Titus and I playing concert halls together, building a glittering classical music career on the foundation she and Amos had laid for us – an entire life mapped out in front of him. A beautiful life. I knew heavy metal didn't factor at all into her plans.

In that moment, I understood Titus – I knew how hard it was to live in the shadow of a great artist. And *my* father had the good sense to disappear on me, so he would always be judged in stasis, whereas I would be able to grow and improve and one day, I hoped, surpass him. But Titus ran after a moving target, and his parents' success was a wolf chasing him down, snapping at his feet, ready to devour him unless he ran faster, worked harder, played better.

We were more alike than I'd ever guessed.

The room started to clear as guests moved to their suites upstairs or to their cars for the long drive back to civilization. Madame Usher frowned at me and nodded toward the door – her first acknowledgment of me since I waltzed into the party. Faye the musician had overstayed her welcome. Faye the servant was once more called to work.

I helped the guests find their coats and scarves. Dorien's parents stepped toward me. His mother looked me over, and she smiled. She actually fucking beamed. And all I could think of was that time she'd thrown her own son access the floor and told me he was beyond redemption.

"Thank you for a wonderful evening, Faye," she said, as if the weight of our history didn't bear down on us. "I hope you will come to visit us next weekend at the compound."

"Um…" I flicked my gaze to Dorien, who was helping his father into a scratchy woolen cloak.

"Bye, Mother." Dorien shoved them out the door. His eyes met mine over his shoulder, and he mouthed something to me that might've been an apology, but I didn't stick around to see. I looked away before I could consider what I saw in his eyes – the hurt, the fear, the regret. It wouldn't do to start feeling sorry for the dickweasel.

Amos clasped my hand in his. "It was lovely to meet you, Faye."

"And you too." I couldn't help but think there was something in the way he looked at me, like he didn't see a person, but the *idea* of a person. Even though his touch was warm, a shiver ran down my spine.

Ivan and Elena stood at the bottom of the steps while Master Radcliffe farewelled his guests. Ivan gripped her arm so hard I could see red welts on her skin, but she didn't cry out or brush him away. Instead, she leaned over and kissed his cheek, leaving a bow-shaped crimson streak across his skin that made me smile.

Heather kissed her parents on the cheeks, fingering the brooch at her mother's throat and flashing a broad smile. As soon as they disappeared into the night, she dragged Dorien upstairs. His eyes followed me as he climbed the staircase toward her room, and his face was a blank slate – utterly devoid of emotion. The storms in his eyes had faded into a mask. I tried to ignore the knife twisting in my gut as Heather's door shut behind them.

"What are you waiting for?" Madame Usher barked at me as soon as I shut the door behind the last of the guests. "I expect this house back to normal before you retire for the evening."

Of course she did. Hatred burned white in my veins as I ducked into the ballroom, staring at the mountains of dirty glasses and crockery, the napkins scattered over tables and stuffed between the sofa cushions, the crumbs that needed to be vacuumed away and the greasy fingerprints dotting the lid of the piano.

"We'll help." Titus' lips brushed my ear as he came up behind me. His hands slid around my waist, and I sank against him, drawing his red musk and myrrh scent deep inside me, taking strength from the sizzle of heat that passed between us.

And they did. Titus stacked glasses while Ivan wiped down the surfaces. Madame Usher watched from the top of the stairs as we removed the trash and dirty dishes to the kitchen, her mouth set in a frown. But she didn't say anything.

When the last of the dishes had been stacked in the dishwasher, Titus took my hand, his enormous fingers dwarfing mine. Ivan leaned against the doorframe, saying nothing, his icicle eyes boring into me.

"We will make Dorien regret ever hurting you." Titus' voice was rough. He wrapped his strong arms around me and pressed his lips to my forehead. The touch sparked a fire inside me – a flame that had burned bright ever since I held my violin to my chin and played my song of defiance. A flame that burned bright for two Broken Muses, even as the third tried to snuff it out with his callousness.

"I don't want to think about Dorien," I growled.

"Neither do I." Titus' lips found mine, his kiss hot, needy. He'd been dancing on a bed of nails since his parents arrived, and now all that emotion poured from his lips into me. I took it in greedily, demanding more of him, desperate to feed the flame and starve his pain of the oxygen it needed to fester.

Hands slid around my middle, and warm skin pressed against mine. Ivan dragged his teeth along the edge of my neck as Titus deepened his kiss. If you wanted a surefire cure for cockpoodles trying to ruin your life and a ghostly presence haunting your ass, being the center of the world's hottest sandwich did the trick.

I felt Dorien's absence in every touch – and it felt *right*. Without the Prince of Darkness drawing all the life in the room into himself, Ivan and Titus could be truly themselves. I wanted to explore every ghost that lingered on the edge of their souls.

"Come upstairs with us," Titus whispered against my lips, his deep bass voice reverberating through my body, right down to my toes.

Mmmmm. Yes.

The three of us linked hands and left the kitchen, stepping out into the grand foyer. My eyes darted around the space, searching for any last speck of dust or a wayward glass Madame Usher could use as an excuse to punish me. My eyes fell on the gap on the wall – that dark square of bright wallpaper where a portrait once hung. Madame Usher said the portrait was with a restorer, but I'd been at Manderley nearly two months now and it hadn't been returned. I would've thought she'd want the foyer looking immaculate for her guests.

"Do you know whose portrait hung there?" I asked the boys.

Titus shook his head. "Some famous dead dude. I never paid much attention."

Instead of answering, Ivan lifted my hand, twirling me beneath his arm in a dance to the music that existed only in his head. As I came around again, he caught me around the waist, pressing me against the curved pillar of the balustrade. Wooden cherubs jabbed into my back, but I didn't care, not with Ivan's lips pressed on mine, his fingers tracing the line of my neck and sending delicious flames of fire through my veins.

As his tongue explored mine, Ivan became more sure of himself, more probing. He skimmed my arms, trailing fire across my bare skin with his fingers. He circled his thumbs on the insides of my wrists. He cupped my neck and tilted my head back until the room spun with color and light and the strength drained from my knees.

"I don't think you should sleep alone tonight," Ivan rasped into my throat, pulling me closer. I'd seen this possessive side of him before, with Elena, but he'd always held back around me, allowing Dorien to lead. Not anymore. Now he held me as if I were the one candlelight that held the darkness at bay, the only thing in a bleak and bitter world that could ever be truly *his*.

"I don't think so, either." I took Ivan's hand, and Titus in the other. "I know Elena is in your room, but what about—"

"Mine." Titus pulled me close, and I didn't know if he meant his room, or that I was his. I didn't care. I felt like I was his. His and Ivan's. And they were mine. Chains of fate bound us together in this prison. We turned to the staircase. Standing between the two of them, I felt as though I stepped into a piece of music, that the melody carried me along on a journey only it could see, and I was powerless to do anything but surrender.

I lifted my chin. I was Faye de Winter, and I *earned* this night.

I needed—

My eyes flicked to the top of the staircase, and the heat fled my veins.

No.

Fear tightened in my chest as a face watched me from the top of the stairs. Eyes made of shadow and secrets, a cute turned-up nose, and a black hole for a mouth.

It can't be.

But it was.

Clare.

IVAN

Faye staggered back, her face pale with fear.

"What is it?" I wrapped my arms around her waist, pulling her close. Her breath rasped against my cheek, and I could feel her heart pounding against her chest. She was *terrified.*

Of us? Of me and Titus? Did she think we would hurt her?

I will kill Dorien for breaking her trust, for making her doubt—

"I thought I saw…" Faye pointed a trembling finger to the top of the stairs. I realized she wasn't thinking about Dorien, and the relief of that disgusted me. Faye was in danger from more than just Dorien's callousness, of that I was certain. She needed us to stay alert, to keep her safe. "Can you see it? That face? *Clare's* face."

"No." All I saw was a table with a couple of lamps sitting under a mirror on the landing. "Maybe you just saw your reflection move in the mirror—"

"From down here?" Faye's eyes darkened. "Trust me, she wasn't in the mirror. She was in front of it, sort of between the railings."

Right where Clare would've been standing before she fell down the stairs...

"I bet it was Dorien playing some stupid trick." Titus stomped up the steps and peered at the railing. He shuffled the objects on the sideboard. "I can't see anything that looks like a face."

Faye rested her forehead against my shoulder, her whole body trembling. I wished I could protect her from all this *shit*. But I couldn't even protect Elena. The only thing I could do was—

"There's nothing here," Titus repeated. "Faye, come upstairs."

Something in the certainly of his voice spurned Faye. She nodded, her mouth set in a determined line. I gripped her hand as she took the stairs slowly, her eyes fixed on Titus as he waited at the top.

By the time Faye reached the landing, she seemed to have recovered a sense of herself. Titus wrapped his arms around her, and she collapsed into his embrace. She peered at a collection of objects arranged on the hall table, and a strange weariness passed over her face, so quick I might've imagined it. "I think... maybe the shadows and the railing made these look like her face. But I can see now it was just my eyes playing a trick."

"There's been more than enough tricks tonight." Titus drew Faye against him and tilted her head back for a smoldering kiss.

Yes.

I stepped up behind Titus, my hands circling Faye, running down her body as she sank back against me. I loved the way she melted into us like that. She was so strong that she refused to let what Dorien did break her spirit. She could be with us without his shadow haunting our embrace.

As my lips grazed her long neck, I felt eyes burning into my back. I broke away to peer over my shoulder. Dorien leaned against the doorframe in his room, his back rigid, his eyes fixed on mine. They burned with loathing.

I wanted to shrink from his gaze. I'd seen others burn under the heat of his ire, but Dorien had never looked at us like that before, like we were an enemy that needed to be crushed. It was always the three of us against the world. Until Faye. Until he turned against us.

Titus must've seen him, too. He did not break his kiss with Faye, but raised a long-fingered hand and threw Dorien the finger. Dorien watched for a few more moments, then slunk back into his room. The door locked with a *CLICK*.

Good. I hope he lays awake all night listening to us make Faye scream.

Titus unlocked the door to his bedroom, pushing Faye backward until her legs hit the edge of the bed. I walked around and slid in behind her so that when Faye sat back on the bed, she nestled between my legs. Her beautiful ass rubbed against my crotch, and it was all I could do to hold myself back from release right then.

Faye's lips swelled with passion. She licked her top lip as she looped her finger through Titus' belt and pulled him closer. Her fingers worked the buttons of his trousers, opening them and sliding them down his hips to reveal his cock, as rigid for her as mine, the tip already glistening with his need.

As I watched, Faye leaned forward. Her lips closed around Titus' shaft, a sigh of pleasure rolling from her throat as she took him deep into her mouth. Titus tossed his head back, delicious sounds pouring from his own lips as Faye stroked and licked and sucked.

I slid back to kick off my own trousers. Titus' fingers danced up Faye's legs, pushing the skirt of her dress higher, revealing her rich skin and luscious curves inch by perfect inch.

I took over from Titus, pulling the fabric over Faye's thighs, drawing it across her stomach, lifting it over her breasts so they spilled into my hands. Faye let Titus' cock slip from her mouth for a moment to lift her arms. I slid the dress over her shoulders, and Titus grabbed it and tossed it away. My breath hitched as I ran my fingers over her exposed skin. Everywhere I touched her felt like touching fire, like stoking some long-dead part of me until it flared to life.

I threw my shirt off. I wanted my skin against hers. I wanted to crawl inside her until we were one.

"Condoms," Titus growled, his voice tight. "In my top drawer."

Faye watched me with those wide eyes as I dug a foil square from the drawer and rolled the condom over myself. I inched closer to her, my cock brushing her soft skin. My insides coiled tighter, and it took everything I had not to unload on her right here.

Faye rose up on her thighs and sat back down, sighing as I slipped into her warmth. She closed around me and I was inside her, exactly where I wanted to be.

"Ivan..." Faye moaned. She gripped Titus' shoulders and pushed herself up, slamming back down on me, taking her pleasure, demanding it. Her body quaked and she tossed her head back so her dark hair streamed over my shoulder. I buried my face in her neck, breathing in the lavender and orange-blossom sweetness of her as she worked herself upon me. And all while Titus bent over her, his fingers flicking her clit as he sucked her nipple in his mouth.

With each stroke, Faye cracked me open. With each thrust, she tore apart the carefully-constructed walls that bound my fractured heart.

I never had anything in my life that belonged to me and me alone. That was the way I wanted it. I never wanted something if Elena couldn't have it, too. Titus and Dorien and I had many, many women together like this on tour. Groupies who wanted one of us, all of us, who demanded a night of being treated like a goddess by Broken Muse. We called them Muse Girls, and they even had a club of sorts – a group on Facebook where they compared us and formulated new plans to get close to us.

But not one of them compared to Faye de Winter.

I hadn't had a woman without Titus or Dorien. I didn't think I knew how. There had been girls I liked on tour, but when I'd get back to my hotel room some nameless fear would take over and I'd kick them out. As soon as one of the guys would leave the room and leave me alone with a Muse Girl, as soon as she looked up at me with pleading eyes and begged me to fix something broken inside her, I felt this fog descend on me, like if I stood alone with them long enough they'd see the truth I hid.

That I was the one who was broken.

That I didn't want to *possess*, as Dorien did. That I wanted to be part of something, part of a family.

Faye de Winter demanded more. So much more. She demanded worship. She commanded adoration. She *deserved* to possess and to be possessed, to have nothing less than everything I was.

Right now, my jagged edges cut into my skin, but instead of shrinking from the pain, I embraced it. Faye's skin slipped over mine. Her fingers slid in hot trails down my arms, and it felt like a claiming, like she branded me as her own. I wanted to be hers. I'd do anything to be hers, even as she broke me into pieces and put me together again.

My fingers tightened on Faye's thigh as she slammed down on me, her crimson lips forming an O as the scream of an orgasm tore from her lips. The sight of it threw me over the edge, and I came with the tremor of the earth shifting beneath me.

Titus drew back, his eyes meeting mine, the pupils thick and dark with lust. And I wondered what it might be like to kiss the taste of Faye from his lips, to feel truly as if I found my family.

As if I was whole.

As we tangled together in Titus' bed – all limbs and long hair and secret smiles, exploring fingers and desperate need – I watched Faye's face as she climbed off my cock to straddle Titus, and I tangled my fingers in her long hair and bent her head to kiss her. And I thought that maybe, with this girl, I could imagine being whole.

13

DORIEN

What have I done?

I laid on top of my bed, not bothering to remove my clothes or climb under the covers. I wouldn't sleep tonight. Not with Faye's muffled screams echoing from Titus' room. Not with the steady pounding of his iron bedstead hitting the wall.

I fisted my hands into my eye sockets, but I couldn't drive out the images of the two of them with her, *without me*. Of Faye reveling in their worship. Of *my girl* finding herself in Titus' kind hands or Ivan's glacier eyes.

Without me.

My whole body itched for action. I could've stuck in my headphones and driven out the sound of them fucking. I could have gone for a walk around the grounds, or even out to the poison garden or the mausoleum, where the secrets of Manderley hung thick and sweet in the air. I could have battered down Heather's door and tossed her out a window for what she made me do tonight.

But I stayed rooted in place, listening. Hating myself.

This is my punishment.

Every murmur.

Every gasp.

Every moan.

A knife through my heart. And it was exactly what I deserved.

With each excruciating sound, I turned over what my parents had said to me earlier. Their sudden fixation on Faye mixed in my mind with Heather's smug smile, and with her mother walking around with the Key of Truth pinned to her dress. Even as blinded as I was by Faye's appearance, I couldn't help but notice it.

Eustace Danvers *wanted* me to notice it. It was a performance for me and my parents. I thought of my empty bank account, and I wondered about this new urgency for me to visit the compound and date Faye. I put that together with their new mistrust of the Danvers even after they'd arranged for me and Heather to marry a decade ago, and this 'day of ascension' and Father Aaron's escalating anger. And I wondered if Father Aaron was all-too-aware he'd bled my parents dry, and was moving on to greener pastures—

"Titus… more…" Faye's breathy voice filled my head. I tossed my pillow at the wall and reached for my headphones. I jammed them on my ears and flicked it to a playlist Titus made me of the loudest, heaviest, darkest music he could come up with. The first haunting riffs of Blood Lust's 'Garden of Sorrow' filled my head, the thrashing guitars and deep bass blissfully blocking out any sound from the next room.

I can't take this any longer.

I may have lost Faye forever, but that didn't mean I gave up fighting for her.

All of this was connected. Faye's appearance at Manderley, her mother's poisoning, all the weird stuff she said happened we couldn't account for, Heather and her parents suddenly having intimate knowledge of the Temple and of my suppressed criminal record. I knew what the connection was – Madame Usher.

She was the spider at the center of this web. What I didn't know was *why*.

I pulled over my laptop and opened my file. *'Concerning the Fall of the House of Usher.'* It sounded like an awesome song title. The ghost of a melody flickered between my ears – a song of battle lines drawn. My fingers itched to find Titus and Ivan and hash out a composition. But I doubted they'd ever speak to me again, not after I hurt Faye.

I didn't blame them, but still.

I read over the list I made – all the strange things that had happened since Faye de Winter arrived at Manderley. At the end of the list, I typed up everything that happened tonight – how Heather came to me with information she shouldn't have known. How she convinced me to use the chloroform from the old apothecary set to knock Faye out and carry her into the forest. Why Heather's mother wore the Key.

How had Faye managed to escape the bag? I'd run back out to the woods as soon as I could get away from Heather to free her, but she was gone. The zipper had been broken from the *outside*.

One thing was certain – as long as Faye remained at Manderley Academy, she was in danger. Having me and Titus and Ivan for protection wouldn't matter for shit in the end. We were no match for this kind of evil.

In Cauda Venenum. The poison is in the tail. Even if I cut off the head, the scorpion could still strike a deadly blow to the only people in the world I wanted to save.

14

FAYE

That night, I dreamed of Manderley.

I dreamed of my mother dancing, swirling through the empty ballroom as candlelight cast fireflies against her skin. "*Mi cielo,* come dance with me." She held out her arms, her smile so bright it made my heart ache. I tried to move toward her, but my feet stuck to the floor.

"I can't." I tugged at my legs, clawing at my skin, jabbing my fingers at the soles of my shoes. But it was as if someone had superglued me in place.

"*Mi cielo,* come dance." My mother held out her hand, and I leaned forward and reached and reached and I was so close I could feel the breath of her fingers—

A shadow burst from the wall behind me and grabbed her hand, whipping her away in a frenzy of spinning hair and whirling limbs. My mother threw back her head and laughed as the shadow creature gyrated against her, their bodies moving as one even as its dark fingers wrapped around her throat...

"Mother!" I yelled, clawing at the floor. I knew that I had to save her from that shadow, that it was the ghost of Manderley, the dark spirit that dwelt in this house and turned everything to ashes and rot. I knew it would devour her beauty whole and snuff out her light forever, but I couldn't move. All I could do was watch helplessly as the shadow leaned in, closer, closer, its mouth of darkness pressing into my mother's neck as it laid a trail of deadly kisses—

"Faye, wake up, wake up…"

I moaned and rolled over. The hairs on my arms had raised up, and a sickly heat sprinkled my body. I rubbed my skin, drawing my mind back to reality. *It was just a nightmare. A creepy shadow didn't come out of the wall to take Mom away. You're with Titus and Ivan, and you're safe. It's just—*

"Faye, are you okay?"

That voice almost sounded like…

Dorien.

I bolted upright, yanking the covers over my naked body. Dorien leaned over the bed, his face inches from mine.

"Sprite." He stretched closer, his lips darting across mine, not quite touching, but threatening to touch. "Good morning. I hear you had quite a night. Do you—"

I drew back my hand and slapped him across the cheek.

Dorien's head snapped back. He let out a sound like an animal snarl as he tripped over Titus' desk, smacking his elbow into the wall. He scrambled to his feet, still holding his hand against the spot where I'd slapped him. When he spoke again, there was none of the arrogance in his voice. "I deserved that."

"It's the least you deserve." The horror of last night rushed back to me – being attacked in the attic, sucking in that sweet drug that sent me under (I suspected it was chloroform), waking up in that bag and not knowing where I was, and that terrifying text written inside the zipper. "I should call the police. I could have *died* out there."

Beside me, Ivan bolted upright, his hands curled into fists. "Come any closer and I'll hurt you."

"Faye's already taken care of it, trust me." Dorien winced as he rubbed his cheek. "I was going to come back and get you. As soon as the party started, I slipped out and ran back. That's why I left you that flashlight. Did you see my message?"

My stomach flipped. Of course. It was written on the inside of the bag, up near the zipper where he knew I'd see it. "You wrote 'I'M COMING BACK FOR YOU'? Do you have any idea how freaky that was?"

Dorien rubbed his cheek. "No, actually. In hindsight, I can see how that might've seemed a bit ghostly. How did you get out?"

"You don't get to ask the questions here," I shot back. His answer revealed he wasn't the one who let me out, which meant I didn't want him to play any part in figuring it out. "I guess it was also you who left my clothes in the kitchen, or who gave me the jewelry? If you think a few rubies can make up for drugging and kidnapping me, then you—"

Titus' arm snaked around my middle, and he stared up at me with wide eyes. "You didn't tell us about the jewelry."

I fingered the necklace, which was still around my neck. "I was a little distracted. Plus, I assumed it was one of you guys. Someone placed this on top of my clothing in the kitchen before the party."

Ivan shook his head. "This necklace… it looks very expensive."

Titus sat up. His fingers grazed my bare skin as he lifted the stones to inspect them. A shiver of pleasure coursed through my body from his touch, and my mind flashed back to last night, to all the things we did in this bed.

Dorien was in the next room. He must've heard *everything*.

Good.

"Someone who wasn't one of us helped you escape that bag and then left out your clothes and jewelry," Dorien said. "We need to figure out who it was."

Ivan glared at Dorien. "Why should we believe you had nothing to do with it? That this isn't another plan from you and Heather to terrify Faye into quitting?"

Dorien's shoulders sagged. "For fuck's sake, after everything we've been through together, you believe that I'd do this because I wanted to hurt Sprite?"

"Then *why?*" I meant to demand answers, but my voice trembled. After everything we'd been through, after all the promises he'd made to me, he was still trying to put me in my place, to prove he was better than me. "Why did you do it?"

"I didn't have a choice." Dorien squeezed his eyes shut. His face twisted into an expression of such exquisite pain that for a moment, a fucking *moment*, I wavered. I wanted so badly to believe that he hadn't really betrayed me, that this was all some mistake, some fresh plot.

But then I remembered the sweet stench of the chloroform, the foot kicking me in the side as he and Heather dumped the bag in the forest, the tortured expression on Clare's face as she flew toward me in the mausoleum – a trick of my mind, I was now convinced, trying to force me to accept that Dorien was rotten.

"You always have a choice." I fought to keep my voice even. Dorien's eyes fluttered open. Every moment he was here, pleading with me with his tortured eyes, was a knife twisting in my chest. He warped and mangled me until I no longer recognized my own misshapen heart.

Dorien sucked in a ragged breath. "All Heather cared about was that she would be the one to play with me for our parents. She had... she knows something about me, which meant I couldn't refuse her. But I tried to sabotage her. I didn't use enough chloroform. I slipped the flashlight into your pocket so when you woke up you could read my message. I honestly didn't mean for it to be scary – I just wanted to let you know I'd come back for you. As soon as Heather went to her room to change for the party I ran back to free you, only the zipper was broken open and you were nowhere to be seen. I thought you might be nearby, and I called and called but I couldn't find you, so I went back to the house."

That was the voice I heard calling my name when I was in the mausoleum, going on about the voices in the walls and saving Mander-ley. It was Dorien, not some ghostly figure. I was still feeling the effects of the drug, and being in that gloomy place, of course I'd imagine things...

This should have been a relief, but so many emotions bounced around in my head I couldn't even think about Clare's ghostly face right now.

Dorien knelt on the end of the bed. His knee brushed against my leg through the covers, and it was enough to send a sizzle of heat through my body. I wanted so badly to believe the words falling from his too-pretty lips, but how could I when trusting him brought so much pain?

"I know you don't believe me right now," Dorien's hand slid down my legs as he crawled across the bed toward me. "I would never hurt you, Sprite. I love you—"

The words hit me like a freight train.

I love you.

The cockweasel.

How fucking *dare* he?

There was a time in my life when I would have given anything to hear Dorien Valencourt utter those words to me. When I believed I was so worthless, so unloveable that my own father had run away because he didn't want to be with me. I clung to a broken friendship, wishing for what could never be.

And he throws that back in my face?

"No." I covered my ears. "No, no, no. You don't get to do that."

Dorien surged forward, but a dark hand thrust into his solar plexus, holding him back. Titus growled, "Get out of here. You're upsetting Faye."

"I know. I fucking wish I could take everything back. But I can't. I fucked up, and I love you, Sprite. Those two facts are not in dispute." Dorien slid off the end of the bed, leaning his back against the bureau. He looked defeated, drained of color and that indescribable essence that made him so entrancing. "I didn't come to convince you to take me back. I know that ship has sailed. I don't deserve you. I need you to know that you're not safe here. I've been looking into it and—"

"Damn right she's not safe. Not with you." Titus slid off the end of the bed, and Dorien shifted toward the door. "You're not going near Faye again."

"You don't understand." Dorien reared up so he was nose-to-nose with Titus. "It's all connected. Faye's mother, Madame Usher, Clare's death, my parents' stupid fucking cult. All of it."

What Dorien said echoed my own disjointed perceptions, but the words *I love you* floated inside my skull, blocking out any other thoughts.

I love you.

He can't mean that. He can't say it. He doesn't get to say it now, like this.

"Fuck *off*, Dorien." Titus grabbed him under the arms, dragging him across the floor and shoving him into the hall.

"You can't trust anyone at Manderley," Dorien yelled as Titus slammed the door in his face.

Titus turned the lock. Dorien pounded on the door, shouting my name. Ivan gathered me into his arms. I sank into his shoulder, breathing in his scent – the chilled apple and the salt-tang of the ocean, all the ice and lust that hardened his eyes soaked into me, steadying me.

"I will protect you," Ivan whispered into my hair.

"We won't let him near you again." The bed sank as Titus climbed up beside me, leaning his chest over my back, his arms lacing between Ivan's to cross over my chest. "Dorien Valencourt is dead to us."

15

DORIEN

The next day, I didn't leave my room. I lay on my bed and stared at the Broken Muse tour poster on my ceiling – the tour we were forced to cut short after Prague. Twenty-two cities over six weeks, playing larger clubs and festivals and opening for a symphonic metal band named Blood Lust who was charting big right now. The tour that would have made our careers, if I hadn't fucked it up trying to be the hero.

I should have known I was never the hero. I was the villain in this story.

The band had been the bright hope all three of us needed to keep on living and fighting – Ivan, who tasted freedom for the first time on our tours and dared to dream of a future out from beneath Madame's thumb. Titus, who was constantly tugged between two worlds, between the family he loved and the music that fed his soul. And me – Broken Muse was my baby, my vision. Titus and Ivan added their spark, but the songs were mine – my pain, my darkness. In those concert halls and dimly-lit clubs, I poured out all the things I'd never been able to say.

Back then, we'd felt invincible, as if embracing the darkness inside us through our music had become its own beautiful light. But Madame Usher took this light and turned it into our prison.

I turned over the horror show that was my life in my head, trying to see a solution where I got everything I wanted and Madame Usher was left with nothing. But I knew it was already too late.

I let Heather talk me into that evil thing.

I lost Faye. Forever.

And if Father Aaron was courting the Danvers, as I was starting to suspect, soon Jacob wouldn't even have the Valencourt name for safety.

I hurt Faye to keep Heather away from my brother. And I would do it again to keep Jacob safe, even if it meant destroying my own soul in the process.

But that was the problem. As long as Jacob remained at the Temple of Earthly Truths with my parents, I'd continue to be trapped too – a marionette dancing as Heather or Madame Usher or Father Aaron pulled the strings. That was no longer an option. I wouldn't play games with my brother's life any longer.

I had to get him out.

I had to make sure he never, ever got sent back.

I had to remove the leverage they had over me.

Even if that meant stepping back into the lion's den with a slab of meat strapped to my balls.

In the drawer of my bureau – shoved at the back behind my passport, multi-plugs for different parts of the world, old ticket stubs and festival lanyards, all the detritus of a career on the road – I found what I was looking for. The wireless mic I purchased in the early days of the band, when we were playing small clubs instead of concert halls and we needed the best gear. The mic could record as well as transmit.

I shoved aside the stack of music books on my desk, set down my laptop, and opened the recording software. Hours of tracks from Broken Muse practice sessions scrolled past the screen. We recorded everything in case one of us hit on a stroke of genius we wanted to remember later. My chest tightened as I looked at the list of recordings. The last date stood out at me – our last practice session before we hit the road for our European tour. Before Prague. Before I fucked everything up.

I jammed my headphones on my ears and checked the mic and software. I'd used this mic to storm all over different stages. I knew it had a decent range. I had to hope it would do the job when I needed it most.

As I packed up my things, I glanced out the window. My room looked out over the stable house where Master Radcliffe lived. I could see lights on in the window, and Elena sitting at the piano in his parlor, her fingers dancing over the keys as he stood behind her. He leaned in close, his hand touching hers, and a jolt of rage bubbled inside me. I lifted my gaze up, across the overgrown back garden, down to the edge of the path that led to the gazebo, and the poison garden and mausoleum beyond. The stream trickled down the mountain, swelling now from the rains and too freezing cold for the skinny-dipping we'd done with Faye when she finally gave in to the pull of our attraction. And beyond the stream, the towering trees descending the slope of the mountain, then ascending again, becoming a sweep of green as the mountains loomed over us all.

I would free Faye and my brother. I would bring Manderley Academy crashing to the ground.

16

FAYE

The week after the party was one of the most uncomfortable I spent at Manderley, and that was saying something. The house was a war zone – only instead of battles played out with guns and tanks, the weapons employed were intimidation and secrecy.

Heather, Dorien, and Madame Usher stood on one side, facing off against me, Ivan, and Titus. Aroha and Elena and Master Radcliffe stumbled into the crossfire. Our lessons had become tense standoffs, but no one wanted to admit defeat and not show up, so I endured each moment of Heather's smirk and Dorien's probing eyes with my chin high and my fingers dancing over the strings. I pretended I was my mother, raising her sword across the boardroom, accepting a duel with glee.

I pretended, but I didn't feel like a warrior inside. I felt *sick*. I didn't want to look over my shoulder all the time, or feel the prickling in my neck every time I walked the halls alone. When I closed my eyes, I saw Clare's face, her mouth open in that horrible scream as she loomed over me in the attic or came at me inside the mausoleum.

Had I really seen her?

Three times she appeared on the night of the party – in my room, in the mausoleum to deliver her creepy message, and on the stairs. Each time I could chalk the image up to a hallucination caused by distress, exhaustion, fear, or the drug Dorien used to knock me unconscious. But why would I hallucinate the face of a maid I'd never even met? I wondered if it was because of those strange words I found scrawled in the pantry – THE WALLS ARE TALKING.

I didn't believe in ghosts, but I also didn't believe in blindly ignoring what was right in front of my eyes. My mom did that – ignoring weeks of messages warning her to pay her insurance premiums or get cut off – and it destroyed our lives.

I needed answers. And I knew I could find some if I went to speak to Dorien, but I wouldn't give him the pleasure. That meant I had to do a bit of old-fashioned detective work myself.

As I stacked the dishwasher after another silent meal, Elena popped her head around the kitchen, her blue eyes twinkling. Even though she had the same ice-blue irises as Ivan, hers always caught the light in a certain way that made them sparkle. It was the same fae magic that seemed to swirl around her wherever she went.

"I *demand* to know what's going on with you and the Muses," she said.

"I thought your brother would've told you."

"He won't talk about it except to fume over how much he hates Dorien." Elena tipped her head toward me. "Ivan has worshipped at Dorien's feet ever since they formed that band. But now he wants to hang his testicles from a chandelier with rusty piano wire, and I wasn't sure if you wanted me to rescue Dorien's nuts before he goes through with it."

"Do you want to go for a walk?" I glanced through the narrow window above the sink. A bitter wind had been tearing through the valley most of the day, rattling the windows and sending several roof tiles crashing to the ground. But the wind had calmed now, leaving behind a crispness in the air that spoke of a landscape renewed – an old layer peeled away to reveal what hid underneath.

Elena pulled on her fur-lined coat and followed me across the garden. "You know there are plenty of places we can talk *inside*, beside a roaring fireplace, with a mug of your delicious spiced cocoa."

"Prying ears can't overhear us out here." I glanced up at the imposing facade of Manderley, my eyes darting across the windows that formed Madame's private wing. I noticed lights on in the room furthest away, a shape moving through the narrow gap in the drapes. *What is she doing right now? What fresh torture is she dreaming up?*

Elena and I linked arms and went side-by-side down the overgrown path toward the gazebo. When we were far enough from the house that I could not feel its specter looming through the trees, I told Elena everything that happened on the night of the party.

Once again, I left out the image of Clare – I felt certain now that I hadn't seen her at all, that she'd been a vision I'd invented in my mind to spurn me into action. I'd been swooning after Muses when I should have been focused on the crime or crimes that had taken place here, and why they'd drawn me to Manderley in the first place.

"I can't believe this happened right beneath my nose, and I didn't even know about it," she said as I recounted the story of Friday night. "Ivan never tells me these things. He thinks I should be sheltered from the darkness of this place. I don't want you to treat me like that."

"I get it. That's why I'm telling you now." I saw how Ivan doted on Elena, how he lurked in the corner of her private rehearsals as if he expected a horde of ninja assassins to leap out and attack her at any time. "When I got to the party, I just needed to play. I needed to bleed the horror of it through the music.

After the performance, I don't know... there were so many people there and it all rushed at me at once, like a delayed trauma."

"My brother will protect you," she declared, the certainty in her voice borne of an entire life lived under Ivan's watchful gaze.

"I know. The way he protects you," I said. "Why is Ivan the way he is? Why does he sit in on all your tutoring? Why is he so against you going to Moscow with Master Solokov and Master Radcliffe over the summer?"

Elena sighed. "You'll have to ask him."

"I've tried, but—"

Elena flapped her hand to cut me off. "Ivan was born two minutes before me. He believes it is his job to watch over me always. I know he told you we are trapped here, that Madame Usher is our guardian, our jailer. Ivan feels he has failed me. To him, I'm still the innocent eight-year-old girl who needs protecting from the big bad world. But I am a woman now. I am not innocent, and I refuse to die locked away in this crumbling shithole because he won't do what needs to be done."

I gave her a friendly nudge with my elbow as we approached the gazebo, although I knew her answer was deliberately evasive. "You sound like you're contemplating murder and mayhem. Should I be worried?"

Elena smiled. "Not murder, but a little mayhem. Broken Muse tried to escape Madame before, and failed. Now they must let me try my own methods."

"Will you tell me? I'm down with a little mayhem."

Elena shook her head. "Maybe soon."

I stared up at the crumbling gazebo, with its rotting wood floor revealing jagged and gaping mouths into the darkness beneath, and the vines curling through the broken lattice and circling the roof, as if trying to drag the whole structure down beneath the void. A bitter breeze caressed my arms, and I shivered. "So many secrets here."

Elena took my hand in hers, squeezing my cold fingers between her warm gloves. "Manderley is built on secrets – they're like twisted roots growing deep underground. There's nothing that can untangle them."

"I say cockpoodle to that. I am going to bring them into the light," I said. "Starting with who poisoned my mother."

17

DORIEN

"You have failed me." Madame Usher spread her thick fingers over her desk. Stacked neatly on her left were thick books of musical scores. On the other, worn leather tomes I could only assume were spellbooks for summoning demons.

Madame Usher rose. I didn't bother to reply. She didn't expect one.

I stood in front of her desk, my hands clasped in an attempt to hold myself back from reaching over and wringing her pale, fleshy neck. Even though I had the height on her, I felt small. Her glare was enough to shrink me into the carpet.

Standing in her office always made me feel like this – perhaps because it reminded me so much of my father's study, of my mother marching me before him when I was little so he could recite a litany of my faults. Later, when it became Father Aaron's office, I spent hours with my nose pressed into the rug, forced into silent penance for my transgressions.

But perhaps it was because this office had always been Victor's domain. He died not long after I arrived at Manderley, and he'd always been a kind, but stern, teacher. My prevailing memory of Victor was of a man who spent his evenings reading on a bench in the garden while Harrison weeded the beds or tended the flowers. Victor would stare pensively to the heavens, wishing for a life he couldn't have. But he loved Manderley with a fierceness that bordered on obsession. It was only when he grew sick that Madame allowed it to devolve into its current state of ruin.

Or perhaps it was simply because Madame Usher's interior decor borrowed heavily from the school of "Dracula Chic." All this room was missing was the coffin where she slept at night to be a complete funhouse horror set.

She walked slowly around to my side of the desk, the hem of her black silk dress sliding along the floor. She reminded me of a snake inching toward her prey.

A clock ticked.

Madame smiled.

SMACK.

She struck me across the cheek – the same cheek where Faye slapped me only five days earlier. The sting of it pounded between my ears as my head snapped back. I didn't dare lift my hand to my cheek or show her any other reaction.

"You were supposed to get rid of her," she snapped. "Not fall in love with her. Your mother is right – you fail at everything you touch."

"I'm not in love with Faye."

The words had no strength. No venom. I knew it and she knew it.

"Don't lie to me," she hissed. "Heather saw you run back into the forest on Friday, and Faye mysteriously shows up at the house in time to perform? I admit you did an excellent acting job pretending to be surprised when she made her entrance. I almost believed you. But you were the only one who knew she was out there. You can't hide from me, Dorien. I always get my way in the end."

Clearly I wasn't the only one, because I didn't free Faye. I didn't say that, of course. Instead, I focused on the new nugget of information I learned. "So you *were* behind Heather sabotaging Faye's performance?"

"Of course." Madame leaned back, and her smile shriveled my balls back into my body. "I am the architect of everything that goes on at Manderley. Heather came to me with information she thought I might find useful. I'd always thought her a silly, dimwitted girl, but she's proving to have more of a penchant for deception than I expected."

"Why are you doing this?" I growled. "You told me that Master Radcliffe wanted Faye at Manderley, but you couldn't stand the daughter of Donovan de Winter under these walls, ruining your reputation with her father's curse, so you wanted me to get rid of her. But that's not true. Faye said you came to her yourself. She said you were Donovan's lover. So why invite her here if all you want to do is get rid of her?"

Madame's eyes flashed. "My business with Faye is my own. You're to do as I say and don't ask questions, or I will ruin you. Or have you forgotten what I hold over you, Dorien?"

My fingers curled into fists. "I haven't forgotten."

Madame glided across the room to pace in front of the hearth. Above the stone fireplace hung a painted frame containing a photograph of her and Victor Usher from their younger days. It wasn't a wedding portrait, for I knew they were married back in Prague, but Madame wore a virginal white dress with lace sleeves and a high collar. Her dark hair framed her face and she gazed up at Victor from in front of the Cupid fountain. Water filled the fountain, and the pristine marble gleamed in the dappled mountain light. Behind the couple, Manderley watched over them like a proud mother hen. Harrison stood on a ladder, painting the porch lattice, his face turned toward the couple with a pinched expression, as if they'd just spoiled Christmas dinner by shitting in the figgy pudding.

Gizella Usher clung to her handsome new husband with his aquiline nose and hawk-like eyes, her face turned slightly toward him, her breasts swelling from her dress. She might've even appeared beautiful and madly in love, if it wasn't for the gleam of triumph in her eyes. Even then, she had seen Manderley not as a home or a school, but a weapon to wield against the world.

Madame stopped her pacing, her eyes following mine. The portrait arrested her, and for a moment she seemed to retreat back into the body of that young girl, so possessed by passion. She was no longer the evil spider, but perfectly and beautifully human.

The emotion passed from her features in a moment, and she became Madame Usher once more.

"I brought three Broken Muses into my home. I made every concession, forgave every sin, and gave you the lives that would otherwise have been denied you. Yet still, the three of you betray me." She spat the harsh words at the blazing fire. "I have seen the way Titus and Ivan fawn all over her, hoping to be thrown the scraps of her affection. How the three of you could be turned simple by such a plain girl is beyond me. But it is over for you, Dorien. I will tell you what will happen now. You will stay away from Faye de Winter. I cannot trust you or either of your friends around her. Do this, or Commissioner Walpole will see no further reason to withhold certain information concerning Aaron Varney's assault. You know he holds sway over the county sheriff's office."

"I can't control Titus and Ivan, and I've already given her up," I said. The truth of it twisted in my heart – a wound I'd never heal.

She spun around, her eyes reflecting the orange flames. "I don't believe you."

"Fine. Do it." I nodded at her. "Have me arrested. I don't care anymore. But know that if you do, I have a few secrets of my own to reveal to the police."

Her eyebrow lifted. She tried to keep an expression of cool detachment, but I could tell she was interested. "Such as?"

Fuck.

All I had were suspicions and slim connections in my file. I had nothing concrete. Nothing the police would be interested in, especially not her precious Commissioner Walpole.

Nothing except...

"In Cauda Venenum," I said.

"Pardon me?"

I sucked in a breath, hardly daring to believe I heard a waver in her voice. "You heard me. In Cauda Venenum. I have that."

I knew what it meant, though not why it was important, but I saw the way Madame Usher rolled her eyes, as if I were some bothersome child who refused to be disciplined but must be indulged. And I knew I'd hit on some chink in her armor that could be exploited. "Very well, Dorien. For now, we have a truce. You will remain at Manderley, but if I find out you've revealed anything, you will feel the sting of my wrath."

~

*B*ack in my room, I pulled on jeans and a black shirt and shoved the laptop and recording equipment into a bag. My cheek still stung from the force of Madame Usher's blow. I needed to get to my parents' place in time to see them before the recital today. I needed to move fast, because I'd be a fucking fool if I thought Madame Usher would accept a truce between us. She might decide at any moment to call my bluff. I had to ensure Jacob was safe first.

As I turned the lock in my door, my eyes fell on the narrow staircase that led to Faye's room in the attic.

The skin on the back of my neck prickled.

I'm being watched.

I hefted the backpack on my shoulder and stepped toward the staircase. "Faye?" I asked the empty air.

I didn't imagine she'd want to speak to me after everything that was said in Titus' room, but I wouldn't give up without trying. I squared my shoulders as I lifted my foot onto the staircase.

A loud creak echoed along the empty hall. In the distance, I could hear voices talking and laughing downstairs, and someone – Aroha, judging by the atonal dissonance and brutality of the piece – practiced in the Yellow Room. The prickling intensified, but when I looked around, I couldn't see anyone else in the hallway or on the stairs.

I placed my foot on the second step.

A face leaned out of the darkness into the square of light cast from the hallway chandelier. My heart skipped.

Clare.

I froze as she slid up beside me, her body formed of ash and air and sorrow. My heart hammered in my chest as she brushed against my skin, leaving a trail of goosebumps in her wake.

I tried to warn you, a voice rasped in my ear. Clare's voice – sweet and musical but tinged with moss and graveyard dirt. Invisible lips pressed against my earlobe, ice cold. *The walls are talking, Dorien.*

Fuck.

I staggered back, my heart leaping into my throat. Clare's face hovered above the stairs, her mouth open in a silent scream.

The walls are talking.

Somehow, through the haze of panic, I managed to tear down the grand staircase. I heard someone call my name, but like fuck was I stopping. I slammed Manderley's front door and leaped over the rotting porch.

I ran to my car, slamming the door behind me and tearing out of the drive. *Get me out of this hellhole.*

My fingers gripped the wheel so hard my knuckles burned

white. I struggled to bring my shaking breath under control. My earlobe still tingled from Clare's icy kiss, while her words turned over and over in my mind.

It's not possible. It can't be her.

I glanced in the rearview mirror, back at Manderley Academy receding into the trees. Did I imagine the white-clad figure standing at the window in Faye's bedroom, staring down at me? Or was it my own guilty conscience?

Clare had been so strange those last few weeks of her life. She kept trying to talk to me about weird things going on around the house – food disappearing, odd sounds – but I wouldn't hear it. I didn't want to think about anything else apart from escaping Manderley and helping Jacob. The day she died, she'd been running after me, trying to get me to listen to her. "The walls are talking," she said. "You have to believe me, Dorien. I know Madame Usher's secret. I know about the man—"

And then she screamed. I turned back just in time to see her body fly down the stairs, to *feel* the snap of her neck as it broke – a twang in the air, like the buzz of a reverberating note at the end of a sonata.

I still heard that crunch in my dreams.

I always thought her ravings were a desperate attempt to hold on to me as I drew away from her, but Clare might've been the only one to discover the truth about Manderley, and now she was dead.

She's dead and I'm seeing her. I didn't listen to her then, but I need to listen now.

I'll do anything to save Jacob and Faye from the same fate.

The road snaked down the mountain. Every mile I put between myself and Manderley only quickened my resolve. By the time I turned onto the road leading to Valencourt Manor, my blood burned with righteous fire.

I'm coming for you, Jacob. I'm not going to let them hurt you any longer.

I knew they had someone watching the gate from the house – Father Aaron may have eschewed modern technology in the Temple itself, but his surveillance system was state-of-the-art. The gate swung open, and I drove inside. Past the mountains of trash and broken furniture discarded from the house. Past the piles of cars with their tires slashed – so those who showed up at the Temple could never leave. Aaron could have sold them for cash, but he preferred to use them as part of his indoctrination.

I was the only one who managed to escape the horror of this place, only to fall into the jaws of another sinister trap.

The concrete on the driveway had cracked in places, weeds twisting through the gaps to choke the bright flowers that once lined the path. Everywhere were piles of trash and old-fashioned farm equipment rusting where it had been dumped. From what I could gather from Jacob's sporadic texts, Father Aaron had plans to farm the land to sustain a larger population, but Valencourt Manor was built on the site of an old timber mill – little would grow in the nutrient-sapped soil.

The drive turned into the woods, climbing through the trees until it fanned in front of a sprawling mansion of wood and stone. There was a time when this house had been a haven to me – a place existing outside of the city where I could forget about being Dorien the perfect son, the musical visionary, the constant disappointment, and run around the woods like a real kid. But then Father Aaron moved in and things got weird. And then they got terrifying. Now, when I gazed up at the manor, all I saw was a prison keeping my brother from me.

My mother glided down the cracked stone steps as I jerked the car to a stop. Her brown robe dragged across the dead leaves, and they clung in wet patches to the hem. "I'm so pleased you came, son."

I nodded mutely. She kissed my cheeks, but I couldn't bring myself to give her any affection in return.

"No Faye?"

I laughed hollowly. "If you want Faye to be your daughter-in-law, then you'll want to keep her far away from this freakshow."

"Of course. Very wise." She smiled, as if we were in on this scheme together, as if I hadn't just insulted the life she'd chosen. "We must ease her into our way of life. It's not easy to let go of earthly things and embrace the True Path. God knows how much you have struggled. Come with me."

As I followed Mother up the steps, I noticed three other cars in the lot – flashy cars like mine that oozed wealth and status. I thought again of Heather's mother wearing the Key of Truth, and the 'day of ascension' that was approaching. A sinking feeling weighed in my stomach as I tried to fit the pieces together.

Inside, the house bore little of its former grandeur. The high ceilings, marble floors and grand staircase still remained, although they were streaked with filth. All the furniture was gone – the finest pieces sold, others tossed into the piles or burned so Father Aaron could hammer home his teachings about casting aside earthly possessions. Bright squares of paint dotted around the walls indicated where lavish artworks once hung. Now, there were only strange phrases scrawled in loopy handwriting – the creed of the Temple of Earthly Truths.

A circle of children played beneath the stairs, tossing painted stones across the floorboards. They wore white versions of my mother's brown robes, the hems grubby from working in the gardens.

"You should all be at your tasks." Mother frowned at the tiny faces. They looked up, startled, recoiling from her stern expression. Genuine fear flickered in their eyes. She snapped her fingers. "Go. Do not let the Holy Father see you idle."

The children dropped the stones and scattered. My mother wiped her hands on her dress, as if she'd completed some great and satisfying work. She waited until I dropped my mobile phone into the tray in the hallway, then indicated toward the kitchen. "We will have tea."

The kitchen had once been a warm place where my parents' cook created piles of delicious food and my mother drank wine with her society lady friends in front of the double-height windows while I played Frisbee or croquet outside on the lawn. Now, it was as cold and neglected as the rest of the house – bare of furniture and mirth. Old-fashioned pots and enormous serving platters designed for many people were stacked in the corners, as were sacks of flour and grains that reeked of rot.

I stepped into the hexagonal breakfast room, where Aaron had forced me and Faye to play that one time she visited for my birthday. This was how I lost my family – over the breakfast room. Aaron started by suggesting Mother remove the table and have us all sit on the floor, to be closer to the earth. Then he removed the cushions, and the oak side table our staff used for serving. Then he got rid of the staff, and the meal of breakfast. Things spiraled from there until the whole house fell under his spell.

I peered out the windows, imagining I could still taste Faye's intoxicating scent perfuming the air. A group of figures wandered across the lawn – Father Aaron with his robe flapping around his reedy legs, leading a group of would-be acolytes around the grounds, pointing out the fountain fed from a fresh-water spring and the fruit trees.

Trees my grandfather planted, so that future generations of Valen-courts could enjoy this place. Instead of a pleasure palace, it's a prison of horror.

"Are you expecting more new recruits today?" I counted eight people in total listening to Aaron with rapt attention – two fami-lies with small children, and a couple of teenagers hanging back and smirking at it all. They thought the whole thing was a joke, that this tiny bald man in a brown robe couldn't do anything to uproot their comfortable lives. My fingers itched to grab them, shake them, make them see the danger.

Run away, now. Before it's too late.

"We shall have guests all day. Your dad has been hard at work spreading the word about our perfect life here. The Holy Lord will be pleased with him."

This was new. My parents never had to work to 'please' Aaron before. Signing over their estate, their savings, their family to him must not be enough any longer.

Footsteps clattered on the marble floor. I turned just as a boy hobbled into the kitchen, followed by two girls with braided blonde hair. They all wore the white robes of the children of the Temple of Earthly Truths.

"Dorien." Jacob rocked forward on his feet and threw his arms around me. He was fifteen years old – he should be as tall as me by now, but he barely came up to my armpits. I let him hold me as long as he wanted, feeling his love soak into my bones.

Why is he hobbling? Has he been injured? I longed to throw him over my shoulder and run out with him, but it would be pointless. My parents were his guardians, and Madame Usher and Heather would ensure I couldn't make a legal case against them. So I plastered a smile over my concern.

"Hey, bro." I ruffled his hair and he smiled, the smile of a boy trapped in a man's body. "Who are your girlfriends?"

Jacob rolled his eyes, like I'd said something really funny. "Girlfriends aren't allowed. We can't have impure thoughts ruin our good work. These are my sisters, Pearl and Emma Danvers. We're in charge of making bread. Do you want to help?"

I peered at the two girls over Jacob's shoulder. *Danvers.* They did have Heather's honey-blonde hair. It was impossible to know for sure, but I didn't remember the two of them from last time I'd been here. They were new recruits, which meant my suspicions were right – Father Aaron was courting the Danvers' family, and my parents were falling out of favor.

But I couldn't speak these things aloud. So I squeezed my brother's hand, grateful beyond belief to see him alive and smiling, even if every other facet of his appearance terrified me. "Sure. Just show me what to do."

Jacob hopped and scraped his feet as he made his way into the kitchen. At one point he had to grip the edge of the counter to remain upright. His face twisted with pain before Mother frowned at him, and he wiped it over with a forced smile. It looked like standing was excruciating for him.

My hands balled into fists. A deep, keening dread settled into my gut. *This is my little brother, and he can't walk. I have to help him.*

For once in my life, I'm doing the right thing.

The two girls pulled a large bowl from the windowsill and placed it on top of an old-fashioned scale. They started to measure out a mountain of flour while Jacob filled a jug with water.

"We need *this* much." He pointed a grubby finger at a mark on the side of the jug. "I make bread every day now. I'm good at it. I like it, too. It smells nice in here. Since my feet hurt I can't go back to the fields, so—"

"Jacob," Mom warned. "Dorien doesn't want to hear about that."

Dorien very much does want to hear about that. I shifted my weight, fighting the urge to touch the mic hidden under my shirt recording all this. She hadn't said enough. Even though my skin crawled with the thought of what Father Aaron had done to hurt Jacob's feet, I had only an uncomfortable conversation between mother and son on tape. No evidence of evil.

Jacob's face flushed with pain. He focused on the water. When the jug was filled, he carried it in two hands, hobbling and lurching across to the flour to dump it in. The older girl, Pearl, removed a large jar of something foul-smelling and dumped a quarter of the contents into the bowl, and then the three of them started to punch and stir and knead the mixture into a stretchy dough.

"Dorien, come help." Jacob's face lit up as he stretched and shaped the dough. "It feels so cold and funny."

I shuddered. "That's okay. I'll just watch."

Bread should come from an artisan bakery in New York. Bread was the crisp tortillas Faye rolled out and fried to perfection while she sashayed her gorgeous ass around the kitchen singing pop songs. Bread was warmth and happiness and sinful carbohydrates. It shouldn't be the product of a child labor camp to sate one man's desire for godhead.

When the loaves were finally kneaded and shaped and set out to do whatever bread was supposed to do, Jacob grabbed my hand again. "I'm going to show Dorien the chickens," he told Mother.

"I'll come with you." She stood up.

SMASH.

"Mother Valencourt, I'm so sorry!" Pearl stood on a stool above the oven, frozen in terror. Broken glass scattered over the counter and across the floor, and a cloud of brown dust coated everything in sight.

"You stupid girl. That was our coffee supply. Father Aaron will not allow us another for six months." Mother wrung her hands. "What are we going to serve our guests this evening? Clean this up, and take yourself to the penalty room for the rest of the afternoon."

The penalty room. That sounded *great.*

The two sides of my mother battled it out – the part of her that still believed in putting on appearances for guests, and the side that wanted desperately to be the perfect acolyte for Aaron. As she rushed to the kitchen to deal with the mess, Jacob tugged my hand, dragging me across the room and holding open the side door that led into the manor's courtyard.

My breath hitched as I followed him around the raised garden beds. He moved as fast as he could on his sore feet, gasping under his breath as he led me away from the house. What he was doing could get him into a lot of trouble. But the fact that he was doing it filled me with hope. Apart from the mobile phone I gave him, I don't think I'd ever seen Jacob defy Aaron's rules before.

We reached the other side of the courtyard. Here, the tall beds filled with vegetables obscured us from view of the kitchen. Up against the side of the house was a long run filled with a couple dozen birds. It smelled delightful. I pinched my nose as I followed Jacob around the back of a rotting wooden coop.

"Down here." Jacob dropped to his knees and pushed aside a board, revealing a crawlspace beneath the house. I thought of the nice shirt and freshly-pressed slacks I'd put on for today's recital. But Jacob's face begged me to follow, and I couldn't refuse him.

I sank to a squat and waddled into the gap. Jacob pulled the board over the hole, casting us into near darkness. Down here the smell was even worse – mingling the smell of the chicken shit with damp and rot.

I knew we didn't have much time. Jacob faced me, the pale outline of his face striped with the light that streamed between the wooden boards. He bit his lip, and I knew it had cost him dearly to get me here, but he didn't know what to do next.

"That girl in the kitchen, did she drop the bowl so we could talk?" I asked Jacob. He nodded.

"I haven't seen you in so long," he whispered. "Pearl says that our whole family is crazy and no one is supposed to live like this, that our house is supposed to be filled with furniture and we're *supposed* to have water coming from the taps. She said she'd help me talk to you, and maybe you could tell the police."

I couldn't help but smile. This Pearl was pretty smart. "She's right. You *are* supposed to have all those things. You're not supposed to feel scared all the time. And I'm going to help you, bud. I'm sorry I haven't done anything already, but that's going to change, all right?"

Jacob nodded. He hugged his legs to his chest. I noticed red welts striping across his wrists and around his ankles as the hem of his robe hitched up. Someone had tied up my little brother. *I'll wring Aaron's neck.*

I fought back the rage. I had to stay calm. I had my brother alone at last. I needed to use this time to get something I could use against Aaron. "How long has Pearl lived here?"

"She doesn't live here. She told me they live in a big house with real furniture and lots of money and she even has a pony. Father Aaron spends most of his time there now. He says he's preparing it for the day of ascension."

"What's the day of ascension?"

"It's when the world falls to ruin, crushed beneath God's wrath. It's when the oceans boil and burning rain falls from the sky, and the righteous are raised up to heaven while the sinners are tortured for all eternity. Father Aaron says if we please God, we will sit beside him in his kingdom."

Yup, that's not good. "And what date is this illustrious event?"

Jacob stared at me blankly. He didn't understand. He'd never been taught about numbers or reading a calendar. I tried another line of inquiry.

"Have you met Pearl's parents?"

"Mmmhmm. They came for our last feast day. Father Aaron let them sit with him at the top of the table. Their names are Fenston and Eustace."

Those were Heather's parents' names. I wished I could show Jacob a picture of them from the party and he could identify them properly, but I didn't have my phone with me.

"Tell me everything, buddy. I need to know what's going on in here."

"You always say that." Jacob put his thumb in his mouth. It was a habit he started when he was two. He had no other comfort in this place, so even though Aaron beat him when he did it, he couldn't stop. The sight of it broke my heart. Jacob should be chasing girls, breaking hearts, thinking about studying for college, not sucking his thumb, or limping, or hiding under the house because he feared *the penalty room.* "You say that and then nothing happens."

"That's because I fucked up. I let my anger get the better of me, and now we need a new plan." I lifted my shirt, showing him the microphone hidden on my belt. "This time is different, I promise. I'm getting you out before the day of ascension, which is bullshit, but the way. Don't believe a word Aaron says. If he says it's time for ascension and I haven't come for you yet, you need to get the mobile I gave you and call me *immediately.*"

Jacob squeezed his eyes shut. He didn't like it when I swore, and he barely understood how to use the phone. He thought it was scary. "Father Aaron is so angry. He says we don't work hard enough. Mother and Father don't bring in enough new converts. The house is falling apart. Father Aaron says this was supposed to be paradise on earth, but God has abandoned us. The only thing that makes him happy now is visiting Pearl's family. Whenever he returns from their house he's in much better spirits. He says they've been touched by God's eternal light."

"Has he done anything to Mother and Father?"

"He made them sleep in a cage with the pigs for a week," Jacob said. "That used to only be a punishment for new converts, to help them to learn to return to the earth. But he thinks Mother and Father need help. He thinks he's been too soft on them, and now he has to undo the damage or they cannot ascend. And now if I do something wrong, he says it's their fault. I don't want to get them in trouble. I was working outside and I was so hungry. I'd been working since dawn and I wasn't allowed any food. There was a beautiful orange on the tree and I ate it. Father Aaron caught me – I thought he was going to yell at me, but he yelled at them instead. He made us cook a big, fancy meal for the Danvers' visit, but he wouldn't let us eat any of it. I didn't get food for three days."

This is torture. Pure and simple.

"It was my fault. I shouldn't have taken the orange," Jacob sniffed.

There was a cold, gaping hole where my heart should have been. "Jacob, can you show me your feet?"

I thought he hadn't heard me. He didn't move or react for the longest time, just kept staring at me with those eyes that were so much like mine, and yet nothing at all like mine. They were eyes that had seen nothing outside the walls of this shithole and yet had seen more than any teenage boy should ever have to see. They were the eyes of a boy with a rich imagination and a kindness toward all creatures that reminded me of what I loved about Faye.

I was just starting to worry when Jacob reached down and slid off one of his holey shoes. The inside of the sneaker had turned pink with blood. He wore no socks.

Bile rose in my throat as I stared at my little brother's foot. He winced as he turned his ankle toward me to show the torn, bloody sole. Someone had flayed off his skin in long ribbons. Burns around his ankle had blistered and wept into open sores, and dried blood crusted between his toes.

Red welts obscured my vision as hot, violent rage pulsed behind my eyes.

Someone did this to my brother.

Someone would *die*.

18

DORIEN

I tried to speak, but it took several deep breaths before I could form words again. "Jacob, how did this happen?"

Jacob shrugged, and that shrug hurt more than seeing what had been done to him. *He thinks this is normal, something he has to endure if he wants to be Aaron's special boy.* "I did a bad thing. Pearl and I were holding hands. I didn't know it was wrong. I didn't feel evil or sinful, but I was wrong. I promise I won't do it again."

"Don't say that." My knuckles cracked from the force of holding my hand in a fist. I needed to smash it into something. Preferably Aaron's smug little face.

"I had to go back to working in the field," Jacob said. "But then it hurt too much. I fainted, and Father Aaron said I could bake bread instead, even though men aren't supposed to bake bread."

"Men can bake whatever they want to bake," I growled. "The only thing men can't do is hurt people who can't fight back. Jacob, this is important. Are there weapons in the house? Guns and stuff?"

Jacob reached into his pocket and pressed something into my hands. "Pearl helped me make that. She's smart like you. She thought of all these things you might want to know—"

"Jacob, Dorien. Where are you?"

Jacob's face paled. He shoved the board aside and crawled out of the gap. I was surprised how fast he moved given the state of his feet, but he must've been forced to walk around on them for weeks now.

I hated to think of my brother being used to that pain.

Death isn't good enough for Aaron. Or my parents. How can they subject a child to this torture?

How could I?

Was I any better than them? I escaped Valencourt Manor to play music, and I'd left Jacob inside these walls, all alone, believing one day I'd come back for him. And then I fucked that up and I let myself fall into Madame Usher's trap. How long had this solution been open to me? How many nights had I tossed and turned in my comfortable bed, holding back for selfish reasons, pretending as if I had a choice, while Jacob slept in a pig pen and had his feet flayed?

I clambered out after him, trying to keep my clothes away from the dirt. Jacob winced as he tugged his sneaker back on. He rolled onto his feet, and for a moment he stood upright. Tears stung his eyes as his weight bore down on his ruined feet. I reached out to him, but he took off toward the sound of Mom's voice.

"I'm here." Jacob stopped in front of her, staring at his shoes. "I was showing Dorien my chickens."

"You shouldn't have run away like that." She looked to me, her face twisted with suspicion. "You know you're not allowed to be alone with Dorien. He cannot help that his head is filled with the sins of the world, but we can't have his wickedness poisoning you, not when you have worked so hard."

"We were just talking about chickens," I said, hoping like hell she didn't ask any follow-up questions. What I knew about chickens could fit into a demisemihemidemisemiquaver. That's the smallest musical note, for any philistines out there.

"Go inside and help Pearl serve cordial to our guests." My mother's cold eyes bore into mine as she placed her hand on Jacob's shoulder and pushed him in the direction of the house. "I want to speak with your brother alone."

Has she seen the mic? I thought I'd hid it carefully under my shirt, but I didn't dare look down to check. Maybe they had some kind of machine that sensed transmissions? I kept my face impassive. I wouldn't give anything away. I needed to make it out of here with Jacob's recording.

Mom looped her arm in mine, dragging me to the far corner of the courtyard, where a high hedge hid us from view of the fields below. I followed where she looked – another car had just pulled up, and Father Aaron raced over to help a woman from the front seat.

It was Heather's mother, Eustace Danvers. The Key of Truth sparkled in the late afternoon sun.

"What did Jacob tell you?" My mother's fingers dug into my arm.

"We talked about chickens. And baking bread. He has bruises around his wrists and ankles, Mother." My hands curled into fists. "How could you let Aaron hurt him?"

"Jacob acts out, especially now Pearl is here. Father Aaron has to discipline him." She turned to face me, her mouth set in a hard line. Out here in the sunlight, she appeared older, her face crisscrossed with wrinkles, her forehead sagging from stress. "Things will be better once Pearl learns to accept our ways. Dorien, we must talk about your marriage. Faye de Winter—"

"I'm not going near Faye," I said. It was the least I owed her. Ten years ago I destroyed our friendship to save her from the Temple. Life had come full fucking circle once more.

"You *must.*" She snuck a glance back to the lawn, where Father Aaron had Mrs. Danvers on his arm and was gesturing to the orchard trees. "Or we will lose everything."

"You already lost everything when you joined this stupid cult."

"Just because you don't understand our ways does not mean they are not valuable. Jacob is growing up without the negative influence of money. He's eating wholesome food. He lives in a utopia without greed or lust or avarice—"

I snorted. "That's fucking rich."

But she wasn't listening. "—it's everything you should want for him, and for your own children. But if you don't marry Faye, it could all be taken away from us."

"Here's a shocking idea," I smirked. "Why don't you stop pretending we live in the Dark Ages and let me *choose* who I marry? Maybe Titus wants me to put a ring on it."

"This isn't funny, Dorien." Mother pursed her lips as she glared at Mrs. Danvers. "We need you to align with a powerful family, with someone Aaron respects and believes he can save, or this all goes away."

"I have no intention of marrying Heather. What are you talking about?"

"Ten years ago, things were so different. After you rejected Faye, I read the auguries and your union to Heather was preordained and God-blessed. The Danvers' influence and their wealth would enable the Temple to grow and blossom. It costs a lot of money to recruit the powerful people who are most in need of saving. Aaron has to infiltrate the right circles. We've given our entire fortune to the cause, but it hasn't been enough." Her face pinched. "Aaron no longer believes I'm his prophetess. He thinks he was mistaken before, that Eustace's energy was so powerful that he mistook it as coming from me. If we don't do something quickly, she will be his Blessed-Bride, and he'll punish me for deceiving him."

"Punish you, how?" Jacob's ruined foot burned itself into my brain.

"He wants to burn this place down. On the day of ascension, we will purify ourselves in a great conflagration, and be made anew. He'll move our community to the Danvers' California estate. I'll no longer be prophetess and Jacob will no longer be his God-son. He won't be safe from Aaron's wrath."

She meant that *she* won't be safe from his wrath. Below us, Aaron turned, leading Eustace back toward the house. Mother stiffened.

"He can't see us together like this. I'll contact you again soon. If you won't choose Faye, I will find another bride who will help restore me in his eyes." Her eyes flashed, and she darted back toward the kitchen.

What the fuck?

I followed her, climbing back over the crumbling steps just as Father Aaron stepped into the kitchen. His presence drained what little life remained in the room. The children stood back, hands behind their backs, faces turned to the floor. Eustace glared down at them as if she wished she could grind them into the dirt beneath her boot. Jacob's shoulder trembled, and Pearl's mouth set in a defiant line. I didn't need auguries to read the future from the tension tugging at the air. If Father Aaron moved the cult to California, my brother would be lost to me forever.

I couldn't stay in that house another minute. Now that Aaron was here, no one would dare say a word I could use, anyway. I fished my phone from the tray in the foyer. "I have to get to my recital."

"Yes. You must play for them, son." My mother thrust a stack of pamphlets into my hand. "Give one to anyone you meet who is searching for answers. We welcome all at the Temple."

She looked over her shoulder at Aaron, searching for his approval, but he was too distracted with his inspection of the rising bread to glance her way. He'd reduced my formidable mother to a pathetic mess, scrambling for scraps of affection. I felt no love for her, only revulsion. This was what she sacrificed our family and Jacob's future to obtain. She could drown in pig shit for all I cared.

But Jacob... he will be free.

"Goodbye, bud." I knew better than to give Jacob a hug in Aaron's presence. My brother nodded, his eyes never leaving the floor. I tore myself from the room and fled outside, feeling like a coward with every step I took away from my little brother.

My hands trembled as I gripped my Porsche's wheel. *I'm sorry, Jacob. I'm sorry I couldn't give you a normal life.*

At the end of the street, I parked the car. My chest felt so tight I struggled for breath. I took out my mobile phone and punched a number I memorized a long time ago. My finger hovered over the CALL button, but when I tried to press it, bile rose in my throat, burning at the back of my mouth.

I tossed the phone aside, flung open the door, and threw up into the grass.

When the heaving stopped, I sat back up, my head spinning.

I have to do this. It felt like a betrayal of my family. It was something I could never go back from. It might ensure I never saw Jacob again. It might send me to jail. But just like when I tried to help Ivan and Elena escape, it wasn't about me. Jacob deserved better than this. And he needed to be kept as far away from Heather's family as possible.

I picked up my phone and hit CALL before I could chicken out again. "Hello. This is Dorien Valencourt for Agent Rochester. Tell him I'm ready to talk about the Temple of Earthly Truths."

19

FAYE

All through breakfast, Elena was in her excited state, bouncing in her seat and talking with her mouth full. After I cleaned up the dishes, I made a quick phone call to the hospital to check on my mom (no change), collected my violin and overnight bag from my room, and climbed into the backseat of the twins' Eldorado – the Cadillac old enough to be a beater. Originally, Dorien was going to be driving down with us, but after I told Elena what he did, she made him make his own way. His car was already gone, and I hadn't seen him at breakfast. But then, he'd made himself scarce most of the week.

I couldn't say I minded. I didn't want to be forced to remember the promises he'd broken.

Ivan got behind the wheel. Elena slid in back with me, leaning over to squeeze my leg.

"We're going to have the best time." She unzipped her purse to show me the clothes stuffed inside. "I have plans for after the recital."

I pulled out a tiny sequined dress. "Does it involve Ivan singing 'Like a Virgin' at a drag club? Because that's the only situation I can imagine where this dress would be appropriate."

Elena giggled. "It does not, but I like the way you are thinking. Brother, how about a little cabaret show tonight?"

"How about you two stop scheming and let me focus on the road."

"Did you know that Ivan wanted to be in musical theatre when he was a little kid?" Elena grinned.

I couldn't even picture it. In my head, Ivan had always been a serious, stone-faced icicle, even as a kid. I wanted more of this story. "Is that so?"

Ivan gripped the wheel. "Elena is telling fairy tales."

"It's true! Our mother used to do laundry for this old lady who lived next door, and Ivan would wrap himself in her winter coat and pretend to be Javert, or tie her black shawls and cackle like the witch Elphaba."

"You are making all this up so I look silly in front of Faye." Ivan yanked the wheel hard around. Elena screamed, but it was a shriek of delight.

All through the trip, the twins bickered. Elena came alive in the car, blossoming from the delicate flower into an excitable bunny. The further we got from Manderley, the more she bounced in her seat, the louder she laughed, the more she teased her brother. I loved watching Ivan with her. It felt like I saw beyond the mask he wore for the world.

Outside of Manderley, we were just normal people. How I longed to be normal for a few hours.

When we arrived at the museum where the recital would take place, Dorien's car wasn't in the lot. Odd, considering he left well before us. We'd been told to be there an hour early for set-up and tuning, and he never missed an opportunity to show he was the professional amongst us. It wasn't like him to be late.

I don't care. Dorien is not my problem.

We took our cases inside, and a woman named Karen introduced herself as the collections manager and showed us the space where we'd be performing – a beautiful octagonal foyer with a double-height ceiling and chandelier made from recycled Colonial farm implements. Wooden staircases swept off to either side. These had been roped off for VIPs and the museum staff. Visitors to the museum would gather around the grand piano and overflow into the adjacent galleries.

Ivan and I unpacked our violins and tuned while Elena sat at the piano and played through some scales. I kept glancing at the glass clock above our heads as the room filled with patrons. It was now only ten minutes to showtime, and he still hadn't arrived.

"Where's Dorien?" Karen wrung her hands nervously. "Many of our donors have come along today especially to see him."

"He will be here," Ivan said in his thick Romanian accent, but he glanced at Elena in alarm.

"I've tried his phone. He's not picking up." Elena raised it to her ear again. "He left before us, so why isn't he here? Do you think we should call the police?"

"I think we should get out there and play." Ivan glanced at his phone. "He's not coming. After that evil thing he did to Faye, I think he—"

Behind us, the crowd shuffled. Whispers circulated the room as a commotion started near the entrance. Dorien burst through the revolving door, nearly knocking down several patrons. He wore the same red shirt he'd been in this morning, the material creased and stained at the cuffs. His hair flopped over his face, and his eyes flashed with something that might've been horror.

"You are late," Elena snapped. Dorien didn't acknowledge her. Instead, he slid in beside her on the piano bench. She wrinkled her nose. "And you stink."

"It doesn't matter," Dorien barked, his fingers darting across a scale.

"Dorien, your sleeve," Ivan hissed.

I glanced down and noticed a dusting of white powder on the end of Dorien's sleeve. My whole body went rigid.

I thought of the baggie of white powder Aroha had the night of Boris Solokov's visit. I'd wondered then where she got it from. The cocaine I found in Ivan's drawer made me believe he was the one supplying her, but Ivan denied it. I also knew what Dorien was capable of when his back was against a wall. And I *definitely* knew he had no money to his name.

Is that where he's been? Out selling drugs for cash?

Ivan glanced up at Karen, who stepped back, her face horrified as she took in Dorien's rumpled appearance. From the staircase, I caught murmuring from the crowd. We weren't the only ones who noticed the powder.

Dorien frowned and started folding over his cuffs, rolling up his sleeves to hide the stain. Tattoos of ravens and bats circled his strong forearms, and it took everything I had not to lick my lips at the sight of him. *He's not yours any longer. He's proven he doesn't deserve you. So stop drooling over his forearms.*

If only I could get my hormones to listen to reason, but the damn things had a mind of their own. And they wanted Dorien Valencourt, on the piano, any time, anywhere.

Elena licked the tip of her finger and pressed it to the white stuff on Dorien's cuff, then touched to her tongue. "That's the worst coke I've ever had. It tastes like flour."

Dorien glared at her as he finished rolling his sleeves. "It *is* flour."

Flour? That was weirder than it being cocaine. Before I could stop myself I asked, "Why do you have flour on your sleeve? You don't even know how to boil an egg, let alone anything that requires baking."

"None of your business. Can we get this over with?" Dorien pushed the piano stool with so much force he tipped Elena off the end of it. She stumbled but managed to regain her composure. Dorien's rigid back and hard eyes said that was the end of the discussion.

Karen introduced us, and we played through our pieces. The

adrenaline coursed in my veins as I drew from the crowd's nervous energy. As Dorien and I launched into my composition, a hush fell over the room. He had the power to do that, even when he was in a stormy mood.

Or perhaps *because* he was in such a stormy mood. *The Bad Boy of Baroque lives up to his title.*

This time, when we played, the music felt like a duel, a battle of wills. His fingers slammed into the keys, creating a grating harshness that I mirrored with my instrument. *Anything you can do, I can do better.*

As we reached the crescendo of the piece, the tension in the room swirled around me, drawing me into a dark tunnel where all I could see, all I could *feel*, was Dorien fucking Valencourt. His demonic music crawled inside my head, poisoning me, bleeding me out with his savage spell. *Not this time.* I pressed down so hard on the strings that one broke with a loud *PING*. The coiled tip leaped up to sting me across the cheek. It was the warning I needed to break the spell, to beat Dorien at his own game. I finished with a screeching note – an improvisation that threw Dorien off and made me the focus. The defiant fairy facing off against the Prince of Darkness, and beating him soundly.

The applause that broke through the spell rippled over my skin, and for once I was grateful. This was why rockstars love performing so much. The adoration and the exchange of emotion with the audience punched me right in the heart. They didn't know what was going on between me and Dorien, but they felt my triumph and his defeat as I did, and that was all the revenge I needed.

High on the applause and the music in my veins, I circled the room in a daze. I only half-heard the praise heaped on me by the patrons. I waited for Elena to be done with a serious conversation she was having with two rich-looking men in dark suits, then we linked arms, the pair of us skipping to the car. "To the hotel, chauffeur," Elena commanded her brother. "We will change clothes and hit the town."

Ivan didn't say anything as he drove us to the hotel. "Do you want me to stay with you?" he asked Elena as he walked us to the door.

"Not even remotely." She slammed the door in his face and broke down in a giggling fit. "Poor Ivan. He worries about me so much. Just because he's forgotten what it's like to be alone, doesn't mean I don't enjoy it."

"Is that why he follows you around Manderley?" I said, thinking of the pair of them sharing a room when there were plenty to spare, and of Ivan searching her out whenever he hadn't seen her for a few minutes. "I noticed he goes to all your classes."

"Yes." She moved to the bed and rooted through her bag. I expected her to elaborate, but she didn't. The abrupt end to the conversation struck me as odd. Had I hit on something?

"What do you think was up with Dorien?" Instead of pushing it, I changed the subject. This friendship or whatever it was with Elena was still so new – a fragile trust tethered us, and I wasn't ready to test that yet.

"You mean, why would he kidnap you and leave you in a bag in the middle of the forest?"

"I know why," I said. "He didn't want me to be the center of attention. He wanted everyone focused on him."

"If you say so." Elena shrugged. "If you're referring to today, I can't imagine why he'd be covered in flour, but I'm just happy he turned up. You and he are so perfectly suited for your composition. The passion between you two today – it was like you were fucking the music. I could not have done it justice."

"Nonsense." Heat crept to my cheeks at her words. "Dorien may be the Bad Boy of Baroque, but you're Master Radcliffe's favorite for a reason."

Elena's face shifted into that doll-like mask of hers, and she returned to rummaging in the bag. Okay, there was definitely something going on. I opened my mouth to ask about it, but she thrust a black leather bodycon dress into my arms.

"Wear this. It'll look amazing."

I glanced down at my concert clothes – a floor-length black skirt and crimson turtleneck. I threw the scrap of fabric back at her. "You're like a size 0. Nothing you wear is going to fit me."

"Except that I brought that for you, and it's got these panels at the side that stretch." She held it up against me, her lips tugging into a satisfied smile. "Trust me. Where we're going tonight, you'll be overdressed."

"You're terrifying." I went into the bathroom and locked the door, peeling off my layers. There was something about undressing in front of a skinny bitch like Elena that made me suddenly self-conscious of the size of my thighs and stomach. I pulled the dress over my head, smoothing the leather.

Sound the fucktrumpets, she's right. The bodycon shape worked my figure to perfection. Thick halter straps gave me killer cleavage while keeping the girls contained – just as well, because no way would I be able to get away with a bra in this dress. It hugged my waist and thighs, accentuating my hourglass shape. I imagined Ivan's expression when he saw me in this dress – I wondered if I could break through that icy exterior of his.

What will Dorien think?

I bit my lip. Why did I care what he thought? Dorien was no longer part of my... harem, I guessed I could call it. I had Ivan and Titus, and the night of the party proved they were *more* than enough.

A tiny fist hammered on the door. "Are you coming out, or do I need to get Ivan to break down the door?"

I sighed. "I'm coming out."

I unlocked the door and sashayed into the room. Elena wore her own party dress – a scrap of dusky sequined fabric that looked more like Liberace's handkerchief than a dress. She squealed and embraced me, her stick-like arms wrapping around my bare shoulders.

On the bed, Ivan watched me with a wariness that set my teeth on edge. Elena must've let him in while I was changing. I couldn't tell what he thought beneath that icy stare. If Elena noticed it, she ignored it, shoving my purse into my hands and practically dragging me out the door.

Across the street from the hotel was an old-school diner. Elena marched me inside. With her waif figure and long legs, she looked like a runway model or a forest elf. When the guy behind the counter saw her striding toward him, he dropped a bottle of ketchup, sending red sauce splattering all down the wall and across the floor.

"C-c-can I help you?" His eyes bugged out of his head. He hadn't even noticed the sauce.

Elena ordered piles of food – chili fries and onion rings and deep-fried mac 'n cheese balls. All the stuff we never ate at Manderley. Ivan found a table near the back, and the three of us slid inside.

"Why so much food?" I asked. "How do you fit it all in?"

"This is a tradition we have for after a performance," Elena said. "Ivan and I come from this small medieval city called Sighisoara. There are a lot of tourists who come to see the medieval buildings. We would play together in the town square, and when we finished for the day, we were supposed to take our earnings home to our parents, but we would always go to this tiny restaurant on the corner of the square and gorge on fried food and meat and cakes, all the things we couldn't afford at home."

"Tell me about your city." I was looking at Ivan, but he glared at the salt shaker, determined not to look at me.

I remembered the words he said to me beside the poison garden before he kissed me. *I wanted to know that what I feel between us is more than just unfinished business between you and*

Dorien. It was. Dorien and I had history, but Ivan and I had a future. I hoped he understood that after hearing Dorien and I play together today.

Elena answered my question.

"It's lovely. It's all cobbled streets and old medieval buildings. Tourists think it is marvelous." Elena reached across to squeeze Ivan's hand. "Of course, Ivan hated it. He thought it was too small for us. He didn't even like Bucharest when we played there. He always wanted to come to America. It is only a pity it was never as we dreamed it, but it still might be. One day."

The food arrived then – plate after plate of piping hot fried things that made my thighs grow two sizes just from smelling them. Elena dug into a stack of fried chicken while Ivan crunched down onion rings like he was hoarding them for winter. Clearly, both the twins were able to eat whatever they wanted without worrying about their weight, but they were both too wonderful to hate for that.

"Even with your voracious appetite, this is way too much food for three of us," I remarked, biting into an onion ring.

"I'll help."

Dorien slid into the booth next to me. He was dressed for a night out – dark jeans and a black tank that showed off those glorious inked shoulders and arms. He slung a leather jacket over the back of the seat. His thigh pressed against mine as he leaned across the table to grab a mac 'n cheese ball, and my throat closed.

"Nice dress." Dorien's eyes dropped from my face to my chest for a moment. Under his gaze, the scrap of fabric seemed to disappear. I felt like I was wearing nothing at all.

You do not get to have an opinion on my dress.

I glared at him and focused on the spread of artery-clogging goodness in front of me. If I had to sit next to Dorien, I'd eat until I fell into a carb-and-sugar-induced stupor and forgot how much I wanted him.

I had so many questions for him, about where he'd gone today, about the flour on his shirt from earlier, about what he'd said in Titus' bedroom. But I refused to break. I wouldn't give him the satisfaction of knowing I still thought about him, trying to unravel his mysteries.

Elena glared at Dorien, and her solidarity made my chest swell with love. The three of us continued talking – the kind of easy conversation that took place between longtime friends that I'd always been locked out of at school. We left no gap in our words for Dorien to fill with his overbearing presence, and he got the hint and stayed quiet. He didn't move, though, and I found it increasingly difficult to concentrate with his leg pressed against my bare thigh.

When we'd stuffed ourselves full to bursting, Elena linked arms with me. The pair of us strutted down the street like we owned the town. Tonight, I felt like maybe we did.

Ivan walked beside us, content to bask in the light of Elena's aura. Dorien walked a few feet behind, his eyes burning holes into my back.

"Where are we going?" I asked as we wandered away from the brightly lit streets filled with bars and restaurants toward an industrial block.

"You'll see." Elena turned down a dark alley. She counted doorways, pointing her pink nails at the roller doors. Beneath my feet, the ground vibrated from some nearby club, but there were no signs or crowds nearby – just rows of shitty-looking warehouses shuttered against the night.

She stopped in front of a nondescript roller door, the bottom corner decorated in orange graffiti. Elena flipped up a small box on the wall and punched a number into a keypad. The door rolled up, revealing a concrete and brick garage. She waved us through.

At the rear of the garage was another door that swung open on an automatic hinge, revealing a dark, damp hall. Inside, the floor vibrated harder, and I caught the faint, tugging beat of house music somewhere in the distance. We dug our phones from our pockets to see as we followed Elena to the end of the hall, where she pushed open a second door.

The music slammed into me – a wall of thudding, pulsing sound. We stood in some kind of old factory turned packed nightclub. Pipes and valves crossed the ceiling. In the center of the room was a giant steampunk art piece that doubled as a platform where a few brave souls danced high above the crowd. Beneath it, bartenders in old-fashioned clothing served colorful cocktails in test tubes and beakers.

Elena yelled something to me, but I couldn't hear her over the din. She dragged me through the crowd to the bar, where a bartender in a full steampunk outfit and top hat mixed drinks with flare. Elena leaned over the bar and moments later, a smoking test tube filled with pink liquid was placed in my hand.

"Drink up," a voice purred in my ear.

Dorien. His velvet voice dropped through my body, straight to my core. My veins buzzed with energy – the music touching something deep and primal and urgent. Everything about tonight felt like a web spun of his dark magic. Did he leave his leg there by accident, or because he knew he had this effect on me, or... or...

I dumped the drink over his head. Sticky pink liquid dripped down his face.

"Ivan, I need a drink." I leaned back and brought Ivan's lips to mine, tasting the sweetness of his longing. Ivan's fingers tangled in my hair, bringing my face closer as he set fire to my body with the heat of his tongue. Over his shoulder, Dorien's mouth was a cruel slash across his sticky face, his eyes dark and fathomless.

"Isn't this place amazing?" Elena slid between us, breaking the spell. Her pink lips touched the end of a straw as she sipped on a rainbow concoction that smelled like a flower garden. She grabbed my hand. "Let's dance."

I glanced over my shoulder as Elena led me away. Dorien remained still, watching me – a dark face in the crowd of vibrant color. Even when I looked away, I felt his eyes on me. It was a little creepy, but outside of Manderley's walls, where I wasn't tripping over ghosts and secrets... I enjoyed knowing I had this effect on him, feeling the possessive need rolling off him in waves.

I felt powerful.

I felt like fucking with him.

Elena dipped and shimmied between throngs of people, leading me to a winding metal staircase with a velvet rope. She pushed the rope aside and bounded up the stairs. I followed her with less exuberance and significantly more trepidation, and Ivan came up behind me. A moment later, we stood inside a gilded cage, high above the crowd. Lights flashed on all sides of us as the dance-floor gyrated far below.

Elena drank in the lights and the music and the attention. She twisted and writhed against me until she swept me up in the spirit. Before I knew it, I was grinding against her, our bodies shimmying together in our skimpy clothes. I let the music fill me, moving my body, healing the scars Manderley left on my skin. Beside me, Elena and Ivan moved together, their bodies a perfect mirror of each other. Their twin magic enchanted the air around us.

Hands gripped my thighs, grinding me against something hard and needy. A salty, apple-laced scent hit my nostrils – ice-hardness that was sweet and luscious inside. Ivan's breath grazed my bare shoulder as he moved with me, letting his body say the things he couldn't articulate. The sweet kiss we shared in the poison garden lingered between us, the promise of something more than the torrid night we shared with Dorien. I wanted to crack the ice that trapped his heart – I just knew that underneath was a lost boy desperate for the love he didn't believe he deserved.

The music pounded in my ears, drilling down to my bones. I was no longer Faye, made of flesh and blood and bone. I became the music – the melody, the chords, the endless, relentless bass beat.

Ivan laced his fingers in mine, dragging me through the crowd. Elena waved and continued dancing, relishing the touch of two men who swooped in on her.

At the bar, Ivan got our drinks, and we wove our arms together to pour the bright test tubes down each other's throat. The zesty alcohol only made me bolder, more desperate to get Ivan alone. There was no privacy in this club, but I was so desperate for his pretty lips on mine that I nearly didn't care.

Behind the bar, a metal staircase wound up to a second story, blocked off with a velvet rope. Ivan nodded to a security guard, who pulled aside the rope and nodded to him. Ivan's fingers squeezed my hand as he dragged me up the stairs. I peered over the side, searching for Elena, wanting to give her a wave in case she wondered where I went.

She no longer danced in the cage. I scanned the surging bodies for her silver elfen hair. She wasn't on the dance floor, and I couldn't see her near the bar. I scanned the edges of the room and—

What the hell?

I paused, yanking Ivan's hand. He bent down to kiss my neck, but his body stiffened when he saw what I was staring at.

Elena leaned over a booth at the back of the room. It was surrounded by a low velvet curtain, so no one could see in, but from up here we had a view down on her. She reached into her bra, removed three bags of white powder, and dropped them on the table. A hand stretched out from the shadows and pressed a stack of cash into her hand, which she stuffed into her bra as she stood up, a satisfied grin creeping across her face.

Sound the fucktrumpets, did I just watch Elena Nicolescu do a drug deal?

20

IVAN

Elena, what have you done?

I watched my sister shimmy through the crowd, her calculating smile playing on her lips. I longed to go after her, but I knew it was pointless. I knew the same tired argument we had again and again would play out. Instead, I whipped my phone out and sent off a text to Dorien, asking him to watch Elena. I didn't want to speak to him, but Elena was more important than our feud. I had to hope he agreed.

A moment later, Dorien emerged from behind the bar and met her on the dance floor. His eyes flicked up to me and he nodded, once. So our friendship was not so severed that he wouldn't do this for me. I wanted to hate him for what he did to Faye, but I couldn't quite fall over the edge of animosity the way Titus had.

My feelings for Dorien were complicated. I hated him because I loved him. I needed him, because I could never possess him, or be possessed by him. I feared him, because he was a bottomless void within which I could lose myself. And if I lost myself, Elena would suffer.

Faye watched me as Dorien led Elena back to the bar. "Ivan, what's going on? What did I just see?"

I grabbed her hand again and dragged her up the staircase. Faye's eyes darted around as she took in the second floor of the warehouse. I don't know what she was expecting up here – some kind of private bar? – but it certainly wasn't the steampunk wonderland of metal gangways, moving chandeliers made of cogs and gears, and huge bulkhead doorways that opened with wheels. This place was called *The Engine Ward*, after some obscure steampunk novel. Elena was telling me the owners had a popular secret club in California named *The Grotto*, and they were trialing the concept on the East Coast.

I stopped in front of one of the riveted doors and punched a code into the keyboard before turning the wheel. The door opened with a hiss.

"Wow." Faye's eyes widened as smoke billowed from the room from a hidden dry ice machine. She stepped through the mist into a high-ceilinged room. Every available inch of wall was covered with pipes and gauges and cogs, and there were several large levers and buttons labeled 'PULL FOR BUBBLES' or 'PRESS TO HANG AROUND.' In the center of the room was an enormous four-poster bed, made of carved wood with metal vines twining around it. Hanging from the vines was an enormous spider, her metal legs reaching for us as she glared at us through a hundred beady eyes.

Faye grinned as she pointed to the spider. "I'm not sure I like the idea of Madame Usher frowning at us while we do filthy things on this bed."

I laughed, but the sound came out forced. The spider did have a certain resemblance to Madame, but I couldn't stop thinking about Elena tossing that cocaine on the table, and the filthy things Faye had planned.

Faye pushed a steamer trunk underneath the spider and

climbed up to inspect its fixings. "I think I can turn this around so she's facing the wall. Are you okay?"

"No. I am not." I had Faye alone. This was supposed to be where I could say the things I wanted to say to her, let her see the person I hid from the world and show her what she meant to me. I could only do that away from Manderley and the shackles that tied me down. *But this is all wrong. Completely fucked up.* "Elena is…"

"I'm not mistaken, right? I *did* just see her hand that guy drugs in exchange for money?" Faye folded her arms.

"She does not know what she is doing."

"She looked pretty in-control to me. Like she'd done this before."

My legs trembled. I flung myself down on the bed, staring up at the spider's ass, trying to avoid Faye's penetrating gaze. "Elena thinks it's her turn to save us. I told you that Madame Usher owns us. She takes the money we earn from our performances. She says she adds it to our trust, but she will never show us the accounts. I know that she spends it, and I don't believe we have a trust at all. Our money pays Master Radcliffe's salary and for everything we eat at Manderley and for all those fancy tutors to visit. And I think it pays for other things – things I don't like to consider."

Faye perched on the bed beside me, her fingers tracing along my thigh, making me momentarily lose focus. "I thought the tutors and guests came because they were her friends, and they believe in the talent she picks and nurtures."

"Most of them would not make the trip to a falling-down house in the middle of nowhere even if Beethoven himself were performing, but she rewards them handsomely. In money, and in other things. In secrets."

Faye glanced up at the spider, and her shoulders straightened. "Yes. I guess she does. Ivan, I need the whole story here. No more giving me pieces of information or trying to 'protect' me by keeping me in the dark. It's bullshit and you know it. It's more about protecting yourself. I don't want us to end up like Dorien and me. I don't want to hate you, but I will if I don't get answers."

I swallowed hard. Faye lay down beside me, propping herself up on her elbow so her dark hair cascaded over her shoulder and fanned over my chest. I folded my hand over hers and stared at them, noticing the callouses and dents from the strings – my same marks mirrored in Faye's fingers. "All our life, I thought our lives would begin when we escaped our parents. Even back then, I knew Elena was special – she was wasted playing on street corners to tourists. I never wanted to be famous, not like her. I just wanted to remain by her side, to bask in the glow of her love, to draw a little of her brightness into myself.

"When Madame Usher offered to take us to America, we never thought to protest. Our parents wouldn't have given us an option; they needed the money that badly. But it seemed like the perfect opportunity." I let out a bitter laugh. "If you'd known how badly I dreamed of escaping to America, you would laugh."

"I'd never laugh at you, Ivan." Faye's voice soothed over the turmoil of my memories.

"I thought America would mean freedom. I wanted Elena to be able to shine. Instead, we are prisoners here even more than we were in Romania. There, at least we were prisoners of poverty. Here, evil has us locked up and has thrown away the key."

"I can only imagine what it has been like for you both, trapped with that horrible woman for so many years." Faye danced her fingers along the inside of my thigh, and I struggled to keep hold of my rational mind. "I've lived at Manderley a few short months and I already want to throw myself over a balcony."

I gripped her hand. "You wouldn't think of it."

Faye laughed. "No. I won't let Madame Usher win. And I won't leave you or Titus or Elena." *Or Dorien*, I thought, but didn't say. As much as Faye hated him right now, her hatred was borne of love. If she didn't love him, she could not hate him so. I knew that dance all too well.

I shook my head. "You do not know the half of it. When she was fifteen, Master Radcliffe took Elena to Europe for the summer to introduce her to some of his contacts there. He believes that she should begin her career back in Europe. In this and only this, I support him. Elena is wasted behind Manderley's walls. Her talent should be on show for the world to see."

"I agree," Faye said. "I've never heard someone who plays like her before. Everyone at Manderley is talented, but Elena is one-of-a-kind."

"I knew you could see it. And although I hate him, Radcliffe sees it, too. But Madame Usher wants to keep us close so she can control us, and our money. Elena begged and pleaded Madame Usher to let her go on the trip, and I believe Radcliffe interceded for us, for she would not leave without me. And so we all went to Europe."

"And something happened on this trip?"

My hands balled into fists. "Elena played for sold-out crowds in Vienna, in Moscow, in Prague. It was incredible to sit in the audience and listen to her light up the world, to hear her talent spoken of in excited whispers. At the galas, she glittered on Radcliffe's arm – his darling, his *protégé*. And one summer's eve in Prague, while they walked over the Charles Bridge under the full moon, he asked her to marry him."

"He… what?" Faye looked completely lost, like I'd just told her I'd decided to play Tchaikovsky on a wet fish.

"Let me correct myself. He did not *ask* for her hand. For we are slaves at Manderley, and what we want does not matter. Master Radcliffe informed Elena that they would be wed as soon as she graduated from Manderley and received her trust, and they would return to Europe as a married couple to begin her glittering international career."

Faye wrinkled her face. "But he's, like, *sixty*."

"Sixty-four, and yet he lusts after my sister." My blood boiled at the thought of it. "But there is nothing I can do. Madame Usher will see Elena wed to Radcliffe, and our fortune will become his. And as he is indebted to her, we will remain Madame's to control. We will never be free."

Faye's mouth formed an O. "This is why you stay with her during her lessons, because of Radcliffe."

"Yes." I balled my hands into fists. "He is always pulling her aside for extra tuition or asking her back to his coach house, or trying to get her alone during our international travels. He looks at her as though he cannot wait to devour her. She says he has been a perfect gentleman, but she does not tell me everything, and I know she encourages him in her own way – if he's on her side, then we have more freedom. It's only because of Elena's charms that I was allowed to be part of Broken Muse. She knows that to reject him outright is to incur Madame's wrath, and that will come back on me."

"How do you mean?"

"Madame won't hurt Elena, because Master Radcliffe won't allow it." My body stiffened. I didn't want to talk about it – my shame. I should be able to fight back against a bitter old woman, but she had always been able to use my love for Elena against me.

Realization dawned on Faye's face. "Those marks on your back."

I nodded.

Faye's fingers traced beneath my shirt, lifting it up and off my head. I sat rigid while her fingers trailed along the scars. I forced back the tears that pricked in my eyes. I wished I was someone else – that I didn't have to be here with her in my broken, imperfect body.

"*She* did this to you." Faye's eyes fluttered shut, her dark lashes tangling together.

"These were after our trip to Prague, when she caught us

trying to escape." I pointed to scars latticing the backs of my legs. "These are older, from childhood. I never let her touch Elena."

Faye's fingers against my skin felt like fire, like a thousand tiny needles boring into my soul. "Ivan, this is abuse. We should report her to the police."

I shook my head. "You saw her at the party with Commissioner Walpole. She has secrets on everyone who passes through Manderley's walls. We cannot trust the police."

"Tell me the rest of your story, then. Why does Elena have all those drugs? What does it have to do with Prague?"

"Elena never seemed serious about the engagement. She seemed to believe the marriage would never happen, or that when the time came she'd be able to charm her way out of it. A few days afterward, she returned from a party at the Rudolfinum in a state of excitement. She said she had a way to get us out of our mess. 'We need money, yes? I know how we can make money.' And she opened her purse and showed me the drugs inside."

Faye's hand flew to her lips. "I can't believe Elena would do that."

"Believe it. We were desperate. We still are. We stitched the drugs into the lining of my violin case and made it back to America without being caught. Then it was a matter of selling them on for a profit. Elena's contact in Prague had the names of prominent orchestra patrons who wanted what she had – a particularly pure cocaine that isn't usually sold on the street. Elena built up quite a discerning clientele, and we sold discreetly whenever and wherever we could, including in the audiences of Broken Muse shows. I didn't want Dorien or Titus to know, because I didn't want to jeopardize their careers. And because..." I hung my head. "I did not want them to know how bad things were for us."

Faye looked at me with those huge, dark eyes, and I wished

more than anything I could be a man who was worthy of her whole heart. I took a deep breath and continued.

"The *Zână* gifted my sister not just with musical talent, but with the mind of a criminal genius. Elena made more money than we'd ever seen in our lives. Some she spent on clothes and makeup and trinkets, but the rest we kept hidden away for the day we would make our escape."

"Since you're still here, I'm assuming that didn't go so well," Faye said.

"It was the final Broken Muse tour, although we did not know it at the time. We had Elena with us as our opening act, on the condition Master Radcliffe accompanied us around Europe. When she wasn't on stage, he kept Elena under lock and key at the hotel. He was at her side at the parties, and she couldn't make the meeting with our dealer. I knew he suspected something, which meant that Madame Usher suspected something. We decided to run. Dorien helped us. He had fake passports made and organized our tickets so we didn't arouse suspicion. He said he would send our money once we were safe. Elena drugged Radcliffe with something she found in the attic at Manderley – some Victorian tonic for insomnia – and ran to meet me at the station, where Dorien saw us off on a train. We were going to head to Russia, wait until we turned twenty-five, and then it would not matter. We would be free of her.

"Madame Usher found us. We do not know how. We were on a train to St. Petersburg, and she had the authorities stop the train. They confiscated our passports and all the money we had left. They took us to a Czech jail. They held me there for days. Without food. Only filthy water to drink and a bucket to shit in. I was not allowed to see Elena, and for three days I thought of nothing but her, of what they might do to her, and that I was powerless to stop them. Finally, the police pulled me into a room. Madame Usher sat across the table, wearing her black lace gown and furs, glaring at me like I'm a piece of dirt beneath her shoe."

"What did she say?" Faye leaned forward, her nails digging into my thigh.

"That she expected more of us, that after all she'd done to give us a better life, we'd disappointed her. That she had done what she could to smooth things over with the Czech authorities, but we were facing serious charges." I shook my head. "To anyone observing, she might have sounded like a concerned guardian, but the truth sparkled in her eyes. She orchestrated the entire thing to bind not just me and Elena to Manderley, but Titus and Dorien as well. She left me in prison. Five days later, they released us to her care with no charges laid. I don't know what she did, but when we returned to Manderley we were met by two new students, Dorien and Titus. Our tour was canceled. Broken Muse was on hiatus. None of us have been free of this place since."

"I believe it." Faye's eyes flickered with malice. "I just don't understand it. What does she have on Dorien and Titus that make them stay? And *why* does she want Broken Muse so desperately? I understand controlling the two of you if she needs your money, but why does she need Dorien and Titus? What benefit does she draw from keeping you three at Manderley, apart from having Dorien available to torture me? All this happened long before Madame Usher found me in my mother's hospital room, so I can't be the reason. And none of this explains why Elena is downstairs selling drugs..."

"Because she still has hope. Because she still believes she can get us out of this. Because she knows I'm useless, and that as much as I wish I could save her, I can't—"

"Maybe you can't," Faye whispered. "But *we* can."

"It is of no use. Master Radcliffe will marry Elena at the end of the school year." I buried my face in my hands. "I'll lose my beautiful sister forever."

Faye crawled up beside me, curling her body around mine. She lifted my hands from my eyes. I stared into her face, saw her wide eyes set with determination. She was a lot like Dorien in so many ways – a force of nature, bending the world to her will. To hold her in my arms was like catching lightning – I felt like I'd been blessed with a remarkable gift, but that gift was made of fire and danger.

Her hellion eyes stared down at me, and her lightning forked across my body, setting my veins alight with panic. "We're going to be free. All of us."

21

FAYE

After Ivan told me his story, he cradled me against his body. His jaw sat heavy, and I knew the hot steampunk sex I was going to have with my ice prince was off the cards for tonight. Instead, I traced the lines of his scars, each one telling a story about what he endured for his sister, for love.

Ivan's breath hitched as I touched him, as I read his past on his body. For him, this was even more personal than sex. This was everything stripped away, pure and raw.

"If it bothers you so much, you could put your shirt back on," I teased him, trying to lighten the heaviness between us.

"I've never been... alone with a woman before." Ivan worked his jaw like he was trying to unclench it.

"What about all those hot Broken Muse groupies on tour?" I stroked his cheek. "Didn't they used to call you the Slavic Stallion?"

"I always shared with Titus or Dorien," Ivan said. "I know myself. I know that I cannot touch someone's body and then throw them away. Not the way they can. I would become attached. I would see love where there was only passion, and I would lose myself."

I wondered how he didn't end up falling for Titus or Dorien, but I realized he might be admitting exactly that.

"Elena would want you to be happy," I said.

"I cannot. Not until she is free."

His words cut into my skin.

"I wish you'd been able to meet my mom." A tear rolled down my cheek. "She was so incredible. She built her PR company from the ground up. In the early days, her office was our kitchen table. Once, this hip hop artist wanted to meet at her offices, so she rearranged our entire apartment to make it look like she rented it as an office. She draped a cloth over the kitchen table and dressed me up in a pencil skirt, and I served him coffee and pretended to be her secretary. It was so completely ridiculous but we pulled it off. That client booked her on the spot and paid us enough money she actually could move to an office.

"But even when she was hustling like mad, she never lost sight of why she was doing it. To give us both a better life. No matter how much work she had, she'd toss her laptop aside when I got home from school and drag me out for ice cream. Or we'd go skating in Central Park or to cause trouble at some fancy industry party." I sniffed as I thought of one of the last times I saw Mom looking normal – we went to a new rooftop restaurant, and the next table over was having a loud high school reunion. She told the waiter she wanted to be seated 'at the fun table' and we spent all night hanging out with this group of ex-theatre students, drinking cocktails and improvising filthy Shakespearean sonnets.

"The very next day, she doubled over in the office and was rushed to the hospital. But they couldn't figure out what was wrong. They didn't know she'd been… *poisoned*." My body shuddered. I still couldn't believe it. Everyone loved my mother.

Or so I thought.

Someone didn't love Marguerite de Winter. Someone hated her enough to poison her. And I needed to get to the bottom of it.

I owed it to the remarkable woman who still lay in a coma in a hospital room I bought for the price of my soul.

"Hey." Ivan's fingers stroked my cheek, touching each tear as they rolled across my skin. "I will meet your mother, because she *will* wake up."

"I miss her so much."

"I understand," he whispered back. "I know what it is to love someone so much that their breath is your breath."

He stroked my cheek with his finger, drawing a line of fluttering butterflies across my skin. Those icicle eyes softened at the edges, melting into pools of endless blue. Our chests rose and fell as one, and our breath mingled into a warm flush as our lips hovered an inch apart, not quite touching but *wanting* to touch. Ivan stood on the edge of a great precipice, and he wanted to fly over the edge with me, but he didn't know if he was wearing a parachute or carrying the anvil that would send him hurtling to his doom.

Me? I was already flying, my wings made of phoenix feathers unfurled wide. I'd risen from the ashes of my father's lies, and I wanted to see Ivan Nicolescu soaring by my side. I wanted us to tumble through the air together, lost in each other. But he had to take the leap – I couldn't do that for him.

A knock sounded at the door. "Ivan?" Elena's voice called tentatively. "Faye? We should leave."

Ivan stared into my eyes, and I read there all the things he wished he could say. The ice slid over his gaze, hardening his body into the shell he wore to protect himself. He slid off the bed and pulled me to my feet. "Next time," he growled. "The only tears will be tears of ecstasy."

"I can't wait," I whispered back.

22

FAYE

*E*ach day at Manderley was a little better than the last. Madame Usher still hated me. Heather seemed convinced that her little humiliations would supplant me, so she filled my bed with worms and put peanut butter inside my violin case. Dorien still stared daggers in my back, like he was convinced he could make me forgive him though sheer force of will.

But I had Titus and Ivan. And Elena's friendship, which became more precious to me every day.

They no longer practiced or performed with Dorien. Broken Muse was no more. I hated how sorry I was that I'd deprived the world of their music. And then I remembered being trapped in that leather bag, alone and terrified, and I didn't feel sorry anymore.

What concerned me is that I hadn't heard anything new about my mother's case. Dr. Nelson kept me updated with my mother's progress (slow, but definite progress). I called the police station every day about the investigation, but they kept giving me the run-around, passing me to different people who repeated the same information – they couldn't release any details at this time.

Finally, I had a call from the investigating officer, Detective Carroll, and it wasn't good news.

"We've conducted a thorough inquiry, and we're closing the case and not investigating further."

"What? But the evidence clearly points to a malevolent act. Surely you've found a suspect who—"

"Unfortunately, the real world is rarely a neat little box the way it is on TV. Your mother ingested toxic amounts of a rare plant sometimes used in herbal remedies. We believe this was administered through a tea. We traced the brand of tea she drank back to a warehouse in Soho, but it's been abandoned. The company has long since skipped town. We have no leads. We've passed everything we have on to the FDA, who investigate cases like this, but these companies can disappear overseas in a flash, so these things are usually a dead end. If anything further shows up—"

"They *poisoned* my mother. How could you just let them get away with it? What if they start up again somewhere else? Surely this company has records, a board of directors, someone to take responsibility."

"I truly am sorry, Ms. de Winter."

"Sorry, my ass." I flung the phone across the room. It hit the wall and the face popped off. I picked it up and sighed. I'd cracked the glass, and I wouldn't be able to afford a replacement. Madame Usher gave me a small paycheck each week, but it was hardly anything, and I was trying to save as much of it as possible in case I had to leave in a hurry.

I flung myself on the bed. *This can't be happening. How can they say there are no leads? We* had *a lead – the herbal tea my mother was taking, and the fact that birthwort is still used in some herbal remedies even though it's poisonous.*

When Dad disappeared, they had task forces combing the entire country. But they can barely spare the time for Mom. I didn't want to believe it was a race thing, that my mother was so much more than her Latina heritage to them, but the grim reality of the world loved to bite me in the ass these days.

Mom wouldn't take this. If our positions were reversed, she wouldn't let this be the end of it. She'd knock on every door, bash heads together, find the clues the police missed.

This is ridiculous. I couldn't believe what I was contemplating. *I'm a violinist, not a sleuth.*

I swore that I would not let Manderley claim another victim. The whole reason I imagined Clare's ghost was because she never had justice. Dorien didn't push her down the stairs, but the police didn't look any deeper than that, and I couldn't help but wonder if that had anything to do with Madame Usher's friendship with the commissioner. No one investigated why she'd been acting strange, or talking about voices in the walls. Clare was all alone at Manderley, and no one listened to her until it was too late. But that would *not* happen to my mother.

I had to try.

I picked myself up and knocked on Titus' door. When he opened it, I didn't give him a chance to speak. "I need to go to New York City this weekend, possibly to do something illegal. Can you drive me?"

~

Our first stop on the way to the city was the hospital. Titus wanted to come in with me while I visited Mom, but I made him and Ivan wait outside. "She wouldn't want you to see her like this – silent and still in a hospital bed."

"I don't want you to have to go in there alone." His warm eyes bore into mine.

"I've been sitting in that room with her since she got sick. Besides, I'm not alone." I held up my violin. "I have music."

Titus backed away, nodding. I knew he understood. I knew

that his music was the doorway into the lonely place where his heart and mind resided.

In the cold room filled with beeping machines, I played *Nigun* for my mother, as well as the composition piece I played at the party, since she hadn't been there to see it in person. Her machines beeped a steady rhythm of unrelenting sameness. No change. Why didn't she wake up?

I need you, Mom. Please come back to me.

Dr. Nelson dropped in to visit just as I was packing up. "Faye, I was hoping to see you. I wanted to give you an update on your mother's progress in person."

I frowned down at her still figure. "I think I can see for myself."

She beamed. "Actually, we've had positive progress. Your mother has responded extremely well to the antidote, and the damage to her organs is not as terrible as we feared. Her PET scan results showed an increased level of brain activity, which is a positive indicator for a patient waking up."

My heart stuttered. "You mean—"

"I mean, we expect her to wake up any day now. I need to warn you, it's not like in the movies. She won't suddenly sit up in bed and reveal the secrets of the universe. She may regain consciousness for only a few moments the first time, and then come back for longer periods. She may not be able to speak, and she may experience temporary or long-term memory loss."

"You mean she might not remember who I am?" The thought of that... I couldn't bear it.

"I don't want to alarm you," Dr. Nelson touched my arm in that kind way of hers. "I'm just trying to prepare you for what might happen. She might be perfectly normal, exactly as you remember her. From everything I know, your mom is a fighter, and she's raised her daughter to be the same."

I squeezed my eyes shut, trying to shove the tears back into my skull. "Thank you."

"I wanted to ask, since I know you'll want to come back more frequently to check on her, if you'd like to grace us with another performance? You were such a hit last time. I don't want to take your time as I know you must be busy with school, but I thought you might have a break for the holidays. Many of our patients will be in here over Christmas, and we do what we can, but I think they could use some brightening up."

"I'd love to play for you," I smiled back.

I packed up my violin with trembling fingers and met my muses downstairs. Titus must've seen the distress in my face, because he swept me into an embrace that threatened to crush the fear from my lungs.

"She might not remember me," I whispered the words into his warm skin, speaking aloud my greatest fear. My mother had been my whole world. What if I got her back but she had no idea who I was?

~

After the hospital, we headed to the police station, where I hounded the guy at the front desk until he handed over Mom's case file. Being flanked by Titus' bulk and stony glare definitely helped expedite the process. My giant teddy bear could look mean as fuck when he wanted to.

I slid back into the car and flipped the folder open. There wasn't much in the file – a few photographs and pages of written statements.

"What does it say?" Ivan peered over the seat.

"Not much." I flipped past the toxicology report – a photocopy of the one Dr. Nelson gave me. There were a few short transcripts of statements – from me, from Dr. Nelson and a couple of people at the hospital, of the homeless man who wrote 'LEAVE' on my mother's forehead. From employees of De Winter PR. Nothing I didn't already know, except...

Natalie. My mother's PA turned newly-minted CEO of her own PR company, with most of my mom's old clients on her books. Natalie's statement felt heavy in my hand, each word a stab of betrayal.

Natalie benefitted from my mother's hospitalization. And she was the one who ordered and prepared the tea. It was right there in her statement…

…along with something else. Something important. My eyes narrowed on the page as I read and reread the details, making sure I had it right.

"Here's the address of the company that sold Mom the tea." I held up the sheet in triumph. "Natalie gave it to the police."

Titus plugged it into his phone. "Let's go."

~

Titus jiggled the lock on the warehouse door. "This place is deserted."

I don't know what I expected to find – a cartoonish lair in a faux mountain with 'EVIL GENIUS THIS WAY' emblazoned over the door, perhaps? – but it wasn't this nondescript Soho warehouse in a row of industrial buildings. The only windows were seven-feet off the ground. I cupped my hands over the grimy glass panel in the door and tried to peer inside, but the filth was too thick and the interior too dark to see a thing.

"Stand back."

I jerked out of the way as Ivan picked up a broken roof tile from the debris and tossed it through the window. The glass shattered, spraying inside. Ivan picked up a second piece of tile and hefted it in his hand. His icicle eyes focused on that broken window with singular focus – the way he looked when he played a particularly difficult piece. Only, now he wasn't contemplating Beethoven's sonatas but breaking and entering.

"Help me up," he said. Titus knelt down. Ivan climbed on his shoulders, pressing one hand against the wall for balance. Titus stood up, propelling Ivan into the air. Ivan gripped the windowsill and used the piece of tile to knock out the glass around the window, creating a hole large enough for him to wiggle through.

Ivan counted down from three under his breath, then swung his leg up.

My hands flew to my mouth as Ivan missed, his body swaying dangerously as he struggled to maintain his balance. "That doesn't look safe."

"Don't worry," Titus grinned. "Once we were on tour in Paris and two groupies locked us out of their apartment, naked, in the snow, with all our clothes inside. I had Dorien sitting on my shoulders holding Ivan while he swung over a narrow third-floor balcony to sneak back in their window. Now *that* was dangerous."

"Don't tell her that story," Ivan growled. "If you'll recall, I slipped on the ice and nearly impaled my nuts on the iron railing, and the girl's father called the *gendarme* so you two hid in the bushes and left me to freeze my ass off in a cell for the night."

"Ivan's right. Don't tell me that story." I glared at Titus, hands on hips. "Just don't let him slip this time. I have plans that require all appendages intact."

Ivan swung his leg again. I gritted my teeth as he made it, pulling his body up and slipping through the narrow gap in the window like he was a professional cat burglar. I held my breath, half expecting an alarm to start blaring or a pack of ferocious hounds to descend upon us. A moment later, I heard a click. The front door didn't budge.

"Over here," Ivan called. A side door swung open, and he leaned out to wave us in, pulling the door closed behind us.

Inside, all was shrouded in darkness. The light from the row of windows along the front of the warehouse barely penetrated the gloom. I pulled out the tiny flashlight Dorien left in the bag for me (I had no intention of giving it back. I lived in the attic of a possibly-haunted gothic mansion – tiny flashlights came in handy) and shone it along rows of metal shelving. Titus moved to inspect a forklift in the corner coated in a layer of dust while Ivan aimed the beam of his mobile phone at some packing boxes.

I swept my flashlight along the shelves, taking in the empty boxes, the piles of rat droppings, the random piles of counterfeit clothing from brands that were trendy a decade ago, and oddly-shaped kitchenware that bore a completely different company's logo.

"It doesn't look like this place has been used for *years*," I said. "And none of the stuff here makes any sense. I thought this company sold herbal remedies. It's weird. My mom was drinking that tea right up until she collapsed. So that doesn't give this company a lot of time to disappear. I mean, how would they know they were under suspicion if we only just discovered the poison ourselves?"

"How did the cops get this address again?" Ivan asked.

"My mother's old PA, Natalie, gave it to them. She was the one ordering the tea. I wondered if she might be the one poisoning my mom so she could steal the company, but then what's going on here? I can't see a trace of a supplement or herbal remedy company ever having product in this place."

Ivan bent down and picked something from a nail protruding from the side of the shelves. "This is interesting. It's not as dusty as the other stuff."

He placed the thing in my hand. I trained my flashlight on the object, struggling to figure out what it was. It looked like a scrap of material – black, with floral lace along the edge. One side was a jagged edge where it had torn, and there was a hole in the lace where it snagged on the nail. It looked like it had come off someone's clothing.

Black lace.

I didn't want to think about the significance of that. Not until we had something more.

We reached the end of the shelves. A narrow door led off the warehouse into a small office. I peered inside and wrinkled my nose. Back here, the air smelled of rot and damp. Papers were strewn across the desk, too encrusted in rat feces to be legible. Titus tugged open drawers and peered into filing cabinets while I stared at the dusty portraits on the walls. They were all a lot older – one was from the 1960s – and related to import businesses, none of which were the herbal remedy company.

Titus straightened up, holding open a leather-bound ledger. His frown told me everything I needed to know. "I found something."

"What?" I rushed to peer over his shoulder.

"You're not going to like it. It's completely fucked up." Titus jabbed his finger at the page. "According to this, this warehouse was owned by an import company that went broke a decade ago. Afterward, it was leased by a company called Menabilly Holdings. The name of the contact at that company is Victor Usher."

23

TITUS

*V*ictor Usher.

It couldn't be true. And yet, there was his name in faded black ink. Madame Usher's husband – the quiet man who first came to my parents in our New Orleans home after the canceled tour to offer me a place at Manderley, who'd convinced both them and me that it was an opportunity and not a curse – leased the building where the company that poisoned Faye's mother worked.

This is not a coincidence.

In that moment, I knew everything Dorien had been going on about was true. Somehow, it was all connected. Marguerite de Winter's illness was not some cruel twist of fate that brought Faye to Manderley. It had been *orchestrated* – a deliberate and malicious act to drive her into Madame Usher's arms.

But why?

And why, after going to such lengths to get Faye to the school, did Madame Usher wish us to drive her away again?

Faye tore the book from my hands. Her fingers remained steady as she held the faded pages under the light, carefully examining each word. The corner of her mouth twisted, and her jaw set in this look of grim determination that reminded me far too much of Dorien to be a good thing.

"How did the police miss this?" Faye breathed.

"I'll tell you how," I growled. "Madame Usher gave Commissioner Walpole VIP tickets to every show on the Vienna Philharmonic's touring season. He must owe her a pretty favor, and she called it in."

Faye sank to her knees, holding the paper up to the light as if it might reveal its secrets. "I know this is bad. But I don't understand what it means."

"It means your mother's herbal tea was purchased from the Ushers." Ivan knelt down beside her. "And from the looks of this warehouse, she might have been their only client."

"They set out to… to poison my mother. This was all planned to bring me to Manderley." Faye clutched the book to her chest as the full weight of it sank on her shoulders. She closed her eyes and swayed a little. Ivan placed his hand on her back, and it seemed to steady her. "What should we do?"

She asked the right question, but I didn't have an answer. Clearly, going to the police was out of the question. They could have found this information by doing a search with the secretary of state. They had to know the Ushers were tied up in this, and yet they closed the investigation. Who knew all it took to buy the police department was a few free concert tickets?

Ivan looked up at me. His eyes were two shards of ice – cold and determined. He would do anything necessary to protect what he loved, and I knew him well enough to know that he loved Faye with a passion he usually only reserved for Elena. But Ivan was a soldier – he wouldn't hesitate to spill the blood of his enemies, but he needed a leader. A general giving his marching order. He needed *me*.

Faye needed me.

My head spun with the weight of their need. Dorien was always the one who came up with schemes. Some of them were brilliant – pooling our musical talents to start Broken Muse. And some of them were borne of rage and desperation, like embracing Madame Usher's plot to destroy Faye in order to escape his feelings for her. But one thing I could say about Dorien – he picked a path and ran headlong toward it. I wasn't a leader any more than Ivan. I followed. I let things happen *to* me. I did what I was told.

All I had to show for my obedience was deception and misery.

I opened my mouth to offer banal words of empty solace. But Faye beat me to it. I should have known she didn't need me to take charge. She would find her path, and it was our job to protect her while she strode boldly into the unknown.

"I think…" Faye blew dust off the cover of the ledger book. "I think we need to talk to the person who purchased the tea."

~

The offices of Natalie Baker PR were located on a trendy street in the Financial District. Faye pointed out that it was only a block away from her mother's old office. We took the elevator to the thirty-first floor and got off in a slick space decorated in stark white with a motif of large red dots that made me feel stuck inside of a Yayoi Kusama exhibit.

"Can I help you?" the receptionist asked, her voice chipper. Faye shot her a filthy look and stormed past the front desk.

"Natalie Baker. It's Faye de Winter," Faye yelled into the glass walls and open-plan desks. "Come out, come out, wherever you are. We need to have a little chat."

Young women in pencil skirts darted out of the way and men with wingtip shoes threw themselves against the walls as Faye stormed through an open-plan office space. On the far wall was a suite of glass-walled offices, their doors decorated with red dots. Inside the central office, a perfectly-coiffed blonde woman with scarlet lips purred something into an earpiece as she typed on her computer.

"Wait, please. Natalie is a very busy lady." The receptionist hobbled after us on her stiletto heels. "You can't just walk in there without an appoint—"

Faye flung the office door open. A woman rose from her chair, her face a storm. She jabbed a pen at the door, but when she saw who it was she dropped the pen into her coffee, splattering dark liquid all over her perfect white blouse.

"Ow. Oh, shit. Sorry, Gary. I'll have to call you back." Natalie made no move to wipe away the coffee stain. She lifted the headphones from her ears and stared in wide-eyed surprise.

"Natalie," Faye hissed.

Natalie bit her lip. She was trying to keep it together, but I could see she was terrified. I couldn't say I blamed her. Faye busting in with her mane of wild hair streaming behind her and the fire for justice smoldering in her eyes – I was a little afraid of her myself.

Afraid. And madly, desperately fucking in love.

"Faye? Long time no see, girl." Natalie gripped the edge of her white desk. I noticed a row of glittering diamantes set in a row along the edge. "Wow, you look amazing. How's your mother? I heard about her slipping into a coma, I'm so sorry—hey, what are you doing?"

Faye turned and locked the door behind her. Outside, the receptionist banged on the window and mimed calling security. Faye yanked down a shade and pointed to Natalie's wing-back chair. "Sit down, Natalie. You and I need to have a chat about my mother."

Natalie gulped as she took in me and Ivan. I folded my arms, letting her get a full view of my muscles and the mean expression on my face. I was a huge, scary black dude, and today I wasn't ashamed of it. Not if it got answers for Faye.

Inside, my head spun. *What did Faye expect us to do here?*

It didn't matter. If Faye de Winter asked it, I would do it. I would do anything for this wild woman.

Natalie sat down, gripping the arms of her chair with crimson-tipped talons. She swallowed. "Faye, what's this about?"

Faye smiled, but there was no mirth in the expression. She curled a strand of dark hair around her finger. "My mother was poisoned deliberately."

"I know. The police told me. I gave them a statement. What a horrible—"

"The doctors call it acute poisoning – she was fed a tiny dose of a plant called birthwort over a period of months, and the poison built up in her system until it made her sick. She's been in a coma now for three months, but the good news is that now the doctors know what hurt her, they think that if she wakes up soon she may recover, albeit without the use of some of her organs."

Natalie gulped. "That… that is good news."

"Is it, Natalie?" Faye kept twisting her hair, pulling it around her fingers until it made red welts on her skin, then releasing it to spring free. "Or is it bad news for you, because if she wakes up and tells the world what you did, you'll lose everything."

"What do you think *I* did to her?" Natalie shot back. She was trying to look tough, but her eyes darted to mine, and I saw the terror there.

"You know this looks bad. You've always been ambitious. My mother gets sick and suddenly you're promoted in her company, and you're in the media talking about how she was *so* flighty and unreliable. *Then* De Winter PR goes bankrupt, and suddenly you've got a brand new company with half the same staff and all her high-profile clients."

"You're right. It does look bad." Natalie wrung her hands. "It looks like I steamrolled over her to get to the top. Of course it does – that's how I *wanted* it to look. That's how your mother and I decided it had to look."

SPRING. Faye dropped the curl and it bounced free. "I don't understand."

"When she first got sick, and it drew out over months and months, Marguerite knew there was a chance she might not recover. When she had her first episode and she realized she didn't have insurance to cover treatment, we held a war council. She'd been mentoring me on the side for years, showing me the ropes so I could run things if anything happened to her. After what happened to your father, she was so worried about protecting you and your future."

"If you were her successor, why didn't you fight harder for De Winter PR? Why did you swoop in and take over the moment she was out of the picture?" Faye gripped the back of the chair as she glared down at Natalie, but something had shifted in her demeanor. She believed this Natalie.

"If I quietly sat in the background like a demure fucking flower, everything Marguerite built would have been picked over by vultures. You wouldn't believe the nonsense the board came up with – the half-wits they tried to promote above me. I fought to keep this company going, and when it crashed and burned, I salvaged what I could. Did I take advantage of the situation? Of course. I'm a woman in a male-dominated, chauvinistic industry. If I don't stomp on toes to get here, I won't get my Louboutins through the door." She smiled. "Marguerite taught me that."

"But the tea…"

"That fucking tea." Natalie slammed her fist on the desk. "I hate myself so much for giving it to her. She started to get sick and nothing was working, and then a sample box showed up in the mail from some new supplement company. It said it treated her *exact* symptoms, and I thought it was just the universe shining on Marguerite de Winter like it always did. She loved that tea. She thought it was helping. She kept trying to get me to contact them to ask if they wanted some PR consulting, because she thought everyone in Manhattan would want this miracle fucking tea. But I could never get them on the phone."

"Why didn't you tell this to the police?"

"I *did* tell them. I explained all of it. I even dug out all the receipts and sent them over. It was a hell of a job, but I thought it might help find out who hurt Marguerite."

Faye dug around in her purse and pulled out the file. She lifted a page from it and handed it to Natalie. "That's your official statement from the police."

Natalie scanned the document, her eyes widening with every word. "This isn't what I said. I swear it. I told them everything. I even gave them a box of the tea so they could test it or whatever. Why would the police change my statement?"

Faye and I exchanged a glance. There was nothing about testing the tea box in the file, or that the tea had been sent anonymously. That confirmed our suspicion that the police had been bought off.

"We're trying to find out," Faye said. "That's why we stormed in here. I know it's a bit unconventional, and I hope your receptionist doesn't get us arrested, but I needed to hear you tell the truth."

"I still have a few boxes of that tea left." Natalie knelt down beside a white sideboard decorated with more diamantes. She pulled out a storage cube. "Here. Take the remaining boxes. Take it to a lab or whatever. Find the bastard who did this to Marguerite. If there's anything else I can do, I want to help. Your mother is the reason I am here today. She's a fucking inspiration."

"Thanks, Natalie. I really—" Faye's hands trembled as she stared at the box in her hands. I couldn't imagine what it must feel like to hold the poison that hurt the person you loved most, and to know that it also held the answers you desperately needed. To love an object and hate it in equal measure.

No. Scratch that. I knew *exactly* what that felt like. I knew because I felt it every time I picked up my guitar. Every time I played riffs that felt like molten lava in my soul, that tasted of power and freedom even as they closed around me like the walls of a cage.

Faye lifted up one of the boxes, holding it on the very tips of her fingers as if the cardboard packaging itself was laced with poison. Her perfect lips twisted, and I knew she'd noticed something new.

"What is it?" Ivan leaned over, his arm dropping around her shoulders.

"In Cauda Venenum," Faye read aloud. "That's the name of this tea. It's the same words above the poison garden at Manderley."

And on Dorien's tattoo, I thought, but didn't say. I could see from Faye's eyes she'd already put together that particular nugget of horror.

"What's going on?" Natalie leaned forward. "Did you find something? I told the police I thought it was someone who wanted her out of the PR business."

"That's what I thought too, but now I'm not so sure." Faye dug out her phone and flipped to the Manderley website. Her finger hovered over an image of Victor and Gizella Usher standing behind the piano in the opulent red room, inviting students to apply for their prestigious program. "One last question. Do you recognize either of these two people?"

Natalie squinted at the picture. "Yes. That woman. She's the one who dropped off the package of teas the first time. I think she's the woman I spoke on the phone with for orders, too, but I can't be sure. She had an odd way of dressing, like the villainess in some old storybook. Why, do you know her? Does she have something to do with this? She looks like such a harmless lady…"

~

"You're amazing," I said when we walked out of Natalie's office a half-hour later. After Natalie identified Madame Usher, Faye looked like she might be sick, but she recovered quickly. Instead, the two women found the common thread that united them, tugging and teasing out each frayed end until it bound them together. Faye unlocked the door, and Natalie had her receptionist bring in wine and a platter of deli meats, and by the time we left they were setting up a coffee date for next time we were in the city.

As we dropped into the car to return to Manderley, I reached over to squeeze Faye's hand. "That was amazing. When you strode in there, I expected you to explode on that woman's face. You were ready to *throttle* her. And yet, by the end of it not only had you'd got all the information you needed, but I think you made a friend."

"There was nothing amazing about it. I knew Natalie was ruthlessly ambitious, but I also knew she cared about Mom. No one is one hundred percent evil." Faye paused. "Except maybe Madame Usher."

24

FAYE

Fresh snow fell as we drove back to Manderley, kissing the towering trees and wrapping the mountains in a snug white blanket. I relished the quietness of the car, with the music turned up loud and Titus and Ivan in the front arguing over how best to tackle the treacherous forest road. I needed space to think.

My mind reeled from everything we learned. It was all so impossible, so completely ridiculous, like a twist in a gothic novel. But it was real.

The Ushers poisoned my mother.

Why?

Nothing about this made sense. It had to be about my father. Madame Usher claimed to love him, which meant her hatred of my mother was borne of jealousy, of possessiveness. But he was long gone. A moot point. A cul-de-sac on the map of history. She could not possess him. Poisoning my mother achieved nothing...

...except to give her something to hold over my head, to control me. The way she controlled everyone at Manderley.

Madame Usher used my mother's illness to draw me close.

She knew I wouldn't give up, that leaving Manderley would rob me of the medical care I needed to save my mother. She brought me to her home, paid for the medical care that eventually revealed her plot, and then tried to drive me away.

I needed answers. Evidence. At least now I knew where I needed to start looking for it.

When at long last we pulled up in front of Manderley, Titus leaned over and clasped my hand. "I know it must feel impossible," he said. "But you can't let on to Madame that you know about this."

I nodded. "I'm going to strangle her."

"With your bare hands. I believe you. But not today. We know we can't go to the police with any of this. We need to figure out what to do next."

Cockpoodles, he's right. I nodded again.

"Where have you been?" Madame screeched as we traipsed into the house, tracking snow over the rug as we draped our coats on the carved stand. She circled around to loom over me, her eyes blazing. "I have a guest coming tonight and there's no dinner, the Red Room is a shambles, and you've left Harrison to light the fires himself with his bad back—"

"We went to see my mother. You never told me about a guest." I fought to keep my voice calm. *You poisoned her. You tried to kill her.*

"Titus, Ivan, you need to practice your Sibelius." Madame Usher turned to them as if I hadn't spoken. "I'd like you to perform for Commissioner Walpole and his wife tonight."

Neither of them moved.

"Go, now," Madame screamed.

Titus looked to me, and I nodded. I hadn't forgotten what we said in the car. I could handle Madame Usher. My muses slunk into the shadows, but I knew they hadn't gone far.

Madame leaned in close, her cloying perfume invading my

nostrils. I longed to gasp for air, but I wouldn't give her the satisfaction of my discomfort. "You are on thin ice, *girl*. When you first came here, I informed you that if the house was not kept to my standards, you would not be allowed to continue here as a student. I'd hate to throw Donovan's daughter out on the streets, but I will do it. Do not chase after ghosts, Faye de Winter, or you won't be the only one who suffers."

She threw her fur stole over her shoulder and stormed off, leaving me shaking with rage, a sliver of fear burrowing into my spine.

~

*A*s I chopped and sautéed and drizzled ingredients for a three-course dinner, my chest tightened as Madame Usher's threat weighed on it. She was trying to use my love for the guys and Elena to stop me. It was the same tactic she used to bring Elena and Ivan to heel, and probably Titus and Dorien as well, although I hadn't got close enough to their secrets to figure them out.

She wanted me to stop digging. That meant I was close. And as much as I couldn't bear the thought of her hurting anyone else, I knew for any of us to be truly safe, we needed to be free of her forever. We needed to bring her down.

It's time for Manderley's ghosts to come out and play.

After I served dinner to Madame and her guests in the dining hall, I grabbed Elena's hand. "Do you want to help me with something? It might be dangerous."

Her eyes sparkled with mischief. "Danger is my middle name."

We snuck outside through the kitchen door and hightailed it across the overgrown back garden before anyone could see us. As we dived into the shelter of the forest, I looked back at the looming stone facade of Manderley. Did I imagine it, or had it grown even more decrepit? Cracks snaked along the ancient stone – a lattice of ruin, as though the house itself felt the pain of those who suffered within its walls. A whole section of roof above Madame Usher's private wing had fallen away, leaving a section of the attic there open to the elements. Even though the flowers in the beds beneath the eaves refused to grow – no matter how lovingly Harrison tended them – the creeping flora of the wood slithered ever closer. Vines attacked the walls and choked the narrow windows of precious light. Master Radcliffe's coach house was now submerged beneath a blanket of weeds and creepers, as though it were being devoured by the earth itself.

The longer I stared up at Manderley, the more the house appeared to be alive, shifting in the wind, her bones creaking and groaning as she glared back at me. I shuddered and turned away.

"You lived here since you were a kid," I said to Elena as we made our way down the slippery path. "Has Manderley always been in such ruin?"

Elena shook her head. "It was Victor who loved this house. He was always outside tending the gardens or repairing the shingles, even in the deepest winter. He was fanatical about Manderley, about keeping it beautiful. He told me once that Manderley had a kind of magic – if she was respected and cherished, she would reward the world with beauty and light. But if she was neglected then all inside her would fall to ruin."

"I remember Victor from Madame's city school. He used to teach Dorien. I can't imagine him doing physical labor."

"Oh, yes. He and Harrison were always heading out to chop wood or repair shutters or tend the gardens. Sometimes they would go hunting and they would leave for days at a time. Madame never seemed to mind – I think she preferred to have the house to herself. In the final years of Victor's illness he was bedridden, unable to tend to the house in his usual way, and Harrison has never been able to nurse her back to her former glory. The flowers have not bloomed since Victor's death, but Madame does not seem to mind the weeds. What need does she have of beauty and light when she has her store of secrets?"

I nodded. Elena was right about that. "I'm surprised she doesn't hire someone to replace Harrison. He's not exactly young and spritely. Or even get him an assistant."

"Mmmm. She's not able to remove Harrison from his house – it's part of his contract. And she won't give up space in her private ring to house new help. Harrison can only do so much, and honestly, since Victor died he's been a bit strange himself."

"Strange, how?" Harrison had always been my ally here at Manderley. I wasn't sure I liked his character being called into question.

"I do not know." Elena frowned. "There's just… something different about him. He and Victor were always close. They grew up together. I know Harrison finds it hard to remain here under Madame Usher, but where else will he go? He's a remnant of a past era."

We emerged in front of the dilapidated gazebo. Elena sighed. "Ivan and I would spend every day in the summer down here after we finished our lessons. The other students in the house were always older than us, and Master and Madame Usher didn't much like to see children. They only seemed to care about us when there was a guest to impress."

"What did you two used to do down here?"

"We played games. I liked to pretend we'd been kidnapped by an evil witch and were trapped in her castle, but in her neglected garden we found this magical gazebo where fairies lived, and they'd take us on all sorts of adventures and invite us to wild fairy parties and defeat the witch so we could be free." She ran her fingers over the rotting balustrade. "Why did you bring me here?"

"Actually, this isn't what we came to see."

Elena lifted an eyebrow. "You're being secretive."

"No more than anyone else in this house of dickweasels." I wrung my hands. I needed Elena with me tonight – I didn't want to piss her off, but I had to get this off my chest. "Ivan told me about what you've been doing. Dealing drugs at recitals and such."

Elena pursed her lips, and her elegant neck seemed to grow an inch.

"Before you get mad at him, I saw you with that guy at the *Engine Ward*. I'd have used all my feminine wiles to wrestle the truth out of him. Here's the thing, I don't give a fuck that you sold drugs to a bunch of rich cockpoodles for a chance to escape this place. What I care about is that we had this secret hanging between us. Secrets are what has trapped us all here in the first place, and they're what she's using to divide us, to pit us against each other. She doesn't believe we can still love a person even when the darkest parts of their soul are laid bare, and she'll use that to destroy us. But I think differently – I think the darkness is beautiful, and *real*. So from now on, no more secrets, right? We're all in this together."

Elena cracked a smile, and it was as if a warm hand pressed against my chest. "Even Dorien?"

I screwed up my face. "Even Dorien. I hate his guts, but he's as much a victim of Manderley as the rest of us. I'm going to stop her, Elena, and I need your help."

I told her everything we'd discovered about my mother's poisoning, and how it had all been part of a plan to get me to Manderley. "We can't go to the police with this, but I need proof. I need something we might be able to use against her when the time comes."

Elena followed me down the overgrown path. Raindrops rolled off the leaves above us, splattering on our heads. I pulled my hood over my face and shoved my hands into my sleeves. The forest opened out around the Victorian greenhouse. In the moonlight it appeared grotesque – the squat building of wood and steel and grass being offered back up to nature, with the exotic fronds and deadly fingers spilling from every crack and pressing against the windows – a ruinous garden desperate to escape its cage.

Elena shivered. "I don't like to come here. It's scary."

"I think it's fascinating." I peered up at the structure. Strange fronds reached down at us from the broken roof. Dead purple flower petals stained the icy ground. A sweet smell lingered in the air that made me feel light-headed. "I'm also certain it's the source of the poison that sent my mother to the hospital. But I need to know that for a fact before I decide what to do next."

"Do you know what are you looking for?" Elena asked as we circled the building.

I dug my phone from my pocket and showed her the picture of birthwort I downloaded from the internet – the plant with the uterus-shaped leaves that had been erroneously used as a birthing aid for centuries. Elena pointed to a corner of the greenhouse. "That one?"

I knelt down and peered at the plant peeking through the cracked glass. It was tangled in another weed, but the leaves were unmistakable. "That's the one."

Elena leaned closer. "There are branches here that have been snipped off."

I looked where she pointed. Sure enough, empty stalks stuck up through the cracked glass. They looked as though they'd been snipped neatly with shears. Quite recently, too, and when I took a closer look at the plant I could see more evidence of regular pruning.

I pulled on the rubber gloves I used for cleaning and tugged the plant from its cracked pot. I slipped it into an empty yogurt container I'd cleaned out and punched with drainage holes, and packed some dirt in around the edges. "It's a long-shot, but I'll see if Dr. Nelson will do some tests on this. She might be able to identify if it's the same strain. Then at least I'll have some evidence to tie Madame Usher to the crime. I might be able to go over the police commissioner's head. For all I know she's invited him here tonight because she intends to poison him, too—"

"Or you can let me help you."

I bit back a retort as Dorien stepped out from the shadows. He looked like shit, with his hair a mess and his shirt splattered with rain and his eyes raging storms of despair. Dorien wore his pain as a noble tragedy. Even in despair he was beautiful, and it made me hate him and long for him at the same time.

"You've done enough helping," I snapped.

"No, I haven't." Dorien darted a look around, as if checking if the guys were nearby and if they'd pounce on him. Satisfied we were alone, he took a step toward me. I wasn't going to give him the satisfaction of backing away. "Sprite, I heard what you said about me at the gazebo. I—"

"You were spying on us?" Elena frowned at him.

"No… well, yes. But I only came out because I wanted to talk to Faye. Because I feel the same way you do, that our secrets are destroying us, and I want to—"

"You want to be honest with me, Dorien. You can start by telling me about the tattoo on your chest," I growled.

"What tattoo?" Elena asked.

In response, Dorien's fingers flew to the buttons. He tugged open his shirt, revealing the gothic letters inked across his alabaster skin. Elena's eyes widened as she read the strange phrase. She turned to me. "I do not understand."

I pointed to the sign dangling above the door. "It's written there, too. And today I discovered it's also the name used for the herbal tea that poisoned my mother."

"What?" Dorien's face paled.

"Don't play dumb. I've got the evidence in my hand. Madame

Usher poisoned my mother, and *you* had something to do with it." Tears pricked in my eyes, but I forced them down. "Why? Why would you want to hurt her just to bring me here to torment me? Do you hate me *that* much?"

"I did not touch your mother. I would never do that to you, Sprite." Dorien's voice cracked. I wanted so badly to believe he spoke the truth. "I swear it upon all the gods who will listen."

"You don't believe in any god."

"Fine. Then I swear it on my love for you, a love that's burned bright ever since we were kids. A love that's inspired every song I've written and haunted my dreams every night. I had nothing to do with your mother's poisoning. If I'd known Madame Usher was doing that, I would have found a way to stop her, no matter the cost."

Fuck you, Dorien. Fuck you for speaking words that make my body sing with music. Fuck you for being the song that only my heart under-stands. How I wish I was indifferent to you, that I could toss away your storm-soaked words until you were nothing but dust and dry rot. Instead, I hate you as much as I love you, and the pain of it is tearing me apart.

Dorien slapped his hand to his chest, over his heart. His inked fingers obscured the gothic script of VENENUM. "I got this tattoo done after Prague. When Broken Muse was over and I fell under Madame Usher's control. I got it to remind me that I could never be naive enough to underestimate her again."

"What does it mean?" Elena asked. She threaded her fingers in mine, and she didn't even wince when I squeezed her so hard I heard her knuckle crack.

"It's Latin for 'the poison is in the tail.'" Dorien said. "It describes a scorpion – its pincers look evil, but it's the tail that will kill you. The Romans used it as a metaphor to remind them to be wary of their enemies – that the attack might come from where they least expect it."

"You got that right." I stared down at the plant in my hands. My fingers trembled.

"I know you don't want to speak to me again. I am trying to respect that. But I also can't live with myself knowing I could help but I didn't offer. You want to bring down Madam Usher? Believe it or not, so do I. And we need to act fast, or your mother won't be the only one in danger. We must—"

I shook my head. "You don't get to follow me out here and start barking orders. I meant what I said, Dorien. I've bled for you. I've cried enough tears over you. There can be no more secrets. If you want us to work together, you need to bleed your secrets for me."

His face twisted. Exquisite pain turned his eyes into storm clouds, and I knew that this man could never be dust to me, no matter how much I wished it. "You know how my parents are in a cult? It's called the Temple of Earthly Truths. The cult leader, Father Aaron, has taken over my parents' estate and turned it into an armored compound. My fifteen-year-old brother, Jacob, is trapped inside. They mistreat him, make him work all day, starve him, tie him up and cut his feet, and Satan knows what else."

Shit.

Dorien turned his eyes toward the heavens as he continued. "I believe Father Aaron has burned through my parents' money, and he's now trying to get money out of Heather's parents by making them new elders in the cult. I don't know what it means for my parents or for Jacob, but it's not good. He's scared, so scared, and I think something terrible is going to happen to him if I can't get him out. Madame Usher may have got to Commissioner Walpole, but I'm going above her head, to the FBI. There's an agent there who contacted me a couple of years ago, on their task force for dangerous organizations. He thinks he can help me get Jacob out, and if we tell him about the poison, he might be able to help us bring Usher down—"

Elena's fingers squeezed mine as I took in the litany of horrors he spoke. "I don't understand, if you knew someone in the FBI, why would you not have gone to them before now? You're in your twenties, you could have got custody of your brother if this cult is as bad as you say."

"Because..." Dorien squeezed his eyes shut. The storm inside him threatened to escape through his sockets. Now it clung to his alabaster skin, shrouding him in tragedy. "Fuck it. Because I did a stupid thing. I was going to get Jacob out. I planned to save all my money from the last Muse tour to sue my parents for custody. I even had the lawyer lined up. But then I tried to help Elena and Ivan, and Madame Usher cut the tour shut, and I had to go back to the States without the funds I needed. My parents had already drained most of my savings to give to the Temple. I didn't know what to do, so I thought I'd try to talk to them, convince them to let me leave with Jacob. I was prepared to do whatever they wanted, even marry Heather, if I could get him out of the cult. But I arrived at the house and Father Aaron, he... he wouldn't let me see Jacob. He said I was a bad influence. He threw tabloid articles about our tour in my face and said a court would never find in favor of a vile sinner like me. I was so angry at him and how he destroyed my family. And... fuck." He buried his face in his hands.

"And?" I prompted.

"I *broke*. I punched him. He didn't expect it. He went down and just held his broken nose and stared at me. And I kept hitting and hitting and hitting him. It was only when I heard Jacob screaming that I stopped. I couldn't even recognize him under all the blood. My mother called the police, and they arrested me. Dragged me off to make an example of. A rich dick like me? Walpole was going to come down hard and ruin my life. And then Madame Usher showed up. She said she'd make everything go away, but I had to enroll in Manderley Academy, and I had to do exactly what she asked me to do."

Dorien's shoulders shuddered. He scraped his nails down his cheeks, leaving scratches that filled with trails of tears. "That's my secret. That's what she has over me – I'm an evil person who beat a man within an inch of his life. If I didn't find a way to make you leave Manderley, then Walpole would arrest me for the crime and Jacob would be trapped in the cult. If I'm convicted, I can't be Jacob's guardian, even if my parents were deemed unworthy. Jacob will go into foster care, and I didn't want to do that to him. He's been raised under Father Aaron's crazy rules. He can barely read and write – he'll get eaten alive in there." Dorien gulped. "I thought if I could just do what she wanted, if I could hold on until the end of the year and win the Manderley Prize, I'd have the money to help Jacob. But I had to hurt you to do it. I sold my soul to the devil and now we'll never be free of her."

A savage battle raged within me – I wanted to wrap my arms around him, to hold him close and never let go, and I wanted to press my fingers into his throat and squeeze until he could no longer utter any words that would hurt me. Because it hurt too much loving Dorien Valencourt. Every word, every breath, every touch was a fresh and exquisite agony.

"Why didn't you just tell me?" I screamed. "If you'd come to me in the first week and explained all of this, I could have helped you. We could have worked together. Do you truly think so little of me that you assume I'd let an innocent kid be made a pawn on Madame Usher's chessboard of lies?"

"After I'd already hurt you so deeply, would you have listened? Would you have believed me?" Tears streamed down Dorien's cheeks. "I took the coward's way. I knew you were stronger than Madame Usher could comprehend. I knew you'd survive anything I tried to do to you, but *this?* I didn't know what seeing you again would do to me, how it would crack me open and let my sickness pour out, infecting everyone around me. I thought that if I pushed you away, if you thought I hated you, then you'd

never see the *true* evil I was capable of. But it's better you do."
Dorien turned away, his shoulders hunched, his face turned to
the moonlight as he drank in the pale shadows. "I'm a monster.
You're better off without me, Faye. But I will never stop loving
you or fighting for you. Cast me out of your life if you have to, or
use me to make her pay. Because the only way to fight a monster
like Madame Usher is with one of your own."

FAYE

"*I*t's settled." Elena bounced into the Blue Room.

"*Fuck.*" My hands fumbled with the vase I was dusting, and I nearly dropped it. I'd been thinking about everything Dorien said to me at the poison garden – as if it were possible to think about anything else since I'd run away from him that night. I couldn't reconcile the Dorien I knew with this brutal man possessed by violence. *I will never stop loving you or fighting for you.* All my life I'd wished for love like that – feral, haunting, beautiful. But could I give myself over to Dorien's bloodstained promises? And what about Titus and Ivan? Because I loved them too. I loved three Broken Muses, and I needed to have my head examined. I was such a tangle of wild thoughts I hadn't even heard Elena enter the room. "What's settled?"

"We will spend Christmas in Europe." Elena flopped down on the chaise, oblivious to the fact I was having a mild cardiac arrest. "Master Radcliffe is going to accompany us, but I'm sure we'll find ways to get up to mischief."

"How did you swing that? I thought we were all on Madame Usher's naughty list?"

"I just flitted my eyelashes at him, like this." She demonstrated some next-level eyelash flitting. "And he is putrid in my hands, as you say."

"Putty. It's putty in your hands."

Elena waved elegant fingers in the air. "I do not care. We are going – Ivan and I. We will visit our mother for the first time in five years. You will come, of course."

"I can't, Elena. My mom's in the hospital. They say she might wake up any day now. I can't just race off to Europe. I have to be here for her."

Elena's face fell. "But we're all going away for Christmas. Which means it will just be you and Madame alone in this house."

I swallowed. That sounded like my worst nightmare. "I'm sure I can manage."

~

Winter descended on Manderley Academy, hiding the untended gardens and cracked driveway beneath a thick layer of snow. Harrison's work became an arduous cycle of clearing the way for us to drive to Christmas recitals and chopping wood for the fires that roared throughout the house all day and night. I carried load after load of firewood upstairs to stack in the bedrooms and the basket in front of Madame's private door. By the end of the week, I could hardly lift my bow.

Heather had settled for ignoring me, turning her head away as I entered a room as if I carried a bad smell with me. I worried that her lack of interest in tormenting me was only because she had something dramatic planned. That worry compounded as I noticed her ducking into Madame Usher's office on several occasions for private meetings, and a smaller version of her mother's jeweled pin appearing at her throat.

I heard the footsteps in the attic only once more, and the soft violin music reached my ears just as I was slipping into my dreams. If Heather was behind it, she'd have to do better if she wanted to frighten me away.

Manderley's ghosts had declared a ceasefire. For now.

On the final Saturday before the Christmas break, Titus, Ivan, and Elena went into the city to perform a chamber concert by candlelight. I longed to go with them – we could have seen my mom on the way – but Madame Usher decided I needed to reorganize the linen closet, so I spent the evening refolding perfectly folded linens while she barked orders at me and I imagined how she'd look impaled on the sword that hung above the fireplace.

My chores done for the day, I served up mulled wine and spaghetti Bolognese for the other students and returned to the kitchen to eat in peace. While I slurped spaghetti, my phone rang, flashing the hospital's number.

Mom.

I snapped up the phone. "Hello?" I breathed.

"Faye, this is Dr. Nelson. Your mother is awake and talking. She'd like to—"

I didn't even listen to the rest of the sentence. The phone clattered from my hand as I leaped to my feet. She's awake. *Awake.*

I can see my mom again. I can hold her in my arms and—

Fuck. I had no car. The only friends I had in this place were playing a gig in the city two hours away. I could try to call a cab again, but that didn't work so well last time – if they didn't laugh in my face it would still take them hours to drive out here to pick me up.

I flew through the house to the Blue Room, which faced the sweeping drive. I pulled back the curtains and breathed a sigh of relief when I saw lights flickering through the trees from the gatehouse. Harrison was still awake.

I picked up my mobile to call his extension. It rang and rang and rang, but he didn't pick up.

His lights are on, and I can see his car in the drive. Maybe he's in the shower or something. I'll run down and bang on the door.

I sprinted upstairs to the attic to grab my purse, coat, and violin. On the way back downstairs I streaked past Dorien as he slunk along the hall toward the library. He opened his mouth to say something, but I wasn't sticking around to hear it. Madame Usher yelled something from the depths of the house, but I had my feet in my boots and was out the door and flying down the driveway before she could find some other inane task for me to do.

Tonight, I didn't give a fuck. Tonight, my mother was awake.

Maybe, just maybe, this was the first step toward this nightmare being over.

Outside, the mountain air bit at my skin as my feet sank into the fresh layer of snow. I shifted my violin case to my other hand as I tugged on my jacket one-handed. My violin case battered against my legs, and I abandoned my jacket to hug it against me so I wouldn't damage the precious instrument inside. I still didn't know who'd given it to me, but I guessed from the way he smiled whenever I raised it to my chin that Titus was involved. I ducked and dodged around the slippery patches of ice, sticking to the softer snow at the edge of the drive and barely noticing the branches scratching at my bare arms.

By the time I reached the gatehouse, my chest was heaving and I tasted blood in my mouth. I never ran that fast unless there were donuts at the end. I gripped the wall and sucked in several deep breaths. My cheeks stung from the cold, and because I hadn't stopped to put on my gloves, I couldn't feel my fingers.

Calm down. You can't see your mom if you give yourself a heart attack.

I stumbled up the steps and knocked on the door of the gatehouse. I couldn't believe Harrison was forced to live out here. Sure, Manderley was a bit of a relic, but this place was depressing. It was a squat stone building, barely large enough to be called a house. Vines encircled the building, obscuring most of the windows. Piles of gardening tools, old bricks, roof shingles, and car tires lined the broken path to the front door. I could see a tarp fluttering in the breeze, plugging a hole in the roof. Would Madame Usher's cruelty not allow her to have Harrison in the big house, or did he choose to live down here, away from her prying eyes?

"Harrison, it's me." The wind whipped my words away. I cupped my hand against the narrow, grubby window that pointed into his kitchen. Light flickered from somewhere deeper in the room – a candle, perhaps? A dark shape moved in front of it, momentarily obscuring the light from view. I pounded both fists on the door. "Harrison, it's Faye. Please open the door. I need your help."

I pounded on the door until my fists stung. I circled the house, jumping over the piles of detritus and flinging aside thick vines to peer in every window. Wet snow plastered my hair to my face and drenched my clothes. I was cold right down to my bones. Harrison didn't answer, and I couldn't see any light inside.

I slumped on the stoop, not caring that the ice soaked through my wool dress. Tears sprung in my eyes. *How will I get to the hospital now? Where's Harrison? I know he—*

"There you are, Sprite. What are you doing out here?"

I swung around. Dorien stood in the driveway, shining a flashlight on the path between us. He wore a red shirt that cast crimson shadows through his hair, and a dark wool coat that flapped around his frame.

"None of your business." The wind swallowed the words, making me sound high-pitched, desperate.

"It's your mom, isn't it?" He stepped toward me. "I can see it in your eyes."

I wanted to tell him he didn't have the right to see anything in me, but I was too full of emotions that were threatening to burst the floodgates any moment, so I nodded. "She's woken up, but Titus and Ivan have gone to the stupid recital and I need to get to the city and Harrison has decided today is the day to become a deaf hermit—"

"I'll drive you."

I shook my head.

"I know you hate me now, and that's a hundred percent fair. But you don't have any other options. I promise, if you get in the car with me, I won't try to convince you not to hate me. We'll drive to the hospital in complete silence. You'll see your mom. I'll call Titus and get him to collect you after the concert."

I stared up at him, trying to read his mind in his features.

Dorien stared right back at me, his slate-grey eyes remote, unreadable. "You can't sit out here all night. If you catch frostbite and your fingers fall off, you'll never be able to scratch Heather's eyes out."

I tried to laugh, but I was so cold and so distraught it came out as a hiccup. I stared at Dorien's outstretched hand, and against my better judgment, I took it.

As soon as my fingers touched his, that fire that flared whenever we were together danced along my veins. The magnetic pull of Dorien Valencourt called to me, and I had to summon every last ounce of strength to resist.

"Okay. Let's go."

Dorien kept my hand in his as we picked our way back up the drive. The wind howled through the trees, battering us. Dorien wrapped his arms around me and kind of shoved me forward. I wanted to not like the warmth of his body against mine, the protective feeling of his body trying to shield me against the wind. I wished the heat in my veins and the flutter in my heart could be real, that Dorien really was my dark prince and not the monster who would haunt my dreams.

I scrambled inside his Porsche, slamming the door against the snow squall. Dorien climbed in beside me and planted his foot to the floor before I'd even fastened my seatbelt. He took Manderley's winding driveway like it was a racetrack, even though it was impossible to see in the horrible weather. As we exited the high iron gates of the school and careened down the mountain road, he rested his phone in a cradle and tapped the screen. Loud, strange dark electronica pulsed from his expensive speakers.

"What the hell is this shit?"

"I figured you weren't going to talk to me," he said. "So it's either this or we sit in stony, uncomfortable silence."

"I never said I was going to stay silent." I grabbed his phone and switched it to a musical theatre playlist. I cranked the heat up as I belted out the lyrics to *Cats*.

My mother is awake. Awake.

My mind spun through everything that had happened since she collapsed and fell into that coma – everything I had to do to keep her alive. I worked all those crazy hours. I sold my soul to Madame Usher and climbed into bed with Dorien against my better judgment. But in this moment, it was completely and utterly worth it.

I tried to think of everything I wanted to tell her, and remind myself she might not be up to talking, or that I hadn't even waited to hear what Dr. Nelson might say about her condition. I wrung my hands around themselves in my lap and twisted my stomach in knots and tried to convince myself I wasn't sneaking glances at the beautiful boy who drove into the gloom.

By the time Dorien turned into the hospital parking lot, I was a wreck of nerves. I threw the door open before he even put on the brake, and darted out. He called after me, but like fuck I was waiting for him. There was a group of people huddled by the elevators, so I took the stairs two at a time. As I raced into my mom's ward, Dr. Nelson appeared like a magical fairy godmother. She wiped a hand across her face, tucking her lank hair behind her ear, and a tired smile played across her features.

I fell into her arms. "Thank you," I whispered.

"Just doing my job." She pulled away, giving me a slight push toward my mother's room. "You can see her now. She's been waiting for you."

She's been waiting for you.

That implied my mother was coherent. That she didn't have brain damage. That she remembered who I was.

I pulled open the door to Mom's room. Fear gripped me, rooted me in place as I stared at the figure in the bed – the tiny woman with the skinny arms staring at the ceiling. The tall, beeping machines that had kept her alive still hemmed in around her, beeping and clicking and chirping. *It's all a trick. She's not awake. It's another cruel joke by—*

Mom blinked.

She fucking *blinked.*

Her head swiveled toward me, and her eyes lit up with recognition. With love. Her dry lips curled back into a wobbly smile. "What are you waiting for?" she croaked out. "A written invitation? Get over here, *mi cielo.*"

I rushed to her bedside, desperate to put my arms around her but not knowing if I'd hurt her. "Mami?"

"Faye de Winter, get the fuck over here right now."

I threw my arms around her. She felt so light, practically weightless. My heart soared. I thought it might fly out of my chest.

I don't know how long we held each other, her stroking my hair, me touching her dry, fragile skin. I know that at some point my tears spilled over and soaked her hospital gown.

When she pulled away, there were tears in the corners of her eyes. She stroked my face. "I'm so sorry to have scared you. I promise to never do that again."

"Don't make promises you can't keep." I laughed, and the sound was so foreign in this room that it startled me. "I know better than anyone that you run headlong into danger and trouble."

"And that's exactly why I came back to you. I couldn't have you becoming boring without me."

"What has Dr. Nelson told you about your condition?" Dr. Nelson warned me that when patients come out of a coma, it can feel completely disorienting. You didn't want to lay everything on them in the first ten minutes.

Mom leaned back and fluffed her pillows. "The doctor and I have had a nice chat. She wanted to save all the highlights of my little sojourn for when you got here, but I dragged it out of her. I've been MIA for a few months, and you've done a remarkable job coping on your own."

"Mom, I…" So much had changed since she first slipped into the coma. I didn't know where to begin. Instead, I held her tighter. "Don't ever go away like that again."

26

DORIEN

I waited in an uncomfortable chair for over an hour, staring at a poster advocating for prostate checkups until my balls shriveled up into my body. My mind spiraled to the darkest place it knew – a place where I dared to hope that Faye's mother might be okay, that she might be the missing piece we needed to nail Madame Usher for what she did. That Faye might forgive me.

Hope is a broken-winged bird that looks to the heavens and remembers what it is to fly. I had Faye's love once, and now I would be forever haunted by the ghost of her kiss. In my dreams I will see the sky through her eyes, and the hope that I might have her back will undo me utterly.

The doors swung inward, and Titus and Ivan raced toward me. "Where's Faye?" Ivan barked in his typical Romanian charm.

"Upstairs, with her mother." I stood up, shoving my phone into the pocket of my jeans.

"You're leaving?"

"She doesn't want me here. I'm trying to respect that."

Titus raised an eyebrow. I shot him a dark look. "Look after her, please. There's something I have to do."

"Dorien, wait—"

I didn't wait. Every muscle in my body screamed at me to turn around and go back to Faye, to hold her close and never let her go, but I summoned a strength I didn't know I possessed and pushed myself out the doors and into my car. Titus and Ivan would give her what she needed, and that was the important thing. If I had to lose Faye, I'm glad it was to them. They were better men than I could ever hope to be.

She got in the car with me. I clung to the dark hope unfurling its wings inside me. I needed something to cling to, especially with what I was about to do.

I parked on a side street a few blocks from the hospital. I peered out the windows as slushy snow drenched the glass, searching the street for someone who might be watching me. A raven hopped along the gutter of the house opposite – was it Huginn or Muninn, one of Madame Usher's spies? No, I was being fanciful. The snow came down harder now, thick sheets that obscured the buildings and cars from view. Dim headlights pierced the gloom.

Lavender and orange-blossom lingered in the car. I took a deep breath in, allowing Faye's scent to steel my nerves. I checked my watch. He should be here any minute—

Someone rapped on the window. I leaned across and shoved open the door.

The man who folded his sodden frame inside my car looked like an actor playing an FBI agent. He was a walking cliche with the All-American flat haircut, the college athlete thick neck and shoulders tugging at his impeccable suit, and those eyes that had seen too much. He slammed the door against the deluge and wrung out his tie.

"Dorien," he said, holding out his hand. "Agent Gavin Rochester. Thank you for contacting me."

His handshake was firm, reassuring. "Thank you for agreeing to meet on short notice."

Rochester nodded. "I understand it's difficult to get away in your current situation."

A dry laugh escaped me. "You don't know the half of it. There is so much I need to talk to you about."

"Why don't we start with the evidence you gathered on the Temple, and we'll go from there."

I held out the flash drive toward him. I thought he'd throw it into his briefcase, but he slid the flash drive into the jack on his phone and hit PLAY. I listened to the track on the drive back to Manderley, to make sure I'd captured everything Jacob said, and that had nearly killed me. Now, with Rochester in the car, hearing my boots crunch on the gravel and my mother's harsh voice greeting me made it all worse. *I should have done something sooner. I should never have let things get this bad.*

Jacob's voice came out, so small and quiet. He started talking about his feet. My chest closed up, and I struggled for breath. I wound down the window a fraction and let the freezing rain splatter my face. It didn't help the ache in my chest, but it did hide the tears.

When the track finished, Rochester remained still, his eyes darting across to me. He slipped the flash drive into his briefcase. "This is good," he said. "We can work with this. Combined with the other evidence we have, it's enough for a warrant."

My fingers played with the paper Jacob gave me. "Jacob and Pearl Danvers made you this map, too."

Rochester spread the map across his lap, taking in the floor plan of the house and grounds, with what had to be Pearl's neat handwriting in the key. He'd labeled Aaron's weapon stores with pictures of guns, the sleeping quarters of the five families that made up the Temple, and shown the security fences and the positions of the cameras. He may not have been able to write well, but Jacob's drawing skills were pretty incredible. He'd even included a scale in the top right corner, next to the key.

"That's a very clever brother you have," Rochester said.

"I know." *And it's time he got to shine in the real world.* "What happens now? I'm concerned about this 'day of ascension.'"

"You have reason to be. Our task force has seen an increase in activity amongst the Temple in recent weeks – not just their recruitment activities, but Varney has been moving money and goods around. These are often signs a cult is preparing for a major event. Not every cult ends up like Jonestown, but with Aaron Varney involved, we need to act fast."

"I don't know anything about him."

"He's an extremely dangerous individual. He used to home-school for a young family in Maine. The father had made a fortune in the shipping industry, but it involved long hours and lots of travel, and he wanted a fresh start to see his kids grow up. So they purchased an old hotel in the mountains and started renovating it. One of their first guests was a teacher who'd recently lost his job – Aaron Varney. Aaron enchanted the whole family with his stories and games – especially the mother. Over time, Aaron convinced the couple to give up more control to him. First, he moved into their hotel as a full-time teacher, then he started to make changes to their schedules – 'suggestions' for healthier meals or activities for the children. Then he started to introduce religious teachings, which became more and more extreme. If any friend or family member expressed concern, Varney convinced the family they were trying to crush their fire, and they were cut off or driven from the property. Next, Varney started selling off the family's possessions and gained control of their finances to help fund his missionary work. He became increasingly agitated, speaking of armageddon and a battle of good and evil, of purging the earth with fire. The beautiful old hotel went up in flames and took the couple with it. Their two children – a son and a daughter – managed to escape by walking sixteen miles in a snowstorm to the nearest village. By the time an investigation was opened, Aaron Varney had disappeared."

Rochester paused, looking me dead in the eyes. "That couple were my parents."

Fuck. A cold shiver trickled down my spine as I studied Gavin Rochester's face, seeing behind his All-American looks to the darkness within. I'd never met someone before who knew what it was like to lose your family to a religious nutcase with a God-complex, to see your supposedly-sane parents slip under a spell that allowed atrocities to be committed on their watch. Aaron had already destroyed one family; I couldn't let him rob the world of Jacob's light.

I balled my hands into fists and punched the steering wheel. *I hate this. I hate being so helpless.*

Rochester watched me pummel the wheel until my knuckles stung and I gasped for breath. He didn't admonish me or give any sign he found me disturbing. "We're going to do everything we can to stop Aaron destroying anyone else's life," he said. "I need to take the recording and the map back to my task force and get a warrant, and we'll plan our next move. I'll keep you informed every step of the way. If anyone from the Temple contacts you again, record the conversation if possible – if it's safe for you to do so – or at least write a transcript while it's fresh in your mind. Note the day and time. And get a hold of me immediately. Here." He handed me a crisp business card. "This is my personal line. Call any time. For any reason."

"Thank you." I pushed the edge of the card into my finger, slicing my skin so a single droplet of blood marred its pristine surface. "I have to tell you something else. I don't want it to impact the case. I'm… I'm ready to face the penalty for covering it up if it comes to that."

With my eyes screwed tight and Faye's scent lingering in my memory, I told Rochester *everything* – about assaulting Aaron, about trying to help Elena and Ivan in Prague, and how Madame Usher bribed me to cover it up. I itched to tell him about Faye's mother's poisoning, but I knew she needed to do that herself when she was ready.

Rochester recorded the conversation. "I'm not going to lie, the assault is probably going to come up if anything goes to trial. Aaron's lawyers will dig up any dirt they can find to discredit you. Things will get ugly. We'll do what we can to protect you, and it's likely a good lawyer could make a case for self-defense – you were defending your impaired brother. But you may have to answer for your crime. I'll warn you now, even if everything works out fine and we get the bastard, you might not get the happy family you're imagining. Most of the cases I've worked on like this where one family member gets out from an extremist cult, they remain estranged from the family even after deprogramming. Jacob may never forgive you for taking away the only family he's known."

I nodded. "I understand. All I want is what's best for Jacob. And it's not as if we were a happy family before Aaron came along."

"As for this Gizella Usher, I'll make some inquiries. If the commissioner is that deep in her pockets, that's something we need to keep an eye on. Are you safe at that house?"

I wasn't, but no way was I leaving Faye there alone to face Madame Usher's wrath. "Safe enough for now. Start by looking into Clare Fairbanks – she was a maid who died at Manderley earlier this year. She fell down the stairs; or at least, that's what the police decided."

"You're not so sure?"

I rubbed my eye sockets. "I don't know what to believe anymore. Clare was chasing after me when she fell. She wanted to tell me a secret she'd discovered about Madame Usher and the school. She was my girlfriend, and I treated her like shit. That's probably going to come out, too. I heard her scream, and I turned back immediately. I didn't see anyone else at the top of the stairs, but there is so much in that house that doesn't add up, and

Walpole oversaw the investigation, and I think there might be something more there if you dig."

Rochester's shook his All-American head. "You get mixed up in a lot of weird shit, kid."

I laughed bitterly. "You have no idea."

27

FAYE

I stayed by Mom's bedside for hours. My eyes drooped with fatigue, but I couldn't bear the idea of falling asleep and risk not having her there when I woke up.

Instead, we talked. I knew I was supposed to let her rest and give her space, but Mom was desperate to have some kind of normalcy. She needed to grasp the new world she'd woken up in. So I told her everything that had happened since she fell into the coma – about losing the business, losing our apartment, about Madame Usher's offer, and all the weird stuff that happened at Manderley. Mom's face twisted in a painful way when I mentioned Madame Usher, and I knew she was thinking about Dad.

The nurses tried to make me leave, but Dr. Nelson gave them the hard word that I was allowed to stay.

Dr. Nelson poked her head in just as I was telling Mom about my violin getting smashed. "My shift is over, so I'm heading home for the night. Marguerite, I wanted to check on you. Is everything okay?"

"I have my Faye with me." Mom beamed. "The only thing that could make this day better is a pitcher of margaritas."

"I'm afraid I can't help with that." Dr. Nelson smiled. "Faye, there are some very beautiful men waiting downstairs for you. Should I let them up?"

Mom sat up, her eyes on fire. "These are your boyfriends?"

"I'm not sure it's a good idea—"

"Send them in. I *demand* to meet these boys who tormented you and then won your heart."

Dr. Nelson ducked out, and a few minutes later, I heard a commotion in the ward – deep voices talking, boots clomping on the tiled floor, beads clacking together. The door flung open, and in stepped Titus, Ivan… and Dorien.

What's he doing here?

Dorien hung back as Titus and Ivan swooped toward me. He leaned against the door as if it was the only thing holding him upright, and took in the hospital room and the wall of blinking machinery with those storm-dark eyes. A corner of his mouth twitched, and he had his hands shoved into his pockets.

Mom's eyes narrowed as she recognized him. "Dorien Valencourt, what an… interesting surprise."

I loved how uncomfortable Dorien looked. Marguerite de Winter could still make grown men tremble.

"Mom, this is Titus Thibodeaux and Ivan Nicolescu." I touched each of the Muses in turn, ignoring Dorien because I hadn't invited him here and I needed him to know that. "This is my mother, Marguerite de Winter."

"It's a pleasure." Titus leaned over and kissed her on the forehead, his braids falling over the sheets. She took his hand and squeezed it, then held Ivan's. Dorien stepped forward, but Mom shook her head at him.

"He insisted on coming with us," Ivan said. "If you do not wish him to be here, I'll deal with him."

"I drove her here, asshole," Dorien shot back. "You want me here, don't you, Sprite?"

"*Want* is too strong a word," I said.

My mother gave my hand a weak squeeze, as if to say, 'That's my girl.'

"Dorien took you to the hospital?" Ivan fixed Dorien with his icy stare. "You should have called us. Or asked Harrison."

"It would've taken too long for you to drive back and collect me," I said. "And I tried to find Harrison, but it was so strange. Lights were on in his house, but he didn't answer the door. Dorien offered, and I didn't have any choice."

Ivan folded his arms and shot Dorien another glare. Dorien stepped away, pressing his back against the wall. I noticed his shirt was soaked from the rain, whereas Titus and Ivan were dry – he'd been outside. I wondered what had drawn him out into the storm, and then I hated myself for wondering.

"How do you feel, Ms. de Winter?" Titus asked, changing the subject from Dorien. Titus was always the first to sense tension coiling in the air and try to find a way to dissipate it.

"Like I've been hit by a truck. Faye's told me everything that happened since I went under. It sounds as if you've all had quite the experience at that fancy school of yours."

"Everything?" Titus lifted an eyebrow to me.

"She left out the sex, but I've filled it in with my imagination." Mom grinned. "I'm *very* imaginative."

I shifted in my seat as Titus burst into his deep, beautiful laugh.

"I'm glad you boys are looking after my Faye." Mom said this with her eyes fixed on Dorien. "I don't like the idea of her being in that woman's house. I don't think it's safe for any of you."

"It's not, but we're going to fix that. Mom, do you remember after Dad disappeared, Madame Usher came to our apartment? She tried to give you an envelope, and you had an argument in the kitchen, then she left with the envelope."

"I'll never forget."

I bit my lip, then continued. "What was in the envelope?"

"It was money." Mom's jaw clenched. A shudder ran through her body. "She tried to pay me to send you to her school."

That... didn't make any sense. Tuition at Manderley cost tens of thousands of dollars. Why would Madame Usher want to *pay* my mother to send me there, especially when my father had only just disappeared?

Mom read my questions in my eyes before I could speak them. "Gizella is a formidable woman – it takes one to know one. That's why I refused her, because I can recognize the cunning in her eyes. I do not know why she had such an interest in you, but I did not like it. Not after she and Donovan..." Mom's eyelashes fluttered shut. "Perhaps she thought if she couldn't control him any longer, she could instead exert her power over you and in some sick way remain close to him. But I believe mostly she wanted to take you from me, the way she believes I took Donovan from her."

My stomach clenched. "I don't understand. How can she blame you for Dad's disappearance?"

Mom's eyes flickered shut. Panic rose inside me that she might be fading back into the coma. Dr. Nelson said it could happen. But no, those fierce green orbs fixed on me again, filled with the fire that mirrored my own. "Because Donovan did not disappear, *mi cielo*. After everything you've been through, you deserve the truth. Donovan de Winter is dead. I killed him."

28

FAYE

The world stopped.

My blood froze in my veins.

Sound the fucktrumpets.

What the fuck did she just say?

I killed him.

I stared down at the woman who had raised me, and for the first time in my entire life, I looked at a stranger. My knees wobbled. Titus rushed to grab me as I gripped the edge of the bed, fighting to keep hold of my lunch. He sank down into the chair and pulled me into his lap, wrapping his enormous arms around me. His braids fell over my face like a curtain, and I sank against him gratefully. I needed him to be my strength right now.

I killed him.

"I think you'd better explain, Marguerite," he said in his deep, kind voice. "Faye needs the truth, no matter how ugly."

I couldn't look at Mom. Part of me wanted to cover my ears to stop her tainting every memory of who I thought she was. But I needed to hear this. And she needed to say it. She took another sip of her water and began. "Gizella was the reason Donovan and I fought so much. I guessed about their affair long before she told me from the way he acted around her – as if she could do no wrong, as if she alone understood the great artistic yearning that rose up inside him. He hired her as his manager, and she demanded more of his time for practice and touring, more money for his trips abroad and his wardrobe, and his lessons that stretched long into the night. She wanted him to purchase an expensive instrument from a famed luthier that he could never hope to pay off. He told me that she was the only one who believed in his music, even after I worked three jobs to keep food on our table. Finally, I told him I would give no more. I would not see our daughter suffer because of his selfishness. He had a family, and he needed to live up to his obligations as a father. He did not want to hear it. He left for a tour with Gizella. He never even kissed you goodbye."

She paused to gasp for breath. I knew we shouldn't be taxing her like this, but she opened this wound. I dared a glance at her through Titus' hair. For a moment, I saw my mom as she was in those last years before Dad disappeared – tired, drawn thin like the cheap curtains that didn't quite fit the windows of our run-down apartment, her eyes rimmed in red as she stirred a saucepan of soup on the stove – our only meal for the day. I remembered her and Dad screaming at each other. Her calling him selfish, him saying she was a stealer of dreams. Doors slamming. Me hiding under my bed or climbing onto the roof with my violin, playing Bach until I drowned out their shouts.

She loved Dad in the beginning. She felt his music in her soul, the same way his recordings still captivate audiences a decade after he disappeared. But my father wasn't some immortal weaving magic betwixt his violin strings – he was a man, capable of great and terrible things in equal measure. He might play like an angel, but to her, he would always be the demon who accused her of stealing his dreams while he devoured hers.

I inherited so much from my mother – my thick, dark hair,

my Mexican nose, my fiery nature, my penchant for the bad boys, the heartbreakers, the demons in disguise.

I would always love her. I would love her even if she was a murderer. I squeezed Titus' knee. "If this is too painful, you don't have to tell me—"

"Nonsense, *mi cielo*. Pain is part of life. I can't imagine what you've gone through, being a servant in that woman's house, knowing of her relationship with Donovan..." she coughed violently. "You must hear this – you must know the guilt I've carried with me all these years. You must understand why that woman is dangerous. The last night I saw your father, he came to the door in a panic. You were asleep upstairs and he... he was supposed to be performing in Canada, but here he was, on our doorstep, his hair a mess and his eyes filled with demons. He said he needed ten thousand dollars by sunrise or he would be killed. He had been borrowing money from an Eastern European crime organization to fund his expensive tours and lifestyle, and to buy the violin I refused to purchase. He'd fallen behind on his payments and they had finally called to collect. I told him he would not get another penny from me, that he had robbed his daughter of enough already. I slammed the door in his face. The very next day he did not show up for his recital. He was never seen again. Your father is dead, *mi cielo*, I tell you, because I killed him. I could have saved him, but I didn't."

Relief and love swept through me. I'd imagined my mother choking the life from Donovan with her bare hands, or plunging a knife into his chest. I pictured her taking his body to Central Park and digging him an unmarked grave, like the murderer on a TV mystery show. In her mind, refusing him that money was the same crime, but I couldn't see it that way. All I could see was the woman who'd always looked after me, and Madame Usher's poison seeping into our life, rotting the heart of our family.

I flung myself from Titus' arms to wrap myself around her. I pressed my cheek to hers, and our tears mingled together. "I love you, Mom." I closed my eyes. I didn't want to say this, but we couldn't have any secrets between us now. "We think Madame Usher might've tried to poison you. She owned the company that made the poisoned tea, and I found birthwort in the garden at Manderley with some of the branches snipped off."

Mom coughed. Titus handed her a water glass, and she took a sip. "I believe it. She blames me for his death. She told me so. What do the police say about it?"

"We can't go to the police. Madame Usher owns them – she's in bed with Commissioner Walpole."

Titus wrinkled his nose. "Hopefully only figuratively."

I glanced across the room at the dark prince hunched in the doorway. "Dorien thinks we should go to the FBI. He has a contact there, but I'm not sure about it. I'm not sure about him."

I will never stop loving you or fighting for you.

"You're not safe in that house." Mom's eyes narrowed. "You get out, you and your beautiful boys, before it's too late. I don't care about justice, only that you are safe. And when I can rise from this bed, *mi cielo*, I will go to that big house and strangle her with my own hands."

29

FAYE

I barely remember a moment of the final week of classes before Christmas break. The shadow of Madame Usher's crimes hung over all Manderley like a shroud. Weirdly, having closure over my father's death made dealing with Madame Usher bearable. All my life the Great Donovan de Winter loomed over me, but now I could see him for who he truly was – a small, selfish man who'd abandoned his family for the lure of fame and fortune. Madame Usher was welcome to his memory, because I didn't want it.

I hoped his ghost would be all that kept her warm in her frigid prison cell when we finally took her down.

Every day after I finished my private lessons with Master Radcliffe, I flew to my room to video chat with my mother. Sometimes Titus and Ivan joined me, but they seemed to sense that I needed this time alone with her. Instead, they puttered around in the kitchen, making the food and doing my chores so I could spend more time with her when we couldn't drive in to see her.

Our future was still so uncertain. Now that Mom was awake and I knew the truth about Madame Usher, all I wanted to do was drop out of Manderley. But Madame Usher, for all her (considerable) sins, was still footing Mom's medical bill, and I had no financial resources from which to draw if that dried up. Mom had spoken to Natalie, who had an old hotelier client from De Winter PR on her books that she sweet-talked into giving Mom a free room during her recovery, so at least she would have somewhere to live, but the rehabilitation process would be long, as Mom would be having surgeries over the next six weeks to deal with the damage to her organs.

"We've got the Christmas concert at the hospital on Thursday." I sat cross-legged on the bed, the laptop propped up on my pillows as I brushed my hair while I talked to her. "The boys will head home afterward and I'll stay with you. Elena wanted to come too, but she needs all the time she can get to pack her suitcase – her room is even messier than yours. I wish you could meet Elena; she's amazing, but she'll be in Europe with Ivan for Christmas."

"Why aren't you going with them?"

"Elena asked me, but I couldn't leave you." My brush hit a particularly snarly knot and stuck fast. I gave it a violent tug. "And now that you've woken up, I have plans. I downloaded a whole bunch of new horror films for us to watch together. Maybe Dr. Nelson will discharge you for a few hours and we could rent a fancy hotel room somewhere or go out for a fancy dinner."

Mom made a stern face.

"Okay, I don't mean a nice hotel room. I don't have that kind of money. But I'll settle for a cheap motel with clean sheets. Anything so that we can be together."

"Faye de Winter, stop being such a wet blanket. I'm not going to be the reason you avoid running off with your friends and getting up to mischief. You are nineteen years old and you never got the chance to be young and frivolous, and I won't stand for it."

"What are you talking about—"

"You are going to Europe, and I won't hear another word about it. You'll be away, what, ten days? That's nothing. You and I have the rest of our lives to watch horror films and develop our womanly figures with junk food."

"But—"

"Not another word."

Even I could not refuse Marguerite de Winter, no matter how much my heart stuttered at the thought of her being alone over Christmas. I couldn't help but feel a tinge of excitement as Elena screamed and jumped about and immediately called the airline to book me a seat next to her.

But just because I'd be gone over Christmas didn't mean that my mom would miss out. I got Harrison to trim a branch off one of the overhanging spruce trees, and I planted it in a large pot with tons of earth and stones. Titus, Ivan, and I loaded up his car with loads of decorations and Christmas treats, and on the day of the Christmas concert we drove it to the hospital and set up Mom's room. When we arrived in the pediatric ward where the concert would be held, we found the place decorated with bright streamers and balloons. Mom was in a wheelchair, tearing down the corridors and cackling with laughter, chased by a line of giggling children.

We set up in the corner of a large playroom. While we tuned, nurses wheeled in patients, and families crowded around the tables where festive food had been set out. We played through a selection of Christmas favorites. During the final number, Ivan slipped away, leaving me and Titus to perform a rendition of *Silent Night*.

I faced Titus, watching his fingers dance across the strings while he drew the bow with his usual gusto. My mind flashed back to that night I caught him in the woodshed playing electric guitar, his features wild with rapture as he flung his whole body into the music. He'd looked alive then in a different way than now – he was going through the motions, playing the notes he'd been taught to play. But he didn't feel the music in his bones the way Dorien and I did. Not this music, anyway.

I didn't understand why Titus kept up the pretense he wanted to be a classical musician. Unlike Ivan and Dorien, he paid for his place at Manderley. He could leave any time and pursue the heavy metal he truly loved. His parents were so kind and lovely, just like him. I knew Titus desperately sought their approval, but I couldn't understand why they wouldn't approve of anything he did.

We finished with a few bars of Rudolph the Red-Nosed Reindeer, which turned into a few more bars when everyone started clapping and singing along. Titus beamed into the crowd as the kids in front got up to dance, and suddenly he was playing with zest and singing along. *This* was what he craved – knowing that his music moved people, that it made them *feel* something, and that he could live in the moment with them. He didn't get that from classical music.

After we finished with a flourish and a bow, Mom wheeled up to us. Tears streaked down her cheeks. "You were magnificent." She squeezed my hands.

"Let's take you back to your room." I grabbed the chair handles so she couldn't run off and cause chaos, and so I wouldn't think about the tears streaming down my own cheeks.

As we pushed Mom into her room, her face lit up as she took in our surprise. Ivan had done a great job, winding the tinsel around the rungs on her bed and across the windowsill, setting up the Christmas tree on the nightstand and stringing it with baubles, and laying out all our festive treats across the over-bed table.

"*Mi cielo*, you shouldn't have." Mom laughed as Titus plonked a pair of fuzzy reindeer antlers on her head. I laughed and hugged her, relishing her wriggling, laughing, and *living* in my arms.

Dr. Nelson stepped out of the bathroom with a bottle of fizzy grape juice, which she popped with much fanfare. As we passed around plastic cups, she said, "I need to get back to my rounds, but I couldn't miss this. Now, Marguerite, I'd like to point out that you shouldn't overexert yourself, and take it easy on the sugar."

"Good thing you're here to look out for my health, Doc." Mom held out a plate of Mexican chocolates for Dr. Nelson. "Please, remove these delicious temptations from my sight."

"If you insist." Dr. Nelson popped three in her mouth as she left. I shared around the presents I'd wrapped under the tree – homemade chocolates for Titus and Ivan and Dr. Nelson, and for Mom, a performance of *Nigun* right there at the foot of her bed where she'd be able to hear it.

"Ivan and I have a gift for you both." Titus unclipped his cello case, and Ivan raised his violin to his chin. They launched into one of Broken Muse's most famous songs – a hauntingly beautiful dirge of lost love and longing called 'Requiem for a Dying Swan.' A morbid choice for a hospital room, but without Dorien's piano, they gave the piece a lightness and a faster tempo that made hope sing in my heart.

I didn't want to leave the hospital, but if we didn't go soon we'd be late for our flight. Mom pulled me to her chest and kissed my forehead.

"I want you to throw this sensible, grown-up Faye out the plane window," she scolded me. "You'll be in one of the most beautiful cities in the world. Have fun, do drugs, skinny dip in the hotel pool, shag that beautiful blue-eyed boy of yours. That's an order."

I laughed and stood back, staring down at her and trying to commit every curve and plane of her face to memory. It felt like I was leaving her for longer than ten days.

Titus squeezed my hand in his, reminding me of his promise that he'd watch over her while I was away. I didn't want Madame

Usher trying to finish the job. "I won't let anything happen to her."

"Young man, if I were you I'd be more concerned about what might happen to *you*." She waggled her eyebrows at him. "Hasn't my daughter told you about me? I'm a menace. I hope you can salsa dance, because this ass is too damn fine to spend New Year's Eve sitting in a lumpy bed."

~

Ivan and I met Elena and Master Radcliffe at the airport. Now that I knew the truth about Radcliffe's intentions toward her, I couldn't believe I never noticed it before. The way he doted on her, always touching her arm and leading her places like she was a delicate Victorian flower. I thought he was just a kindly old man in awe of her talents, but now his behavior bore a sinister edge.

Ivan *definitely* noticed – his frosty eyes followed Radcliffe everywhere. I hoped he'd relax once we were on the plane. Elena knew exactly how to handle Radcliffe, giving him little jobs to do and treating him in a fatherly way. I trusted her when she said she was safe from his sexual advances until there was some kind of official engagement, and none of us would let that happen.

Ivan, Elena, and I had seats in a row together in economy, with Master Radcliffe sitting up the front of the plane in business class. Elena chose a movie she wanted to watch and made all three of us start it at the same time so we could enjoy it together. Ivan broke out a stash of Christmas chocolate he'd saved from the hospital, and I leaned my head against his shoulder as I fought to stay awake.

I was still worried about Mom, but it was hard not to get caught up in the excitement of our trip. The only time I'd ever been to Europe was a crazy trip Mom and I took to Istanbul a few years ago. We mostly spent our time there shopping and eating our body weight in *baklava*. This trip was the first time I'd be leaving America without her, and I'd be visiting Prague – a city with a long musical history I'd always wanted to visit – and Romania, Elena and Ivan's homeland.

We arrived in Prague mid-morning, and Elena made it clear we would not be allowed to sleep until evening, no matter how much my body protested. Snow blanketed the city's spires and bohemian buildings, making it even more magical. We settled into our apartment on the edge of the Old Town, and Master Radcliffe whisked Elena off to meet some old conductor friend of his. I made a quick call to my mom to let her know we arrived safely, then Ivan placed his gloved hand in mine and marched me across the city to the ancient Prague castle.

We joined a crowd of freezing tourists wandering the vast castle grounds. I'd expected a grey stone fortress filled with narrow staircases and turrets, but Prague Castle was more of a walled city, where Bohemian monarchs and Holy Roman emperors added, expanded, rebuilt and altered a whole complex of palaces, reception halls, gardens, fortifications, and churches.

As we entered the foreboding St. Vitus Cathedral beneath elaborately carved doors, I turned to Ivan. "Dorien thinks we should go to the FBI about Madame Usher poisoning my mother."

"I don't care what Dorien thinks. I care what *you* think." We stepped into the towering nave of the gothic cathedral, and for a moment I lost my train of thought as my gaze was pulled up and up and up by the elegant columns and arches fanning out across the vaulted nave like a forest of stone, and rainbow prisms of light filtering through intricate stained glass. A choir practiced Christmas hymns behind a wrought-iron screen beyond the transept. Their voices filled the space with a discordant resonance that made the old church feel alive. A delicious shiver ran down my spine. Even with all the problems facing us back home, I still couldn't believe I was in this magical city with Ivan.

I remembered Dorien's confession in the poison garden, how his whole body trembled as he forced out his darkest secrets. *I will never stop loving you or fighting for you.*

"I think… this is his way of reaching out and trying to mend what he broke. And maybe he's right – the only way to fight a monster like Madame Usher is by becoming monsters ourselves."

"It sounds as though you have made up your mind."

I shook my head. "Even if I trust Dorien – which I'm still not sure I do – can we trust this agent of his? What if Madame Usher owns him, too? Dorien said the guy approached him years ago. We know she plays a long game, so she could have set him up somehow. I can't risk exposing my mom to whatever's going on. I think we just need to wait and see, and find as much evidence as possible to build a case against her. If Dorien—"

"I do not want to spend another moment talking about Dorien Valencourt." Ivan's words rolled over my skin like liquid flame. Before I could speak, he yanked me into a dark corner of an ornate chapel and pressed his lips to mine.

His kiss shocked the protest out of me, and suddenly I wasn't thinking about Dorien anymore, either. How could I, when I was being held by a man whose body *trembled* with need of me? Ivan's hands entwined in my hair, the warm tips of his fingers brushing against my cheeks as he devoured me. His own cheeks were flushed from the cold – pools of blushed skin outlining his razor-sharp cheekbones.

Ivan's eyes locked on mine. Staring into those glaciers was like leaping off a cliff into ice water. The shock of the cold might kill you, but the thrill fills your body with such heat that you've never felt more alive. Ivan wore his sadness as a badge of honor, and all I wanted to do was kiss away the stories he told himself about who he was and what he deserved. Ivan tried not to be seen because he didn't believe he was worth the attention. But he was, and I saw him. How could anyone miss him? He was enchanting – not of this world, but some fae prince of a shadow realm.

He might not see it, but Ivan carried the magic of the *Zâne* within him. He wove beautiful, pain-drenched magic with his fingers, his apple-and-sea-salt scent tainting the air around him with ice and lust.

Tourists streamed past the door as Ivan dragged me behind a wooden screen decorated with the images of saints. He shoved my back against the wall, exploring my body with needy hands. My heart thudded in my chest. *We're going to get caught...*

I don't care.

I want him.

I crave him.

My body was on fire, and the only thing that would quench it was to dive into Ivan's glacier eyes. His hands snaked beneath my shirt, squeezing my nipples roughly until I moaned. Ivan's pressed harder against me to muffle my moan as he slipped a hand into the waistband of my jeans. Two fingers slipped inside my heat, his palm pressing against my throbbing clit.

I gasped against his lips as the heat inside me flowed through my skin. I clenched around his fingers. Touching me in this ancient building felt so filthy and sordid and so totally unlike Ivan that I wanted to tear his clothes off right then and—

BRRRRP.

A loud whistle blew right beside my ear. I jumped ten feet into the air. Ivan's hand slipped out of my waistband as he glared at the guards crossing the church toward us. The whistle hadn't been right by my ear, but the acoustics had made it seem as if the guards were closer than they were. But they definitely knew what we were up to, and they were determined to reach us and show us just how much God did not approve.

"Run." Ivan grabbed my hand. My wet shoes slipped on the floor as we bolted for the exit, escaping into the bracing cold. A crowd of American tourists wandered through the square, and we ducked into their midst just as the guard emerged and ran in the opposite direction, whistle blowing.

"That was crazy." Ivan laughed. A strand of his white-blonde hair had escaped from beneath his beanie and fluttered across his forehead. God, I loved to see him laugh, to lose himself in a moment. The blush in his porcelain cheeks deepened into a rosy glow, and the severity in his eyes softened to a blue shimmer.

"I can't believe we did that." I held my hand to my chest, trying to calm my racing heart. The wetness in my panties wasn't going away any time soon, not if I remained in close vicinity to Ivan Nicolescu.

Ivan took my hand and we wandered deeper into the castle, deliberately not speaking about what just happened. The ice around Ivan's heart had cracked, and I knew calling him out on it would make him freeze up again. Instead, I dragged him toward a cart selling hollow rolls of delicious-smelling warm pastry.

"What are these?" I pointed to the treats.

"Those are *trdelník* – a spit cake. You'll find these carts all over the city, even though the dessert itself is not a traditional Czech recipe but comes from Slovakia and Moravia. We have a similar dessert in Romania. Here in Prague, it is very popular with tourists, especially with ice cream." Ivan stepped up to the cart and returned a moment later with two of the towering cakes warm from the spit with their insides filled with ice cream.

I bit into the warm, sugary pastry. Cinnamon and cold ice cream struck my tongue. It was delicious. We finished our snacks while visiting the quaint shops along the castle's 'Golden Lane,' licking melted ice cream from our fingers.

"When we were here in summer they filled the trdelník with strawberries," Ivan said.

"I would love to come here in summer," I beamed up at him. "We could tour the concert halls and see the Mucha museum and walk through Petrin Park when it's not covered in snow."

Ivan turned away, but not before I caught a glimmer of sorrow in his eyes.

"Does this city make you sad?"

"Being with you could never make me sad," Ivan said. "But this city will never be only architecture and beer and *trdelník* to me. This is where Elena and I made our last stand against Usher, and we lost everything. I worry that she chose to come here to close the door on our plans to escape Manderley. She is swanning around on Radcliffe's arm – the girl who leaped onto a train with me last year is gone, and my sister is a stranger to me. You notice she does not push Radcliffe away? She practically encourages him. I worry that she thinks if she agrees to marry Radcliffe, he will be our key to freedom. I don't know how I can make her see that's a lie. She's too precious to sacrifice her life for me."

Always Elena's happiness was in his thoughts. I didn't want Elena to marry Radcliffe, either, but I hated that Ivan thought he wasn't worth sacrifice. "She won't have to do that," I said. "I promise, we will all escape her."

Ivan shook his head. The cold slid back into his eyes as he slunk deeper into his ice cave. "I cannot let you choose me."

"Who's choosing anything?"

Ivan blinked. "We can't all be with you, Faye. Dorien won't stomach being one of three, and Titus needs to be able to put you on a pedestal and worship you. I wanted to fight for you, but now I see that loving you means I have to give you up."

"Ivan, you're not making any sense." I reached for him. "I don't need a martyr, and neither does Elena. If you don't want to be with me, say that. Don't hide behind this absurd—"

"It's not absurd." He jerked away. "I am bound to Elena, and she will always come first. You deserve someone like Titus – or even like Dorien – who will place you above all others. It is that simple."

"You're being ridiculous." *Where is this coming from?* "I love you, Ivan. I can't choose—"

"We should get back to Elena," Ivan interrupted, taking off down the cobbled street, his coat flapping around his long legs as he widened the distance between us.

I just told a boy I loved him for the first time, and he ran away from me.

I raced after Ivan, my mind a tornado. The three Broken Muses sent my thoughts into a tailspin. The weight of my history with Dorien shrouded everything that passed between us, and I knew that as much as I hated him now, I'd never stop loving him. Then there was Titus, the impossibly kind boy who shed his skin around me and became completely and fully himself and encouraged me to do the same. And Ivan… Ivan of the glacier eyes, who wasn't made of ice at all, but who felt everything *too* keenly. Ivan who believed that he hadn't earned the right to love and be loved.

I didn't know how to show him that was bullshit. Especially not when he made a perfectly valid point. When Dorien told me that the three Muses wanted to share me, I'd accepted it readily because it was a fucking dream come true. This… harem I'd acquired was the least weird of all the things that had happened at Manderley, and all three of them lit up my body and my heart.

But it wasn't realistic. It was Manderley's dark magic corrupting us, making us believe in a future that couldn't be. I couldn't keep all three Muses. It would only end in all four of our hearts torn to shreds.

The time will come when I'll have to choose one of them. But who will it be?

30

FAYE

Christmas in Prague was even more magical than I could have anticipated. Snow blanketed the city, and delicious smells of warming stews, trdelníks, and roasted nuts wafted from every corner. We went to a carol service in St. Nicholas Cathedral – the massive Baroque nave packed to bursting with people holding candles and singing carols. I didn't see our guard friend anywhere, thankfully. Afterward, Ivan and I got mulled wine (fruit lemonade for him) and warm trdelníks filled with ice cream and wandered back through St. Charles' Square to watch the astronomical clock chime the hour.

Ivan had been distant since his outburst, and I could see his grim thoughts weighing heavy on his mind. We continued our sightseeing around the city, keeping our conversations light and free of drama. He avoided touching me and stood two feet away from me at all times. We accidentally brushed together on a crowded tram, and a flame of heat engulfed my body. I wanted to finish what we'd started in the church, in the steampunk room above *Engine Ward*, but I didn't know how to bring Ivan back to me.

The constant presence of Master Radcliffe weighed on us

both. I couldn't believe I'd ever respected him. He fawned over Elena, treating her like a spoiled princess. She lapped it up, but I could see it was a ploy to keep him at arms' length. As long as he believed her to be an innocent porcelain doll who couldn't read a city map, let alone walk around the corner to purchase her own toiletries, he would not touch her. But I knew their engagement loomed – Radcliffe had been patient with Elena and with Madame Usher, but soon he would demand his bride.

After Prague, we boarded a train to Romania. For the first leg of the journey, Master Radcliffe had booked a private compartment for himself and Elena. Ivan and I had seats in first class, facing each other across a table. I drank Czech beer and we played cards as the landscape rolled by. Sometimes, Ivan would stop, his eyes darting to the window, and his whole body would go rigid. Every time the train guard walked past, Ivan would drop his eyes to the table. I knew he was remembering the night of their failed escape. I wished he'd talk to me, but when I tried to bring it up, he shut down.

We changed trains in Vienna. The next train wasn't nearly as comfortable, and we all had to sit together around a narrow table – Ivan and I on one side, and Elena and Master Radcliffe on the other. Ivan stared daggers at Radcliffe for the whole trip – the master kept shifting in his seat, uncomfortable under Ivan's relentless gaze.

Good. He should feel awkward. Pervert.

We arrived at the station in Sighisoara in the early morning and alighted, making our way past an Orthodox cathedral and over a river. Ivan pointed to a towering church on top of the hill. "There is the Old Town, built by Transylvanian Saxon merchants as a commercial and strategic center."

The Saxon medieval heart of the city was so beautiful, it took my breath away. Snow dusted the sloping roofs and piled in the corners of steep cobbled streets. Everywhere were tiny shops crammed into alleyways and beneath stone arches selling t-shirts and mugs bearing the epically-mustached visage of Vlad Tepes. Restaurants lined a cobbled square where musicians and street performers added to the otherworldly atmosphere. Men in medieval garb and vampire capes walked between carts serving hot food and jugs of mead, ringing bells to advertise walking tours in a range of languages.

I couldn't help but think of Dorien, and how much he'd enjoy the campiness of the vampire schtick. In a souvenir shop, I fingered a garish t-shirt of a vampire bat grinning with a pair of googly eyes.

"Who's that for?" Ivan asked as the shopkeeper wrapped up my t-shirt.

"No one," I answered as I rang up the purchase. Buying Dorien a tacky souvenir didn't mean I'd forgiven him.

We made our way through the square, past a sign advertising 'Vlad Tepes' birthplace,' (Ivan informed me with a laugh that it was a complete farce). The twins' mother lived in a ramshackle house on the edge of the old town, consisting of three rooms and an attic for storage. Their father died not long after they were sent to America. Madame Usher's regular payments helped keep the house, and Elena and Ivan sent as much of their meager funds as they could spare back to help keep their mother afloat. It was another way Madame Usher kept them tied to Manderley, and I could see from the love shining in their eyes they would never leave her with nothing.

She was an older woman with arthritis in her hands, though tall and strong. She kissed my cheeks and insisted upon serving tea. She didn't speak a word of English, and Radcliffe and I sat mute while Elena talked a mile a minute and Ivan frowned into his cup.

After tea, we visited their father's grave. He was buried in the cemetery behind the church Ivan had pointed out on the top of the hill. Up close, the church's gothic shape seemed at odds with the serene Saxon cemetery spilling down the hill behind it.

"This is a beautiful place to rest," I said to Ivan's mother as I placed flowers on the modest gravestone. It really was – from here, their father had a view out across the city and to the formidable mountains beyond. She did not understand me, but she sensed the meaning of my words for she linked arms with me and chatted all the way.

We had a hotel overlooking the main square, where tents were being set up and a bonfire built for New Year's Eve festivities. Ivan and I watched them while I called Titus and updated him on our travels.

"How's Mom?"

Titus didn't answer right away. "Dangerous."

"How so?"

"She snuck us both out of the hospital last night," Titus said. "She found some underground salsa club where she insisted on dancing all night before jumping in with the band. I had to drag her away to get her back in her bed before Dr. Nelson started her rounds. I've never had a hangover this bad in my life. Your mother is something else."

"I know. She's wicked."

"And so are you. I miss you," Titus said, and I could hear the sincerity in his voice. "I wish you were here to rub my temples and cook me hangover food."

"Not likely. The men in my life cook their own hangover food. And I miss you, too." I thought of Ivan's harsh words the other night, and my stomach twisted at the thought that I might not be able to keep all three of my muses. How could I give up Titus? How could I give up any of them... even Dorien?

"I dread to think what your mother has in store for me for New Year's Eve," Titus moaned. "I'm not sure I'm cut out for a de Winter."

I hung up and pulled on a long-sleeved wool wrap dress that hugged my curves in the best possible way. It was crimson, of course. We invited Elena to come out with us, but she and Master

Radcliffe had disappeared somewhere. She sent Ivan a text saying she'd meet up with us in the square after dinner.

Ivan and I toured the Dracula 'museum' – which was a dark room above a restaurant containing an old coffin and some dusty candelabras. As we moved around the coffin, a guy hiding inside leaped up and cried "blah!" and I nearly wet myself. I had to give him two euros to take a selfie with him. It was completely ridiculous, but it put Ivan in a great mood. We shared a platter of grilled meats and sausage and blood-themed cocktails at the bar downstairs, and Ivan couldn't stop mimicking my yelp after the guy jumped at me. He kept lunging at me, mimicking Count Dracula and collapsing into giggles. It was so completely adorable I almost forgave him for the relentless mocking.

Almost.

But as the night wore on, Ivan's agitation returned. He kept checking his watch and glancing toward our hotel. I knew he was thinking about Elena. The music in the square was in full swing when Elena appeared, alone, wearing a jersey dress over black leggings and an enormous fur-lined coat with sleeves that hung down past her fingers.

"Where have you been?" Ivan demanded.

Elena replied in Romanian. Ivan snapped at her, but she dismissed him with a laugh. She dragged us into the square as crowds of young people moved to join the dancing in front of a folk band.

She took my hands and the three of us spun giddily, stomping our feet and swaying our hips to the lively, hypnotic music. I dared to think that things might be mending between Ivan and Elena, that the wild abandon of the dance had shaken our secrets loose. Then Elena stopped, dragging us underneath an archway in a dark corner of the square.

"I have to tell you something," Elena said. Even though I gasped for breath after the dancing and my hair was plastered across my face in sticky clumps, the dancing had put a little color into her cheeks, making her even more radiant. "I need you to be happy for me. I cannot live if you are not happy."

Beside me, Ivan stiffened.

Elena held her head high. She slipped her hand from the pocket of her coat and held it up. The light glittered off a diamond engagement ring.

"Maxim asked me tonight, over a candlelit dinner. I have said yes. We will marry at the end of term," Elena spoke in a breathless whisper, her voice choked with emotion.

Ivan's fist pounded the wall. "No. You can't."

"You had to know this was inevitable. Why else would he pay for this trip? He wanted to ask Mother's permission and do everything right." Elena said. "It is a formality, of course. I have said yes to him, Ivan. I must say yes."

I tried to read Ivan's temper, but he'd retreated into his ice cave where I couldn't reach him. His body went stiff, and he stared at his sister as if he didn't know her at all.

"Do you want to marry him?" I asked. "Are you in love with him?"

"He is a good man," Elena said, but the way she pursed her lips and drew her eyes away, I knew the truth. She did not believe her own words. She was afraid.

"You have a choice," I said. "This isn't the fucking seventeenth century. Girls can make their own way in the world."

"What would you both have me do?" Elena threw up her hands. "If Madame Usher throws us out, we are penniless. The only thing Ivan and I can do is play music, and one word from her, and our names are mud in classical circles. For over a decade I've let Ivan protect me, watching him suffer to keep me safe and happy. It's time I did something for him. If marrying Maxim frees us both from our cage, then I will do it a thousand times over."

"But you're leaving one cage to enter another," I begged. Ivan stared at a spot behind my head. He'd gone a million miles away.

"Do not shackle yourself to this man. Give us time, and we'll destroy Madame Usher."

Elena shook her head. "It is a foolish dream, Faye. You are just like Dorien, consumed by ancient ghosts and fiendish plots. You believe we are all characters in one of those horror films you love so much – that we'll triumph because we are good. But this is real life, and there's no good and evil. I'm not the pure virgin who needs saving, and I've already given too much of my life to that vicious woman. I *want* to play music. I *want* to travel the world and bathe under the brightest lights of the concert halls of Europe. I am fading away behind the walls of Manderley, and my brother is killing himself protecting me from every shadow." Her eyes swiveled to her brother. "Don't you see? If I marry Maxim, I don't need you any longer. You are released from your burden and you can have your own life."

"I don't have a life without you," Ivan's words rasped, harsh and cold with concealed pain.

"It is done," she said. Her hand fell on his shoulder, and she pulled her brother into her embrace. He did not return it, standing as stiff and still as a corpse. Elena's words turned over in my mind as I watched her try to call her brother back from his dark place, and I could see the situation as she did. How even a loveless marriage to an old goat could look tempting if it meant escaping Manderley's walls.

But what I couldn't shake was the look in Elena's eyes – that look of cold calculation. That look of dread. Elena Nicolescu had no intention of making an old man her husband, of that I was certain. What I didn't know was what she planned to do about it.

31

FAYE

I never thought I'd say it, but after Elena's announcement, I couldn't wait to return to Manderley. Ivan had been in a rotten mood, unable to hide his hostility toward Master Radcliffe or to deal with his feelings about me even a little. In Bucharest, we toured the Palace of Parliament and took in the Romanian National Opera, but the thrill of travel had lost its spark.

You want to know what's not fun? A fourteen-hour flight and two-hour car journey sitting between twins who aren't talking to each other. When I opened the car door at Manderley, I almost bent over and kissed the rotting porch.

Titus flew out the door and swept me into his arms, laying delicious kisses along my cheek. "Your mother wished she could be here, but she got me to leave a surprise in your room – Mexican chocolates and a recording from my phone of her jamming along onstage with a mariachi band."

"Thank you," I whispered into his cornrows. I couldn't wait to hear the tale behind that video.

Footsteps sounded in the hall behind him. Madame Usher appeared out of the corner of my eyes. A rush of emotion assailed me at the sight of her – mainly loathing, mixed with the tiniest hint of pity, the way a house cat might regard a spider before tearing its legs off. "Faye, I'll see you in the Blue Room."

She disappeared before I could reply. Titus squeezed my hand. "Do you want me to come with you?"

I shook my head. "I'll be fine. I won't drink anything she offers me, and there are no stairs nearby she can push me down. What else can she do to me?"

"That sounds like the words of someone tempting fate." Titus and Ivan followed me along the hall to the Blue Room. I pushed the door open and slipped inside. I did feel safer knowing they'd be in the hallway listening to every word, ready to swoop in if I needed them.

"Sit down."

Madame Usher sat in the wingback chair in front of the fire. She indicated the chair opposite her. Unable to bring myself to obey her command, I perched on the edge of an old piano stool under the window, as far from her as it was possible to get while still being in the same room.

"It's come to my attention that your mother has woken from her coma," Madame Usher said. "The terms of our agreement were simple. I would provide care for your mother in exchange for your services as our maid. Recently, you have been lax in your duties, and your absence over the holiday period is the final straw. Now that your mother no longer requires care, I see no reason for you to continue here at Manderley."

My stomach twisted. Of everything she could have done to me, I didn't expect this. She'd gone to such lengths to keep me here while using the Muses to torture me. She'd spun a deadly web around me. Why would she suddenly snip the cords and set me free? "My mother still has underlying health issues, and she'll require ongoing treatment…"

"This is not up for debate." Madame Usher stood, smoothing down her lace dress. "You are dismissed from the academy and my service. Pack your things and have them ready by the close of school on Friday. Harrison will drive you to meet your mother. Our business will be concluded."

I stood up. "This is ridiculous. Dorien refuses to do your dirty work any more, so you decide to drop me? At least drop the pretense that you wanted me here in the first place. You had to control the last piece of Donovan de Winter's legacy because you can't handle the fact that he's dead because of you—"

"Don't you speak his name in this house," Madame's eyes raged. "You have no right to claim his legacy. You are not fit to kiss his boots, let alone share his name. You are not his daughter. You cannot be – his light would shine through you like the sun. Instead, you are dulled by the stupidity and selfishness of that bitch wife of his."

"Selfish? My mother?" I wanted to laugh. And smash her face into the hearth. Either option could win at this point. "Donovan de Winter put his career before his family. He didn't think about us once when he was out living it up on tour with money he borrowed *from the mob*. He's wearing concrete shoes at the bottom of a lake somewhere, and I couldn't be happier."

"Get out." Madame Usher shot to her feet, tipping over the tea table in front of her chair. Cups and saucers shattered on the floor. She jabbed a finger at the door. She hadn't raised her voice, but her eyes were murderous.

"With pleasure." I stood and moved toward the door, taking my time about it, letting her know that I wasn't afraid of her. "I'll be glad to be rid of this place."

I slammed the door behind me, enjoying the way the antiques stacked in the hallway rattled. From somewhere in the wall behind me I heard a groan, like someone keening over a broken heart. But it was just the house re-settling.

I sucked in a deep breath, then another, trying to formulate a plan. A figure stepped out of the storage room, where I'd picked up the Becker violin that had got me into such trouble with Madame Usher.

Heather.

"Good riddance to bad trash," Heather twirled a strand of honey-blonde hair around her finger, making no secret of the fact she'd been listening in. "Count yourself lucky that you're walking out of here alive. I had different plans for you, but sounder voices prevailed."

"Stay classy, Heather." I grinned at her to show her I didn't care, but her words rattled me. *Did she just threaten my life? I don't want to leave the Muses alone with her.*

Heather stepped forward, and I noticed she held a violin in her hands. It wasn't her usual instrument, but the infamous Becker. Something about seeing it in her hands triggered a blip in my mind – a memory that I couldn't quite grasp. Heather lifted the Becker to her chin and played a funeral dirge. "You may be free of Manderley, trash, but I'd watch your back if I were you. The Temple will find you under whichever rock you crawl beneath. They don't appreciate having their plans interrupted. They'll make sure you pay."

32

TITUS

"She can't do this," I growled to Ivan. We crouched around the corner near the Blue Room, with our backs pressed up against the wall. There was a crack in the paneling here where a draft sliced through, and it meant we could hear most of what was said inside. It also made the hairs on the back of my neck stand up, but whether that was from the cold air or Madame Usher's chilling words, I couldn't tell. "She can't send Faye away."

"Of course she can," Dorien muttered, from his own crouched position a little further down the wall. "We can't stop her."

I stood up, my fingers curling into fists. I'd never been a violent person, but at that moment, I wanted to knock Dorien's stupid, smug head off.

"Madame Usher is kicking Faye out of Manderley." I could barely get the words out through my rage. "She'll be gone by Friday."

"Isn't this what you wanted all along?" Ivan's eyes flashed as he swung around to confront Dorien. "Isn't this what the whole year has been about? You and Heather would convince Faye she's being haunted so she runs as far from Manderley as she can get."

Dorien squeezed his eyes shut. "I only went along with it because I thought she'd be safer far from Manderley."

"That's not what you said to us. You wanted to scare and intimidate her into leaving, instead of admitting to her the truth." Fuck, I hated him. "You might've been friends as kids, but if you thought that would work, you don't know Faye de Winter at all."

"Yeah, well, maybe I was fucking lying to myself," Dorien snapped. "But it was never about me. I never wanted any of this. You know what Madame Usher has over me."

"She has something over all of us," Ivan shot back. "We didn't use that as an excuse to drug Faye and dump her in the woods."

"You're right." Dorien turned his face away. "I should have talked to you both. I should have gone to the FBI earlier, when Rochester first contacted me. I shouldn't have pushed Ivan and Elena onto a train in Prague. I failed everyone, especially Faye and Jacob. Heather had me by the balls. She threatened to take guardianship of Jacob, and I... I get tunnel vision when it comes to him. I didn't see a way out."

"How would Heather even do that, though?" I demanded. "She's not related to Jacob."

"Simple. Usher gets her lapdog Walpole to put me away for assault. Heather swoops in as a 'concerned friend of the family,' and since my parents are bonkers and we don't have any other family who'd take him, she'll end up with custody. She knows I won't leave him, so I'm bound to her forever." Dorien laughed bitterly. "That's how this will go down as soon as they hear the FBI is involved, but believe it or not, I think it's the lesser of two evils. I think Father Aaron is gearing up for some Jonestown-level bullshit, and I want Jacob far away from him."

"Maybe it's for the best." I slumped against the wall, wishing I had some weed to take the edge off this blow. I *wanted* to hate Dorien, but we'd been friends for so long that I understood his fucked-up logic. I'd do anything for my brother, too. The real evil supervillain here was Madame Usher, and playing us off each other was part of her plot. "If Faye leaves Manderley, at least she's no longer in danger from Madame Usher. I've got money in the bank, I'll help her find a place, pay her mother's medical bills. My parents adore her – I bet they'd even let her stay with us—"

Dorien shook his head. "Faye's mother was poisoned outside of these walls, and someone broke into the hospital to write 'leave' on her face. I don't believe she's safe *anywhere*."

I buried my face in my hands.

Sound the fucktrumpets, as Faye would say.

"Faye needs us more than ever," Dorien said. "And she needs us united. I know I've been a fucking little shit, and you're both completely justified in punching me in the nuts and never speaking to me again, but will you do this with me? Will you help me bring down Manderley Academy?"

I slid my hands away and stared up at Dorien. He held out his hand to me, palm facing up. His mouth – which usually formed a self-satisfied smirk – turned up at one end into a nervous half-smile. Our history etched across his features. Broken Muse had been one of a kind. We'd tasted true power from the stage – we captured the stars in our music and played beautiful melodies that told of terrible things. We spoke a language that transcended speech – the literature of the heart. Together, we conjured the more enduring and elusive form of magic. Yet all along, one woman wielded an even greater power over us, and she was using that power to destroy the one thing we all loved.

Fuck that. I wouldn't let our ruined friendship with Dorien stand in the way of protecting Faye. Ivan looked to me for guidance – he'd do whatever I agreed, although I noticed he'd shifted his foot back, as if preparing to knee Dorien in the nuts. As tempting as that was…

I reached up and accepted Dorien's hand. "Count us in. Madame Usher will never hurt Faye again."

33

FAYE

Titus and Ivan wanted to spend the final night with me, but it felt wrong somehow. I'd come to Manderley alone, and I needed to spend my last night in that attic room – the same room Clare Fairbanks lived her final days – alone.

Only I wasn't completely alone. The mournful, haunting music wafted through the wall between my bedroom and the storage room. The tune had become such a fixture of my life here that I didn't find it threatening any longer, although I still wish I knew where it came from. I no longer believed it was Heather – she would have quit long ago when I failed to react to it. The music felt as though contained some vital clue meant for my ears only – a message that I hadn't figured out how to decode.

It bugged the hell out of me that I'd never got to the bottom of Manderley's secrets, but I wasn't done yet. I had my mother to care for now, and I'd have to get a job or seven to have a hope in hell of keeping her alive. But I still had the Muses. I would still dig into Manderley's secrets. I would solve this mystery.

I will get justice for my mom. I will save Broken Muse from the prison of their secrets.

I stayed in bed as long as I dared. Fuck going downstairs to make breakfast. I wouldn't find Titus in the kitchen, his delicious fingers moving over my hips while I bent to get something from the fridge. There would be no Ivan peering at me from across the table, those icicle eyes exposing my darkest urges. I would no longer pass Dorien in the halls and catch a whiff of his hypnotic scent – cinnamon and frankincense, dappled with sweet violets – that assaulted my senses with the weight of our history.

I showered for the last time in the tiny bathroom, pulling my hair back into a messy bun. I pulled on a pair of jeans and a red V-neck I knew made my tits look amazing. I wrapped my black trench coat around my shoulders, balled up Madame Usher's itchy wool dress, and tossed it into the trash, stomping it down.

I picked up a picture of Mom and me, the one I'd found in my old photo album and had framed. I debated throwing it out the window, watching the glass smash in all directions across the cobbles of the kitchen garden. But no, Madame Usher would only force Ivan or Elena out there to pick up the glass. No matter what I did, she still owned them.

But she no longer owned me.

I tucked the picture on top of the *Grimm's Fairy Tales* book – the only memory of my father I wanted to keep. I threw my duffel over my shoulder, picked up my violin case, and shuffled down the narrow attic steps.

Manderley stood silent – no sounds of utensils scraping and tinkling glasses from the dining room, no ghostly notes from behind the closed doors of the practice room. The grandfather clock in the entrance hall counted down to my expulsion.

My fingers gripped the balustrade as I descended the staircase. Slowly, they came into view. Everyone in the house had gathered to see me off. Nine pairs of eyes watched me – some glowed in triumph (Heather) while others glistened with tears (Elena) or drew heavy with resignation (Harrison). I couldn't bear to look at Titus or Ivan or Dorien – I wouldn't give Madame Usher the pleasure of seeing me burst into tears.

At the bottom of the stairs, Master Radcliffe greeted me with a kiss on both cheeks. "Goodbye, Faye. It has been a pleasure to teach you. I hope you will continue with your musical career."

I didn't say anything. I knew if I opened my mouth, I would call him all sorts of words I'd regret. I didn't want to hate him – he'd been kind to me, and I knew that he was trapped here like the rest of them, weighed down by some terrible secret Gizella Usher waved over his head – his own personal sword of Damocles. I knew that Elena was his ticket out from Madame Usher's thumb. But then Elena's engagement ring caught the light, and I remembered that look of dread on her face back in Romania. I recoiled from his touch.

Elena stepped forward now, pressing her face into my neck. "I love you," she whispered.

"I love you, too," I whispered back, burying my face in her hair.

Heather smirked at me. She hung off Dorien's arm, although he shrunk from her like she smelled bad. Over the last day as I packed up my things, I noticed him talking quietly with Ivan and Titus. I asked Titus if they were friends again, and he said, "as much as anyone can be friends with a selfish prick like Dorien." Which I guess meant yes. I hated how happy that made me feel. The three of them needed to look out for each other while I wasn't here.

Beside Heather, Aroha had her hands shoved in the pockets of a black hoodie. She stepped forward, touching her nose to mine as her father had done. "Kia Kaha, Faye. That means, 'stand strong.'"

I nodded again. I sensed that part of Aroha was trying to reach out. She saw in me something of herself. I'd forgiven worse things from Dorien. But now I'd never get the chance to connect with her.

Next, it was Titus and Ivan. They enveloped me into their arms, embracing me together, their cheeks pressed against mine, their fingers stroking my skin, reminding me that they would always fight for me. That we were a family. That I had their love to shine a light in the darkness.

"I'll find a way to save you," I whispered to Ivan.

"Maybe it will be us who save you," he whispered back.

Dorien flung off Heather's arm and surged toward me. "Sprite," he said.

That one word was enough. The tears I promised myself I wouldn't cry itched at the corners of my eyes. I swallowed hard and turned away from him. I heard the sharp intake of his breath and knew I'd hurt him, but I couldn't touch him or look at him right now. Dorien would undo me completely, as only he could.

"This farewell is needlessly drawn out." Madame sniffed. "Harrison, you should be going. I'd hate for you to be driving the treacherous roads in the dark."

Harrison reached down to pick up my bag. As he did, an antique vase sailed over the railing from the second floor and smacked into his skull.

He fell to his knees, clutching the side of his head and moaning. The vase bounced into the corner of the side table and exploded into a million pieces. Heather and Aroha leaped back as shards of pottery flew across their feet.

"Harrison!" I ran to his side, trying to inspect the wound. Blood spurted between his fingers, and he let out a low moan. "Someone call an ambulance."

"Don't be ridiculous. He's just—" But Madame's words cut off when a second vase hurtled through the air. She dived for cover just as the vase hit the wall behind her, where her head had been only a moment before.

What the fuck?

A picture came next. The corner of the gilt frame slammed into the floor, scratching a deep gash along the polished floorboards before it toppled over, sending more fragments of glass skittering across the floor. Heather screamed as a bust of Beethoven flew at her head. She dived away, sheltering under the stairs as torn scorebook pages fluttered down in a tsunami of confetti and destruction.

Objects, paintings, and a bronze horse figurine flew from the balcony above, raining down on us. Ivan grabbed my hand and dragged me under the stairs. The others crowded in around us, pressing hard against the wall. Still, the destruction continued as precious antiques smashed on top of each other, grinding their remains into the floorboards.

The fury of it stilled me – every time a new object dented the walls or smashed against the floor, Madame Usher shuddered a little, as though her body had been assaulted.

But who's doing it?

We were all here – all of us. Heather huddled beside me, her skin pale with fear. Aroha stood stoic at the back of the group, her hood pulled up around her dark hair. Dorien tried to creep closer to me, but Ivan and Titus placed themselves between us. Elena had her arms around a trembling Harrison while Master Radcliffe tried to speak words of hollow comfort. Madame Usher's sickly floral perfume choked us all as she stared at the carnage with pursed lips.

Who's throwing this shit over the stairs? Who could—

It stopped.

The house fell silent and still, the only movement the swirl of plaster dust rising from the debris in the hall.

The grandfather clock ticked.

My heart roared in my ears.

"What the *fuck?*" Heather screeched.

Dorien was the first to step out into the open. He picked up the edge of a frame and held up the corner. It was the portrait of the Ushers from Madame's office. The glass had shattered and the frame bent, and a shard of wood from a serving tray pierced the canvas right over Victor's head.

"You have to call the police," Heather cried. "Harrison, get your gun. There's an intruder in the house. You have to—"

"That will not be necessary." Madame glared at the pile of broken antiques, her chest heaving. "Harrison, fetch the broom."

"But Madame, he needs a hospital—"

"Not another word from any of you." Madame turned her face to the ceiling, and there was something in her features I'd never seen before. Something that on any other human might've been read as fear. "The ghost of Manderley has spoken. Faye shall stay with us."

34

FAYE

"What in the fucktrumpets is going on?"

I paced across Ivan and Elena's floor, wringing my hands. My boot kicked a pile of Elena's makeup, sending tubes of lipstick skittering across the floor.

I waited for a response, but none came. Ivan's lips remained in a tight line, while Titus sat at the window, sucking on a joint like it would divine the answers. Elena sat at her dressing table, applying lipstick to her perfect lips. Her hand trembled so much she was starting to look like the world's hottest jittery fairy clown.

"That… was impossible." Ivan crossed the room and sat beside his sister, wrapping his arms around her shoulders. She rested her head on his shoulder.

"We were all under the stairs," Elena whimpered. "Who could have been throwing those things?"

Titus glared at Dorien. "Fess up. How did you do it?"

"I didn't." Dorien threw his hands in the air, his eyes fixing on mine. "I swear, Sprite. I had nothing to do—"

"So when you declared that Faye needs us and that we should

bring down Manderley, that was just you waving your dick around?"

I glanced between the three Muses. "You guys are... friends again?"

"Not friends," Ivan muttered.

"We agreed that if we're going to stop Madame Usher from hurting anyone else, we're better off working together," Titus added, taking another long drag. "Which is why I'm surprised Dorien immediately went off and pulled this stunt without telling us—"

"I had nothing to do with it—"

"I believe you." I swallowed. "I'm going to tell you guys something, and you're going to think I'm crazy, but..."

Titus leaned forward, the joint dangling from his lips. "Go ahead."

"Right before Dorien and Heather drugged me, I saw Clare. She was standing in front of the door to my room. I could see right through her."

"Could it have been a trick of the light, like when you thought you saw her face on the stairs?" Titus sounded hopeful.

"See..." I wrung my hands. "I wonder if I actually *did* see her face there, too. I also saw her when I was walking back to Manderley and found the Usher mausoleum. I kept trying to convince myself it was a trick. That I was scared and cold. That I'd had too much of whatever Dorien used to knock me out. But today was no trick. And there have been other things – the music I hear at night, my father's book appearing in the Yellow Room. My violin being smashed. Dorien said he didn't do it and now... I think I believe him. And today..."

"Are you saying you think Clare's ghost is haunting Manderley, and she threw all that stuff to convince Madame to let you stay?"

"I don't know!" I threw up my hands. "I don't believe in ghosts. All I know is what I've seen and heard, and what we all saw today. Weird stuff has been happening ever since I came to Manderley, and it seems to be getting worse. It's as if... something has shifted. Madame Usher's power over this place is cracking, and through the cracks all this stuff is—what the hell are you doing?"

Dorien surged toward me, holding out his phone. "Read it."

Ivan's eyes narrowed at the screen. "What is it?"

Dorien jabbed his finger at the file's title. *Concerning the Fall of the House of Usher.* I had to crack a smile. Dorien could never resist a chance to be dramatic. He scrolled through lists and doodles and dates and images. "It's all my research on the strange things going on in this house, and on your mother's poisoning."

"What do you know about it?" I asked.

"When you told me about the tea, *In Cauda Venenum*, I started hunting around." Dorien zoomed in one of the photographs. "Clare and I found a case of old Victorian apothecary bottles in her room in the attic. That's where we got the syrup of ipecac I used to make you sick that first night. There was a notebook too, with observations about different drugs and their properties. There was a whole chapter on poisons, and another on birthing aids. The weird thing is, that book disappeared, along with several of the bottles. I thought Clare kept them, but now I'm not so sure. And I never put it together before you told me about the birthwort, but what happened to your mother sounds *exactly* like Victor's symptoms leading up to his death."

"Holy fuck," Titus breathed. "You're right."

I narrowed my eyes. "What do you mean?"

Dorien scrolled down to a list he made. "Victor started to complain of stomach pains. He could hardly eat anything, and sometimes he'd double over during lessons. He was so weak that he couldn't climb the stairs to the private wing, so Madame Usher moved him to a suite of rooms on the ground floor. She brought herbalists from all over the world to the house. They gave him tinctures and teas to help him, and put him on strict diets Clare had to prepare. Every meal Madame Usher would take the food from Clare and deliver it to Victor herself. We weren't allowed to see him, and she spent every moment she wasn't in lessons at his bedside, until one day, she emerged and told us he was dead."

"You think Madame Usher killed her husband?"

"There's only one way to find out. An autopsy was never performed, and no one suggested anything other than natural causes. But if your Dr. Nelson could test his tissues for traces of birthwort..." A smile tugged at the corner of Dorien's mouth. "What do you say, Sprite? Fancy a little grave-digging?"

35

TITUS

*A*fter our meeting broke up, we all drifted our separate ways, too restless to commit ourselves to much. No one saw Madame Usher for the rest of the day, but we could hear shouting and objects smashing from within her private quarters. Twice, I stood in front of that locked door, debating the intelligence of breaking the door down under the pretense of seeing if she was okay, but both times I backed away.

"Do you think we should move you into one of our bedrooms?" I asked Faye. "Or one of us will sleep in the attic with you. I don't like the idea of you being alone at night if Clare's ghost is hanging around."

Faye shook her head. "If I really am being haunted by Clare, she's on my side. I feel safe with her. Besides, I kind of like it up there. It has personality, and it makes me feel like I'm the heroine in a gothic horror film. We all know the heroine is the only one who survives."

I couldn't argue with that logic.

Faye was right – something had shifted in Manderley. It was as if, with that display, the house had disgorged some kind of secret and it was now shrinking within itself. The high ceilings and gilded portraits that had always felt vaguely threatening to me now seemed smaller, almost homely. The shadows in the corners had dissipated. The grandness of the place had faded behind the cracked stone and peeling paint. It didn't hurt that many of the antiques were gone now, dashed to smithereens by our ghostly protector.

Perhaps because I grew up in New Orleans, where the living and the dead existed side-by-side, but I was more willing than anyone else to accept the idea that Clare was still with us. Dorien was having an emo moment about it, and Ivan was just… Ivan.

Faye pulled burgers and buns out of the freezer, and I made my mother's famous fried chicken and slaw. The five of us ate dinner around the kitchen table, warmed by the heat from the fire. Ivan brought in a couple of bottles of port from the Red Room cabinet and poured generous glasses for everyone but himself. No one stopped us.

I was admiring Faye wrapping her gorgeous lips around a huge piece of chicken when I sensed someone standing behind me. I turned to see Aroha leaning against the doorway. "Hey."

"Fuck off," Ivan growled.

Faye held up a hand before Ivan could say more. She swallowed her bite. "Would you like to join us?"

Aroha took a step forward, then seemed to think the better of it. "Don't you all hate me? I tried to burn your hand."

"Why don't you tell us why you did it, and then we'll decide if it's worthy of hate?" Faye said. "I'm interested."

Aroha shrugged. "It's the whole *place*, you know? You met my parents. They're so *desperate* for me to fit into this world, but I don't and I don't want to. None of you know what it feels like to walk into a room and be the only brown girl there. To know that your skin is seen, but you aren't. You all *fit* here. You make sense. I don't, and I thought I was okay with that. I'm proud of my history, my culture, but I also fucking miss home. I want to write and perform music, but I didn't realize how lonely that path would be."

"You want music on your terms," Faye said.

"Right." Aroha nodded. "And I know you're thinking, what did you expect, enrolling in a stuffy, upper-crust school like Manderley? Because I've come from a long line of warriors, but I'm fucking terrified of going on stage. I wanted to confront that. I thought if I could master Manderley, I could do *anything*. But I'm not mastering Manderley. I'm falling to pieces. And you know sometimes when you're falling into pieces, you want to drag others with you? That's me, guilty as charged. Faye looked like an easy target. I know you won't believe me, but right up until Ivan pulled me away, I didn't believe Heather was really going to burn your hand. I thought we were just giving you a fright. But then I saw her face when Titus stopped her, and I realized that bitch be crazy. I'd hitched my horse to the wrong cart."

Ivan met my eyes, unconvinced. I didn't want to trust Aroha either, but it wasn't up to me. Faye patted the seat beside her. "Try the chicken. It's delicious."

Aroha sat, gingerly, on the edge of the stool. "I tried to burn your hand."

"And I haven't fucking forgotten it," Faye said. "We're not friends. Yet. But everyone in this room has done fucked up shit they're not proud of, so you're allowed to sit with us. Titus, pour her a glass of port. We're celebrating. It's a new era of Manderley."

I watched Faye as she passed burgers around the room, her wild hair streaming down her back, her head tossed back as she laughed at something Aroha said. I saw again what she'd learned from her mother – to be big and bold and beautiful, but the biggest thing of all was her heart.

Across the room, my eyes met Dorien's, and I read his mind in those grey storms. If Faye could find it in herself to begin to forgive Aroha, then could she – *would* she – forgive him?

～

"Ｙou don't have to watch this," I grunted as I leaned my weight against the heavy stone lid, using the wall of the Usher mausoleum as leverage as I shoved the carved lid open a quarter of an inch.

I'd rarely visited the mausoleum. Dorien and I occasionally stumbled into the clearing when we took drunken walks in the forest, which wasn't often because that place was spooky. And filled with bugs. Honestly, we were indoor dudes. Ivan had explored more of the forest trails, but even he tended to steer clear of the mausoleum. We hadn't even come down here for Victor's internment. The place was creepy as fuck.

Faye twirled a lock of hair around her finger. "You assume because I'm a girl I can't stomach a little grave desecration? Step aside, Thibodeaux, I want a piece of the action."

I obeyed. Faye assumed my position, her back against the lid. She planted her feet on the edge of the step and pushed.

Absolutely nothing happened.

"Okay, fine." She slumped against the coffin, sweat glistening on her brow. "Maybe I'm more of a 'hold the flashlight while my boyfriends desecrate the grave' kind of girl."

Ivan handed her the flashlight. "Together?" I asked. He nodded. The two of us planted our hands against the lid and kicked off from the wall. A cloud of dust and dead leaves blew up around us as we scrambled for purchase. I strained, and Ivan growled, and we managed to shove the broken lid open a foot – wide enough for our purposes.

I bent down, knife and tweezers and baggies ready to collect tissue samples. Ivan grunted as he gave the lid a final shove. Faye leaned over and aimed the flashlight beam. A stale smell rushed out to meet me and—

"What the fuck?"

We peered into the tomb.

It was empty. Victor Usher was not inside.

FAYE

"Where the hell is his body?"

The four of us huddled together under the gazebo. Titus' arms fell around my shoulders, and from the way Dorien kept looking at him, I knew he was jealous as fuck. I wished that didn't affect me so much, but it did. I'd never had guys fight over me before, and it gave me a little thrill. At least, until Ivan's words echoed in my head. *We can't all be with you.* He'd been remote ever since we got back from Europe, never being in the same room alone with me. And it knew it was his way of trying to influence my choice. But I didn't want to choose. I wanted all three of them – even Dorien. I was a selfish bitch like that.

"Maybe Madame Usher had it removed precisely so that no one could gather evidence from it," Dorien suggested.

My face fell in my hands. "It doesn't matter. That was our shot at proving she poisoned both Victor and my mother, and it's gone."

"Not necessarily." Dorien dug out his phone. "I might be able to do something."

"What now?" I wasn't sure the world was ready for another of Dorien's cunning plans.

"My contact in the FBI is looking into Madame Usher for us. I know it's a risk because Madame bought off the police. That's why I didn't tell him about the poisoning."

"You should have talked to us before you told him *anything*," Ivan growled. "These are our lives you're messing with. What if he's on her payroll? What if he goes straight to her?"

"He hasn't done that yet, or we'd know about it. But you're right. I shouldn't have done it. I played all our cards because I trust this guy. I think he'll come through for us, but in case he doesn't, we've got Faye's creepy stalker friend – the one who so generously emptied my bank account for a worthy cause."

"Cory?" I hadn't expected his name to come up. "What could he do?"

"He could dig into Madame Usher's accounts, maybe cause a little chaos." Dorien's eyes were a storm of mischief. "It's your decision, Faye. If you want to do it, make the call. Otherwise, we'll keep digging around."

I remembered the horrible, crawling feeling of Creepy Cory's eyes on me as I moved around the bar where we used to work. The way he'd stand too close or deliberately brush up against my breasts as we moved around each other to pour drinks. He made me feel unsafe, and I was already in the crosshairs. Having him help me with Dorien's revenge invited him back into my life. He'd blown up my Facebook with messages and pictures before I blocked him again. I didn't particularly want to open that wound.

But then I remembered huddling under the stairs as vases and painting rained down from above. I remembered the strange message scrawled in the walls of the pantry. THE WALLS ARE TALKING. And I knew that something was going on in this house that neither the FBI nor Creepy Cory could help us with.

This was always about Clare, and we've been too distracted to see it.

It's about getting justice for her. And that starts with figuring out how she died.

I nodded. "If Creepy Cory can cut off some of her resources, it might help us stay one step ahead of her. But that's not all we're going to do. We need to solve Clare Fairbanks' murder."

37

FAYE

As we trudged up the path back toward school, I felt the prickle in my neck of someone watching me. I raised my head to my room, certain now that face I'd seen in the glass all those weeks ago had been Clare. But she wasn't there.

Instead, Heather stood at the window of the Yellow Room. The light danced off her honey-blonde hair as she stared out at us.

A shiver ran down my spine. I knew that Clare's display today might have neutralized Madame Usher for a time, but Heather was still dangerous.

~

Madame Usher didn't emerge from her quarters for another week. The school term continued as though nothing had changed, although everything had.

Master Radcliffe assigned us essays on musical theory and continued our composition class and private lessons. Dorien and I worked on the piece I'd written, expanding it and building the tension, drawing out the third movement for a beautiful, haunting climax. I was starting to think that I could add instrument parts to it, that Titus and Ivan could have a place within the music, too.

Working with Dorien had me all twisted around. With every note he played and every smile he flashed, I drew a little closer to forgiving him. We reached for the same piece of scribbled score and his fingers brushed mine, sending a jolt of heat down my arm and setting the butterflies living in my stomach a-flutter.

Although we didn't speak aloud about what we'd seen and Madame Usher's decision to allow me to stay, everyone seemed to feel the ghostly attack marked the end of my servitude. Titus now helped me in the kitchen, while Ivan and Elena took charge of the cleaning duties, and we all pitched in carrying the wood for Harrison and lighting the fires. Heather tossed a mountain of filthy laundry at me in the hallway, but when I refused to clean it and it remained in a stinking pile in the middle of the landing for three days, she relented and did it herself.

Manderley had entered a new normal, an uneasy truce. But we knew a reckoning was coming. We knew Madame Usher would find a way to reclaim the power she felt she'd lost. And from the way Heather stalked the halls, glaring at each and every one of us, we knew we had made another powerful enemy.

~

All seven students gathered around the Bösendorfer grand in the ballroom for Radcliffe's composition class. As I closed my eyes to focus on his use of *appoggiatura*, I was jerked from reverie by a series of heard thumps and bangs upstairs. My eyes flew open as everyone else turned their gaze to the ceiling. I figured it was Madame Usher raging in her quarters again, but when I heard furniture being pushed across the room above, I realized someone was up there.

"That's my room." Titus stood up, his eyes wide. "Someone's in my room."

Master Radcliffe glanced up from the piano. Something flickered across his eyes – a nervous energy. *He knows what's going on.* "I'm sure it's nothing to be concerned about. It's probably Harrison stacking wood for the fires. Let us turn to the study of *glissando—*"

Titus' eyes met mine, and when I saw the pain swimming there, it hit me. His guitar was in his room. If someone found it and told his parents, something bad would happen.

I didn't know why Titus had to hide his love for metal music, but I'd protect his right to do so with my life. I rose from my chair, setting down my violin. "I think we ought to see what's going on."

Titus wasn't waiting around. He flung aside his cello and rushed to the door, twisting the handle in both directions. "It's locked."

"I'm sure it's just stuck." Master Radcliffe looked pained. "Please, Mr. Thibodeaux, return to your seat and we'll sort it out at the end of the lesson—"

Titus pounded on the door with his fists. "Let us out!"

Wind howled outside, rattling the windowpanes. Tree branches scraped against the glass, their long fingers reaching toward us. Upstairs, more furniture scraped and objects thudded against the floor. A shiver ran down my spine as the wind whispered to me, *Fayeeee...*

Dorien and Ivan were on their feet in a flash. Heather remained in her seat, the hint of a smile playing across her lips. I didn't like that smile. Not at all.

Titus upended a chair, hefting it over his shoulders like it weighed nothing. He was just about to run at the door when it fell open.

Madame Usher stood in the doorway in all her glory – her dark hair pulled back into a stern bun, her black lace dress swirling around her ankles, her stick rapping against the wood floor. A terrifyingly satisfied smile tugged at the corners of her mouth.

"Greetings, students." She swept into the room, ignoring the raised chair in Titus' hands and the expressions of confusion and anger on our faces. "I'm pleased to see you continuing your lessons during my leave of absence. Unfortunately, it has come to my attention that certain rules of this fine school are being flouted, and that is unacceptable to me. My husband Victor left this house and his endowment in my trust to carry on his legacy and reputation, and I will not have that reputation laid to waste. Therefore, I have taken the opportunity to search your rooms, and my, my, what a horde I have uncovered."

"You can't go into our rooms without permission." Aroha surged toward Madame, fists raised. Titus held her back, although he glared at Madame Usher with such a murderous expression I barely recognized my gentle giant.

Ivan and Elena exchanged a glance, an entire conversation passing between their eyes. I knew Aroha was probably worried about her drugs, but I wondered if Elena still kept a supply here.

"This is *my* house, and I'm perfectly within my rights to go where I wish and seize property that brings the name of Manderley into disrepute." Madame Usher snapped her fingers.

Harrison stepped into the room, his shoulders sagging. He held a large case, which he dropped on the rug and unlatched, swinging open the lid to reveal a gleaming guitar.

Titus' flying V.

I stepped toward Titus, reaching out to touch his hand. He was gone to me. He dropped his grip on Aroha, his whole body sagging.

But Harrison wasn't done. On top of the case, he dropped an armload of other items. I recognized Elena's makeup cases – the bright lipsticks and eye shadows she loved spilling from the plastic boxes. Stacks of old books, their pages opening to reveal poetry and scores scribbled in Dorien's distinctive hand. Pill bottles and metal Altoids cases and baggies filled with white powder. "What are you doing with those?" Aroha surged forward. "They're my prescriptions. I *need* them."

Madame Usher thrust a bottle into her face. "This is *weakness*. In my day, a musician who couldn't go on stage would be a poor musician playing alone in a prison cell. You will learn to stand on your own two feet, or you don't deserve your place at this school."

As Harrison tipped more of Aroha's drugs and Elena's sexy clothing onto the pile, I noticed the corner of a leather-bound book sticking out, the words in gold lettering shooting a jolt of pain through me.

Grimm's Fairy Tales.

That's mine. I noticed other items that belonged to me, too – my crimson dress, the jewelry box given to me on the night of the party, the photograph of me and Mom. I reached for the spine of my book, but Harrison pushed my arm away.

"There's no point, my girl," he said, sadly.

"You don't understand. That's my father's book—"

SMACK.

One moment my fingers grazed the corner of the book. The next, I was on my back on the floor, my vision reeling. Dorien stood over me, offering me a hand. I reached up to accept it, and *then* the pain arced across my skull, and I fell back, pressing my fingers into my forehead in a vain attempt to stop my brain leaking out.

Madame had hit me with her stick.

Dorien advanced on her, fists raised. "You hurt Faye. You—"

"I'd rethink the path you're on, Dorien Valencourt," she whispered. "I'd hate to have to call my friend Commissioner Walpole and inform him that you hurt a defenceless old woman. In a room with all these witnesses, I doubt even your parents' money and influence would save you. Do your parents still have money, I wonder, or have they given it all to their vegetable cult?"

Dorien's skin reddened. I thought he would explode. But he stood, impotent, his hands clenching and unclenching. A slow smile spread across Madame Usher's face. She was enjoying her revenge.

"Your parents will be informed of these transgressions," Madame Usher said. "I'm well within my rights to remove you all from this school, but I will give you one final chance. I blame myself – I've allowed you to become too comfortable here, too complacent. I've let you believe that the privileges of this house are given freely, and not earned. That stops today."

"What do you mean?" Aroha demanded.

"I have supplied you with many pleasures and concessions to make your stay here comfortable. Harrison will be removing them all today – the Egyptian cotton sheets, the snacks and fancy foods, the designer clothing, free access to the internet and telephone. None of this is required to provide education. The greatest art is created under oppression, and you with your silk robes and iPhones can't conceive of the true sacrifices one must make for art. I am your teacher, and it is my job to help you on this path. I will do it by whatever means necessary."

Behind her, Heather beamed. I couldn't help but notice nothing on Harrison's pile belonged to her.

Madame Usher turned to leave. The wind howled my name. She turned, slowly, her face carved in stone, her eyes flicking to each one of us before fixing on me.

"You'd all better fall in line," she hissed. "Or I will see each and every one of you ruined. People who dig up secrets end up at the bottom of stairs."

38

FAYE

We watched from the window in the Yellow Room as Madame Usher ordered Harrison to stack Titus' guitar case and all the other confiscated items in the center of the snow-covered lawn. On top of this, he carried down all the luxury furniture and other items from the students' rooms. I recognized the inlaid desk from Ivan and Elena's room, sections of a wooden wardrobe that had been next to Aroha's window, Titus' hookah pipe, and stacks and stacks of crimson silk shirts and combat boots I knew belonged to Dorien. Harrison piled it high – a great edifice of power and indulgence. On Madame's orders, he struck a match and held it to the pile.

Beside me, Elena gasped and buried her face in Ivan's chest. I wanted to turn away, but I couldn't. The flames caught surprisingly quickly. Fingers of orange light wrapped around the legs of tea-tables and tore into billowing silk curtains. They curled the edges of Titus' music magazines and shot out sparks as Dorien's clothes went up in smoke.

Tears streamed down my face as the pages of my father's book curled into black ash, caught on the breeze to scatter across the snow-dusted lawn – a flutter of ash and bone and wasted dreams.

The stories of my childhood – of fairy castles and violent witches – given back to the air and the forest by the wickedest witch of them all.

In the corner of the window, Ivan held Elena in his arms, the pair of them cheek-to-cheek as they watched what few possessions they owned go up in smoke. I turned to Titus, to offer him what comfort I could, but he wasn't there. The door to the Yellow Room swung with an ominous *creeeeeak*. Dorien turned at the sound, and realization passed across his stricken features. I took off toward the kitchen, Dorien at my heels.

As I flung open the backdoor, the heat slammed into me. A wall of orange flame plumed into the sky, licking dangerously close to the tree line. Smoke and ash rolled over the house, casting an apocalyptic haze over Manderley. I coughed into my sleeve as I surged forward, heading toward the Titus' shaped lump in the snow ahead of me.

Behind me, Dorien's breath stuttered.

Titus had fallen to his knees on the snow. His cornrows fanned around his face, the beads clicking together as the mountain breeze stirred through the flames. His eyes glowed as black coals – reflecting the firelight that stole his passion.

I fell to my knees beside him, wrapping my hands around his shoulders. The gesture felt so hollow, so pointless. Flames licked the edges of his guitar case, melting the plastic and rubber into dribbling, eldritch shapes. I wanted to tell Titus that he didn't have to watch, that it was only a guitar, that he would have another. But I did not believe any of it. There was something much deeper going on with him. The fire wasn't just burning his possessions – it consumed a part of his soul.

"It's over," he whispered.

"It's not over," I whispered back. "We have to be stronger than her."

Titus shook his head. He dug his mobile phone from his

pocket and pushed play. I had to hold it right against my ear to hear the voicemail message over the roar of the fire.

"Titus," Delphine's voice came through, her usual sultry tone scarred with pain. "Madame Usher has just called to inform us what she found in your room. How could you hurt us like this? After everything we've done for you. Your father won't see you, not now, maybe not ever. And I… I don't know if I can, either."

Titus clicked off the phone. His mother's words hung in the air around us. I wanted to ask the questions that had nagged at me ever since I found Titus shredding that guitar out in the woodshed, but I couldn't find the strength to ask. Not when his heart was tearing apart in front of me.

It was Titus who decided to speak. "My older brother Micah died when I was five years old." His wide shoulders sagged, and he raised his chin to the sky as if the billowing smoke gathering over Manderley might offer salvation. "He was a lot like my dad – friendly, charming, the life and soul of any party. He'd walk into a room and instantly the whole place would feel lighter. He had that way with people, you know? Now that I've met your mother, I know you understand."

I nodded. Titus tipped his head back, his cornrows a dark waterfall streaming over his shoulders.

"Micah played the cello like an angel – like the instrument was an extension of his personality. He was twelve years older than me, and he used to look after me while my parents were on tours. I adored him, and from the time I could walk I followed him everywhere. I copied his style, his mannerisms, his way of dressing, even his love of the cello. I just wanted to be him when I grew up. Micah loved all music – classical, jazz, but most of all, he loved metal. He had this old turntable in his room, and when my parents were away he'd pull out all the records he'd collected that they derided as 'filthy noise.' 'Listen to this, Titus,' he'd say, and he'd play some Black Sabbath riff over and over. 'This is what freedom sounds like.'

"It happened on his eighteenth birthday. He'd just been accepted to Juilliard, and my parents threw him a big party at home with all their music friends. He left at 6PM to go to a metal concert with some of his friends. I remember sitting on his bed while he pulled off his suit and threw on a black t-shirt with a picture of Lucifer dancing on a pile of skulls, and he laughed and kissed me on my head and said one day we'd go to a concert together."

Titus sucked in a breath. He must've got a lungful of smoky air, because he broke down into a barking cough. My eyes stung and my throat itched from the fire, but no way would I leave his side. I rubbed his back as he pushed out the words, his face streaked with tears. "We don't know exactly what happened, but there was a fight in the mosh-pit at the concert. Micah got trampled. By the time people noticed and security pulled him out of there, it was too late. He stopped breathing."

Shit.

Even though the heat roared all around us, ice seeped into my veins as I held Titus. I knew nothing I could say would repair the wounds today had opened. I could not even imagine the horror Titus and his parents had gone through, losing Micah like that.

A single tear rolled down Titus' cheek – a symbol of the tears he'd already cried, the pain he'd already endured. "My parents left his room exactly the way it was. I used to sneak in there when they were out and play his records. Listening to the music he loved made me feel closer to him. I was so young when he died that I never really got to know him, but I felt like maybe he was listening to Metallica or Iron Maiden up in heaven. It was this thing we could share even though he was gone.

"His absence sucked all the life out of our house. In public, my parents were the happy, bubbly people you met at the party. But it's like they deflate as soon as they're alone – all the color drains from their faces and they're just these grey ghosts. I didn't want to be like them; I didn't want to be grey. I wanted to be full of life and passion, like Micah. When I was twelve, I asked for an electric guitar. I'd never seen Dad so angry. They forbid me from ever mentioning it. They burned all Micah's records and t-shirts and posters, locked his room and forbade me from going in there. I've hidden my music from them ever since."

It explained so much. The battle that raged inside Titus to be both the boy that held his family together and to express himself in the way that felt real and true to him. And Madame Usher had just ripped the heart right out of that boy's chest.

Another hand fell on my shoulder. Dorien leaned down, kneeling in the grass in his designer jeans. He wrapped his arms around both of us and pressed his cheek against Titus. "I swear to you, brother. You will be free."

I wanted to believe him. But as the fire raged in front of us, the heat boring into my skin, I felt so small.

I turned back to the house, picking out figures in the windows of Manderley through the haze of smoke. Ivan and Elena stood at the Yellow Room window, clinging to each other. Aroha leaned out her bedroom window, smoking a cigarette and watching us. Heather stood at *her* window – the only student room Madame Usher hadn't ransacked – with the smirk of a cat that got *all* the cream.

And in the private wing of the house, from a window high in one of the hexagonal turrets, Madame Usher watched us with cruel eyes, her lips frozen in a thin line.

I raised my hand from Dorien's shoulder, and I flipped her the bird.

Dorien laughed, holding me tighter. His laughter mingled with the fire's crackle, becoming the roar of our rebellion. I held two Broken Muses as the ashes of Titus' beloved guitar rained down on us, sticking to tear-stained skin and turning us grey with our sorrow.

No matter what Madame Usher did to us, she would never make us grey on the inside. Not where it counted.

~

*A*s the fire died down, I picked through the ashes, searching for a page from my book I could keep, or the the ruby necklace I'd been given by a ghostly admirer the night of the party. I found a charred piece of the jewelry box lid, but no necklace inside. The fire wouldn't be hot enough to destroy the necklace, and I felt certain Madame had taken it.

Dorien managed to convince Titus to return inside. Ivan and Elena met us in the kitchen. Ivan looped his arm under Titus' other shoulder and the two of them half-guided, half-dragged him up the stairs to their rooms.

I wanted to go to him, but Dorien said he and Ivan needed to speak to Titus alone first, so I stayed in the kitchen. The door swung open and Harrison appeared, his face ashen, a pile of wood in his arms.

"How could you do that?" I whispered, my hands balled into fists.

Harrison's face fell. I felt awful. I didn't want to hate him. He stacked the wood beside the stove with a stiff back. "I didn't have a choice," he said.

"There's always a choice, Harrison."

He shook his head. "Not when the Madame is concerned. You came to Manderley knowing her history with your father. You came because she found a way to remove your choice. That's what Manderley does – and before you know it, you're trapped forever."

"Harrison…" Tears itched the corners of my eyes. "What does she have on you—"

"She says I'm to tell you that lessons will commence tomorrow, but that she expects the ballroom and practice rooms to be pristine. She does not care who does the work, but the work must be done, or worse punishments will follow—"

"I'll help you."

Ivan's voice cut through Harrison's instructions. My ice prince stood in the doorway, those blue eyes watching Harrison with wariness. Wordlessly, I collected my mop and bucket and polishing cloths, and Ivan and I moved to the Blue Room, shutting and locking the door behind us.

"How is Titus?" I whispered.

"He is sad," was the reply.

"You and Elena don't seem so surprised about what happened today. Has she done this before?"

Ivan nodded. "When we were eleven years old, we started to ask questions about why we were kept here, why we couldn't see our parents or access the money we earned from our performances. She did not like that. She needed to remind us that we have nothing and we are nothing without her. She burned everything we brought with us from Romania – including the only photographs of our parents together."

"Ivan, I'm so sorry. I wish—"

"It does not matter. It is past." Ivan grabbed a silver candlestick from the sideboard with such force, he left a scratch behind in the wood. "We should get to work. She will expect perfection."

I started to explain how to use the silver polish, but Ivan was already dabbing the liquid onto his cloth and rubbing the candlestick with the same deftness he used to play the violin. He looked away when he caught me staring. "Before Clare came to Manderley, Elena and I did most of the cleaning. Only when one of the students said something to their parents about 'child labor laws' did it occur to her to find a live-in maid."

I hated the way his shoulders slumped as he worked, how resigned he was to living out this wretched existence. I picked up a silver platter and started swiping at it vigorously, wishing it was Madame's cockpoodle head.

"What was Clare like? I want to hear about her from someone other than Dorien."

"We didn't speak to her much," Ivan said. "Madame Usher

likes things to be a certain way, as you know. She wanted the help to remain the help. When Madame hired Clare, she made out as if it was this great gift for me and Elena because she loved us, because she wanted Elena to focus on her music. And so we did not question it, we never looked closer."

"Tell me what you do remember about her."

"She didn't say much, but every now and then I caught her pulling faces behind Madame Usher's back," Ivan said. "I think she was probably quite funny, like you. She was allowed to sit in on our lessons if she'd finished her daily duties, but Master Radcliffe didn't teach her privately. She would join me and Elena when we practiced sometimes – she played a passable Mozart, but her real talent was composition. When Dorien arrived at Manderley, Clare fell for him hard, and I remember her running around after him, practically falling at his feet. He lapped up her attention, because he's Dorien. He treated her the same as any of our groupies – when he was with her, she'd be the center of his world, but he didn't invite her to hang out with me and Titus. He doesn't let anyone into his heart… not until you. But she wanted more. When their relationship soured in those final few months, Clare became a different person. She'd run out of the room when Madame entered, and she seemed to jump at every loud noise. She stopped coming to lessons, but sometimes I heard her playing in her bedroom late at night."

I was starting to build a picture of Clare in my head, and what I saw made my head spin. I saw a girl like me, trapped by her circumstances, caught up in a game with rules she didn't understand. The more I thought of it, the more I was certain Clare was the key to Manderley's secrets – that was why she appeared to me. She wanted to tell me something, and she trusted me of all the Manderley students to understand.

I needed more. I needed to give things a nudge. And Ivan had given me an idea.

After dinner, I declined to sit with the others, who were still reeling from the destruction of their possessions. I climbed up the stairs to my room, which I hadn't visited since the fire. I paused in the doorway to take in the carnage.

My drawers had been turned out, and all my clothes, bar my scratchy wool dress and a few spare pairs of underwear and stockings, had gone up in flames. My beautiful shimmering crimson recital dress was a pile of ash and broken memories. A lump rose in my throat as my eyes fell on the gap on my night-stand where the *Grimm's Fairy Tales* book sat only this morning, and the space on my bureau where the framed picture of Mom and me stood. But apart from that, I seemed to have got off lightly. Madame must've considered my meager possessions too modest to be concerned about.

Madame Usher thought she could silence us with intimida-tion. But her spider's web could not collect everything. The music in my heart and my fingertips belonged to me alone, and I could weave such magic with it. I could conjure ghosts and make beautiful men fall in love. I could even – if I played things right – bring her down.

I sat on the end of my bed and rested my violin to my chin. "Clare, I'm here if you want to talk."

I held my breath.

I listened.

Drip, drip, drip. The tap in my bathroom drummed a foolish beat.

This is ridiculous. My fingers twitched on the bow. *I don't believe in ghosts. And I certainly don't believe one will talk to me just because I—*

A lone, mournful note sang through the air.

I stared down at my violin, even though I knew I hadn't touched the strings. I remained frozen as the note ran out, swelling and building into a soft melody that echoed around my tiny room.

It was the same song I heard late at night. The song that I'd tried to blot from my memory, convinced it was one of the students torturing me.

Where's it coming from?

The answer was *everywhere*. The music rose around me, mournful and beautiful, sweeping and diving with a yearning trill. For the first time, I didn't just hear the notes, I heard the *voice* behind them – the story told without words, for music speaks in ways that letters never could.

Clare.

She's here.

The hairs on my neck and arms stood upright. My spine tingled, and the urge to flee the room itched in the soles of my feet. Instead, I raised my bow to the strings and played a simple harmony to accompany her.

My phrase reverberated through the small space, filling out the song to create a rounded *lacrimoso* as I entwined my story with Clare's. I paused, expecting the ghostly music to disappear, to be left feeling stupid for believing it was real.

Instead, the music continued, repeating the melody again, inviting me to continue. I stood, my neck bent beneath the low ceiling, and I closed my eyes as I played with Clare and *for* Clare. I did what she'd been asking all along – for someone to listen to her.

All we ever want is to be heard.

The ghost of Manderley and I played together. My fingers swept over the strings as I rose and fell, following where she led. And in our reverie, she gifted me with the one thing she had left in this world – her story, her truth. The one thing that could bring Madame Usher down.

39

FAYE

After I set down my violin somewhere around 2AM, I collapsed into bed and fell into a deep, restful sleep. No footsteps in the storage room nor phantom music disturbed me that night.

I woke with the alarm and went downstairs to prepare breakfast. Madame Usher held court from one end of the dining table while I set out stacks of pancakes, maple syrup, whipped cream, and other toppings. She stared at the food with disdain, but she could find no fault. I think she was hoping I'd serve stale cereal so she had an excuse for more carnage.

Heather kept up a steady stream of chatter with Madame and Master Radcliffe. No one else spoke. Even Master Radcliffe remained oddly silent, and he kept stealing glances across the table at Elena that made Ivan stab at his plate so hard he chipped the edge.

After breakfast, Ivan and Elena helped me clear the table, then we all joined Master Radcliffe and the others in the ballroom for composition. As soon as I entered the room, I became aware of a pair of beady eyes watching from the shadows of the velvet curtains. Madame Usher.

What's she doing here?

This can't be good.

Master Radcliffe stood behind the piano, clearing his throat repeatedly while throwing glances back at Madame. He looked like he didn't quite know what to say.

"Are we going to begin the lesson, Maestro?" Heather asked in her sickly sweet voice.

"Yes, well… um…" he scratched behind his ear. "Has anyone been working on a new piece? We can workshop it together."

An idea sparked. Heather beamed and moved to stand up, but I beat her to it. "I've been playing with something." I held up my instrument, and Master Radcliffe nodded. I raised my bow.

I played the first phrase of Clare's song.

After all the nights of hearing it inside my room, inside my head, I knew the melody by heart. I played the story Clare couldn't speak, pouring all my fury and fire in building the haunting piece to its crashing, bittersweet conclusion.

It was as if I cast a spell in the room. Something living dropped out of the air. The temperature plummeted. A scent permeated the air – a fresh lilac smell, edged with the musty odor of a forgotten room and tainted with blood and betrayal. A memory, but not my own. *Clare's memory.*

I stood bone-still as I played, letting the music carry me, allowing me to view Madame Usher's face as I reached the final, pounding strike of the strings. I imagined this *staccatissimo* as the *thump thump thump* of Clare's body rolling down the stairs, followed by the stark silence as her flame was snuffed out.

I let the silence in the room hang, heavy as the drapes that shrouded the windows from the encroaching forest. I took my time to meet every pair of eyes in the room, to weigh their stunned reactions.

They all recognize this song.

In the corner, Madame Usher rose to her feet, her hands balled into fists. Her eyes bugged out of her head, the way they'd

done the day I brought that Becker violin downstairs to play –
the same violin Heather held tight in her hands.

Finally, my eyes fell on Dorien. I was so shocked by what I
saw in him that my fingers slipped on the strings and a dull note
rang out.

"Clare," Dorien choked out. But he wasn't looking at me. He
was looking *past* me at an empty wall behind my head. I lowered
my instrument and stepped toward him, but he spun on his heel
and fled the room.

"How dare you claim that song belongs to you?" Madame
Usher roared. She came at me, gliding across the floor as if she
were forced by some unholy spirit. Her fingers raised to my
throat, brushing my skin, digging into my flesh. "You don't have
the talent, the *vision* to create music as beautiful as this."

Her fingers tightened, pressing the air from my lungs. I
clawed at her, fighting for breath. Red welts appeared in my eyes,
dancing over her face like warpaint. My chest heaved, and a
burning radiated out from my lungs to consume my body.

I thrashed and bucked and lashed out at her, but nothing
could move her steel hands from my throat.

The red welts swelled.

My ears screamed.

My stomach convulsed.

I am going to die.

Master Radcliffe cried out. The sound came from far away, as
if I heard it underwater. Madame Usher's fingers loosened, and I
stared through the pain with a kind of strange detachment as the
curtains whipped against their rails. The heavy velvet billowed
into the room, even though there was no breeze or draft in
the air.

Ivan and Titus fell on Madame Usher, breaking her grip on
me. I slammed into the floor, my skull roaring the pain, my chest
heaving as I sucked in precious air.

Madame stumbled back, spinning, disoriented. Her foot

hooked under the piano stool. Elena screamed as Madame went down. Her head smashed against the corner of the piano.

She flopped forward, her body limp.

A smudge of blood bloomed across the carpet beneath her temple.

She didn't move.

40

FAYE

The curtains dropped back in place, the invisible breeze no longer fluttering the material. The entire room felt eerily silent.

Silent as death.

"Madame." Heather rushed to her side. She glared up at me and Ivan. "If she's dead, you'll be next."

I grasped my throat, my fingers pressing at the scratches where Madame's nails dug into my skin. My head spun as I focused on that red stain on the carpet.

The song. This all happened because of Clare's song.

"She's not dead." Titus rolled her over. "She's still breathing. I think she's just knocked herself out. We need to move her to a couch and make her comfortable."

I bit my tongue at the idea of doing anything to make Madame Usher comfortable. "I need to go after Dorien."

Titus nodded. I darted from the room, checking in the practice rooms along the corridor. I bounded up the stairs two at a time, but he wasn't in his bedroom, or in my room. As I stood at the foot of my bed, chest heaving, trying to think where to search next, I caught the shape of a figure moving across the lawn below.

Dorien.

I raced back downstairs and out the kitchen door. "Dorien?" I called. No answer. I sprinted across the lawn, taking a wide berth around the burned circle in the center of the garden. He wasn't sitting beside the stream, or floating in it, and my heart lifted a little lighter when I saw the waters running clear. I continued down the path toward the gazebo, calling his name into the wilderness.

He was there, of course. He had his back to me, and he knelt on the rotting floor, his head bowed and a set of earbuds in his ears. He looked up at the trees, and the expression on his face was of such rapt torture that I couldn't bear it.

He didn't acknowledge me as I moved behind him. "Dorien." I planted both hands on his shoulders. "Talk to me. What happened back there?"

"Argh!" He whirled around. The anger on his face turned to despair when he saw me. I couldn't help but think back to when our roles were reversed. Dorien came to find me playing under the gazebo – a wild, angry song that I'd needed to purge the memory of him from my veins. Only that was impossible. A raw, primal hunger stretched between us – a cord of destiny that pulled taut, drawing us closer even as we threatened to destroy each other.

Judging by the look on Dorien's face, I'd most definitely won this round. I never believed Dorien Valencourt could be brought to his knees. But Clare's song had done it.

Dorien took a step toward me, trembling fingers raised. "Fuck, Sprite, what happened to your throat?"

"After you left, Madame attacked me." I touched one of the welts on my neck and felt a fresh flare of pain arc across my skull. "She tried to choke me, and Titus pushed her away, but she hit her head. She's alive, probably on account of that pact she made with the Devil, but she might have to go to the hospital."

Dorien stared through me. He made no movement or sound that he'd heard anything I said.

"I wanted to talk to you," I said. "About Clare."

Dorien tugged the earbuds from his ears, and before he clicked off his phone I caught a snatch of music. It was the same piece I'd just performed, the same haunting melody I'd played with the ghost in my room.

Dorien turned the screen of his phone toward me, showing me the title of the piece. "My Requiem – by Clare Fairbanks."

"Clare wrote that piece?"

Dorien nodded.

My stomach flipped. I couldn't think about Dorien like *that*. Not anymore. Too much darkness stood between us. Even though it seemed as if the universe was determined to throw us together, to make me let go of the anger that acted as a breakwater. He was a dark tide – alluring and dangerous – and I couldn't let down my defenses or I'd be swept away.

Dorien's eyes fluttered shut. His eyelashes tangled together. "I saw her."

"You saw Clare?"

"When you were playing. Her face appeared behind you. It looked… like she was smiling, but it was a cold smile."

I swallowed. "You saw Clare's ghost? Dorien, I need to—"

"She was there, and she's *dead*." Dorien buried his face in his hands. "She's come for me, because she knows I killed her."

41

DORIEN

*A*s soon as the words fall from my mouth, I felt like a great weight had lifted from my shoulders – my spirit shrugging off its bonds.

Faye had been reaching out to me with those long, beautiful fingers. Her hand froze in midair, and those fierce eyes fixed on mine. Good. I'd sensed, ever since I gave her that ride to the hospital, something in Faye changing toward me. She was starting to think about forgiving me. I couldn't allow her to do that. And this would push her away once and for all.

I'd push her into the arms of my best friends – the two people who would love her as she deserved to be loved, as dark and hidden flowers are to be loved – with passion, with sacrifice, with a yearning that transcends the self. My love for Faye had consumed me utterly, and I couldn't allow it to consume her, too. I loved her enough to set her free of me.

"What do you mean, you killed her?" Faye's red lips pursed as she studied me carefully. "You said her death was an accident."

"No, no." I buried my face in my hands. "I drove her to do it. I made her crazy."

Faye folded her arms. "Dorien, I need you to stop being melodramatic and think very, *very* carefully about what you say next. Clare fell down the stairs. Did you push her?"

"I *killed* her."

"You were behind her. Your hands touched her skin. You *shoved* her."

"*No.*" The word slammed into me. I had done shitty things, so many awful things, so much that I was beyond redemption. But I never did that.

Faye sighed. She leaned against the rotting railing of the gazebo, gripping the pole with pale fingers. "You need to calm the fuck down and tell me *everything.*"

I sank onto the floor of the gazebo, my back against the rotting upright. Icy cold seeped through the seat of my trousers. If my ass got frostbite, it would be the least I deserved.

I buried my head in my hands. The weight of it all crushed me into the rotting wood. When my gaze dropped from Faye, Clare's dark eyes and grim smile haunted the inside of my eyelids.

I took a shuddering breath and began.

"Clare worked for Madame Usher for three years, since she was sixteen. She'd had a hard life – her mother died when she was young, and her father was a war vet who returned from Afghanistan with his head messed up. He drank, and he took drugs, and he became the evil that he'd gone to war to fight. Clare was put into foster care when she was ten. She lived with various families, each more awful than the last. Her last family pulled her out of school and sent her up here to work for Madame Usher, and Madame paid most of Clare's wages directly to them. Clare talked about running away a lot, especially at the end, but she had nothing of her own.

"Clare said that at first being at Manderley was a dream come true. She had a room to herself. There was no foster father sneaking into her bed at night. She cleaned and cooked and sat in on Radcliffe's lessons. When she turned eighteen, Madame Usher asked if she'd like to stay on at the house and keep her wages –

she said that if Clare wanted, she would have Master Radcliffe teach her for a time in the afternoons. Clare was so happy to be able to steal a little bit of the joy of music we all took for granted."

"Was she talented?"

I closed my eyes as the memory of Clare's music rushed through my veins. "She was rough. Poorly trained. Perfectly mediocre. But she could compose. She wrote music that hummed in your veins long after the movement was over. In a lot of ways, you remind me of her."

"Tell me about when you met," Faye said. "Tell me everything. I need your secrets now, Dorien. Did you love her?"

The question shocked both of us. It hung in the air – a silent accusation. I lifted my head, and I fixed my eyes to Faye, and I hoped like hell Clare wasn't standing behind her, listening with ghostly ears. "She was a distraction, a warm body, a shoulder to rest my head on. Titus and Ivan were over listening to me wallow in my own bullshit, but to Clare, every word out of my mouth, every note I played, was genius. That's intoxicating. I cared for her. I enjoyed her company. But no, I didn't love her."

"Tell me about when she died."

"We'd been fighting. Clare was acting weird – one day she'd be happy and bubbly, the next day cross and angry. She'd be all over me, and then she wouldn't want me to touch her. She wasn't sleeping at night, said she kept hearing creaks and groans and weird footsteps. She said food kept disappearing from the kitchen, and objects would be moved around in her room, things not placed where she put them down. I thought it was just the other students playing tricks on her – no one much liked her, the weird maid who presumed to study alongside us. I tried to calm her at first, but then it got tiresome, and I started to ignore her. I'm not proud of myself, but you asked for the truth.

"And then, things got really weird. She was supposed to be a distraction from the hell that is my life. Clare wanted answers I couldn't give. She asked so many probing questions about my life, especially about my time studying with Madame Usher. She spoke to herself under her breath, asking questions and pausing as if she expected someone to answer. And sometimes I'd enter a room I thought was empty, only to have her leap out at me from some dark corner. I found her unsettling. So I broke things off with her. She wasn't happy about that. She cried, threw things. Madame Usher talked about sending her away, but Master Radcliffe stepped in and said she'd get over it."

"The day of her death, I opened the door to my room, and there she was, her hair wild, her eyes as wide as saucers. Her nightgown had been torn, and there was blood under her nails. She looked like she was on drugs, and she hissed all these strange things."

"Like what?" Faye leaned forward, her eyes wide.

"I don't remember, exactly. It just sounded like nonsense at the time. She kept saying, 'he touched me,' and I thought she was talking about me. I didn't want another fight, or to be blamed for something I didn't do. I shoved past her in the hall, but she kept coming after me. I reached the bottom of the stairs. I wasn't looking at her. She yelled, 'The ghost in the walls is real, and he's not happy. She's been lying to us all, and she'll burn for it, and you'll all burn with her.' Something like that. It sounded completely insane. Then she cut off into a scream, and there was this horrid *thump.* I turned around just as she slammed into the floor beside me. Her neck bent at this terrible angle. I felt for her pulse but—"

I turned away from Faye as the memory assailed me. Clare's body lying in my arms, her head bent a way no head should ever be bent, her glassy eyes staring up at me, her mouth open in a silent scream. I saw that face every time I closed my eyes, sometimes superimposed over my brother. I couldn't save Clare. I couldn't save Jacob. I was trapped in this cursed house because of my own selfishness, my own inability to control my passions.

Faye looked completely drained by everything I told her. She rested her cheek against the pole. "Her story is so sad. I wish you'd told me all of this earlier, that I'd known what happened in my room."

"But you don't know what happened in your room. All we have is Clare's crazy ramblings. How did you know that music?" I asked.

"I hear it at night," Faye said. "It's the song that's played over and over in my room. It's how I know Clare is haunting Manderley, haunting *me*."

A chill ran down my spine as she spoke those words. I shook my head. "You're wrong. I'm the one she wants. You have to stay away from her. She'll use you to get to me, to punish me. Because of what I did to her. Because I wouldn't listen."

Faye fixed me with that intense stare. "We're listening now. We couldn't save Clare in this life, but she's giving us a clear message. Whatever she was afraid of, whatever she died over, it's still in this house. If what you said is true, it's not just Clare's ghost who's haunting this place."

Another shiver ran down my spine. "I can't believe we're out here talking about ghosts."

"Neither can I, but what did Sherlock Holmes say? When you've eliminated the impossible, whatever remains, however improbable, must be the truth. Clare can't be in the house because she's dead, and yet, you saw her and I saw her. And I knew her song."

I nodded. "And that's impossible because the only person she ever shared that piece with was me. Where does the music come from, *exactly*?"

Faye looked up toward Manderley. "I only hear it in my bedroom. It sort of… flows all around, but sometimes it seems to only come from the storage room, where you walked back and forth all night, keeping me awake."

"I swear, we never did that." I shook my head. All those things Faye thought we'd done to her in the beginning rushed at me. "I wonder how many of the weird things you experienced were actually Clare trying to hurt you?"

Faye shook her head. "I don't think she's malicious. I think she's been trying to warn me, to help me."

"But then why would she destroy your violin? Because I swear to you I didn't do that. I only moved it into the bathroom."

Faye touched her lips with the tip of her finger, and I could see the sparkle of an idea forming in her eyes. "I believe you. I just don't believe she had evil intentions toward me. I wish we could get into the storage room and see what's in there, but the only key to that room is on Madame's key loop. We could shimmy out my window and go in from the outside." Faye slapped her ass. "Well, probably not me, with this glorious rump. But maybe Ivan…"

"There's no need for any of us to risk falling to our deaths." I felt the corner of my mouth twist up at the possibility of answers. "I think it's time we beat Madame Usher at her own game."

4 2

———

FAYE

"Here it is." Dorien lifted an old case from beneath his bed.

Dorien and I stood under the gazebo for a long time after we decided what to do next. He held my hands in his to protect them from the cold, even though he was the one who'd run out wearing only his thin silk shirt. As he told Clare's story and confessed to the dark guilt that haunted him, it broke something open between us. I could feel the cords of our lives twining together again, even though the ends were all frayed and broken.

We talked over our plan, and we were all prepared to make it happen while Madame was at the hospital. But when we returned to the house we found her bandaged but awake, demanding we continue with the day's lessons. She glared at us all as she continued as if she'd never tried to strangle me, daring us to contradict her, to stand up to her. No one did.

So our plan had to wait for another day. Which was today.

"Wow, this is so cool." I lifted the lid on the trunk, admiring the rows of glass bottles and vials inside. There was even a tiny pair of tongs and some glass measuring cups and test tubes, all beautifully presented in the velvet-lined box. A Victorian apothe-

289

cary set in perfect condition, saved from the fire because Dorien had hidden it in the back of the linen cupboard. Manderley might be full of secrets, but some of them were kind of cool. I pulled out one of the bottles and held it under the light to read the label. "What did you use to drug me the first day I was here?"

Dorien ran his finger along the row to find a small bottle. "This stuff called syrup of ipecac. Victorians used it to induce vomiting after a patient swallowed something poisonous. The chloroform is here."

I shook my head as he tried to hand me the bottle. I didn't want to be reminded of what he did on the night of the party. "How do you know how to use all this stuff?"

"Heather's mother is a professor of history. She wrote a book on medicine in the early nineteenth century." Dorien peered at the chloroform bottle in his hands. "Also, the internet."

"I don't think we want to use that one." I glared at the chloroform. "We need to hold that over her face, and I don't want her to suspect we did this. We just need something that will knock her out for a few hours."

"I have just the thing." Dorien held up a larger bottle. A black skull-and-crossbones adorned the label. "Chloral. It was a common cure for insomnia during the Victorian period, until they discovered that prolonged use caused addiction and death. One dose of this and she'll be out like a light."

I stared down at the clearly marked skull-and-crossbones on the bottle. I thought of my mother, still in the hospital after poison had destroyed her body. Did I really want to be responsible for using a dangerous drug on someone else?

In Cauda Venenum. The poison is in the tail. My mother was in the hospital because of Madame Usher. She deserved a taste of her own medicine. I slipped the bottle into my purse. "Leave it to me."

∿

*D*orien no longer had access to Heather's book, and we no longer had our phones or the house internet, but we did have the Manderley library's many history books. I read everything I could about chloral and how it was often used to spike drinks for bars for nefarious purposes – a bartender at a Chicago saloon in the 1890s named Mickey Finn dropped the drug into drinks so he could rob his customers after they fell asleep, lending his name to both the practice and the drug.

Time to slip Madame Usher a little Mickey of our own.

Titus and I prepared the midday meal as usual, and I put Madame's on a tray to bring to her in her office, as she was still feeling weak and didn't want to walk to the dining room. I included a glass of her favorite port.

When I entered the room, I found her seated at a chair beside the fireplace, her eyes fixed on the space above the heath where her photograph used to hang. I set the tray down beside her and backed out of the room before she acknowledged me. I knew that if she saw my face she'd read my deception.

I paced in the hall, my heart racing as I counted down the minutes. When I checked on her again, she was sleeping deeply, her chest rising and falling in a steady rhythm. The port glass was empty. I leaned over her, waving my hands in front of her face, then poking her lightly in the belly. Nothing. She didn't stir.

Now or never. I slid my hand under her leather belt and unhooked the loop that held her ring of keys. It jangled as it fell into my hand.

I froze, my heart thundering.

Madame let out a gentle snore.

Phew. I palmed the keys and slipped from the room. Elena waited in the hallway, her hands at her throat. "I've locked the door to Heather's room."

"Good." I squeezed Elena's hand. "Stay here and keep an eye

on Usher. Call out to us the moment she looks as though she's waking up."

Elena nodded. "Be careful."

I slipped my hand from hers and bolted for the stairs, Dorien and Titus only a few steps behind me. On the attic landing I fumbled for the ring of keys – it was nearly identical to the one she'd given me, so I knew that any keys that didn't match mine could work for the storage room.

I found a long, narrow key with a filigree decoration on the bow, but it didn't fit in the lock. Next was a much plainer key, which slotted in with a little jiggling. I held my breath as I turned the lock and the door pushed open.

Dorien leaned over me and shoved the door with his hand. "Let's see what's—"

"Not yet." An idea formed in my mind. "Back downstairs. Quickly. I think I know what this key unlocks."

The guys followed me along the hall past their bedrooms, to the door bearing the sign NO STUDENTS. The entrance to Madame Usher's private wing. I lifted the filigree key from the ring and tried it in the lock. It fell open, and the door swung inward.

My breath hitched as I saw the same drab reception room I'd seen last time, with the row of footsteps in the dust leading into the private chambers beyond. My feet itched to move forward, to explore the space, but I knew this wasn't the time. We couldn't risk Madame thinking anything was amiss when she came to, and I knew her well enough to know she'd notice if even a single speck of dust was out of place.

Titus held out his hand. "You stay here and search the storage room. I'll run to town and get a copy of the keys made."

I shook my head. "We should all go."

"Faye, Madame Usher is out cold. Even if we do get these copies made before she catches us, I don't know when you'll have another chance to use the keys. If I'm caught, my parents' renown might protect me from her wrath, but I can't say the same for anyone else." Titus slipped the ring into his pocket. "Go upstairs. Find your answers. You deserve that much."

I leaned forward to capture his lips in mine, using up a few of our precious moments to commit his kiss to memory, to sear the beauty of him into my soul. "Go like the wind," I whispered. Titus nodded before taking off for the stairs. A moment later, the front door slammed, and his car roared down the driveway.

"Hey." Heather banged on her door. "I'm trapped in here. Let me out."

I glanced at Dorien. I could see the cogs turning in his mind, the same way we used to read each other as kids. The connection that sparked between us flared to life, the end of our cords knotting and knitting together. Our wounds could never be repaired or stitched over as if like new, but we remake ourselves together.

I clambered up the attic stairs, my breath hitching at the sight of the storage room door still ajar. Darkness spilled from behind it. My chest tightened. That room had been the source of so much fear and anger and resentment. All those weeks I was certain the Muses were up there, using it as their personal playground to make me miserable. Now, finally, we had the chance to find answers.

Dorien extended his hand with a flourish. "Ladies first."

I stepped forward. My chest heaved as I drew a deep breath. The air stretched thin here, as if there wasn't enough to go around. As if something lurked in the darkness, devouring the oxygen.

My fingers grazed the rough wood.

I exhaled.

I pushed the door open.

It was stiff from the lack of use, and budged only an inch before it stuck in its frame – the wood swollen from the rising heat in the attic. I leaned into it with my shoulder and shoved hard.

The door scraped over the floor and banged open, revealing a narrow room shrouded in shadows. I reached for a light switch, but there wasn't one. They must have never installed electricity in this room, not intending it to be used as a bedroom. I dug my phone from my pocket and flicked on the flashlight app, casting the light across the floor in front of me.

My breath caught in my throat.

The entire floor was covered in a thick layer of dust, except for a narrow path across the floor, leading from a spot on the wall to the window. The edges of the path were ragged – this wasn't a piece of furniture being moved – but a trail of footprints. Someone walked this path so many times they'd kicked aside all the dust.

I hadn't imagined it. Someone had been in this room, walking around at night to scare me. But who? I believed now that it wasn't any of the Muses. And even though I believed in Clare's ghostly presence, I didn't think it was her, either. For one thing, she seemed to be mostly ethereal, and these footprints were evidence of a solid, corporeal being. For another, what she'd said to Dorien implied that she'd heard them, too. We were both victims of whoever was walking around in this room.

Dorien bent down in front of the window, moving aside boxes and broken chairs and tables, while I inspected the wall where the footprints stopped. It was lined with the same horizontal clapboard as my bedroom, with no adornment. I studied the wood, poking and prodding in search of a secret door. My fingers grazed over a knot in the wood, and I exclaimed in surprise as one of my fingers slipped through the center of the knot.

It was a hole. I pushed my finger through, feeling a rush of cool air from the space between the walls. I withdrew my finger and pressed my eye up to the hole, not expecting to see anything but darkness.

The hole looked straight through the wall into my bedroom.

"Fucking dickweasel," I growled. Dorien said something, but the blood boiled so loud in my ears I didn't hear him.

Ghosts don't fucking need peepholes.

I ran back around to my room, scanning the walls. My eyes caught on the painting above my dresser – a woman in a flowing white dress playing the harp in a moonlit garden – one of those slightly melancholy Victorian fancies. I leaned in close – the center of one of the flowers behind the woman had been drilled out, leaving a small hole. In the gloom, I never would have noticed it.

I peered through to the storage room, my stomach churning with sick thoughts. A shadow fell over the hole. My heart stuttered, then I realized it was Dorien's eye. He'd found the peephole, too. He blinked. "This is creepy."

"Yup." I fingered the edge of the painting. The hole had been carefully drilled out, the edges filed flat so it couldn't be seen unless you were looking for it. I'd turned my room upside down looking for a secret passage the Muses could have used to make that face at my window, and I'd never seen it. "Why does a ghost need a peephole?"

"An excellent question."

I walked back through to the storage room. Suddenly, I felt dizzy, lightheaded. I couldn't believe I'd been living in that bedroom for months while someone was in here, spying on me. I slumped down on top of one of the boxes, watching Dorien as he shifted furniture and searched the contents.

Was it Madame Usher? She was the only one who had a key to this room. But somehow I just couldn't picture her stomping around in this stuffy room, getting all dusty as she peered through the peephole to watch me sleep and change and... fuck Dorien and Ivan. Gross.

No, Madame Usher always got others to do her dirty work. That meant someone in this house was up here, night after night. My thoughts flew to Master Radcliffe, who had come to

Manderley with the explicit purpose of marrying Elena. But the gross pervert had never shown any interest in me.

"There must be a secret passage that connects this room to downstairs," I said. "I can't see how anyone would be sneaking up here and unlocking this door without me hearing them."

"I thought so, too," Dorien said, flicking through a stack of old paintings leaning on the wall beneath the window. "I've been looking around here, where the trail of footsteps end, but I can't see anything…"

His voice trailed off. He frowned as he bent to look closer at something. I heard the sound of paper tearing.

"Don't damage anything. We need the room to look exactly the same as when we entered it—"

"Um, Faye. I think you should see this."

Dorien lifted something from behind the stack of boxes. It was a large, flat rectangle covered with brown paper. One section flapped free, revealing the gilded corner of a painting. Dorien's mouth set into a firm line as he tugged at the tape holding the corners of the paper.

"This is the portrait that hung in the hallway," Dorien said. "I never looked too closely at them before, but I'm sure of it."

"She said she sent that portrait away for repairs." I knelt down in front of it as Dorien tore the paper away. "So why is it up here—"

I gasped as the last of the paper fell away, revealing a man with a mane of wild, dark hair, piercing green eyes that seemed to stare straight out of the canvas at me. He wore an expression of serene contemplation.

My hand flew to my mouth.

Sound the fucktrumpets.

It's my father.

Madame Usher had a portrait of my father hanging in her hallway. And she hadn't wanted me to see it.

And that wasn't even the most terrifying thing.

My father held an instrument against his chest. Not the violin he played when he was alive – a secondhand Fiorini my mother worked herself ragged to afford. My mother sold it to a collector in Strausberg and used the money to start De Winter PR. This violin he cradled in his arms with all the love one might reserve for one's first-born daughter.

Not just any violin.

A Becker.

A very *familiar* Becker.

It was the same violin I'd picked up from the music room, the one that made Madame Usher freak out. But that didn't make any sense.

My father is dead.

So how does this portrait exist?

43

FAYE

I rubbed my eyes, thinking that I could rub away the impossibility of it. But the image of my father still grinned back at me, holding an instrument he couldn't possibly have held. I tore my eyes from it to glare at Dorien. "How did you not think to tell me the missing picture was of my father?"

"Because I'm a selfish bastard who never notices the world around him?" Dorien's mouth twisted up into that half-grin, the one that never failed to drive me wild. "The walls down there are filled with stodgy portraits of famous musicians. I never even noticed one was missing until you pointed it out."

"You mean this portrait has been missing since you started at Manderley?"

"I think so. I can't say for certain, but I think I would have noticed your dad. But that violin…"

I held my hand over my heart. I was having trouble breathing. "I don't want to think about what this means, but we have to. We have to consider the fact that this portrait might have been made after my father disappeared."

Dorien bit his lip. "She could have had this created from memory, from photographs and shit."

I shook my head. "No way. Look at the face. Look at the quality of the brushwork. This is not the kind of art you make from photographs. It's *living*. That's Donovan fucking de Winter. How did no one notice this?"

"Faye, this is crazy." Dorien glanced around the room. "We should get out of here. I don't know how long we'll have until she wakes up, and we need to make it look like we weren't here."

I glanced down at my feet. We'd both tried to remain on the trail, but when I'd seen the painting I'd stepped over the line, leaving fresh trails in the dust. Not to mention the boxes had been moved around, kicking up a cloud of dust that settled in the air, closing my lungs.

"I'll take care of it." Dorien wrapped the portrait up again and stashed it back behind the boxes. He spent a few minutes shuffling things back into place, closing lids and shutting drawers. Then he scooped a handful of dust into his fingers. "Back out of the room."

I did so, being careful to stick to the trail. Dorien followed me, stepping his feet where he stood before to avoid making any further prints. He tossed the dust into my footprints, erasing the steps.

"It's not perfect, but you say this person is up here at night, so it's probably too dark to notice." He coughed. "Plus, when this dust settles again, hopefully that should help."

I hoped like hell. If Madame Usher and whoever she had up here knew we were onto them, everything we worked on today would be in vain.

Dorien's fingers stroked mine as he turned the lock from the inside and slammed the door shut. My fingers tingled from the ghost of his touch.

I peered up at him. "Dorien, I—"

Dorien's fingers stroked along my arm. His lips parted ever so slightly. In a flash, he'd narrowed the distance between us.

We hovered there, lingering in the moment, not daring to let our lips touch, yet knowing the moment was inevitable. The cord that bound us pulled taut, smashing our bodies together, crashing us into each other like the waves upon a rocky shore.

The kiss tore pieces of me away and dashed them against him, crumbling my defenses to dust and tossing me all about until I didn't know which way was up or down. Dorien stole all the oxygen in the room, pressing against my lungs until all I tasted, all I breathed, was him. All the emotion I'd been stamping down since I saw that portrait of my father welled to the surface.

This is a bad idea.

This is the worst idea.

And yet, it felt like it was the only possible conclusion.

Dorien tore his lips from mine, staggering back until he pressed himself against the clapboard, bending his tall frame to the slope of the roof. His chest heaved.

I glared at him.

He shook his head. "Don't, Faye. Don't make the mistake of forgiving me. I'm the reason Clare is dead, and I won't be the reason you die, too."

"You can't blame yourself for Clare," I said, my lips tingling with want. "Lots of other shit, yes. But not that. It's this house. It does something to people."

"Yes, it makes you believe I'm somehow redeemable." Dorien tore his eyes from mine. He looked terrified as he half-ran, half-skidded down the steep steps.

I pressed my hand to my chest, willing my racing heart to calm again. Suddenly, I couldn't bear to remain in the attic, thinking about that peephole in my wall and Dorien's lips hot against mine. I shimmied down the stairs after him. Ivan met us on the first-floor landing.

"What happened up there?" he demanded. "You were gone a long time."

The heat of Dorien's kiss burned against my lips. Ivan's ice eyes bore into mine, and I knew he read the flush in my cheeks and the quickening of my pulse. He grunted and turned away, his shoulders hunching as he strode off down the hallway. I remembered what he'd said to me back in Prague. *I wanted to fight for you, but now I see that loving you means I have to give you up.*

I knew that was what he was doing, and it made me want to grab him by the scruff of his neck and kiss him until he agreed to be mine.

But I didn't have time to sort out my bullshit feelings. We raced back to Madame's office, past Heather's door rattling on its jamb. "I can hear you out there," she yelled. "I demand you open this door, right now."

Elena met us at the doorway, her perfect lips quivering with worry. "I was just about to call you. She stirred a few moments ago, but she seems to still be asleep."

I glanced at my watch. Titus had been gone for a little over an hour. He needed at least another hour. I glanced at the empty port glass. Had I given her enough? The books weren't exactly replete with detailed information about how to knock someone out with Victorian insomnia medicine.

I sat in the chair opposite Madame Usher, watching her face as her chest rose and fell. She seemed so serene – it was hard to believe she was such an evil spider. The ticking of the grandfather clock echoed through the house, punctuated by Heather's cries.

"We should have given Heather some of that stuff," Dorien mused.

"Next time," Elena promised.

Ivan wouldn't look at me.

I couldn't sit still any longer. I was desperate to search Madame's private chambers, but we couldn't get in there without the key, and I'd given that to Titus. We had to save that for another day. But there was one room where I did have access.

"Dorien, search her desk drawers," I said. "Look for any evidence we might be able to use against her."

"Don't disturb anything," Elena cried.

"Relax," Dorien opened a second drawer. "I know what I'm doing."

Not wanting to question why he'd claim to be an expert at snooping into people's private affairs, I removed my own keyring and went out into the hall. I opened the door to the storage room. The rows of dusty instruments watched me in silent vigil. There was always something about seeing musical instruments displayed in neat rows like terracotta warriors that gave me the creeps, as if they were waiting for the ghosts of their former owners to return.

My gaze fell to the Becker I'd picked up all those weeks ago. It was definitely the same one in my father's portrait. Heather must've returned it to this spot. My heart thudded in my chest as I picked it up. The temperature in the room dropped, and the air around me hummed with tension. I ran my hands down the body, searching for... what? I didn't know. For some sign my father had played this. For some occult symbol or portrait of his ghost.

I turned the violin over. An inscription stood out from the dark wood – I'd been in such a hurry last time that I hadn't noticed it. I held the violin beneath the one small window, focusing the light on the tiny words.

My heart flew to my throat.

A cold shiver ran down my spine.

"To my beloved Donovan. May we make beautiful music forevermore. Your Gizella."

Underneath was a date.

From nine years ago.

One year *after* my father disappeared.

44

FAYE

*S*ound the fucktrumpets, this is my father's violin.

Given to him by Madame Usher.

But that's not possible. Because he's dead.

The instrument fell from my fingers as the room grew frigid. Out of the corner of my eye, I saw something move in the shadows. My racing heart pressed against my ribcage, desperate to escape.

What is this?

What's going on here?

"Wh-wh-who's there?" I choked out, my body frozen in fear.

"Faaaaye..."

My name hissed into the icy air. A cold breeze ruffled the sleeves of my shirt.

Creeeeeak.

Someone's here.

I swallowed and spun around to face whatever horror awaited me, just as the breeze stopped and the temperature returned to normal.

There was nothing. I expected to see Clare's creepy face with her gaping mouth, or something much, much worse. But there was just a rack of cellos covered in dust hung on a dark-paneled wall.

Get a grip, Faye. You're freaking yourself out.

I stared at the violin on the floor. I had every reason to be freaked out. But there had to be a logical explanation for why this violin and the portrait seemed to imply my father had been with Madame Usher after he disappeared.

What that explanation could be, I couldn't fathom. But it had to exist. Or… or… I was going mad.

I picked up the Becker and turned it over again. Thankfully, I hadn't scratched it when I dropped it. My hands trembled as I fixed it back into its stand. Wild thoughts swirled in my head.

Madame Usher bought that violin for him.

Madame Usher knows what happened to my father.

I returned to the office in a daze. Elena and Dorien tried to engage me in conversation, but I didn't hear a word. Ivan just watched me with those penetrating eyes, and I knew he read the truth – I'd seen something that had freaked me out. But I couldn't find the words to explain. Not right now. I needed to focus on getting the keys back to Madame Usher, or I'd go completely mad.

Just as I was starting to panic, Titus rushed in, pressing the ring of keys back into my hand. "I broke every traffic law that exists, but I got the copies. Now we have access to those rooms whenever we need it. Did you find anything of interest in the storage room?"

I nodded. I didn't trust myself to speak. Dorien swiped the copied keys Titus held out. "*Interesting* is not the right word. We'll explain later."

Titus' large hands circled my shoulders. "Faye, something's wrong. You look white as a sheet. Did—"

"Hurry," Elena called out. "I think she's waking up."

I tore my eyes from Titus and ran across the room. Madame

Usher stirred, her hand falling across her face as she moaned. *Fuck.*

I leaned over her, trying to touch her as little as possible as I lifted the tab in her belt and slid the keys back onto the loop. They clanged together, the sound like a gunshot. Madame Usher groaned again. I jerked my hand away, my heart pounding.

She jerked awake, lunging at me and grabbing my arm. Her skin felt clammy, like a wet fish. "What do you think you're doing in my office?"

"I—I—I was worried about you." I organized my face into a look of concern. "There was a phone call for you, and we couldn't find you anywhere. Then Elena found you asleep in here. I was just checking your pulse. You know, you're not as young as you used to be, and you can never be too careful—"

Madame leaned forward, rubbing her temples. "I... fell asleep? In the middle of the day?"

Titus stepped forward. "You did. Do you want one of us to help you to your quarters?"

Madame shoved his hand away. "No. I'll do it myself." She gripped the side of her desk, holding herself steady as she turned to glare at us. "I'd better not find out any of you had something to do with this."

I knew if I so much as glanced at any of the others, it would give the game away. Instead, I turned my gaze to the floor, giving her that meekness I knew she so desperately sought. I could guess the others followed my lead, because Madame said nothing else. She shuffled into the hallway. A moment later, the door to her private wing slammed shut.

Dorien rushed toward me, and I was too freaked out to protest as he swept me into his arms. I breathed in the scent of him, but not even the fragrance of my childhood, of the boy who was forever entwined with my love of music, could staunch the cold horror creeping through my veins.

There's a peephole in my room, and a painting of my father after he died.

His violin is sitting in the storage room.

What does it mean?

Now that I knew about the peephole, I didn't want to set foot in my attic room ever again. But I also couldn't alert Madame Usher – because I was certain she was behind whatever was going on – that I knew about it. Instead, I took to changing clothes in the bathroom or downstairs in the boy's rooms. Whenever I stepped over the threshold, the hairs on the back of my neck prickled. I felt eyes following me everywhere – not just in the attic, but all over the house.

I remembered Clare's message in the pantry. 'THE WALLS ARE TALKING.' And I couldn't help but wonder if the peephole had been there when the room belonged to her. What might've been whispered through the wall by an unknown intruder to make her believe she was in danger?

FAYE

Madame Usher began to make plans for Elena's wedding. She set the date for the end of the semester and blew up the phone lines until she convinced some poor rental company to lug a pole tent all the way out to Manderley. She gave me and Elena the task of hand-lettering and stamping gold-rimmed invitations to mail out to a long list of contacts from all over the classical music world.

Elena's wedding party would double as the end-of-year function for Manderley, where we students could show off our repertoire to a room filled with potential employers and contacts. It would also be where the winner of the Manderley Prize would be announced.

I had a distinct feeling she didn't expect some of us to survive until then.

"We will find a way to stop this." I slammed Madame Usher's seal into a blob of wax. Globs of wax splattered across the antique table, and I knew I'd have to chip them off later, but I was too pissed off to care.

"Please, Faye, do not bother. Many people live in loveless

marriages," Elena said. "It is not pretty, but it is life. Think of your own parents."

"Are you sure my parents are the shining example you want to use here?" I kept nudging Elena about it, but she would shut down the conversation to talk about floral arrangements or the dress she was having made by a Romanian designer.

Meanwhile, I'd tentatively allowed Dorien back into our circle. I still hadn't forgiven him, but I couldn't pretend I didn't still have feelings for him. After I'd endured all I could of Elena's wedding plans, he invited me to walk with him down to the gazebo.

Snowflakes dusted my nose as he slipped his hand in mine, and my heart skipped. The ghost of his kiss lingered on my lips, and an electric tension buzzed in the air around us as our feet crunched over the snow. The cord that bound us tugged at my chest, and I knew it was only a matter of time until I'd forgiven him completely.

It was too damn hard to resist those storm-darkened eyes and that cocky-ass grin, especially since I'd been dreaming of him since I was a kid.

As we approached the gazebo, I could see it was already occupied. Titus knelt on the rotting wood, his huge shoulders hunched, the tips of his braids dragging in the snow. He looked completely broken.

My heart shattered, all the promise of Dorien's lips on mine sucked from the air. Because no matter how much I worried about what the future would hold, I couldn't choose between the Muses. I loved three of them equally – I loved Dorien's passion, Ivan's protectiveness, and Titus' kindness. And right now, Titus needed me.

I dropped Dorien's hand and made to run to Titus, but Dorien held me back. "Don't, Sprite. He needs to be alone. If you go over there now he'll be so worried about how you feel that he won't be able to open up."

I sagged into Dorien's arms, my gaze never leaving Titus' slumped form. "You're right. But I can't do nothing. I'm guessing he still hasn't spoken to his parents?"

"No. And it's his birthday next weekend. Amos and Delphine were planning to spend a week in the city, stay over at school to watch him perform, and take him out to shows. They were going to take us, too." Dorien shook his head. "I'm guessing it won't be happening now."

How can they do this to him? Do they think they're the only ones who feel the loss of Micah? I knew how deeply their words cut Titus, who only ever tried to please them. Hell, he'd denied something primal about himself to try and fit in the box they wanted to throw him in.

My heart hurt not going to him, but I knew Dorien was right. Titus couldn't give his pain to me in this way – he needed to bleed it out through music. And only one kind of music would do the trick. I placed my hand over Dorien's. "I want to do something special for Titus." An idea formed in my head. "I don't want to worry Ivan about it – he's got Elena's wedding on his mind. I can see it twisting him around himself. Will you help me?"

"What do you have in mind?"

I grinned. "Something wild. Trust me, it has Dorien Valencourt written all over it."

~

On the morning of Titus' birthday, Dorien snuck out of Manderley early and drove away to make the final arrangements. I made Titus his favorite breakfast – blueberry pancakes with stacks of bacon and maple syrup – but he pushed the food around without eating it. I didn't like to see him so defeated. His smile was one of the only bright things that shone through the gloom of Manderley. To have it snuffed out because of Madame Usher's cruelty was more than I could take.

Titus retreated to his room after breakfast. Elena tried to speak to him through the door, but he blasted Wagner at top volume until she left in disgust. Luckily, I had keys to the student rooms, so I unlocked the door and barged in.

He sat on his windowsill, one leg dangling outside as he smoked a joint. "Go away," he growled.

I snapped my fingers. Dorien and Ivan emerged from the hallway behind me. Before Titus could react, they grabbed his arms and legs and tackled him out the door and down the stairs.

"What the fuck is going on?" Titus struggled as they dragged him to the twins' Eldorado.

"We have a surprise for you." Dorien opened the door and beckoned for Titus to have a seat. He slumped into the leather, his face a picture of misery.

"I don't like surprises," Titus growled. I knew he was thinking of his brother's death, and his guitar burned to ash.

"You'll like this one. But you can't know where we're going." I held up the blindfold they'd used on me. That got a grin out of Titus.

"Naughty Sprite." I loved that he'd started using Dorien's nickname for me. Titus allowed me to tie the blindfold. I climbed in the seat beside Dorien. We waved to Ivan and Elena, who decided to stay behind, and we took off.

Dorien drove the twins' car the way he drove his own – with a reckless disregard for traffic laws. I gripped the dashboard as we narrowly missed sideswiping a tree. Sibelius blasted from the stereo. Titus yelped as we hit a pothole and his head slammed into the roof.

Dorien pulled down a mountain track that was even more overgrown and treacherous than Manderley's driveway. After a time, the dense trees gave way to new plantings – forest blocks grown for timber. Dorien turned the car onto a dirt track. Titus gripped the handle as the car hurtled over the bumps.

His poor head must be one giant bruise by now. I hope our surprise makes up for it.

"Where the fuck are you taking me?" Titus sounded worried. In the front seat, Dorien and I grinned.

"Haven't you seen this horror film?" I asked. "The beautiful and talented musician lured into the woods by his supposed friends, only to be locked in the torture cabin and forced to saw off his own hand?"

"You're terrifying, Sprite."

I could see our destination up ahead, poking through the trees. Dorien pulled over on a patch of gravel, the wheel crunching over dead leaves. I helped Titus out of the car, positioned him facing the structure, and whipped off the blindfold.

"Um… so you weren't kidding about the torture shed?" Titus frowned at the crumbling brick and iron buildings in front of us. Piles of rusting machinery stood around it, and a tree snaked out a giant hole in the roof.

"It's a timber mill. Or rather, it *was* a timber mill. Now, it's a crumbling crapshack."

Titus looked confused. "Why have you brought me to a crumbling crapshack?"

I grinned wider. Dorien turned the key, and the trunk popped open. "Look inside and you'll have your answer."

Titus lifted the lid. "Holy shit." He staggered back, his eyes wide. "Holy fucking shit."

I loved his reaction as he took in the contents of the trunk. Nestled in a velvet-lined carrying case was a brand new electric guitar. Not just *any* electric guitar, but a St. Moritz SG replica 'Monkey' – the guitar Black Sabbath legend Toni Iommi used on *Paranoid*, *Master of Reality*, and *Vol. 4.*

"Why… why do you have this?" Titus cradled the neck of the instrument like it was a newborn baby.

"It's yours, man," Dorien said. "To replace the one that burned."

"How did you…"

"Creepy Cory did a little messing about in Madame Usher's accounts." I shoved my hands into the pocket of my hoodie to ward off the chill. "With all the payments going out for Elena's wedding, she won't even notice it's gone. Ivan said it was probably his and Elena's money anyway, and they wanted to get you an awesome present."

Titus' eyes glistened. "This is… it's incredible, but it's pointless. Madame Usher is searching my room regularly, and I can't go back to the woodshed again. She'll confiscate this the minute we return. You have to take it back."

"We're not taking it back, and you're not bringing this instrument anywhere near Manderley. There's an old root cellar out the back to service the miller who used to live on-site. It's waterproof, and we've added insulation. You can store it here. I've had the farmer set up a generator for you. Come on."

Dorien gestured for Titus to follow. I took his hand and squeezed it, staring into those depthless eyes. Titus' lips curled back, and the smile I'd been missing for weeks broke free of its cage. He had one of those smiles that took over his whole face. When Titus smiled, the whole world became brighter.

We picked our way through the fallen leaves and broken machinery and entered the main brick structure. Inside, the detritus of the old milling machines, conveyor belts, and railway lines stood as they'd been left. Dorien had come up here after classes yesterday and cleared away some of the debris, leaving a flat area large enough for Titus to run around in. Dorien jogged ahead of us and disappeared behind a hulking pile of machinery, emerging a moment later wheeling a Marshall amp stack.

"You need to hear yourself play, and so does the rest of the forest."

Titus dropped my hand and raced to Dorien, wrapping him in a crushing embrace. He looked giddy, like a kid on Christmas morning. In a few minutes, they had the guitar plugged in and amped up.

Titus stalked to the middle of the old mill. He strummed. A low purr reverberated from the amp. His grin could have lit the world.

He launched into a low, menacing riff. The music pounded through the space, reaching into every corner, punching deep into my chest. Titus used the riff as a theme, circling it back and playing with the shape of it, carving out meaning with each repetition. He angled the neck, bringing it close to his face as his fingers danced over the strings, tearing out a punishing solo.

Like Dorien, he loved to play fast, to build and build the tension of a piece until it exploded with sound. When he drew his bow across the cello, he could invoke an otherworldly dark power. But this was like nothing I'd ever heard before. The purr of the guitar pounded in my chest. I could *feel* the power of it coursing through my veins. My pulse quickened and hot need ached inside me – although that might've been the sight of my love descending into the chaos of the music, embracing the darkest depths of his heart.

Titus looked so completely natural with the guitar slung low and his tatted fingers curled around the strings, his long hair flying behind him as he banged his head along with the riff. All the tension that coiled inside him released in a wave of emotion. He *needed* this.

This is where he belongs.

I realized that what made Titus such a unique cellist was the tension of what he tried to force the instrument to do. He played cello like the lead guitarist in a metal band, all hair flying and unrelenting passion. He didn't fit in that world the way he fitted here.

He was wild, untamed, *demonic*. His music needed to be unleashed.

Watching Titus made my heart soar and the ache between my

legs throb with desire. But after a time, my ears started to ring. I walked outside and sat on one of the old wooden wagons that brought logs to the mill from deeper in the forest. I swung my legs in the breeze and listened to the tendrils of sound blasting through the holes in the roof, and imagined Titus' tatted fingers caressing me the way he did that guitar—

Dorien flopped down beside me, interrupting my filthy thoughts. He pulled a pipe and bag of weed from his jacket and lit up. "I don't entirely understand the appeal of the music, but he's *good.*"

I nodded. "He is. I just wish his parents would see it."

"They never will. To them, heavy metal – and even what we play in Broken Muse – will always be the evil music that stole Micah from them." Dorien sighed. "If I'd been their son, I wouldn't give a shit, but Titus cares too much about what they think. He wants to be their good little boy, but he's anything but good."

"I think he's *very* good." Despite myself, I licked my lip. I'd never been a big metal fan, but I had to admit, it was sexy as fuck. "What about you? You've gone a whole day without thinking about Dorien Valencourt. Does it feel good to do something nice for once?"

"I'll show you *nice.*" Dorien leaned over me, planting his hands on either side of me. His lips hovered inches from mine, his body coiled with tension. My heart thudded against my chest. I knew he wanted to close that space between us, but after he'd lost control and given in to that kiss back at Manderley, he was waiting, holding back, allowing me to give permission.

And in that space he created, this *thing* danced between us. The cord of our destiny wound tighter and tighter, ready to snap. What I felt for Dorien made me reckless. But in this old forest with the lingering notes of Iron Maiden soaring out, I embraced that recklessness.

I rocked forward.

I pressed my lips to his.

The world exploded into flame. The touch of our lips sparked a fire that burned through my veins, turning my entire body into this molten puddle of desperate *wanting*. Dorien's lips drew mine open, and he plunged his tongue deep, tasting me like he'd been starved for weeks, which I guessed was true.

We were used to communicating without words. We poured our hearts into our compositions and spoke our deepest fears with the sweep of a tragic note. We spoke a language that transcended our egos, which was why we'd been drawn together after all these years to have a second chance at building something wicked and beautiful. I spoke to Dorien now, using the music of our bodies to tell him that I forgave him, that I was ready to open my heart to him. That I would give him everything, but I demanded everything in return.

Dorien's hands remained welded in place on either side of me. He groaned as he pushed himself against me, grinding his hard cock between my legs. His whole body shook with need as he walked the tightrope between what he wanted to do to me and what he thought I needed. *He still doesn't realize that all I need is him.* My feet came up of their own accord, hooking behind him, pulling him tighter against me.

"What if someone sees?" I whispered.

"Look around you." Dorien broke our kiss to flash me that shit-eating grin of his. "Who's going to see but those cows under the trees over there? They look like they could use a show."

Dorien's hands slid beneath my jacket, shoving up my shirt and bra to roll my nipples through his fingers. I gasped into his lips as my whole body shuddered with need. I couldn't wait. My fingers tugged at his fly. I would have him *now*.

"There are condoms in my bag," he growled.

"It's okay," I whispered. "I'm on the pill, and I had a clean test. So if you—"

"Oh, I've had my test results sitting in my drawer for weeks, waiting to show you." Dorien's eyes glinted. "Ever since that weekend when Ivan and I had you over the piano stool, also known as the happiest weekend of my life."

I leaned forward and kissed him, drawing out the truth of his words through his wanton mouth. We melted into each other, our twin flames burning together. Magic crackled in the frigid air. What we were doing here – it was more than sex. It felt like the start of something, the opening of a wound so the healing could begin.

"Faye de Winter, it's not my birthday." Dorien's hands trailed down my arms. He looked at me with none of that arrogance that had marked our relationship so far. Here was the boy I'd fallen in love with when I was just six years old – my dark prince, my destiny.

I was so lost in Dorien's eyes I didn't even notice when the music stopped. I leaned in to kiss him again. My lips brushed his before something large and hard forced its way between us. A curtain of dark braids cascaded over my face as Titus' immovable chest separated us.

"It's *my* birthday," Titus growled. The corner of his mouth twisted up, and I thought he was mad before I saw the twinkle in his eye. He planted his legs on either side of me, and I felt his cock press into my thigh. My body trembled, and I felt myself melt against his hard body. Like, I was no longer human, just a puddle of Faye goo.

A cool breeze whistled through the trees, carrying away all the bullshit we needed to discard. Out here, away from Manderley, we could be who we truly were. Titus was the heavy metal guitarist with the kind heart. Dorien was the broken bad boy who needed to forgive himself. And me? I was Faye de Winter, and I could take what I wanted. And I wanted *all* of Broken Muse – mind, body, and soul.

"That's right. It is." I sank to my knees in front of Titus, tugging open his fly. The leaves cushioned me on the hard ground as I pushed down his boxers and drew out his shaft, long and hard, the tip already wet for me. I reached out with my tongue to lick the tip, tasting the saltiness of him.

Titus sucked in a breath, his muscles knitting. Fuck, that was hot. I loved seeing him shed the misery that shrouded him at Manderley and surrender himself to me. Titus spent so much time caring about other people, I wanted him to feel kindness, attention, worship.

I sucked the tip of his cock into my mouth, circling my tongue around and pressing into the little dip. I curled my lips around my teeth and took him in, inch by glorious inch. He was so big I had no hope of fitting all of him in my mouth, so I gripped him with my hand, stroking in time with my mouth.

Titus' head rolled back, his cornrows flicking out like a halo. His whole body was a tight coil of tension, and had been since the day he lost his guitar. Playing metal again had started to loosen Madame Usher's strings, but I could do more. He *needed* this. He fisted my hair, pushing himself against my face, driving me deeper.

"Faye," Titus gasped out. My name sounded like honey on his lips.

I wanted to finish him, to taste him on my tongue, but Titus had other ideas. He lifted me to my feet and spun me around, pushing me against Dorien. Titus ran his hands down my sides, skimming over my curves, mapping my body with kisses and caresses while his stomach heaved with suppressed need. "I don't know what you think about this, Sprite, but Dorien and I could make you feel so good right now."

My heart skipped. The heat of their bodies burned away any inhibitions I had left "I think… I could like that. But I didn't exactly pack up supplies for…"

Dorien's grin widened as he reached into the picnic bag he packed and pulled out a package of lube. "I was never a boy scout, but I do believe in always being prepared."

I gave his chest a playful slap, which only made his devilish grin wider. "You're a cockweasel. All your sweet-talking, and you planned on getting lucky all along."

Titus swiped the lube from his hand. "It's my birthday."

"Of course." Dorien leaned back on the wagon, placing one hand lazily behind his head. The other beckoned me to climb up on him. "It's the birthday boy's choice. Come here, Sprite."

I shimmied out of my leggings and straddled him, rubbing myself against his cock. Dorien reached out and cupped my face, stroking my cheeks with his thumbs as he brought me closer for a kiss. He looked at me with such reverence. "You are so beautiful right now."

I *felt* beautiful, in a way I never had before. A power pulsed in my veins. Two guys wanted to put aside the bullshit that held them at arms' length from each other to make me feel good.

I'm a Muse Girl.

Even better – I'm the Muse Queen.

Dorien's cock jerked between my legs, reminding me that this moment wasn't made of sweetness, but of dark desire. I shimmied closer, straddling him and sinking down onto his cock. My body fluttered, like I was filled with butterflies with flame-tipped wings.

Dorien's grin widened as I ground my hips to drive him deeper. He felt so good, stretching me in all the right places. It felt different than last time, when I'd been so unsure of what we were to each other. Now, as I raised myself up on my knees and slammed down on him, the invisible cord that bound us wrapped tight against my skin. Dorien's grey eyes locked on mine, and I knew that I was his and he was mine, and nothing could break us.

Titus came up behind me, wrapping his huge, inked arm around my chest. His braids fell over my shoulder, and I felt the cord tugging at me, opening, relenting. I wasn't only bound to Dorien. I belonged to Titus, too, as he belonged to both of us.

"This will feel cold for a moment," Titus whispered. I heard the squirt, and then felt cold liquid running between my ass cheeks. Titus used his hand to spread the lube where he needed it. He pushed one finger inside my ass. It felt weird, but good weird. I had part of him inside me, part of Dorien inside me. I wanted this. I wanted *more*.

Titus used his finger to match Dorien's rhythm, and after a few strokes, it stopped feeling weird and started feeling really, *really* fucking good. I ground my pelvis against Dorien, rubbing my clit against him until my whole body hummed with need.

Titus pushed a second finger inside me, and I gasped against Dorien's lips.

"You're going to fucking love this, Sprite," he whispered. "But you have to surrender completely. Let Titus and I make you feel like the goddess you are."

I nodded. I was done fighting, done with pain and want and mistrust. I was ready to have Broken Muse, all of them, in every way imaginable. Titus wrapped his arms around me, and his strength coursed through my veins. I leaned forward to give him more room, pressing my chest against Dorien and feeling his heart thud against mine. Being between them like this, so close, so full of them, it felt like I had music in my *veins*.

Titus removed his fingers and pushed the head of his cock inside me. I gasped against the tightness of it. Dorien chuckled, his fingers digging into my hips. Titus' huge arm across my chest held me upright.

"Relax, Sprite. Let us take control."

I didn't have much choice. Between the two of them, I had no room to move, to force my will upon them. I had to surrender to them, to us. I gripped Dorien's shoulders and let my eyes flutter closed. Titus' breath rasped in my ear, and Dorien's heart thudded against my chest. I gave myself over to the new sensations assailing me as Titus pushed himself another inch inside me, his cock rubbing against Dorien's through the thin wall that separated them.

So full of them.

They started to move – a perfectly synchronized beat that had me lost. An orgasm slammed into me, and it didn't stop as they moved inside me, like one long cock threading its way through my body, undoing me completely. The cord no longer wrapped around us – now it was inside us.

My body tossed and shuddered on a swell of pleasure. I lost myself – my body became a pulsing ball of heat and light and peace as my Muses took care of me, giving me every dark deed and broken sin they'd held back. Stars danced in my eyes as their darkness became mine. And even though there was no music here – the only sound our breath, the birds, and the rustle of branches in the breeze, I fancied I could pluck notes from the air.

The song of us.

The scents that always accompany my music swirled around – Dorien's cinnamon and frankincense dappled with sweet violets, Titus' rose and myrrh and red musk, and other scented memories, too – the pine-fresh smell of the polished piano-stool in the ballroom where Dorien and Ivan first had me, the homely taste of delicious things baking in the house kitchen as Titus and I stood over the stove, the bitter smoke of the pyre that burned our possessions.

My eyes flew open just as Dorien came, his mouth twisting up in that adorable way it did, as if even in bliss he couldn't resist playing games. He sagged back against the wagon, remaining inside me as long as he could before he went completely limp.

Titus' hands closed around my thighs. He pushed up into me, and I saw the stars again as the two of us exploded together – a supernova of pain and hurt and healing.

"Happy birthday to me," Titus whispered as he sank back on the wagon. I pulled myself into the crook of his armpit, placing my head against his broad chest, listening to his heart thunder against his ribs. Like the rumble of the electric guitar, Titus' body purred with raw power and energy. No wonder he chose this music – it literally flowed in his veins.

Dorien fell into Titus' opposite arm, completely comfortable lying naked against his friend. He reached across to stroke my cheek, his breath kissing the air. "You belong to us, Sprite. We'll always love you. We'll always fight for you."

~

On the drive back, Titus couldn't sit still. After he pulled himself off me he'd headed back inside to shred for another two hours straight. I expected him to be sound asleep, but it was as though the music had ignited a flame inside him. His fingers drummed on the back of Dorien's seat until Dorien threatened to cut them off.

"Can we go back again?" he asked.

"Sure, man," Dorien turned into the mountain road that led to Manderley. "I'll drive you down next weekend when I take Faye to see her mother."

That's right. Mom was being discharged from the hospital next week, and she'd be moving into the hotel room in the city paid for by Natalie's company. Natalie said it was the least she could do, given everything Marguerite de Winter had done for her.

"We should bring Ivan next time," Dorien reached back to squeeze my knee. *I guess this means I'd forgiven him?* I wasn't sure. I think I'd forgiven him some time ago. Forgiveness wasn't a single act. It was a constant process of relearning how you felt about someone, and about yourself. And although I trusted Dorien again, I also trusted *myself* that if he betrayed me, I'd be able to survive it.

46

FAYE

*D*orien swung the Eldorado beneath Manderley's high iron gates. He cursed as a figure dashed in front of the car, waving its arms.

"It's Harrison." I rolled down the window. "What's wrong?"

Harrison leaned in the window, his breath coming out in ragged gasps. "Get up to the house. Quickly now."

"What happened?"

Harrison shook his head. He slung the rifle over his shoulder and headed off into the woods.

Why the fuck does Harrison have his rifle?

Dorien, Titus, and I exchanged glances. What now? Madame Usher couldn't possibly know where we'd been all day. Was this about Ivan? Elena? Fuck, did Ivan finally give in to his brotherly instincts and do something to Master Radcliffe?

My heart leaped in my chest as we pulled up into the parking area. I could see other cars parked next to the fountain. I was out of the car and racing up the porch steps before Dorien even turned the engine off. Madame Usher met us in the hall. "Where have you been? I called the Dumfrees Institute and they said you had no recital today."

"Didn't we tell you that it got moved to next weekend?" Dorien lied as smooth as silk. "We thought we'd visit with Faye's mother since we were out."

"I know that's a lie. I called the hospital. You weren't there." Madame Usher grabbed my hair. Tears sprung in my eyes as she yanked my head so I was kneeling on the floor. My scalp screamed. "This is *your* doing. I know you're sticking your nose into your mother's investigation. You've been meddling in things you do not understand, digging up old ghosts. Well, you've gone too far this time."

"Let go of her." Dorien stepped forward. Titus was faster. He shoved Madame Usher against the wall. She shrieked in fright as he held her head in his enormous hand, his muscles tight, his kind eyes murderous.

"You'll never touch Faye like that again," he growled. Madame Usher squirmed, trying to free herself. But Titus was the size of a freight train and angry as hell. "We're not playing your games any longer. I'll tell you what's going to happen now. We will—"

"Drop that woman right this minute, Mr. Thibodeaux, or you'll be in even more trouble."

I whirled around at the booming voice. Titus froze as Commissioner Walpole stepped out of the shadows, his arms folded. Behind him, the dim lighting revealed more figures – Dorien's and Heather's parents, and another robed figure with a bald head and eyes like an eagle – all-seeing, predatory. I remembered him from the one time I visited Dorien's house as a kid. Father Aaron, the cult leader.

My head spun. *What's going on here?*

The commissioner stepped toward Titus. "You heard me, young man. I can make a lot of trouble for you. And your parents."

Tension crackled in the air around us. Titus released his fist, his dark eyes unreadable. Madame Usher dropped to the floor, clutching her throat and coughing violently. Commissioner Walpole rushed to help her to her feet. I heard footsteps on the landing above, and Elena, Ivan, and Aroha poked their heads over the railing. Ivan's icicle eyes burned at the edges with questions. I shook my head, advising him to stay where he was.

"Really now, is this any way to begin a celebration?" When Eustace Danvers' smiled, the jeweled brooch at her throat bounced. She stepped toward Dorien and held her arms wide. "We came to offer our congratulations and welcome you into our family, son."

"What are you talking about?" Dorien demanded. He planted his feet wide, not backing away as she embraced him awkwardly, but standing his ground, as stiff and immovable as stone.

"Heather called us this morning to give us the good news." Mr. Danvers beamed, extending his hand. "I must say, we're extremely happy. We always believed you two would make a great match – the classical world is about to meet the new power couple."

I stared in shock as their words sank in. Heather told her parents Dorien proposed to her? But *why?* Dorien opened his mouth, but no sound came out. My dark prince looked completely floored.

Father Aaron stepped out from behind the Valencourts, his smile broad as he clapped Dorien on the shoulder. "Congratulations, Dorien. You've made a fine choice, as we knew you would. Your marriage will unite two powerful families and bring forth a new age of prosperity for the Temple."

Beside him, Dorien's mother stood, mute and remote. I glared at her, willing her to speak up, to protest this ridiculous marriage. First Elena marrying Radcliffe, and now Dorien had this marriage forced on him? What was this? We didn't live in Victorian England.

Dorien rallied, collecting the storms in his eyes and aiming all that fury at Father Aaron. He stepped forward, shaking his head. "I think Heather's made some mistake. I've been away from the house all day, so I couldn't possibly have—"

"But you did it this morning, silly boy," Madame Usher said, her voice syrupy sweet, like she was chiding Dorien for forgetting his lunchbox. The cloying floral scent of her perfume itched in my nose. "Under the gazebo, with the snow falling around you. It was quite the romantic proposal. Your social media is already blowing up with the news."

What? I yanked my phone from my pocket and scrolled to the Broken Muse Instagram page. The first photograph on the feed was a picture of a gazebo, looking hauntingly beautiful under a dusting of fresh snow. Heather stood beneath it wearing a black lace dress with flowing gothic sleeves, her honey hair perfectly styled and dappled with snowflakes, her face rapturous with love.

My heart stuttered as I peered closer. Dorien was wearing the same red shirt he'd worn when I'd followed him outside after I played Clare's piece. He hadn't taken one knee, but knelt on both knees, his head slightly bowed – the exact position he'd been in that day. Yes, and there was the corner of his phone sticking out of his pocket, and his suit looked a little odd across the breast, where someone had colored over the white cord of his earbuds.

Fuck. Someone took his picture when we were under the gazebo that day, and Photoshopped it into this of Heather. My finger hovered over the comments. The photograph already had twenty-three thousand likes. *This is out in the world now, even though it's not true.*

It's not true.

Footsteps clattered on the stairs as Ivan, Elena, and Aroha joined us. Ivan grabbed the phone from my hands. "This isn't what happened," he snarled. "You can't just fake an engagement and expect us to play along."

"Ivan, don't be so rude to our guests." Madame's voice was indulgent, like she was scolding a naughty puppy. That meant she still believed she had control of this situation, that this wasn't the end of the horrors we could expect.

Dorien looked from Madame Usher to Father Aaron. His shoulders hitched. I knew he was calculating his next move, weighing the cost. I saw the resolve in his eye, and I knew what he was going to say before he spoke. "Mr. and Mrs. Danvers, I'm so sorry, but I can't marry your daughter. There's something you need to know. Once, I viciously assaulted Aaron Varney. It was only because of Madame Usher's connections in the police that I wasn't charged. I should be in jail right now, and even if Commissioner Walpole doesn't take me in today, it won't be long before this comes out in the media. You don't want that stain on your family."

"I admire your sentimentality, Dorien," the commissioner said. "But you need to be truthful. There's no point covering up for Faye de Winter's crime."

Um, excuse me?

Father Aaron shook his head at Dorien as his eyes met mine. I felt like a field mouse caught in the talons of a hawk. "Yes, Dorien. You must never be afraid to raise your voice in truth. You are too young and talented to send yourself away for *her* crimes. Even though it's traumatic for me to remain in the room with that evil woman, I stand here as a member of your family to ensure you don't throw your life away."

"Dorien, listen to Father Aaron." It was the first time his mother spoke. Her voice sounded robotic, like she was speaking from a script. "This girl is dangerous. She's been stalking you ever since you rejected her, sneaking into our home, taking pictures of you. She hurt Father Aaron. She even got herself enrolled in this school because you were here. And now she wants you to go to jail for her? Don't let her manipulate you like this, not when you have a chance at a beautiful future with Heather."

I shook my head. "This is ridiculous. I've been nowhere near your house. I don't even know that man. This is complete horseshit—"

"We knew you'd double down on your lies; so delusional. So I kept these." Aaron held up a stack of photographs. Dorien ripped them from his hands and fanned them out for us all to see.

I gasped.

"These... these are fakes." But even as I saw them, I knew that my protests were pointless. The photographs were screenshots from a security camera feed, and they were expertly doctored – whoever had these made could pay for top-notch deepfake. It really did look like my face twisted with rage as I slammed my fist into Aaron's face, straddling him to get a better angle as a pool of blood spread out beneath him.

"That's for a jury to decide." Commissioner Walpole held up a pair of handcuffs. "Which is where you'd be heading, if I had my way. Lucky for you, with such a large and important event to prepare for, Father Aaron is willing to overlook this attack."

Father Aaron inclined his head to Dorien. "As long as Dorien can continue with his wedding plan unmolested. I'd hate for *anyone* in the Valencourt family to experience the torture of separation from those they love."

The implication was clear. Dorien married Heather, or I went to prison, and something unspeakable happened to his brother, Jacob. Dorien's face twisted as understanding dawned on him. He made his decision in a split second, his jaw set with determination. I knew it was the wrong one. I surged forward, holding my hands out to Walpole so he could cuff me. "I'm confessing to a crime. You need to arrest me or—"

Ivan slapped my hands down just as Dorien said, "You're right. I've been a fool for not seeing things before. Of course my marriage to Heather will go ahead. Mr. and Mrs. Danvers, I'm excited to be part of your family."

"Oh, how wonderful." Mrs. Danvers clapped her hands

together. "Dorien, Heather is waiting for you in your room. She's *so* looking forward to discussing your wedding plans."

47

FAYE

*D*orien's features twisted with rage. His hands balled to fists at his sides, but as his gaze jumped from face to face, I saw the hopelessness settle into him.

If he refused to marry Heather, I would go to jail for his crime. And I knew that didn't even compare with what they could do to his brother. He was doing what he promised – protecting me. And in doing so he'd nailed shut his own coffin.

Dorien moved toward the staircase. I grabbed his arm, my nails digging into his flesh. "Call their bluff," I hissed. "Everything they have on me is fake, we both know that."

"Yes, and we know the commissioner is in her pocket," Dorien growled. He leaned down and brushed his lips across mine. "I'll be okay. Maybe I can get Heather to see reason."

Maybe pigs will fly. Maybe Mozart will rise from the grave to perform Phantom of the Opera. *Maybe Madame Usher will jump off a cliff.*

Dorien climbed the stairs as though he climbed the gallows. His shoulders squared, and a fierce determination settled on his features – his dark soul bent toward a singular purpose. That scared me more than the hopelessness. They'd trapped Dorien in this house and piece by piece eroded his freedoms until he had nothing left to lose, and like a caged lion, he was now at his most dangerous.

He disappeared over the landing. A moment later, I heard his door creak open and then click shut behind him.

The grandfather clock ticked.

"Come, let us discuss the wedding plans." Madame Usher herded the adults back toward the Blue Room. "We're hosting Elena's nuptials here at the end of the semester. If you wish, we could make it a double wedding…"

The five of us remained in the foyer, every face turned toward me. I couldn't hear raised voices from the floor above, and I didn't know if that was a good sign or not. The grandfather clock tick-tick-ticked in the gloom. The silence terrified me.

Titus gathered me in his arms. "It will be okay," he whispered. "Dorien's talking to his FBI agent, remember? He'll be able to see this evidence against you is fake. They'll get into the compound and arrest Aaron and save his brother, and all this will go away."

I nodded, but I wasn't so sure.

The secrets of Manderley ran deep – scar tissue that would never heal.

Ivan stood behind me, his body trembling with rage and indecision. He'd tried to stay away from me because of his own belief about what I wanted and what he deserved. But I saw in his icicle eyes the moment his love overcame him, and he collapsed against me, pressing his lips to my cheek and holding me close.

Elena slammed into me, joining our embrace. From the staircase, Aroha made a gagging face, but she flopped her arms around us. We remained still, wrapped together by the binding cords of Manderley, breathing as one, waiting, hoping.

Tick tock. Tick tock.

I couldn't take it any longer. I extricated myself from the group and slunk up the stairs, straining to hear a sound. The walls groaned, and I fancied I heard the creaking of footsteps darting across the room above my head, but I was so used to those sounds now they didn't even register.

I paused in front of Dorien's door. "Dorien?"

"Faye, don't come in. Don't—"

The fear in his voice spurred me on. I knew all this had been a set up. Heather had done this to him, and she wasn't finished yet. If she thought she could, then she had another thing coming.

I flung open his door.

What?

No.

Blood. So much blood.

48

FAYE

*D*orien stood in the center of the room, his naked torso bathed in soft light. In his hands, he gripped a bloody knife. His eyes flicked to me, and the knife clattered to the floor, the blade leaving a long cut in the polished wood floor beside the body.

The body.

A slab of still flesh slumped on the rug. Jagged wounds cut into the back of a red gown. Blood dribbled from the wounds, pooling and staining the rug pink.

A pair of glittering red pumps poked out from beneath the hem of the dress.

Heather.

"Faye, this isn't what it looks like," Dorien's voice was sandpaper, scouring away the layers of my heart.

"Interesting." My own voice sounded far away, like I was trying to yell underwater. I could barely hear it over the roar of blood in my ears. "It *looks* like you brutally stabbed Heather to death. I'd love to hear an alternative explanation."

"I didn't do it," Dorien cried. "Faye, you have to believe me. I came in here and she was already dead. I picked up the knife because… because I wasn't thinking and she's fucking dead. But I didn't hurt her. I would *never*."

I searched his words for one shred of truth, one possible explanation I could latch onto that would prove to me he didn't do this.

I found none.

There was no other way into this room. The door had been locked – I heard him turn the key. The only other people who had keys were me and Madame Usher, and we were both downstairs. I scanned the windows. They were shut tight, and they looked out over the garden. No handy trees or drainpipes for an intruder to shimmy down. There was no other entrance to this room. No one had come, and all the other residents of Manderley were downstairs in the Blue Room with the guests.

My mind drew up another murder, another young girl brutally killed in this house. Clare lying at the bottom of the stairs, her neck snapped, and only Dorien's word that he'd been in front of her on the staircase.

I ran over his history of violence. That aggravated assault Madame Usher covered up. The secrets he held close like precious jewels. The lies – all the times he told me he had nothing to do with the bullying, when there was no other explanation apart from a ghost.

I trusted him.

The grim, determined look in his eyes, the straightening of his shoulders as he climbed the stairs. The tiger in the cage who sharpened his claws.

It can't be.

But it is.

There's no other explanation.

Dorien murdered Heather.

TO BE CONTINUED

~

Musician.
Heartbreaker.
Murderer.

Manderley Academy 3, Spirited

Dorien Valencourt is in deep shit.
His cheeky grin and stormy eyes won't help him this time.

But I will.
I've found love in the darkness.
Three broken muses possess me,
Mind, body, and soul.
I won't give them up for anything,
Especially not for a witch with a blackened heart.

In a school ruled by shadows and secrets,
I'll shine a light in the darkest places.
We'll expose a long-buried violation,
And force a villain to confront her sins.

If only our secrets don't devour us all.

With Titus and Ivan at my side,
we'll free Dorien from his cage.
We'll drag these skeletons into the daylight.

The ghost of Manderley will have her revenge.

A dark mystery unfolds around musician Faye de Winter in the final
book of this gripping gothic college reverse harem bully romance by
USA TODAY best-selling author Steffanie Holmes. Warning: Proceed

with caution – this tale of three spoiled rich boys with unsettling secrets and the girl who refuses to put up with their shit contains dark themes, a creepy house, a smoldering second-chance romance, college angst, cruel bullies and swoon-worthy sex.

Read Manderley Academy 3, Spirited

~

I should have kept my mouth shut.
I should have let them win.
Now the kings of the school are out for my blood,
... and they're not the only ones.

Need more dark, gothic, and delicious reverse harem bully romance in your life?

HP Lovecraft meets *Cruel Intentions* in the paranormal reverse harem bully romance readers are calling, "The greatest mindfuck of 2019". Warning: Not for the faint of heart – this story of three broken bad boys and the girl who stood her ground contains dark themes, crazed cultists, books bound in human skin, high-school drama, swoon-worthy sex, and potential triggers. Grab book 1, *Shunned,* in KU now.

FROM THE AUTHOR

You've been waiting a long time for the second book in Faye's series, and for that I'm so grateful. Thank you for your patience with this artsy-fartsy author, especially as she navigates life and writing during a global pandemic.

In writing Manderley Academy, I drew on numerous novels, poison manuals, and true hauntings for inspiration. If you're a fan of gothic literature, you may notice some of the illusions and names in homage to my literary heroes and heroines. At the centre of it all is Manderley – named in honour of the grand house at the centre of Daphne du Maurier's *Rebecca*, one of my favourite books of all time. If you haven't read it, I encourage you to do so, although you may not be able to turn the lights out until you reach the last page.

Faye's travels in Prague and Romania were inspired by my own trip last year. Yes, the Dracula museum is real, and some poor schmuck has the job of lying in a coffin waiting for unsuspecting tourists. Yes, I now own no less than 5 tacky Dracula t-shirts. And yes, *trdelnik* is addictive.

I've created a playlist for the Broken Muses of Manderley Academy series. You'll find it on Spotify here. I've tried to include every song I mention in the text, as well as some I love that I feel Faye and the Broken Muse boys would adore. I've included some more modern music, too – a bit of goth, a smidge of metal (for many metal musicians, like Titus, are classically-trained and heavily inspired by classical roots). Maybe it will spark your own 'Come to Dorien' moment, or you'll find some cool new tunes to jam along.

As always, it takes a village to bring a book to life. I'd like to thank my cantankerous drummer husband for reading this manuscript and giving me so many ideas to make it better. And for being my lighthouse. And for putting up with me blasting Bach at full volume.

To Kit, Bri, Elaina, Katya, the SpecFicNZ community, and the Noods for all the writerly encouragement and advice. To Meg and Eveis for the epically helpful editing job, and to Lori for the stunning covers. To Sam and Iris, for the daily Facebook shenanigans that help keep me sane while I spend my days stuck at home covered in cats.

To you, the reader, for going on this journey with me, even though it's led to some dark places. Book 3 is up for pre-order and it's going to be WILD. Get it here.

If you're enjoying *Manderley Academy* and want to read more from me, check out my other dark reverse harem bully romance series, *Kings of Miskatonic Prep*. HP Lovecraft meets *Cruel Intentions* in this dark paranormal reverse harem bully romance that's definitely not for the faint of heart. Hazel is the most badass FMC I've ever written, and I think you'll love meeting her. You can start the series with *Shunned*.

I send out a weekly newsletter that includes book news but also real life spooky stories and the inspiration behind my books. Recent emails have included the history of chloral and birthwort, the last woman convicted of witchcraft in England, and my night in a haunted chateau. Join here.

If you want to hang out and talk about all things Broken

Muse, my readers are sharing their theories and discussing the book over in my Facebook group, Books That Bite. Come join the fun.

I'm so happy you enjoyed this story! I'd love it if you wanted to leave a review on Amazon or Goodreads. It will help other readers to find their next gothic read.

Thank you, thank you! I love you heaps! Until next time.

Steff

Read Shunned now

Who the hell builds a school on top of an inaccessible cliff?

Whoever built Derleth Academy, my new school. I answered my own question as the car's wheel skidded over the rough gravel on the way up the steep peninsula. A scream escaped my lips as the car lurched toward the edge of the cliff, one wheel spinning completely free.

Muttering under his breath, the driver for the school slammed the car into reverse and backed us onto the road before slamming on the gas again. We continued our wary climb along the narrow gravel path.

Surely the Academy can't be completely *cut-off.* The school had to bring up food and supplies. Parents must visit on the weekends. My driver was certainly giving it his all, tearing around the corners like he was on a Formula 1 racetrack and not a goat path hugging the side of a mountain. I gritted my teeth and gripped the back of the seat as rocks rolled from beneath the wheels and clattered over the sheer drop into the raging waters below. One wrong move, and we'd tumble down a two-hundred-foot cliff and be dashed against the cliffs so hard and fast that boats would mistake our remains for rock paintings.

Not the way I ever imagined I'd go.

We passed into thick vegetation, the cliff and ocean on one side giving way to looming trees that blocked out the grey sky. I let out the breath I'd been holding. Branches scraped the sides of the car, and my phone beeped with protest as we moved out of cell range. *No contact with the outside world,* the school brochure read. *At Derleth Academy, we foster a competitive academic program requiring the full attention of our students. Distracting technology or personal items will not be tolerated.*

In other words, I couldn't call for help. It was the opening sequence to every horror film, ever.

Not that I had anyone to call. Not anymore.

"Almost there," the driver said, swinging the car around a hairpin corner and launching my stomach into my throat. It was the most words he'd spoken to me the entire trip. "You can see the school through the trees."

I squinted into the forest, trying to make out some kind of building that might pass as a school. But I couldn't see a thing. We rounded another corner and—

Well, that's terrifying.

We rolled between two towering stone pillars obscured by creeping vines, past an ornate sign that read DERLETH ACADEMY. A wide, pristine concrete drive flanked by an avenue of towering trees and wide, manicured lawns led up to an imposing stone building, stretching in all directions with narrow arched windows, spiky towers, and a row of leering gargoyles along the roof.

What is this place? It looked more like Dracula's castle than a prestigious preparatory school.

I couldn't believe the wealthiest people in the country sent their children up that winding road to get educated. *Who's the headmistress, Morticia Addams?* But according to the brochure, that was exactly what they did. In droves. Derleth Academy had a waiting list a mile long, and you couldn't even pay to get in. You had to be *invited*.

Somehow, I, Hazel Waite – an overachieving orphan from the wrong side of Philly – ended up on their radar.

I flashed back to the day two weeks ago, when a banging on the door of my dingy apartment dragged me from a deep slumber. A woman with coiffed hair and a designer suit that cost more than a car staggered backward in surprise when I glared at her through the chain wearing only my pajamas and what must have been a terrifying scowl. Well, *she* wasn't the one being dragged from a pleasant Jason Momoa sex dream during the four-hour reprieve between night shift at the diner and cleaning rooms at a retirement home.

"Are you Hazel Waite?" she asked, her brown eyes wide and curious.

"No. Piss off." I glowered, slamming the door in her face. She was probably from CPS, trying to force me into foster care. Fuck that. I only had seven more months to survive before I turned eighteen. No way was I going to spend it in the hell that had killed Dante.

The woman didn't go away. She sat out on the road in her sports car and waited me out. I had to leave for work or I'd lose my job, and it wasn't easy to find work when you were underage and using an obviously fake ID. As soon as I left the house, she ambushed me.

"I'm not here to hand you over to the authorities," she said hurriedly, shoving a thick envelope into your hands. "I'm a scholarship administrator from Derleth Academy in Arkham, Massachusetts. Your current school put you forward for one of our four senior scholarship positions – a fully funded year at a first-class prep school, where our students go on to attend the top colleges in the world. I know the first quarter has already started, but it's taken me this long to track you down. You've only missed a week so far."

I stared at the envelope in my hands, at the red, black and gold school crest – a crooked five-pointed star inside a shield with some kind of Latin phrase beneath it. *This has got to be a joke.*

"I know what you're thinking," the woman said. "It's not a joke or a trick. I promise you that it's not. If you come to Derleth, we will assume guardianship duties until you turn eighteen. You'll be housed, clothed, and have all your schoolbooks and other needs met, as well as receiving a first-class education. You're a promising student, Hazel, and I know you've been dealt a cruel lot in life. This could be where you turn everything around. Don't answer me now. Read over the paperwork, and I'll return tomorrow for your decision."

And now, just ten days after I signed my soul over to this school in exchange for paid tuition, room, and board, I stared up at the imposing facade and wondered if I'd made a terrible mistake.

Sure, my life was miserable. I was drowning in grief, and even working two jobs I could barely pull in enough money to survive. College was out of the question, because I couldn't finish high school without going into foster care. But at least all that was familiar territory. That was the world I'd grown up in – the world of pain and struggle and loss. Derleth Academy was the exact opposite. Every element of this building screamed wealth and privilege and *you don't belong here.*

The driver pulled to a stop on the wide circular drive beside a towering stone fountain. A black woman in a drab grey smock darted out of the shadows of the porch and approached the car. I held my hand out to her. "Hello, I'm Hazel Waite—"

The woman ducked her head, avoiding me. She popped open the trunk, hauled out my heavy suitcase and bookbag, and hurried off to the house with them before I could offer to help.

Weird much? I swiped a dreadlock off my face. My friend

Dante's foster sister had done them for me last year, back when things were perfect and the most I had to worry about was whether my mom would ground me for getting dreadlocks.

An awful feeling twisted in my gut. I wished Mom was here, hating my loss, right now. But she was gone, gone, gone, and so was Dante, and it was just me and this terrifying school and no other options.

Three figures descended the grand stone steps toward me: A woman with translucent skin and a flowing black dress, flanked on either side by two students wearing the Derleth uniform. Fallen leaves skittered away from the woman's hem, and she moved with such poise that she appeared to float over the steps. With her severe features and a gauzy black ribbon pinned in her hair, she looked more like she was attending a funeral. Behind her, the two students – a guy and a girl – glared at me, distrust emanating from their every pore.

The woman stopped on the second-to-last step, peering down her nose at me as if I were a bug that wasn't even worth squashing. "You'll have to do something about that hair. We enforce a strict dress code in my school, Ms. Waite. I'll not have you flouting it on your very first day."

This must be the principal, Hermia West. My Morticia Addams guess wasn't far off. This woman looked like she drank the blood of students to sustain her beauty. The way her grey eyes stabbed right through me sent a cold shiver through my body.

There was nothing in the student handbook about dreadlocks. Although, of course, I'd only skim-read the thing on the bus from Philly. The handbook was boring. And *long.* "I'm sorry, Ms. West. I didn't know—"

"Ignorance is no excuse. That's 3 demerit points for you. And you're to refer to me as Headmistress."

Beside her, the boy sniggered. I turned my gaze to look at him, and my heart nearly stopped. *Wow, he's beautiful.* I had no idea boys that hot existed outside of magazines and Hollywood movies. He stood practically the same height as Ms. West, his broad shoulders accentuated by the tailored cut of his red-trimmed blazer. Prefect and merit badges decorated both lapels. Dark brown curls caught the grey light filtering through the clouds, throwing back beautiful shades of russet and silver. His clean-shaven face and high, majestic cheekbones appeared angelic, but his ice-blue eyes were cold and cruel.

The girl moved closer to him, touching his arm and shooting me a possessive glare, like a cat in heat. She had the appearance of a cat, too – slanted green eyes accentuated with heavy makeup, pointed chin, and the lithe body and long legs of a panther. Beautiful but deadly.

"This is Trey Bloomberg and Courtney Haynes," Headmistress West said. "I've appointed them as your student guides. They will show you the dorm, library, and dining hall, go over your schedule and classrooms, and ensure you understand *all* our rules. You will dine with the student body in two hours' time, and tomorrow you begin classes. I've had a copy of your schedule and the school handbook placed in your room. Memorize them, for failure to comply will result in further demerits. Here's your dorm room key."

In my pocket, my phone gave another defiant chirp. *Great.* I'd practically worn down the battery looking for a signal on the death road.

Headmistress West descended the last step to drop an ancient-looking metal key into my hand. Her pointy black boots lined up with my scuffed Docs. She loomed over me, her disapproval seeping into my bones. "You have a phone in your pocket." It wasn't a question.

"Yes."

Behind her, the boy smirked. I felt naked, exposed. My legs itched to make a run for the woods. Headmistress West held out her hand, unfurling long fingers topped with red-painted nails, the tips pointed like talons. "Hand it over. We don't allow outside technology on campus."

Instinctively, my hand flew to my pocket. "I won't use it to call or text. It doesn't work here, anyway, so what's the—"

"Ms. Waite, failure to obey a teacher's command is an automatic loss of 10 points. You seem most anxious to find out what punishments await the students at the bottom of the class list."

A lump rose in my throat. My phone contained photographs – snaps of my mom smiling demurely or brushing her hair in the mirror before she went out to work at the strip club. Of Dante and I hanging out around the neighborhood, smoking on the rusted playground beside his house, tagging the concrete wall behind the boxing gym on the corner. Every other one of my possessions had been destroyed in the fire. Those photographs were practically all I had left of them.

Trey and Courtney covered their mouths with their hands, barely disguising their laughter. Courtney leaned over and whispered something to Trey. They both cracked up. Despite myself, my cheeks flushed. *Better get used to this.*

Headmistress West, of course, ignored them. She wasn't backing down on this phone thing. My fingers closed around it, the comfortable weight of it in my hand reminding me that it was one of the last connections to my old life.

What does it matter? They're gone. Looking at their photos won't bring them back. But this school could be the only chance I have at a real future.

My hand trembling, I dropped my phone into her talons. As soon as it left my hand, I itched to get it back. Headmistress West slipped the phone into a fold of her dress, where it disappeared from sight.

"Follow me." The headmistress swirled on her heel and floated up the stairs. Numb, I fell in step behind her. Trey came up beside me. His arm brushed mine, and a jolt of warmth rocketed through my body. I dared a look up at his face. As we moved into the shadow of the porch, the colors in his hair changed, becoming a deep brown and blood red. A curl flopped over his eye, and I noticed flecks of silver on the edges of those arresting blue irises. My fingers itched to reach up and swipe that curl off his face, to touch his smooth skin, feel his cheek move beneath my fingers, to cut myself on his cheekbones. A familiar longing pooled in my stomach, an ache that I'd never been able to sate before, and now never would.

I'd never seen a boy that *perfect*.

Trey's fingers brushed me again. My breath froze in my mouth as his hand lingered on my elbow. To anyone looking at us from a distance, it would appear as though he was helping me, steadying me up the steep steps. The touch on my skin was white-hot, lighting up parts of my body that hadn't felt anything since Dante… since before the fire. *How can this boy with such cruel eyes have this effect on me?*

When he caught me looking, Trey's perfect lips curled back into a sneer. His fingers tightened on my arm, squeezing my skin. Tighter, tighter, until he was cutting off circulation. I yelped in protest.

"You don't belong here," he murmured, his perfect lips forming hateful words. "You should leave now."

He said it so casually, like he was chatting about the weather, and that self-satisfied smirk never left his face. My stomach twisted, the air driving from my lungs as though he'd punched me.

"No thanks," I said brightly, pretending that I misunderstood him. "I'm good."

"We don't want you, and we're used to getting what we want. We're going to eat you alive, new meat." Trey flashed me a smile that was all teeth and violence. The venom in his eyes frightened me. *This is not a guy to mess with.*

Too bad he seemed to already have it out for me, and I hadn't even got inside the school yet. My plan to keep my head down and stay invisible fizzled before my eyes. Already I could see how the school year was going to play out. *We don't want you here.* Trey spoke for the entire student body. He was a King in this school. It was written in his smile, dripping from the menace in his words.

I'd pissed him off. Just by existing. Just by setting foot on the hallowed grounds of his kingdom. *Well, fuck you, Trey Bloomberg.* I could handle a year of insults and loneliness if I got my diploma at the end of it. My life was already hell on earth – if Trey Bloomberg thought he could break me, he'd have to try a lot harder.

I wrenched my arm away from us. "Don't touch me." Behind us, Courtney giggled.

"Yeah, Trey. You should know not to handle garbage. She's a gutter-trash whore who's probably fucked so many guys that your dick wouldn't even touch the sides."

The comment stung. I thought of my sweet mother, all candy smiles and sticky skin as she stripped off her sweat-soaked lace g-string and six-inch heels after her shift and pulled on the cloud-pink pajamas I found for her in a thrift store. A hard lump rose in my throat. I shoved the image aside. *Not now.*

Wait until you get to your room, until you're alone, then you can break down.

"I guess we're not going to be braiding each other's hair," I muttered to Courtney.

"I wouldn't touch that rat's nest on your head if someone hid a *Faberge* egg inside," Courtney sneered. "I bet it's got real eggs in it, though. Insect eggs, laid by the gross things crawling around in there."

Instinctively, my hand flew up to my face, to touch the dread-lock that always fell over my eye, to tuck it behind my ear – a gesture that Dante would so often do when he noticed my loss in my eyes, which was all the time because I liked them unruly. Ever since the fire, I'd been touching my own hair more and more, seeking the comfort of the familiar weight of a hand moving the dreadlocks. But it wasn't the same. It would never be the same.

Courtney wrinkled her face in disgust, while Trey continued to smirk at me. The force of his loathing sank my stomach to my knees. He didn't even know me, but it didn't matter.

At the top of the stairs, the headmistress turned and frowned at me. "Don't dawdle," she snapped. "The school doesn't bite."

"She's wrong," Trey whispered. "Are you ready to find out just how bad we bite?"

The lump of hard, bitterness burned at the back of my throat. They were right. I didn't belong here. I was the poor gutter-trash girl from the wrong side of the tracks, and they were *royalty*. They were the monarchs. *They're going to make my life miserable, and there's nothing I can do.*

Read Shunned now

Tough luck, bully boys – I won't hide away.
I'm not afraid.
But maybe… *I should be.*

HP Lovecraft meets *Cruel Intentions* in book 1 of this dark paranormal reverse harem bully romance. Warning: Not for the faint of heart – this story of three broken bad boys and the girl who stood her ground contains dark themes, crazed cultists, books bound in human skin, high-school drama, swoon-worthy sex, and potential triggers.

START READING NOW
books2read.com/shunned

ABOUT THE AUTHOR

Steffanie Holmes is the *USA Today* bestselling author of the paranormal, gothic, dark, and fantastical. Her books feature clever, witty heroines, wild shifters, cunning witches and alpha males who *always* get what they want.

Legally-blind since birth, Steffanie received the 2017 Attitude Award for Artistic Achievement. She was also a finalist for a 2018 Women of Influence award.

Steff is the creator of *Rage Against the Manuscript* – a resource of free content, book, and courses to help writers tell their story, find their readers, and build a badass writing career. (www.rageagainstthemanuscript.com)

Steffanie lives in New Zealand with her husband, a horde of cantankerous cats, and their medieval sword collection.

STEFFANIE HOLMES NEWSLETTER

Grab a free copy *Cabinet of Curiosities* – a Steffanie Holmes compendium of short stories and bonus scenes – when you sign up for updates with the Steffanie Holmes newsletter: www.steffanieholmes.com/newsletter.

Come hang with Steffanie
www.steffanieholmes.com
hello@steffanieholmes.com

Briarwood Reverse Harem series

The Castle of Earth and Embers

The Castle of Fire and Fable

The Castle of Water and Woe

The Castle of Wind and Whispers

The Castle of Spirit and Sorrow

Crookshollow Gothic Romance series

Art of Cunning (Alex & Ryan)

Art of the Hunt (Alex & Ryan)

Art of Temptation (Alex & Ryan)

The Man in Black (Elinor & Eric)

Watcher (Belinda & Cole)

Reaper (Belinda & Cole)

Wolves of Crookshollow series

Digging the Wolf (Anna & Luke)

Writing the Wolf (Rosa & Caleb)

Inking the Wolf (Bianca & Robbie)

Wedding the Wolf (Willow & Irvine)

Want to be informed when the next Steffanie Holmes paranormal romance story goes live? Sign up for the newsletter at www.steffanieholmes.com/newsletter to get the scoop, and score a free collection of bonus scenes and stories to enjoy!